MW00574376

the PURSUIT

Novels by Rebecca Belliston

Life

Liberty

The Pursuit

Sadie

Augustina

the PURSUIT

CITIZENS OF LOGAN POND
BOOK 3

REBECCA BELLISTON

GATED PUBLISHING

This book is a work of fiction. Names, characters, places and incidents are products of the writer's imagination and are not to be construed as real. Any resemblance to persons, living or dead, actual events, locale or organizations is entirely coincidental.

PRINT ISBN 13: 978-0-692-76423-7
PRINT ISBN 10: 0-692-76423-2

Copyright © 2016 Rebecca Lund Belliston
www.rebeccabelliston.com
Cover Design Copyright ©2016 Gated Publishing

Ebooks/Books are not transferable. They cannot be sold, shared or given away. To do so is an infringement on the copyright of this work. All rights reserved. No part of this book may be used or reproduced in any manner whatsoever without written permission, except in the case of brief quotations embodied in critical articles and reviews.

For my friends

Who bring me so much happiness

We hold these truths to be self-evident, that all men are created equal, that they are endowed by their Creator with certain unalienable Rights, that among these are

Life, Liberty and the Pursuit of Happiness.

That whenever any Form of Government becomes destructive of these ends, it is the Right of the People to alter or to abolish it, and to institute new Government, laying its foundation on such principles and organizing its powers in such form, as to them shall seem most likely to effect their Safety and Happiness.

Declaration of Independence
The United States of America

one

Carrie Ashworth's head spun in the trapped summer heat. She grabbed the wall and squeezed her eyes shut, hoping this wouldn't happen for the rest of her life, feeling like she'd stepped off the Tilt-A-Whirl. Thirty minutes post-hospital, and she was worn out.

With an arm around her waist, Greg Pierce helped her upstairs to her bedroom, but each step made it worse. At the top, the hallway rotated in front of her.

Greg left her leaning against the wall and cleared a pile of blankets from the mattress on her bedroom floor. Greg peeled back blanket after blanket.

"Where did you get all those?" she asked, not recognizing most of them.

Greg smiled but didn't answer. "Ready to sleep?"

She was, but she stayed leaned against her door jamb, too tired to move to her mattress.

The meningitis had wiped out most of the last few days, but some things she remembered vividly—like freezing to death, which seemed impossible given the hot, stuffy room. He left one blanket, the one nailed over her window to ease the strain on her light-sensitive eyes. A folding chair—her kitchen chair—sat in one corner where he had fretted over her. His NY Yankees baseball cap lay next to it, and a cup of water sat beside the mattress. She remembered those. She remembered the pain, vomiting, and absolute terror.

A shudder ripped through her. So close. She had come so close to never coming back. Grave number nine in their clan cemetery.

As if reading her thoughts, Greg's expression softened. "Come on, Carrie girl. Time to rest."

Crossing the room, she lowered herself onto the mattress. Maybe if she slept for a day—or two—she could shed the dizziness, light sensitivity, and migraine. Hopefully those issues weren't permanent. Unlike her ear…

She rubbed her bad ear, the one that registered things as muted and dull and left her feeling lopsided.

"Wanna change first?" he asked.

"No, I'm fine."

Even though she craved her comfy sweats, she was too tired to change by herself, and she refused to ask Greg, who would only be too eager to help. What she really craved was a long, hot, bubble bath. Not that she remembered what that was like. She hardly got lukewarm ones, because by the time she boiled water for Amber and Zach, the water cooled before it was her turn. A bath, even a cold one, would have to wait until she had the energy to cart in water from her well.

"Here, let me take your card," Greg said, slipping the lanyard from around her neck. It held her new citizenship card.

Her ticket to freedom.

Carrie caught a glimpse of her photo and grimaced. "Any chance they'll let me retake that picture?"

"What, this? I kinda like it. You look like the poster child for the zombie apocalypse."

She would have swatted him if she wasn't so tired. Not that he was wrong. She vaguely remembered him and Oliver coaxing her awake for the photo. At least Greg was teasing her again. For a while, he had looked worse than she felt.

"You can always ask when you take Amber and Zach into town to get their cards," he said. "I'm sure Ashlee Lyon will retake your picture. She knows what it took to get you legal."

That was more than Carrie knew.

"Speakin' of zombies," Greg said, "you gotta get feelin' better. Look at this mop. I'm in serious need of a haircut. Rumor has it that you made me pretty irresistible with the last one."

She smiled.

Definitely irresistible.

With her eyes, she followed the sharp line of his jaw, the shape of his thick brows. Summer had tanned his skin and lightened his brown hair a shade as well. He looked good. Really good.

Winking at her, he said, "Alrighty. Stop checkin' me out and go to sleep already."

Cocky guy.

She closed her eyes, exhaustion consuming her. The medicine needed time to work. She had insisted they leave the hospital in Aurora, Illinois prematurely to save the clan's money, but she hated wasting time to sleep. Too many neighbors had caught this government-inflicted plague, weeds had overtaken the clan's garden, and they still needed to contact other clans and warn them what was coming. She had to get better fast. So she would sleep. But just for a bit.

"You're scowlin' again." Greg rubbed the spot between her eyebrows. "Are your eyes still bothering you? Want me to…"

His lips kept moving, but with her good ear pressed to her pillow, his words muddled into hearing-loss oblivion.

"No, I'm fine." She grabbed his hand and lowered it. "You should go."

"Wow. Love you, too. Was it somethin' I said?"

She gave a tired smile. "No. You've just slept less than I have." And it showed: his disheveled clothes, brows wrinkled with worry, and his drooped shoulders—one of which still hadn't healed from West Chicago. At least his bruises were gone, but he still looked weary to the bone. She felt it. "I'll sleep better knowing you're sleeping, too. In your own house," she clarified so he didn't park himself on her dirty carpet again.

"Fine." He stretched out his back. "I've gotta go around and administer the first round of shots to all the other sickies anyway. Speaking of which…" He grabbed a small white box. "It's your lucky day. You get the first one."

He opened the lid to reveal dozens of syringes.

The cure.

"Are you sure I need another dose already?" she asked. They hadn't left the hospital that long ago.

He glanced down at his empty wrist—an old habit. "When I checked the clock in Oliver's car, it was around six. Besides, I've gotta practice on somebody."

3

Practice? She didn't love that word.

Greg didn't have an ounce of medical training. No one in the clan did. But with six others starting symptoms, someone had to give it a try. Luckily the nurses had shown him how to administer the shots. Apparently, they hated President Rigsby as much as he did.

"Live free or die," they had said, thrilled to be helping a group of illegals.

Carrie eyed the box of syringes. Better for him to practice on her than his grandparents, who were so old and frail their skin would bruise.

She rolled up her sleeve.

Greg pulled out the first syringe and ripped off the plastic covering as if he knew exactly what he was doing. But then the syringe stopped. He froze.

"What's wrong?" she asked.

"Know any techniques to make it easier?"

The needle didn't look too big, but she had received the rest of the medicine via intravenous fluids. The back of her hand was still bandaged and sore, but she forced herself to look brave. "I'll be fine. I'm a big girl. Just go fast."

"Not easier for you." He wiped a thin sheen of sweat from his forehead. "Easier for me. I'm not real fond of needles. They make me...uh..." He glanced at the syringe and quickly looked away. "Ah, man. Not cool."

His summer tan had faded into a pasty white. She started to smile.

"You're afraid of needles?" she asked.

"No. I'm *terrified* of needles. Take this."

He handed the needle to her and jumped to his feet. Then he threw open her window and hung his head out, taking in huge gulps of fresh air. A slight breeze blew inside, bringing in the smell of summer. Greg stayed half in, half out.

Carrie couldn't help it. She laughed.

How could something as tiny as a needle scare Greg Pierce? The needle wasn't even going into *his* arm. It took her a minute to regain her niceness.

"Are you okay?" she asked.

"Fine," he said in a tiny squeak, head still outside.

Smile fading, she thought of the other clansmen who needed shots every six hours. The needle wasn't too huge. She'd just administer it to herself and then the others.

"Did the nurse say how to give it?" she asked.

He looked over his shoulder, blanched, and faced the open window again. "Just slide it into the skin. Oooh. Slide. Not cool."

For some reason, his anxiety relieved hers. She craned her head to see down the side of her arm. Unfortunately, the awkward turn of her neck brought back the dizziness in full force. She clutched her mattress, needing to anchor herself to something solid.

"I'll do it," Amber said, coming in from the hallway. "I don't mind needles."

"Are you sure?" Carrie asked.

"Yep. I've got this." Carrie's little sister grabbed the needle like a butcher grabbed a cleaver. "How high up on the arm, Greg?"

"I don't know. The regular spot. Just do it already!"

"Wow," Amber smirked. "I didn't know you were such a baby."

"Be nice," Carrie said. "He hasn't eaten or slept for days. The last thing we need is for him to pass out and—"

Amber stabbed Carrie's arm, driving the needle deep into the skin.

"Ow!" Carrie yelped. "Not so hard."

"All done." Amber slid the needle out and dropped it into the box.

"It's over?" Greg asked, stealing a glance.

"Yes." Carrie rubbed her arm where it burned from the cold medicine.

Standing, Amber held the small box of syringes. "I'll do everyone else's if you want, Greg."

"No. I got it. I'll be fine. I can do this. I…" He eyed the box. "You sure you know what you're doin'?"

Amber rolled her dark eyes. "Better than you do. I want to check on Braden anyway. Who else needs medicine?"

"My grandparents and Richard. Do theirs first," he said. "Then Terrell, Rhonda, and Braden last."

Amber scowled. "Why does Braden go last?"

Carrie eased herself back onto her pillow. "Because the others can't wait while you and Braden chat."

"Oh, good thinking," Amber said, brightening.

"No," Greg said pointedly. "Braden's last 'cause he's the healthiest and youngest. No lollygagging at his place either. You get two minutes.

And no kissing, not even once. You might not have caught this beast yet, but we've gotta be careful. I don't want to think about what'll happen if we run out of medicine."

And what Greg hadn't said but what Carrie dreaded was that, even with the cure, others might have permanent issues like hers. President Rigsby had manipulated this strain of meningitis to be deadly. Kill those without citizenship, save those with it. The easiest way to stop the impending civil war. It had spread like wildfire. Carrie couldn't bear to think of millions suffering an outcome worse than hers, but from what Richard O'Brien had said, the ER had been packed with yellow card holders and government workers alike. Legal citizens. People the President of the United States shouldn't be trying to kill.

The last week hit her all over again.

She pressed her hands to her stomach and focused where she could. Here. Now. They had quarantined her clansmen. They'd all be fine.

They had to be.

As Amber left with the small box of medicine, Greg knelt next to Carrie's mattress again. He bent down as if to kiss her, but she held up a hand.

"I thought you told Amber no kissing," she said.

"I meant no kissin' for people who weren't vaccinated. Lucky for me, I'm immune."

"Greg..."

"Oh, come on." He wagged his eyebrows at her. "You just said I was irresistible."

"No, *you* said you were irresistible."

"Only because you were thinkin' it."

She chuckled. "Still, you're not sure that they immunized you during training. Plus you look exhausted. So it's my turn to take care of you. Go home and sleep. If I need anything, Zach can run across the street and get you."

"Alrighty," he relented. But instead of moving away, his finger slowly ran along the skin of her cheek across to her lips. She felt every move, every warm ridge of his fingerprint, still not quite accustomed to his touch. His green eyes locked on hers and he whispered something. At least, she hoped he had whispered it because she didn't hear it.

Shifting, she said, "What?"

"You're so soft," he said a little louder. "You know, Miss Ashworth, you still owe me a midnight walk around the pond."

"Sounds perfect," she said while thinking, *I love you.*

He leaned down as if to whisper something in her good ear, but at the last second, he darted to the left and stole a kiss right off her lips.

"Greg!"

He grinned. "You like kissing me. Admit it."

Her lips tingled, but her cheeks went hot, giving him the response he'd been waiting for.

Laughing, he stood again. "Alrighty, I'm gonna let you sleep now. Unless you want some—" He stopped, craning his neck toward the open window. "What was that?"

Carrie strained, but obviously heard nothing. "What?"

"What the heck?" He peered outside and suddenly turned to stone. "Why is *she* here? And Dylan's with her? Great. Just great."

"What?" Carrie said, trying to sit. "Who is it?"

He turned. "I'll be back later. Try to sleep."

Then he flew out of her room and down her stairs. She heard the front door open seconds later.

Curious, her thirteen-year-old brother, Zach, came into her bedroom and went to her window. Zach's brows also furrowed as he peered outside. "Who's with Dylan?"

That did it.

Carrie struggled to sit, but she pushed through the dizziness. Using the wall for support, she worked her way to the window and saw Dylan Green escorting a twenty-something blonde down the street, a woman Carrie had never seen before. Under normal circumstances, that was strange enough. But in the last six years—more specifically the last three—their clan had cut off all contact with the outside world. They never had visitors in their neighborhood.

Ever.

With a jolt, she wondered if that was Greg's old girlfriend from North Carolina, come to find him. Carrie tried to remember her name.

Nicole.

The woman was crying, but even from a distance Carrie could tell that she was beautiful. At the same time, Carrie noticed her reddened eyes and one cheek that looked rosier than the other, almost like someone had slapped her. Dylan Green gripped the woman's arm as they walked down the street, looking furious. Dylan wouldn't have hurt her, would he? Even a trespasser?

It was a sign of Carrie's sad, sick state that it took her that long to notice what the woman wore. A dark green government uniform. That wasn't Greg's old girlfriend. That was a government employee.

In Logan Pond.

With thirty-four illegals.

"Oh no," Zach said, backing away from the window. "They found us."

two

Greg peered around the brick of Carrie's porch. His mind raced with a thousand questions. First and foremost, why was Ashlee Lyon in their neighborhood?

Six years of hiding. Week after week of precautions.

Gone.

He didn't know how much Oliver Simmons had told his coworker about their clan. Enough to get Carrie legal, but more than that? Enough for Ashlee to pop in for a visit? No. Not after so many safeguards. Nobody more than Oliver knew what would happen if the government discovered them.

Frantic, Greg scanned the street.

People had scattered at the sight of the government clerk. How far they'd run, he wasn't sure, but it didn't matter. The damage was done. Ashlee's blonde head whipped back and forth, searching the homes that obviously weren't abandoned. Dylan, as illegal as the rest, looked ready for war as he marched her down the street. Her face was flushed from crying, but Greg had the feeling she'd been crying before she got to their neighborhood.

It had been maybe thirty minutes since Oliver drove them home from the hospital. What could have gone wrong in that short of time? Why had Oliver risked everything in sending Ashlee to them?

Or had he sent her?

Either way, the last thing "dead" Greg needed was to be resurrected and forced into serving in Commander McCormick's unit again. But

Dylan seemed to have one destination in mind. He and Ashlee headed right for Carrie's house.

For Greg.

Greg slunk behind the brick.

As Dylan and Ashlee turned up Carrie's driveway, Greg's eyes zeroed in on something. Not only was Ashlee's face flushed, but one cheek was redder than the other and her lip was swollen and bloody. Dylan wouldn't have done that. Which meant one thing.

Jamansky!

Greg stepped out into the early evening sun, resurrecting himself. Startled, Ashlee jumped back and let out a piercing cry. Her hands flew to her mouth, clamping off the sound, but it still took her a second to regain her composure.

"Greg?" she whispered.

"Ashlee," he said evenly. "Why are you here?"

Tears streamed down her splotchy, mascara-smeared face. "You're not dead? They told me you died in the line of duty. David showed me the death notice himself. How are you not dead?" Hiccupping a sob, she ran forward and threw her arms around him. "Federal patrolmen came. They told us, and I thought...I thought..."

As she entered full freak-out mode, Dylan gave Greg a strange look. Greg patted her convulsing back, unsure how to explain. The last time Greg had seen her had been the day Jamansky stormed into the office and ordered Greg to be handcuffed and carted off to training. The day his mom died. That had been a lifetime ago. Even then, Greg hadn't known *You-can-just-call-me-Ashlee* very well. Certainly not enough for this kind of reaction.

Her tears soaked his shoulder.

"Why is she here?" Greg asked. "What happened?"

Dylan threw his hands in the air. "Don't ask me! I spotted her near the entrance. I thought she was from another clan until I noticed her uniform, so I confronted her. She said she was looking for Oliver. When I told her that he'd just dropped off Carrie a little bit ago, she started freaking out. She says she has a message for Carrie that's life or death. She knows all about our clan and situation, but look at her! She's one of them!"

Greg peeled Ashlee off of him and held her by the shoulders. "Ashlee, what's goin' on? What happened?"

She hunched over, hands covering her face. "He's gone. I missed him."

"Who?"

Her eyes, swollen and overflowing, lifted. "Oliver! Please, Greg. I have to talk to Carrie. Is she home?"

"Yes," a weak voice said behind them. "I'm here."

Whirling, Greg saw Carrie slowly working her way downstairs. "Go back to bed," he growled. "We've got this."

Either she couldn't hear him or chose to ignore him because she pushed toward her front door, looking whiter than snow. "You're Ashlee. You work with Oliver, right?"

Nodding, Ashlee wiped her eyes, smearing more mascara as she appraised Carrie's haggard appearance. Neither woman looked too great. "And you're Carrie. Are you...are you okay? He said you were dying."

"I'm getting better," Carrie said, even as she leaned against the door to keep from falling over. "Oliver told us that you helped to get me legal. Thank you."

That seemed to be the wrong thing to say.

Ashlee dissolved into tears again. "Oh, Oliver."

"Ashlee," Greg said, losing patience, "try to focus here. What happened?"

She took a shuddering breath and looked up. Her gaze locked on Carrie for a moment before shifting back to Greg.

"Jamansky knows," she said.

Greg's brows furrowed. "What do you mean he knows?" Yet even as he said it, his stomach clenched. David Jamansky. Chief of Patrols. Oliver's boss and Ashlee's boyfriend.

Jamansky knew.

Ashlee's chin lowered, and they lost her to emotions again. It didn't matter. More and more pieces fit together. Ashlee was there, swollen lip, beaten. You-can-just-call-me-Ashlee, who had never stepped foot in the Logan Pond subdivision before, had trudged all the way from Downtown Shelton on foot to give Carrie, a woman she'd never even met, a message.

Life or death.

"Ashlee," Greg said. "What does Jamansky know?"

Through heart-wrenching sobs, she was able to manage one word: "Everything."

———— ♦ ————

David Jamansky rolled to a stop by the south entrance to the Logan Pond neighborhood. He should have brought a map. He'd barely glanced at the one in the station in his haste to get out the door. Now he wasn't sure he'd come to the right spot. Trees and debris blocked the entrance into the subdivision, almost like tornado damage, but the debris was too perfectly situated to block the road. Anger coursed through him. Of course the illegal squatters had blocked off patrolmen's access to their subdivision. They couldn't drive. They hadn't owned cars for years. The only people left with transportation could end their pitiful lives.

David pounded the steering wheel, wondering why it had taken so long to piece things together. An entire illegal clan living right under their noses.

Six years!

He thought about hopping the curb but didn't want to risk the patrol car's alignment. Pressing the throttle to the floor, he sped toward the other entrance. If they blocked off the north entrance as well, he'd go in on foot. They would not keep him away. Not now.

Thankfully, the north entrance was open and clear.

He started to turn into the neighborhood, but pressed the brakes with a sudden thought. He knew nothing about this clan. They could be violent or part of the rebellion. They could ambush him the second he stepped foot inside their territory.

But as soon as he thought it, he dismissed it. He'd done plenty of sweeps through here, and they'd never attacked him before. Even when he ransacked the place back in March, they let him have free rein. This clan was a peaceful one, a weak one that had befriended an even weaker patrolman. They wouldn't want an altercation with a truly skilled—and heavily armed—officer.

Glancing in the rearview mirror, he noticed how red and sweaty he still was. His jaw throbbed and ached like crazy, and every muscle in his body still felt tight with fury from the scuffle. If Oliver Simmons had broken his jaw, David would personally visit him in prison and slit his throat. Luckily Oliver had only got in a few punches before the other patrolmen took him down. David finished him off after that, hopefully breaking a few of his ribs. That had felt good. And while Ashlee hadn't inflicted any injury on him—at least not physically—their argument had affected him just as much. His girlfriend's part in all this, her betrayal and schemes, were yet to be punished. She claimed to know little of what Oliver Simmons had been involved with, but David knew better than to believe that lying wench. He'd finish her off later.

First things first.

Carrie.

Taking a deep breath, he tried to calm his nerves. He couldn't look ruffled for this meeting.

The way he figured, Oliver had turned David's girlfriend against him. Now he'd repay the favor. Only David planned to take it much, much further.

Oliver Simmons would spend the rest of his life paying for what he'd done. Jamansky had decided that on the first night he spent sleeping on a hard, smelly, cement prison floor. It had been solidified when the prison gang cornered him and beat him to a pulp.

And now...

Ever since Mayor Phillips had sprung David from prison, David had been biding his time, waiting for payback. Now to find out that Oliver's crimes hadn't stopped at squealing on him for working the black market? No, the hypocrite had a secret far more dark and illegal.

David ground his teeth so hard, pain shot up his temples.

For years Oliver had been hiding a girlfriend—the beautiful, young Carrie Ashworth—*plus* an entire clan. He'd neglected his sweeps, lied about patrols, stolen supplies to give to them, turned Ashlee against him, *and* sent Jamansky to prison.

Yes, Oliver Simmons would pay dearly.

But never had revenge been so sweet or involved someone so enticing.

David pictured Carrie's face to slow his breathing. He'd only met her once and only for a brief minute in that diner in South Elgin. But it had been enough. Carrie Ashworth was the quiet, innocent-looking type: freckles, blushes, and all. He'd instantly felt the connection with her, but the poor woman had been stuck on a date with lame Oliver—a guy who was at least a decade older than her. But the moment David had introduced himself, he'd felt her beautiful blue eyes follow his every move. She had been attracted to him, he could tell. Sure, she blushed and tried to hide behind her hair as they spoke, but he had understood her game. She wanted him to pursue her.

Now he had.

A slow smile crept over his face.

Oliver Simmons had done at least one thing right: getting Carrie legal. That would simplify things. Since Oliver hadn't left her house that long ago, David just had to figure out how to approach this—how to approach her while she was surrounded by two dozen illegals. What excuse could he give to keep her and the others from scattering like they had so many times before? Because he didn't want Carrie to hide anymore. She was legal now. Legal and his.

Revenge was so sweet.

Stretching up to the rearview mirror again, he finger-combed his light hair. His coloring was nearly normal. His jaw didn't look swollen, and any bruising wouldn't show for another day. He was wearing his Chief of Patrols uniform, which was fine. Carrie probably liked a man in uniform—especially a man of his power and rank.

Good enough.

Putting the car into drive, David Jamansky pulled slowly forward.

three

Carrie sat on her old, torn couch as Ashlee talked a thousand miles a minute. How Jamansky found the deed to Carrie's home. How he'd seen Oliver's name on the paperwork and pieced everything together.

Turning her neck made Carrie feel fuzzy, so she twisted her whole body to face Ashlee. Even then, she rested her head on the couch, begging herself to hold on to consciousness a bit longer. Because according to Ashlee, Jamansky didn't just know about their illegal clan, he knew about the raid in March—something that made Carrie sick with dread.

Jamansky knew Oliver had been behind his arrest.

Greg ran both hands over his hair. "Jamansky had been paging Oliver all morning. We were at the hospital, so Oliver ignored him. But..." He looked at Ashlee. "What will he do to him?"

Ashlee started crying again. "I don't know. I'm too late. He attacked me today and you that one day—and your mom! Look at what he did to your sweet mom when she hadn't even done anything wrong. What will he do to quiet, sweet Oliver who he hated even before everything? He knows Oliver sent him to prison in the spring. He knows everything!"

Carrie's insides caved.

Oliver.

"You're worried about Oliver?" Dylan Green yelled through the window. He stood on Carrie's porch to minimize the germ exposure. "What about the rest of us? The Chief of Patrols? How could you have told him?"

"He was hurting me. I couldn't breathe, but he wouldn't stop." Ashlee covered her face again. "He was hurting me."

Greg glared at Dylan. "She didn't tell him anything he hadn't already pieced together."

"That's not what it sounds like," Dylan shot back.

Ashlee Lyon cried harder.

Carrie rubbed her arm. "It's okay. It's going to be fine," she said, shooting Dylan a warning look. Making Ashlee more hysterical wouldn't help anything. They needed information, not an interrogation.

Greg blew out his breath. "We better call an emergency meeting. Dylan, tell the adults to meet at my grandparents' in five minutes."

Carrie jerked around—a bad move. The world flashed black. "People can't go to their house, Greg. They're quarantined."

Dylan threw his hands in the air. "I knew things were ruined. Jeff and I told you this would happen. You've ruined everything!"

Carrie's cheeks burned with shame. *Jeff, Jenna.*

Greg whirled and pointed at Dylan. "I'm way too sleep-deprived to deal with your garbage right now."

Dylan just turned his wrath on Greg instead. "We warned you *and* Carrie. Two stupid lovebirds, and now we have a whole patrol squad—"

Greg stormed across the room, threw open Carrie's front door, and came nose to nose with Dylan on the porch. Startled, Dylan fell back a step. They were nearly the same height, but after six weeks of rigorous military training, Greg had twice Dylan's bulk. Greg's whole body was lines of deep, clenched muscles.

"Go warn all the adults," Greg said, low and deadly. "Now. Let them know we're on high alert until further notice. Have all the healthy ones meet by the pond in five minutes. Make sure they keep a safe distance from each other."

Muttering, Dylan headed down the sidewalk. When Greg came back inside, he looked even more rigid. He started pacing Carrie's living room. Ashlee gave Carrie a questioning look, but Carrie didn't even know where to start. Too much history. Too much pain.

Jeff and I told you this would happen.

"It was you," Ashlee whispered.

Carrie turned, but Ashlee was staring at Greg. "Oliver told me that Carrie was in love with someone else, but I didn't know it was you,

Greg." Her eyes overflowed again. "I didn't even know you were alive. Oliver loves Carrie so much, and now—"

The front door suddenly burst open, and Amber rushed inside. "Ashlee! You're here!"

Ashlee Lyon jumped to her feet. "Oh, Amber. I'm so glad to see you."

The two embraced as if they were lifelong friends even though they'd only just met. Amber had gone with Oliver into town to get Carrie legal. A few hours spent together, yet they hugged and hugged.

When Amber pulled back, her expression darkened. "Your boyfriend found out?"

Nodding, Ashlee broke down again.

"Hold up," Greg said. But he wasn't watching them. He leaned sideways to see out the front door Amber had left open. "Oliver's here. He's back!"

Carrie's heart leapt. She leaned to see out the window. The sunlight pierced into her skull, but she spotted a patrol car—Oliver's car—inching past the Trenton's yard.

"Oliver's back!" Ashlee Lyon said. "Now I can warn him."

Carrie's breath unhitched in a massive sigh of relief. Oliver would know what to do. Or…had Jamansky flipped out and fired Oliver? Did Oliver have bruises worse than Ashlee's?

It didn't matter. He'd come.

He was safe.

Dylan ran up to Oliver's car, probably to yell at him for exposing their clan. If they weren't so far away, Carrie would have stopped him. Oliver didn't deserve any blame.

Dylan halted abruptly in the middle of the road. For the space of two seconds, he stared at Oliver's car. Then he stumbled backward, tripped over the curb, and took off sprinting in the opposite direction. Away from the patrol car. Away from Oliver.

"No," Carrie breathed. "That's not Oliver."

Greg's jaw clenched. "Jamansky."

"What?" Ashlee cried.

Carrie's pulse kicked into full throttle. She tried to see better, but Greg grabbed her arm.

"Back. Get back!"

Disbelief spread through her. She was too shocked to run, to hide like she should. Greg kept tugging on her, urging her toward the kitchen, but she twisted out of his grasp. She had to see. Pressing her face to the front window, she saw Oliver's car with the small dent in the side. But another man sat behind the wheel. Someone with a full head of hair. Oliver's boss.

David Jamansky.

Her heart thumped against her bad ear.

Jamansky had stopped in front of the Trenton's house, watching Dylan retreat. Carrie waited for him to go after Dylan, to pull out his gun and start shooting. Instead, the car started rolling forward again. Inch by inch, one house after the next.

Chaos erupted in her living room.

"Why is he alone?" Greg said. "He'd be a fool to arrest us all with just himself!"

"He found me," Ashlee said, practically hyperventilating. "He followed me!"

Greg spun around. "How? You said nobody followed you."

"No one did. I don't know!"

"If he knows things," Carrie said, "why isn't he doing anything? Why did he leave Dylan alone?"

Ashlee's gaze snapped up to her. "It's you. He's obsessed with you and now he knows where you live."

"What?" Greg said, eyes bulging.

Carrie swayed and caught hold of the couch. Jamansky had asked her in the diner where she lived. She lied and told him an entirely different city far from here—far from Oliver.

His car was close enough that she could make out his face. He was leaning down and sideways, back and forth to scan the house numbers. If she could see him, then he could see them, too. Reason suddenly returned to her, and with it a flood of terror.

Ashlee couldn't be seen.

Neither could Greg who had been declared "dead."

Her illegal siblings.

"Get down!" she called. "All of you!"

Ashlee dropped to the floor. Zach and Amber did, too. Greg backed against the wall where he could still peer out the window while Carrie tried to remember where her citizenship card was. The hospital lanyard.

She peeked outside. Jamansky stopped in the road in front of her house. He glanced down at something, a paper. Then he turned into her driveway.

"Go!" she cried. "Out the back. I'll distract him. Go!"

Greg's expression hardened to steel. "There's no way I'm leavin' you alone with that guy."

"Yes, you are. I have citizenship."

"He knows everything, Carrie!"

"He doesn't know everything, so go!" She pushed Greg toward the kitchen. "You have to get everyone safe."

"There's not time." Greg ran over and slammed the front door shut. "Zach, take the girls upstairs and hide. Whatever you do, don't come back down. I don't care what you hear."

Frantic, Carrie's brother scrambled up the stairs and out of sight, abandoning them. Amber grabbed Ashlee Lyon and dragged her upstairs, but Carrie didn't budge.

Greg jerked back around. "Carrie, now!"

He was going to turn himself in. Greg the Special Op. The second he was reinstated, he'd outrank Jamansky. Oliver's boss wouldn't be able to touch him, but Greg would be gone. He'd be one of them again.

His bruises hadn't even fully healed yet.

"They can't have you back," she said.

"Upstairs now!"

A car door shut outside.

"Listen," she said urgently. "I'm legal now. David can't hurt me, but you aren't. You said yourself that he came alone. If he wanted to arrest us, he would have brought a whole squad or gone after Dylan. Just let me see what he wants. Please. You promised to stay dead." Her voice caught. "You promised."

With a huff, he scanned her front room, looking for a place to hide. The only furniture she owned was her old couch out in the wide open.

"Please," she begged. "Hide Amber and Zach."

Greg growled. "Don't open that door. Whatever Jamansky thinks he knows, you own this house now. He can't search it without a warrant."

Then he flew upstairs.

Carrie backed against the door. When that wasn't enough, she deadbolted it for the first time in six years.

Her heart hammered against her ribs. It hurt to breathe. It hurt to think. The room went in and out of focus, and her extremities turned to ice. She slid down the door and wrapped her arms around her knees. She couldn't faint now.

Jamansky's footsteps slapped up the front walk.

This house was no longer government property.

It was hers.

He couldn't search it.

Why had he come alone?

Her gaze stayed on the stairs, begging Greg to stay away because Jamansky wouldn't care what rank Greg had earned in his military training. The two men had too much history. Jamansky would kill Greg on sight—and after what Jamansky had done to Greg's mom, Greg might do the same.

Jamansky knocked loudly.

Huddled against the front door, she squeezed her knees to keep from screaming.

Go away!

Something tumbled down the stairs. Her lanyard with her citizenship card. She didn't dare leave her spot to retrieve it.

Jamansky knocked harder, hard enough she felt the vibrations against her back.

"Hey, Carrie," he called. "It's David Jamansky, Oliver's boss. Remember me? We met at the diner."

She remembered that voice all too well. Smooth and confident. Strangely, he didn't sound angry. In fact, he sounded as friendly as he had when she'd met him. That scared her even more because he'd smiled and laughed then, too.

The handle clicked above her head. The door didn't budge, but she shoved all her weight against it.

Make it stop!

More pounding. The door jumped against her back with each hit.

"Carrie, I'm here as your friend! I mean no harm to you or anyone. Officer Simmons told me you've been sick. He said you've been in the hospital and he just dropped you off. I know you're home. Carrie!"

She froze.

Ashlee couldn't have told Jamansky all that because Ashlee hadn't known. Which meant Oliver told Jamansky that much at least.

"Please," Jamansky tried again. "Oliver sent me with a message for you—an urgent message."

A message.

Oliver would have only sent a message through his boss if things were desperate. Her eyes lifted to the stairs. Greg would kill her, but she had to know. Pushing herself up, she rose to her feet, ignored the spinning room, and unlocked the door.

She only opened it a few inches, enough to see him smiling on her porch.

"Hey, Carrie," he said. "It's great to see you again. Oliver said you just moved in, so I thought…" Words trailing, his eyes widened on her scraggly hair and wrinkled clothes. "Oh, man. You look awful. Are you okay?"

She clutched the handle and leaned against the door, so dizzy she could hardly stand up. He wore his dark green patrol uniform, which meant he had at least a gun, Taser, and a nightstick strapped to his belt. He didn't need a whole squad to put up a deadly fight.

"Actually, no," she said. "I'm really sick." And getting sicker by the second.

"Oliver told me you caught this"—he paused, choosing his word—"virus. You must be miserable. Can I get you something? Do you need medicine?"

"No. I just need to sleep. You said you had a message?"

"Yes, but first let me help you." He started to push open the door.

She clutched the handle. "No. I'm fine."

"You look like you're ready to pass out. Seriously, you need to lie down."

She tried to hold strong, but he pushed the door open the rest of the way. Then he took her arm and pulled her inside of her own home. Her skin crawled at his touch, but she didn't know how to stop it—how to stop him from entering.

"Where's your room? Upstairs?" he asked. "I can help you back there."

She dug in her heels. "No, I'm fine. Really."

"At least sit down."

As he led her toward her couch, he suddenly stopped. His brows knitted together in a flash of recognition. Her couch. The distinctive olive-green color. The gashes in the side. He recognized it from his government searches through it.

In that second, in that one look, she knew that he knew.

She hadn't just moved in. She'd been living here illegally all along. But he shook it away and helped her sit.

The second she was down, she pressed her head against the arm of the couch. She didn't like being in such a vulnerable position, but she needed something to ground herself on before she passed out.

"When did you get sick?" he asked, feeling her forehead. "Man, you're burning up. You were fine when I saw you last week."

"Um…" She wet her dry lips. "My symptoms started a few days after that."

A few days. She'd shaken David's hand. He'd sat uncomfortably close to her in that booth. Had he given this disease to her—and in return, to everyone else?

"You really look awful, no offense." He straightened. "I think I should drive you back to the medical unit in Aurora."

"No, no."

"What about something from the store? Or maybe medicine?"

Store. Medicine. It's like he spoke another language.

"I'm fine, really." Normally she was a patient, un-pushy person, but this small talk would drive her mad. All she could think was Oliver, Oliver, Oliver.

"I'm sorry, David, but…why are you here?"

"Oh. I wanted to be the first to congratulate you on the new house. I saw your name on the paperwork, and I had to come see for myself. You're in my territory. How great is that? Have you met your other yellow card neighbors? They live down the street. An older couple, CJ and Mabel Trenton."

"May," she whispered.

"Oh, that's right. May Trenton," he said easily. "Nice lady."

She stared at him. Was he insane?

He'd led the group that ransacked May and CJ's home in March. He'd shot their chickens and milk goat, terrifying everyone. He'd attacked Greg and Mariah six weeks ago, hit Ashlee a few hours ago, and Carrie had no energy to sift out the truth from the lies. He knew she hadn't just moved in, and she knew Oliver hadn't willingly told him about their clan.

Noticing her expression, he softened. "I'm sorry, Carrie. I've only told you a half-truth. I came because I wanted to see you—that's true. But I also came because I have a message for you. A message from Oliver. He's...well..."

"Yes?" she said.

"Oliver's gone." He looked at her full on. "I'm afraid he's not coming back."

four

Greg crouched in a corner of Carrie's closet, cursing himself for leaving her. Of course she would open that door. Of course she'd let that creep in.

Anytime he tried to escape the closet, Amber grabbed his arm and hissed threats that Carrie would never forgive him. So he crouched low and strained to make out the soft conversation downstairs. Nothing coherent, but things sounded eerily calm. As long as it stayed that way, he'd keep his promise. Stay dead. But if there was even the tiniest hint that she—or anybody else—was in danger, he would be down there in seconds.

8A374B1552M.

He rattled off his authorizing numbers in his mind, something Commander McCormick insisted he do if he and Isabel were ever caught. Of course if Jamansky tried to verify Greg's story, Greg would have to explain to his former commander why he'd disappeared from West Chicago. Regardless, Greg knew one thing for sure:

Jamansky would not touch Carrie.

The military taught him plenty of ways to incapacitate a man without a weapon or sound. But if he went down there, shots would be fired. Carrie could be caught in the crossfire. He could drop out her second-story window, sneak around the house, and slip in the back door…

Something didn't add up.

Ashlee said Jamansky was *obsessed* with Carrie. He'd sidled up next to her in that deli booth, trying to goad Oliver—which it had—but they'd only talked a few minutes. Barely long enough for anything. Now Jamansky was downstairs, having a friendly conversation. This, right after he found out what Oliver had done. It didn't make sense. The timing of it.

Unless…

Revenge.

The word filled Greg's mind, and with it, a lurch of foreboding. Because if Jamansky wanted to lash out at Oliver, there was one place he could hurt him worse than any other.

Carrie.

Greg wasn't the only man who loved her.

He scrambled out of his crouched spot and slid open the closet door.

"Greg!" It was a multi-person warning.

"Just stay," he hissed back.

Then he crab-walked across Carrie's bedroom floor, checking each spot for creaks in the floorboard. When he reached the bathroom, he lifted the metal vent from the floor. Carrie and David's voice carried up through the heating ducts just in time for Greg to hear Jamansky say, "I'm afraid he's not coming back."

"Oliver is…not coming back?" Carrie repeated in a choked voice.

"No. I'm sorry," Jamansky said. "Oliver's gone."

Greg felt like somebody had punched him in the gut. It was worse than he feared. Oliver wasn't just injured or sitting in some prison cell.

He was dead.

A cry of shock ripped from Carrie's throat. "No. No. NO!"

Greg scrunched up on the bathroom floor, nearly pulling out his hair.

Jamansky had killed Oliver.

———— ◆ ————

The patrol car sped down the highway, but every bump and jar sent Oliver Simmons writhing in pain. He tried to adjust his position, but they'd wrenched his cuffed hands behind his back, preventing him from sitting upright. The metal cut and burned his wrists. He lay on the back seat, bruised. Devastated.

He moaned.

Officer Portman, one of his young partners—*former* partners—glanced in the rearview mirror, saying nothing as he drove. Bushing checked over his shoulder. Oliver didn't know where Jamansky had ordered his coworkers to take him. Maybe to throw him off a cliff.

If only he would be that lucky.

He kept replaying that moment in the township office.

"Live free or die!" he had shouted at Jamansky. *"There are things far worse than death!"* It was the rebellion's motto, but Oliver meant every word to the depth of his traitorous soul.

He would never forget the look on Jamansky's face as he turned back.

"Oh, believe me, I know," Jamansky had sneered. *"Which is why you don't have a bullet through your head. Get him out of here! No, wait. I want him to see this."* Jamansky had sauntered over to the map of Shelton and traced the roads with his finger. *"342 Woodland Drive. 342 Woodland Drive. Ah, there she is."*

She.

"Carrie," Oliver groaned.

What would Jamansky do to her? To them?

Bushing turned back around. "We're almost there, sir—I mean, Simmons. Can you move?"

Oliver's body was a giant mass of pain. The last kick sent him sliding across the tile into a cement wall. Now every breath brought a sharp stab of pain. Jamansky had cracked several of his ribs. His nose felt broken and swollen with crusted blood. And yet all of it was nothing.

Carrie.

The clan.

What have I done?

When the patrol car finally slowed, Oliver used his elbow to push up enough to see his destination.

Walls, thirty-three feet high, greeted him. Fences with looped barbed wires. The compound was filled with tall guard towers, rounded, barred rooms, and a state-of-the-art security system unmatched throughout Illinois—possibly unmatched in the US. He knew this because he'd brought prisoners here before. Not the typical illegal squatters. No. They reserved this place for the truly dangerous. Murderers. The criminally insane.

Traitors.

A large sign hung on the guard tower next to them:

Joliet State Penitentiary. Maximum security.

five

Oliver wasn't coming back.

Dead.

Carrie covered her face as the grief consumed her. Oliver hadn't left that long ago. She had hugged and thanked him for buying her house— her liberty. He pretended like it was no big deal, like he hadn't been saving his meager paychecks for years to buy a life-saving gift for a woman who wasn't even in love with him. He said he would come back later to check on things.

He said he was coming back.

"Whoa, hey," Jamansky said. "Hold on, Carrie. I meant to say that Oliver isn't coming back for a while. He's not gone *forever*. Don't cry."

She looked up through blurred tears. "What?"

"Officer Simmons had to go away for training, that's all. With the rebellion in our area, the federal government wanted to give some of our patrolmen specialized training in Virginia. Oliver is my most experienced officer—at least without rank—so I had to send him. Think of this like a...promotion."

"What?" she said, wiping her cheeks.

"A promotion. I tried calling him all day to let him know, but he was with you—as he should have been. But that left him no time to say goodbye. He had to rush home and pack because he leaves for Virginia first thing in the morning, even before the sun is up. But he'll be back soon, so no tears. I can't bear to see you unhappy."

More lies. They had to be. Yet desperation forced her to consider the possibility that Oliver wasn't hurt or in prison or dead.

Training.

A promotion.

Greg had left for training and almost hadn't come back. And even more, Oliver never would have left for that long without telling her—not willingly. He wouldn't leave them to fend for themselves, or worse, be stuck in the hands of Jamansky. Not without a warning.

Had he sent Jamansky as a warning?

She rubbed her pounding head. "How long will he be gone?"

"Two months. Maybe longer. But enough about him. I'm worried about you. You look miserable. I can't believe he brought you home. Why? Did he run out of money or something? That wouldn't surprise me a bit. He always overspends."

She shook her head against the arm of the couch.

His expression darkened. "No point in covering for him—not after he forced you to leave early." He sighed. "Whatever. I'll just take you back."

"Back?"

"To the hospital. You need to go back there until you're steady on your feet."

If she ever would be again.

Standing, he extended his hand to help her up. "Come on. Can you stand on your own or do you need me to carry you out to my car?"

Before she could answer, a loud thump sounded overhead.

Both of them glanced up.

"What was that?" Jamansky asked, hand flying to his gun.

Carrie's heart jumped when she realized what it was—*who* it was.

"Oh, that's…my cat," she said lamely.

"Your *cat*?"

She nodded desperately. Her two hundred pound, overprotective cat that was going to get them both killed if he didn't calm down. Fast.

Too late.

David slid his gun out of the holster and, gripping it in both hands, inched backward—not toward the front door, but into the corner of her living room. His eyes darted around her house, to the stairs, to the window.

"Thank you for your offer," she said, desperately trying to redirect *both* men, "but I just need to sleep this off. The hospital sent me home with plenty of medicine, so I'm better off resting here. Please."

For a long tense minute, there was no sound. Not upstairs or down. She didn't know if it truly was silent, or if her thundering pulse covered up what little she could hear. Greg could be shuffling toward the stairs and she wouldn't know. David stayed tensed in the corner, gun drawn, scanning every inch. If Greg stepped into the open, he was a dead man.

Terror clawed through her. "Please, David."

David finally straightened, eyes coming back to her, although with none of the cordiality from before.

"Oliver told me everything, Carrie. He told me about this house and your situation. I even know about your"—he motioned to the ceiling—"friends."

She felt the blood drain from her face. "What?"

His eyes narrowed in a challenge.

Game over.

Bluff called.

Her clan. Her friends. He knew she was hiding people upstairs. The room spun because there was no way he knew that "dead" Greg had been the thumper, nor that Ashlee Lyon, his bruised girlfriend, now hid in Carrie's room. Because if he did, there would be war.

She gripped the couch. She had to keep him from searching her house—or better yet, get him to leave.

David slid his gun back into the holster and sat next to her again, close enough that his knee pressed against hers. Close enough that he could pull her in front of him to use as a shield.

"Look, Carrie," he said, louder than necessary, "I'm the new protector for your clan, so you don't need to worry, and neither do your friends. I know your clan is peaceful, so I'll take care of you—all of you—like Oliver has done. Only I'll do it better."

He reached out to take her hand, but she flinched back.

His brows lowered. "Oliver asked me to watch over you, so tell your buddies upstairs that everything will be fine while he's gone—if not better because I'm the boss. I call the shots now. I know you're not part of the rebellion, so I'll keep you safe."

She felt like she was swimming upstream, water gushing over her. She couldn't get above the surface long enough to see where the shoreline was, where true safety was.

His eyes hooded with concern—and annoyance. "You don't trust me."

"I..."

"I saw one of your illegal friends down the street, but I left him alone, didn't I? We're friends, aren't we?"

His nostrils flared as he waited for a response.

She knew she should nod. Knew, but couldn't.

"How about in an act of good faith," he said, "I tell you something so you know that you can trust me. The next government sweep through here is Friday. My two youngest patrolmen are scheduled to do it. They're inexperienced and idiotic, so I'll make sure they don't search any homes owned by citizens. To my knowledge, that's this house and the Trenton's, right?"

She told herself to nod. Head up and down.

"Good. It should be Friday, late evening. Does Oliver tell you anything else?"

Her mind was mush. She shook it slowly.

With a forced smile, he seemed to relax a little more. "Good. With time, you'll see that I can be your greatest ally, Carrie. More than Oliver ever was."

"Thank you," she said softly. It seemed wrong to thank him—not after what he'd done to Mariah, Greg, Ashlee's face, Scott Porter's house, and potentially to Oliver. But she couldn't think of anything else, so she refocused on her one goal: his absence.

With shaky, unsteady feet, she pushed herself up. "I should sleep now."

She struggled to the door and opened it. Though it took a moment, he followed.

Jamansky stopped in her doorway, tall body looming over her in a way that made her feel claustrophobic—almost trapped—against the door. His eyes locked on hers, deep and penetrating. It felt like a violation somehow, so she lowered her lashes and waited for him to take the hint and leave.

Finally, he stepped back. "It's nice to know where you live now, Carrie. And you live so close, too. Tell you what. Since you won't let me drive you back to the hospital, I'll come back and check on you tomorrow. I work until 6 p.m., so I'll stop by after that. Hey, maybe I'll bring you dinner. Don't worry. I'll bring something better than that awful burger Oliver got you at Harvey's. Do you like Chinese? There's this place in Sugar Grove that makes some mean Szechuan chicken. How's that sound?"

In a sudden rush, her brain kicked back into gear. She realized what he was offering. He'd visit her tomorrow, and then what? The next day? The day after that? Becoming their protector, their friend, their…Oliver?

The hair on her arms stood up. This was wrong. This was very, very wrong.

"No," she said. "Thank you, David, but you don't need to come back and check on me."

Ever again.

"I know. But I want to." He dipped his head slightly. "See you tomorrow, Carrie."

Even with her impeded hearing, she heard his dark chuckle as he jogged out to his car.

six

"It's time to abandon Logan Pond," Greg said.

When nobody responded, he turned. The healthy adults had congregated by the muddy pond. In an effort to maintain a safe distance, they stood several feet from the person next to them, making it a spread-out group. Every one of their mouths gaped. Every one, that is, but Dylan's. Dylan scowled at Greg.

"What about the garden and chickens?" Jada Dixon asked. "What about our homes? When this patrol chief comes tomorrow, can't we just hide in the Trenton's like we always do?"

"Who's to say he won't come back with his whole squad and search warrants?" Greg said. "No. I say we leave tonight."

"But if Carrie isn't here when he comes back," Sasha Green said, adjusting squirmy Jonah Kovach on her hip, "won't that look more suspicious?"

"*More* suspicious? He already knows everything!" Had nobody listened to a word Greg had said? With the sun lowering, he felt time running out. It would be hard to move people in the dark. "Look, safety comes first. That's been your motto from the beginning, so I say it's time to abandon ship. The question is, where do we go? Maybe we just set up camp in the woods somewhere until we get a better grip on things, put the sickies in one spot and the healthy ones in another."

"Greg…" Jada Dixon said carefully. Her husband, Terrell, was one of the sickies, so she'd come alone. "I think you're overreacting a little. It sounds like this patrolman was friendly. He left Dylan alone and he even told Carrie when the next raid is." She turned to the group "Can you imagine what it would be like to have the patrol chief on our side? We wouldn't have to hide anymore."

Murmurs of agreement swept through them.

"Let's wait to see if he makes good on his promise about the raid on Friday," Sasha said. "Why else would Oliver have told him about us?"

Greg pinched the bridge of his nose. "Oliver didn't tell him. Oliver. Didn't. Tell him!"

"Why not?" Dylan said angrily. He pointed at Ashlee. "Oliver told her. Oliver probably told his whole precinct about us."

Ashlee stood near some brush, even farther from the group than the others. With each illegal who had gathered, she seemed to take another step back. Her chin dropped at Dylan's words.

"Oliver didn't tell her about us until he asked our permission," Greg said. "But Oliver never trusted his boss. Not once. Not ever. For cryin' out loud, Oliver was behind this guy's arrest last spring! Since Jamansky was released from prison, he's done nothin' but make Oliver's life miserable. I'm tellin' you, whatever this patrol chief knows, he knows by force and force alone. Oliver's not in some government training in Virginia. He's either dead or behind bars."

People gasped—ironic reactions considering none of them had been particularly friendly to Oliver Simmons. The only clansmen who really knew him, the only people who knew enough history between Jamansky and Oliver to understand the gravity of the situation, were too sick to attend the meeting.

Desperate, Greg turned to Ashlee. "You know Jamansky better than any of us. Am I overreacting?"

"No," she said. "You can't trust him. He's definitely lying. You should stay away from him." Hugging herself, she added softly, "We all should."

"Says another government pig," Dylan spat. "We've got green cardies all over the place. Maybe they're trying to force us out because they know we'll give them a fight."

"Yeah," Sasha said, quick to agree with her husband. "If we abandon our houses now, Greg, we might never come back. They'll target Logan Pond, maybe even turn it into government housing. These are our homes. We can't just leave them."

Greg threw his hands in the air. After the financial collapse, these people hadn't wanted to abandon their homes, not even after foreclosing. But they had—until President Rigsby tried to force every American into the slave camps he called "blue card municipalities." Now they'd rather go down with their houses than use common sense.

It was ridiculous.

"Come on," Greg said. "If y'all are right, there's no harm in sleepin' somewhere else for a few days. But if I'm right, if Jamansky's out for blood and we don't leave, then we spend the rest of our miserable lives in prison."

"Can't we at least see what he wants first?" Sasha asked.

Greg's gut clenched, and fury flooded his veins all over again. "I already know what he wants."

"Oh, I get it," Dylan said, shaking his head in disgust. "Is this about the safety of the clan, or because some guy made a pass at Carrie?"

Greg folded his arms. "The safety of the clan. Obviously. This guy is out for revenge on Oliver. He knows Oliver loves Carrie. He also knows that the rest of us are here at two hundred bucks a head if he turns us in."

"If that's the case," Dylan said, "why didn't you just take him out today? He came alone. You could have easily ended this before it escalated."

The comment stung because Dylan was right. Greg should have ended this. Justice for Jamansky.

Then again…

"Carrie could have been caught in the crossfire," Greg said. "It wasn't worth the risk."

Dylan grunted at that. "I say we take this patrol chief out when he comes back. Ambush him before he ever reaches the sub."

Even knowing it was a bad idea, Greg nodded at the possibility. "We could cut him off on the main road. In training they taught me—"

"Gentlemen, please!" Ron Marino interrupted with a dark scowl for both of them. "Taking down the chief of patrols will only bring down the wrath of the entire government on us. We have to think this through rationally."

Rationally.

That felt just out of reach for Greg. He'd only slept a handful of hours over the last two days. Now he felt every lost hour of sleep.

"What does Carrie think?" Ashlee Lyon asked softly.

Good question. Carrie wouldn't mind everyone else abandoning the neighborhood—anything to keep them safe—but she wanted to stay and see this through. She planned to confront Jamansky about Oliver's whereabouts, as if calling him out on his lies would go over well. As if one flimsy little yellow card could protect her when a green card hadn't protected Ashlee.

Greg stiffened all over again. Jamansky had pulled his gun within feet of her.

Szechuan chicken.

If he got his way, David Jamansky would never see Carrie. Ever again.

"Carrie and I didn't talk long," Greg said. "She practically passed out once Jamansky left. Which reminds me." He stopped to scan the group. "Has anybody else started with this virus?"

Thankfully, people shook their heads. That was something. He had meant to run around and check on everybody after the hospital. Then Jamansky happened. Hopefully with their quarantines in place, they had stopped the spread of the disease.

Greg turned to Amber. "How did the shots go?"

"I'm almost done," Amber said. "Your grandma woke up for a second when I poked her. Terrell asked what took you so long. I just have Braden left."

"Alrighty. Then let's get all the women and kids out now, before it's fully dark. The men and boys stay behind to pack up the rest of the homes."

"And the sick people?" Jada asked.

"We'll take them with us," Greg said. "Try to keep them separate somehow."

Although the thought of moving Carrie when she was already so wiped out sounded daunting. And she was a day ahead on medicine from the others.

Ron Marino shook his head. "I'm still not comfortable deciding anything without CJ, May, or Richard here. What if we meet again in the morning, Greg? The patrol chief isn't coming until tomorrow evening. Maybe the medicine will kick in enough that the others can voice their thoughts."

"I agree," Sasha said. "Morning."

Others nodded with them.

In other words, they didn't trust Greg's judgment. Maybe they were right. A good night's sleep might clear his head.

"Fine. We meet first thing in the morning," he said. "As for now, there's still enough daylight for me to head into Sugar Grove."

Ashlee Lyon's head snapped up. "Sugar Grove? Why?"

"See if I can figure out where Oliver went." He hated the thought of dragging out his already-long day, but it had to be done. "Where does he live?"

"In the government housing like the rest of us," Ashlee said. "But you can't go there, Greg. It's too far and too dangerous."

"Where in the housing?" he said, undeterred.

"About halfway down United Drive, but I have no idea what house number. It doesn't matter anyway," Ashlee said. "He won't be there. You know he won't. You can't go."

"Maybe *he* can't go," Dylan said, "but you can. Why don't *you* find out if Jamansky's story is legit? Prove to us you're on our side."

That surprised her. "You're right," she said, tearing up again. "It should be me. I wouldn't have to go to Sugar Grove, though. If I can access my computer in Shelton, I'll know exactly where he is. I owe him that much."

"No way, no how," Greg said. "You're not goin' back to your job *or* Sugar Grove."

"Why not?" Dylan said. "She's willing."

Greg pointed. "Have you seen her face?"

As one, the adults studied the government clerk. Ashlee dropped her chin again and played with a gold button on her green uniform. Her right cheek was still splotchy, and her neck bore red marks in the suspicious shape of a man's hand.

"She's in more danger than any of us," Greg said. And what he didn't add was that if Jamansky forced her to talk again, there was a lot more she could divulge. Now she knew names, faces, homes, and strategies. That Greg was alive and Carrie didn't believe a word Jamansky said. "She risked her life to warn us. She can't go back."

"But..." Ashlee said. "Where do I go then? I can't go to my parents' place. David will look for me there. All of my other friends work for the government."

"Stay here," Greg said simply. "Carrie already offered for you to stay at her house if you want."

36

"What?" Ashlee said at the same time five other clansmen did.

But immediately Carrie's little sister ran over to her. "Oh, yes!" Amber said. "Stay with us! We'll keep you safe from your jerky boyfriend."

Storming through the long grasses, Dylan grabbed Greg's arm and yanked him off to the side. "What do you think you're doing? You can't just let someone into our clan without a vote, especially someone like *her*."

"Fine." Greg turned back and called, "Anybody opposed to lettin' Miss Lyon stay for a bit?"

The group looked too stunned to vote.

Greg didn't care.

No vote was the same as no objection.

"Great. Welcome to the clan." He turned back to Amber. "Go to my grandpa's garage and see if you can scrounge up some clothes for Ashlee."

Carrie's little sister was hyper as she pulled Ashlee Lyon out of the group. "Oooh, you can come with me to Braden's," he heard her saying. "You *have* to meet him. He's totally dreamy, but he's mine so don't be getting any ideas."

Greg sighed. At least one thing was resolved.

As for the other...

"Let's at least post guards tonight. And we should probably sleep everybody at the two legal houses as well, just to be safe."

"Two?" Ron Marino said.

"My grandparents' and Carrie's. Technically both are germ fests, but if we sleep healthy people downstairs and sick people up, it'll have to do."

The group seemed to agree.

"What time will that Jamansky guy be back?" Sasha asked.

Just hearing Jamansky's name made Greg clench up all over again. The smooth tone of his voice. The haughtiness. *"It's nice to know where you live now, Carrie. And you live so close, too. I'll come back tomorrow—maybe bring you dinner. Szechuan chicken. How's that sound?"*

Whatever revenge Jamansky might be planning for Oliver, whatever schemes he had for getting their clan, the guy was still interested in Carrie.

"Around six," Greg said darkly.

Ron nodded. "Let's put one guard down the main road for early warning, and another at the north entrance. If there are any issues, we immediately evacuate Logan Pond. Who wants the first shift?"

seven

Amber knocked on the Ziegler's front door. Ashlee Lyon stood back on the sidewalk clutching the pile of ragged clothes they'd found: men's sweat pants and an old Chicago Cubs shirt. It was pathetic that Terrell didn't have more choices in their stash, but Ashlee insisted she didn't mind. How could she not, though? The woman was gorgeous, with glossy-blonde hair that had been curled with a real curling iron, perfectly filed nails painted bright red, and mascara that had smeared some but was still magnificent. Amber had never been old enough to wear makeup before the Collapse. After the less-than-friendly reception by the pond, the beautiful clerk looked more concerned about meeting more illegals than she did about her demoted appearance. Silly woman. Braden's family would love her.

Love.

Amber squirmed at that. What if Braden noticed how pretty Ashlee Lyon was? She was in her mid-twenties, maybe six or seven years older than Braden. Hopefully old enough to keep him from getting distracted.

Amber knocked louder. Through the side window, she spotted Mr. Ziegler coming down the hallway, wiping his hands on a towel.

"Hi, Amber," he said, opening the door. "What can I do for you?"

Amber clutched the small box. "I have medicine for Braden,"

"You do?" His eyes closed as if in prayer. "That's wonderful. Absolutely wonderful." Calling over his shoulder, he said, "Kristina! Amber brought the cure!"

Mrs. Ziegler came stumbling up from the basement. "Greg got the medicine? How?"

How had the news not spread to them? Neither of Braden's parents had gone to the adult meeting, but even then, people seemed to know about Greg's find in the hospital. Braden's parents must be quarantining themselves, too.

"Long story," Amber said, "but Braden gets shots every six hours for the next week."

"Actually," Ashlee Lyon corrected from behind, "it's every twelve hours for the next five days."

Mr. Ziegler leaned sideways to see out the front door. When he spotted the woman in the dark green uniform, his brows shot up. "Who is she?"

"Oh, this is Ashlee Lyon, Oliver's friend," Amber beamed. She almost added, Oliver's *new girlfriend,* but figured that was premature. But if her hunches were right, Ashlee Lyon had already moved past Jamansky. The little interchange Amber had witnessed between their nerdy patrolman and the clerk had been cute. They both thought she'd been asleep in the back of his car, but she hadn't been. She'd watched Ashlee lean over and kiss Oliver's cheek in thanks.

Oliver seemed clueless, and Ashlee Lyon was way hotter than the guy deserved, but Amber couldn't be more thrilled. Nor could she wait to tell Carrie, who would be even more thrilled since Oliver had chased her long enough.

"But…" Mrs. Ziegler squeaked, backing up behind her husband, "she works for the government."

"It's fine," Amber said. "She's a nurse, kind of. She knows all about this plague thing."

"I'm not a nurse," Ashlee Lyon corrected. "I just work in the township offices. But they trained me to give these shots. All legal citizens are receiving them now, so I've already done several."

"Then shouldn't you do it?" Mr. Ziegler said.

"No, I can handle it," Amber said brightly.

Mrs. Ziegler rubbed the back of her neck with a worried glance at her husband. Amber's mood soured. She couldn't wait to reach adulthood. Maybe then Braden's parents would take her seriously. After all, she was going to be their daughter-in-law someday. They could at least pretend to like her.

"I'll watch her closely," Ashlee Lyon said.

"Look," Amber snapped, "we really don't have time to sit around and chit-chat. Braden's dying, so if you don't mind…"

Braden's parents finally swung open the door.

"By the way, Mrs. Ziegler," Amber said as they headed up the stairs, "you don't look too hot yourself. Your coloring is off."

"It's just my head," Braden's mom said, clutching the railing as she dragged herself up the next step. "I'm fine."

"That's how it started with Carrie," Amber said. "A headache. Neck pain. Greg stole extra shots for anyone else who comes down with it. Maybe I should give you a shot, too."

Maybe if she was nice.

"Don't worry about me," Mrs. Ziegler said. "Just help my son."

Amber had been in Braden's room many times over the years. She, Maddie, and Lindsey used to hide in his closet since it was the deepest and darkest place in the house—plus it drove him crazy. Torturing Braden had once been her favorite winter pastime. But then Braden had shot up, filled out, and become unbelievably gorgeous. Amber hadn't been in his room since the two of them became a couple. His walls were covered with peeling Star Wars stickers. Now that he was eighteen, he hated them, but she thought they were adorable.

Creaking open the door, she saw him curled up on his floor. He'd pulled his Millennium Falcon blanket tight around him even though his room felt hot and stuffy. As she crept close, she noticed his summer tan had faded to a sickly yellow, his cheeks looked sunken, and light-colored stubble lined his jaw. Seeing him so miserable sobered her right up.

What would she have done if Greg hadn't stolen the medicine?

What would she have done if Braden had died—or Carrie, or any of them?

Kneeling next to the love of her life, she ran her fingers through his sandy-colored, sweat-damp hair.

"Hey, good lookin'," she said, trying to coax his perfect, turquoise eyes open.

No response.

His hands felt like ice, but the rest of him—arms, neck, and face—burned fire hot.

Ashlee looked over her shoulder. "Has he been drinking water? It's important to keep them hydrated."

"We've been trying, but he's been so sleepy," Braden's dad said.

"Can you help him?" Mrs. Ziegler asked in a small, frightened voice. "Is it too late?"

"No. Carrie was worse than this, and she's already getting better." Although Amber didn't mention Carrie's lingering issues.

What if Braden lost his hearing or vision?

Thankfully, Braden was young and strong. He would get better faster than the others. He'd be fine. Smiling and back to normal soon. He would.

If that was the case, why did her heart pound?

Probably because she never dreamt eight people in their clan would have died over the years. Her parents. Greg's mom. Richard's first wife. And those illnesses hadn't been this severe or…this engineered.

President Rigsby wanted them dead. He couldn't find them, so he sent this instead. Amber hated him with all her soul. He was a murderer of the worst kind because he pretended like he wasn't even behind it, but they all knew.

When she had sat with Braden in the clan cemetery, counting the graves, he had promised to never let her die. He promised to keep her safe, but he never made the same promise for himself. Now his brain was swelling. *The brain!* How could that not cause major issues?

Eyes burning, she stared down at the white box of syringes. What if she *was* too late?

"Are you okay?" Ashlee Lyon whispered behind her.

"Yes. Sorry." Amber opened the small box and pushed up his sleeve. Heat and fever followed.

"Wait." Ashlee Lyon grabbed her hand. "Where's the rubbing alcohol?"

"The what?"

"Didn't the nurses give Greg alcohol swabs so the injection site wouldn't get infected?" Ashlee whispered urgently.

"It will be fine." The last thing Amber needed was for Braden's parents to freak out even more. Besides, she'd already given six shots without sterilization. They'd all gone fine.

"At least get the air bubbles out. Like this." The township clerk flicked the syringe several times with her bright red fingernail, making a soft *thunk* in the room. Then she pushed the stopper up until a tiny bit of medicine leaked out. Amber really hoped those steps weren't vital. If so, Carrie, May, CJ, Richard, Terrell, and Rhonda Watson were in trouble.

"Just straight in," Ashlee Lyon said, handing it back. "Perpendicular to his arm in the upper part of his muscle."

"I know, I know," Amber said. Refocusing, she pushed the needle in. Braden sniffed awake at the sharp sting. Amber quickly slid the needle back out and rubbed the injection site. "Sorry," she whispered.

His wild eyes searched the room until they found her, kneeling above him. He blinked several times, squinting against the soft evening light. "Amber?"

"Hey," she said, relieved. His eyes could still focus.

"Heya...gorgeous." His words were slow and slurred, but a corner of his mouth lifted. It was the saddest, most tired, most pathetic smile he'd ever given her, but it warmed her heart. It only lasted a moment before he winced. "My...head..."

"I know." She raked her fingers through his hair again. "But I'm here to save your life. You'll be better soon."

"It's about time."

His eyes drifted closed again. His breathing deepened soon after, hopefully returning him to a painless place.

Amber stood and looked at his parents in the door. "I have some bad news."

Mrs. Ziegler clutched her shirt. "Did it not work?"

Amber fought the urge to roll her eyes. It had been all of thirty seconds. "I'm sure it will. We just have to move him—move all of you, actually. You can't sleep here tonight."

At their cries of dismay, she explained their unexpected visitor.

"We have to get him all the way to the Trenton's?" Mrs. Ziegler said, looking even more worn down.

"No, just to my house since we own it now," Amber clarified. "Some people are using their water wagons to move the sick people. I brought ours if you want. It's on the sidewalk."

"Okay," Braden's dad said. "Any chance you ladies can help me get him down the stairs?"

Mr. Ziegler grabbed Braden from behind, hands under his arms to carry the bulk of his upper weight. Amber and Ashlee Lyon each took a leg and got the task of walking backwards down the stairs.

Moaning, Braden suddenly kicked out the leg Amber held. She tripped, cried out, and toppled down two steps. The others struggled to keep hold of him.

"Faster!" Mr. Zeigler yelled.

Amber quickly grabbed Braden's leg again and started back down.

They set the love of her life in the all-too-small wagon. Braden's head slumped back, arms flopped over the sides, but he no longer moaned. As his dad wheeled him down the sidewalk, Amber watched his ashen face for any signs of life.

None.

When they reached her house, Amber said, "Sick people have to go upstairs." A daunting prospect.

Braden's dad dropped the wagon handle and wiped his brow. "Can't we just put him somewhere else?"

"No. He has to go upstairs," Amber insisted. And what she didn't add was that Braden was going in her room where she could watch over him all night long.

Mr. Ziegler sighed. "I better go find Greg."

eight

Carrie woke to the smell of soft smoke. With her good ear, she could just make out the crackle of fire in her downstairs fireplace. She'd never known Amber to start breakfast on her own—she'd never known Amber to even wake up before her—but it was a nice gesture.

The first rays of dawn seeped through the thick blanket covering her window. Yawning, she stretched, grateful to have slept so soundly. She could feel her strength returning.

Sitting up slowly, she tested her balance. The room tilted some—or maybe she just felt lopsided with her bad ear—but she was able to stand relatively well. So she worked her way into the bathroom.

Bright morning sun streamed in through the bathroom window, stabbing her vision. Once her eyes adjusted, she made the mistake of looking up. The mirror, honest as ever, showed a pale woman with ratty, tangled hair, and a wrinkled blue blouse that looked like it had been through the war. She hated that, of all people, Greg Pierce had seen her like that. Thankfully—and surprisingly again—the bathroom water bucket was full. No nagging or anything. Amber really had done some growing up the past week.

While Carrie still didn't have the energy to haul in water for a bath, she decided to work on improving her appearance, and with it, maybe her health.

She plugged up the sink and poured cold water into it. Then she grabbed a rag and started sponge-bathing. Her mind wandered to her yard, hardly believing it was hers. Unlike May's backyard, Carrie's sloped down to the pond, which would make growing food challenging. With two huge gardens, their clan would have plenty of excess crops to sell or trade. They could even raise goats and chickens.

Her heart swelled at Oliver's gift. Not only had he given her a home, but part of her mom back as well since Carrie's mother had been the true green thumb. Some of Carrie's most treasured memories had been time spent talking to her mom in the flower beds. Now she could restore the yard to its former splendor. But…that would have to wait. May's garden took priority since it already had crops. It was probably overrun with weeds, and she had no clue when it had rained. It was the first time in six years she hadn't tracked the weather.

When her skin felt cool and clean, she went to work on her rat's nest. Bending over brought the dizziness back with a vengeance, but she dunked her hair and scrubbed her scalp with the soap Terrell got on the black market. The cold water was refreshing. The cleanliness felt divine. By the time she wandered into her room and dressed in her stained jeans and drab yellow t-shirt, she felt more like herself than she had in a long time.

She reached behind her mattress for her weather journal to see when it had last rained. Strangely, it wasn't there. Turning, she scanned her room and spotted it on the floor next to the folding chair Greg had occupied during her illness. She cringed, picturing him reading all the pages of cloud patterns, rainfall amounts, and her own numbering system to guess temperatures.

"I have a scale for how the air feels on my skin," she remembered spouting off the day they met. *"Ten is blistering hot, one is freezing, and seven is perfect."*

If Greg hadn't hated her before, that had solidified it.

"Since when is seven half of ten?" he had challenged.

She hadn't bothered explaining, but in the months following he'd often scoffed, *"What's the weather today?"*

Now he'd seen for himself. Every last embarrassing day from the last six years. Maybe he'd picked it up thinking he would find secrets scrawled about himself, his name with giant swirly hearts around it or something Amber-esque. That would have been less embarrassing.

She snatched up the notebook and cracked open the pages just to check. All still there. Charts. Graphs. Even smiley faces next to sunny days. He was never going to let her live this down.

Sighing, she flipped to the last page to see when it had rained. Two new entries had been written in different handwriting. Male handwriting.

FRIDAY:

Morning: partly sunny

Afternoon: scattered cumulus clouds

"Cumulus?" Carrie said aloud. Did Greg even know what a cumulus cloud was? Intrigued, she kept reading his tiny script.

Evening: windy

Daytime humidity: Are you serious? How am I supposed to know a thing like that?

Peak temperature: 7 (Based on your previous entries, you'd probably give today a 9, but being an honest man, I couldn't. It gets a heckuva lot hotter in Carolina. Sorry.)

She smiled in spite of herself.
His next entry looked more hurried.

SATURDAY:

Morning: Rainy

Daytime humidity: 100%, I guess

Afternoon: Hot and muggy

Evening: I can barely breathe, your room is so dang hot. But you won't stop shivering even though I've dumped every last blanket I can find on you. You're scaring me, Carrie girl. You gotta get better. Come on. Fight it.

Please get better. Please.

She stroked the words etched into her history.

His entries stopped there, leaving the last two days unaccounted for. She could have backlogged them to keep up her perfect streak, guessing the weather while they'd been in the hospital. Instead, she closed it and hugged it for a long moment.

Greg.

Finally, she set it aside and headed downstairs. With Amber awake and cooking, Carrie could get her medicine early. Each hour on the medicine would bring increased strength, which was good because she needed to hit life at full speed.

Twelve hours to garden.

Twelve hours to figure out how to make David Jamansky tell her where Oliver really was.

Two steps into the family room, Carrie stopped. Amber wasn't in front of the fireplace. In fact, no one tended the crackling fire, but Greg was sprawled out on the floor in front of it, dead asleep. His deep breathing filled the room. A small basket of eggs sat next to her dark fry pan, glowing orange with firelight.

A smile spread through her all over again.

Greg looked so peaceful, mouth hanging open, muscled arm draped over his eyes. Unlike her, he hadn't cleaned up yet. Dark stubble ran along his jaw, his brown hair went every which way, and his favorite UNC shirt looked rumpled. But she loved it—loved him. He'd come to make her breakfast and conked out while waiting for the coals to heat. He'd probably filled her water buckets, too.

She thought about kissing him on the cheek—or better yet, the lips—but not only did she lack that kind of boldness, he needed the sleep.

Creeping across the room, she held her palms out to test the fire. It felt hot enough. She sat on the warm tile and grabbed the first egg, wondering how he liked his eggs cooked. It seemed like she should know that already. While she worked, she kept her back toward the fire to dry her hair faster.

A sudden thought made her cheeks flush as hot as the flames. She'd wandered out of the bathroom in a towel without realizing she had company. She didn't think Greg had seen her, but apparently he no longer felt the need to knock on her front door. The man really didn't—

"Good morning," a soft voice said.

Carrie whirled around, pulse spiking.

"Sorry," Ashlee Lyon said. "I didn't mean to startle you. Greg said I could stay here last night. He said you offered."

Resetting her heart, Carrie smiled. She'd completely forgotten about Ashlee. "Of course. Did you sleep well?"

"Not really." Ashlee tiptoed around Greg's sprawled-out body to join her by the fireplace. "No offense, but I'm not used to sleeping on the floor and your house is so hot. I don't know how you live without air conditioning. Amber let me sleep in her room, which was nice, but my mind kept racing, worrying about David and Oliver and everything." She stared into the fire that was dying down to bits of glowing embers. "What time is it anyway?"

"Maybe five thirty or six. The sun rises early this time of year," Carrie whispered, trying to keep her voice down so Greg could sleep. Clueless, Ashlee kept going full-voice.

"You don't happen to have a phone, do you? I'm supposed to be to work by eight. Not that I'd know what to say if I called. I mean, what would I say? 'Hey, David, are you done beating me up?' And do I want him knowing where I am anyway?" Her shoulders slumped. "Never mind."

"Sorry," Carrie offered.

Ashlee looked down at Greg snoring softly. A tiny smile lit her beautiful features. "I'm so glad he's not dead. I totally bawled my eyes out when the federal patrolmen told us. Of course David just laughed. He said Greg wouldn't survive basic training. I guess Greg gets the last laugh now, huh?"

Carrie nodded fondly.

"He sure is a hottie, too," Ashlee went on. "Even when he sleeps. Maybe especially when he sleeps, because his tongue is sharper than a knife. But I think he knows it. Do you think he knows he's a hottie?"

Carrie froze, cracked egg in hand. "Um...maybe. I guess."

The immature side of her wanted to say, *Back off. He's mine!* But considering he'd only been "hers" for less than a week, she had no real claim to his affections.

Her eyes flickered back to Ashlee. Not only was the woman beautiful, but she looked healthy, with curves, unlike the starved twigs the rest of them were. Someone had given her Chicago Cubs sweats to wear that she'd cinched around her waist. She had flawless skin and bright red nails, in contrast to Carrie's nails that were usually dirt-crusted and cracked from working in the garden.

Carrie suddenly remembered how Greg had sweet-talked his way into citizenship. That had been Ashlee, the woman who had fallen for his charms enough to ignore his illegal past.

Ashlee seemed to notice her reaction and waved a hand dismissively. "Oh, don't worry. Greg never gave me the time of day. But he sure is some nice eye candy, isn't he?" She sighed. "Definitely glad he's not dead."

Awkwardness filled the room. Carrie was even more grateful that Greg was sleeping so soundly. His ego didn't need any boosting.

She grabbed the last brown egg—the eighth, which was two more than their standard allotment. Greg had brought his own. With her returning health, Carrie was starving, but Ashlee probably was, too. She doubted Greg had eaten much in the last few days as well. Eight eggs for five people. A small breakfast, but it would have to do.

Ashlee stared at the dwindling fire, gaze far away. "I thought I'd wake up knowing what to do with myself. David knows I'm gone by now. I bet he's torn my house apart looking for me. What will he do when I'm not at my parents' place either? Burn down my house?"

Carrie turned. "Would he?" Then again, Jamansky had ordered Oliver to burn down Scott Porter's house in Ferris.

"Maybe not. The government owns my house, and David stays there half the time anyway. But I bet he'll go on a rampage and have the whole precinct out looking for me."

"Well, you're safe here. Stay with us as long as you'd like. We're happy to have you."

Ashlee stared at her, eyes still puffy and red from the day before. "Thanks. Is there somewhere I can clean up?"

"Sure. Use the upstairs bathroom. There's still some water in the bucket next to the sink. Soap, too."

"A bucket?"

"Yes. Sorry. There should be an extra towel in the cupboard. Oh, and even though we don't have running water, you can still use the toilet. There's another water bucket next to it for refilling the tank. Just lift the tank lid to fill it after you flush. There's also a small basket of leaves on the floor for...well..."

Ashlee grimaced. "Toilet paper? Is it too much to hope that you have makeup?"

"No makeup, but you can use my hairbrush," Carrie offered lamely. "Top drawer. And we have extra toothbrushes in CJ's garage. I'll grab one for you when I'm done."

Ashlee's revulsion was hard to miss. Their life. Their lack of supplies. The poor woman wore Richard O'Brien's old sweats, and Carrie couldn't offer anything better.

Carrie tucked some damp hair behind her ear. "Breakfast won't be ready for another few minutes, so take your…"

She trailed off, hearing a muffled sound behind her. It almost sounded like footsteps coming up from the basement.

Startled, she said, "Is someone here?"

Sometimes Zach slept downstairs when the upstairs grew unbearably hot. Other than that, she and her siblings rarely went down there since it was nothing but empty space and old memories. But it wasn't Zach who emerged from the basement doorway. It was Niels Zeigler.

"Good morning, ladies," Braden's dad said as if it was completely normal for him to emerge from Carrie's basement at six in the morning.

"Hi?" Carrie said in a question.

Niels scratched his thick, brown beard, still looking half asleep. "You two are up early. I know I'm not supposed to come upstairs, but Kristina asked me to check on Braden. Is it alright if I peek in on him? I promise not to touch anything."

"Yeah, sure," Carrie said. "Um…go ahead."

As Niels headed up her second flight of stairs, she turned to Ashlee.

"What's going on?" she whispered.

"Wow. You must be a deep sleeper," Ashlee said. "Everyone freaked out after David's visit and decided to sleep in your two legal houses: sick people upstairs, healthy ones downstairs. I can't tell you how many people slept here, though. I feel lost enough."

You and me both, Carrie thought.

"Braden slept with us in Amber's room," Ashlee continued. "Zach slept downstairs so two other sick people could take his room: a middle-aged lady and a big guy who, I think, is named Terry?"

"Terrell," Carrie corrected. "No wonder you had a rough night of sleep. Thank you for helping everyone."

Helping strangers she didn't even know.

Carrie eyed her small pan. Eight eggs to feed how many?

Why all the extra precautions when David Jamansky wasn't returning until evening? It had to be Greg's doing. Not that she minded people staying at her house. She doubted Greg had slept downstairs with the healthy clansmen either since he was convinced he was immune from this G-979—and he had acquired the habit of parking himself next to her mattress. She was too embarrassed to ask where he'd slept, but she kicked herself again for sleeping so deeply. And wandering the upstairs in a towel.

A house full of people.

How had she slept through it?

It wasn't until she scraped the scrambled eggs from the bottom of her fry pan that she figured it out. If she'd slept with her good ear pressed to the pillow—which she usually did since she slept on her stomach—she wouldn't have heard much.

A chill ran through her.

She needed to hear. Night raids could happen anytime. Patrol dogs, shouts of warning. She had to hear to keep her siblings safe. Life was too dangerous to sleep through people wandering her house.

Rubbing her ear, she decided she'd have to learn to sleep on her back.

And never roll over again.

"Are you okay?" Ashlee said, peering at her.

A wave of depression washed through Carrie. "Yes. Sorry. Just not quite back to normal yet."

"Well, I hope you don't mind, but I gave your sister a shot. She's not starting symptoms or anything, but she's been exposed to a lot of people. She's not very careful either."

"Oh. Thanks."

Niels Ziegler came back down to the main floor. "Braden looks the same. I guess it's too soon for the medicine." Yawning, he motioned to Greg. "How late was he out doing guard duty?"

Guard duty?

Had she missed everything?

"I didn't hear him come in," Ashlee said. "Late, I guess."

Niels nodded. "Well, I'm going to sleep a bit longer. It's great that you have carpet downstairs, Carrie. A nice improvement from CJ's basement."

He headed back down, door shutting behind him.

Carrie studied Greg's peaceful face that hadn't budged with all the noise. Had he made everyone pack up their houses, too? Maybe she should have explained Jamansky's visit better. Greg had been furious after Jamansky left, but at the time, she'd hardly been able to keep her eyes open. Still, she thought she had put his mind at ease. Jamansky's visit had been harmless. Impossibly confusing and a touch frightening, but ultimately harmless.

"It's despicable," Ashlee said.

Carrie turned. "What?"

"This. All of this," Ashlee said, staring at the closed basement door. "Forcing respectable people to live like this. The disease that would have killed you all. It's despicable. I can't believe I've been part of it. Oliver was right to help your clan. I didn't understand before, but now... He was right, and I..." Voice catching, her eyes started to water. "I was very wrong."

"A lot of us have been forced into lives we didn't choose," Carrie said quickly. "We're just trying to do our best. If it wasn't for your help getting me legal, I might not even be here right now." Grave number nine. "I owe you so much, so don't be hard on yourself. We're all doing the best we can with what life has given us."

"You know," Ashlee sniffed, "you're making it really hard to hate you."

"Hate me?" The words felt like a slap.

"After what you did to Oliver, breaking his heart and all, I wanted to hate you. But I can't, and I don't, and I'm sorry I wanted to in the first place. I can see why he loves you." Ashlee's eyes overflowed. "You're very nice."

Stunned, Carrie didn't know what to say. Especially as Ashlee covered her face. Carrie rubbed her back, words ringing in her ears.

After what you did to Oliver...

"Gah, I'm such a mess!" Ashlee said, wiping her eyes. "I swear I'm never going to cry again!" With a deep breath, she squared her shoulders and forced a smile. "I'd love to eat now. Thank you."

Standing, Carrie went to grab a plate from the kitchen. Her body—and heart—felt heavier than before as she wandered back into the family room to scoop up some eggs for the township clerk.

After breaking his heart...

"Aren't you going to eat?" Ashlee said, taking the plate.

"I will in a bit." Once Carrie saw how many people she had to feed. She grabbed the fire poker to break up the largest coals. With breakfast done, she needed to stifle any heat she could.

"How do you get men to like you?" Ashlee asked softly.

Carrie cringed again. She wasn't sure how much more of this bluntness she could handle. Tucking another wet lock of hair behind her ear, she said, "I don't know what you mean."

"Oliver. Greg. Now David. Not that you aren't kind of cute, but what's your secret?"

"I'm not sure what you've heard, but Oliver and I have been friends for years. And Greg is...well, Greg." She still didn't know why he'd fallen for her. "And David loves you, not me."

"No, David *used* to love me. Not anymore—which bugs me more than it should. I mean, I totally hate his guts, but the fact that he hates me back gets under my skin. I want him to adore me so I can crush him like he crushed me. But he's already moved on to you. Shallow, right? Stupid that I need attention like that, even from a jerk like him?"

"No. I can understand."

That seemed to be the wrong thing to say. Ashlee looked at Carrie, eyes blazing with a sudden hatred. "You just stay away from him, okay? He's trouble."

As if anyone had to tell her. Already she dreaded his return. Even the slight possibility of him being interested in her sent a cold chill through her. What would she say a second time? How would she get him to divulge Oliver's whereabouts, or keep Greg from—

A loud click suddenly echoed through her house. First one click and then a series of clicks, one right after another.

Carrie's eyes darted around in time to see her family room light up. Not early morning light streaming in from the windows, but direct, overhead, artificial light.

In an instant, her family room went from semi-darkness to noonday.

Gasping, she fell back. Her knee hit the fry pan, knocking it onto the hearth with a loud clank. Scrambled eggs spilled everywhere.

Greg jolted upright. "What is it? What's wrong? What happened?"

Carrie looked up, hardly believing it. Her lights were on. And more than just the lights. Soft air blew down as her ceiling fan started rotating. Little particles rained down on them, sending six years of accumulated dust flying off the rails. All through the house, soft buzzes and hums started up as her electricity sparked back to life.

"What the heck?" Greg said, looking up.

Shouts of excitement echoed from the basement. Even from the upstairs, Carrie heard Amber yell, "What? No way! This is so cool!"

Footsteps came tearing up the basement steps. Three people burst into the family room at the same time Amber came flying down from her bedroom.

"What is going on?" Niels Ziegler asked.

"I...I don't know," Carrie said.

Whatever light switches had accidentally been flipped on in the last six years had flickered back to life. No warning. No reason whatsoever.

Carrie smiled. "But I think my power just came on."

nine

The eggs were forgotten. They tried every light switch. If Carrie would have had any small electronics left, they would have tried the plugs, too. Carrie about cried when Amber turned on the stove and it worked. Real heat. As amazing as that was, Kristina Ziegler noticed air blowing from the vents. The air conditioner had kicked on, blowing cold, stagnant air throughout the house. Every healthy person found a vent to stand on. They tried the faucets, but the water was still off. Still, that couldn't dampen their spirits. Amber and Zach danced around the house.

"No more dark nights!" Amber cheered.

The longer it went, though, the more Carrie's joy dissipated. She wanted to think this was Oliver's doing, but Oliver knew they didn't have money to pay for electricity. After spending every last dollar to get Carrie legal, neither did Oliver. Which meant an explanation Carrie didn't like. She could see it in Greg's stiff posture that he had pieced it together, too.

Greg locked eyes with her. He stayed quiet, leaned against her kitchen counter, arms folded while everyone else rejoiced. One thing she liked about him was his ability to always keep the future in sight. *Now* shouldn't come at the expense of *tomorrow*. Maybe that's why the Collapse hit him so hard. For a guy who always planned ahead, the Collapse stole everything he had planned for his future.

He didn't want to ruin this happy moment for her, but one name hung in the air-conditioned air between them:

Jamansky.

He had done this.

As Zach danced past Carrie again, she snagged his t-shirt. "Hey, Zach, run around and turn off all the lights."

"Why?" Zach said, pulling up short.

"Because," Carrie said.

"Wait. Why do we have to turn off everything?" Amber said, overhearing.

The others stopped, too. Carrie glanced at Greg again and explained. "May and CJ have electricity, but they don't use it because they can't afford it. Neither can we."

"But—" Zach started.

"Just go," Carrie said.

Greg pushed away from the counter. "I'll head downstairs and shut off the air conditioner."

As he left, Carrie wandered over to the nearest kitchen vent. She pressed her bare feet to the ice-cold metal, savoring the feel on the soles of her feet. She knew the moment Greg found the switch because the air stopped. She told herself it was for the best. They'd survived all this time without electricity. Thanks to Oliver, she had a house and a yard to call her own. No need to get greedy. But she couldn't help but wonder if Jamansky had restored her power just to torture her clan, teasing them with things they could never have.

Just a new layer to his cruelty.

———— ◆ ————

"What skills do you have?"

"Skills?" Oliver repeated.

The large prison guard looked irked. "Yes. Plumbing? Cooking? Electrical work? We assign you to work areas based on previous skills. Just like the sign says. You do read, don't you?"

Snickers broke out in the line behind Oliver.

He ignored them. It was barely eight in the morning, and the guard looked like he'd already had a long shift. Oliver didn't feel sorry for him. Yesterday, he'd been ushered through paperwork and guards going through the rules. Today was his first full day in this prison work camp. Today he would be unleashed to the rest of the inmates, guys who looked like they might try cannibalism for the fun of it.

Skills. What skills do I have?

He stared down at his stiff, baggy, orange jumpsuit. His brain still felt foggy from a night spent sleeping on hard cement that reeked of urine. Every spot Jamansky had kicked him seemed to have swollen overnight into something excruciating. He could barely breathe without pain stabbing his lungs. His nose felt bruised, and the rest of him felt broken.

Someone behind him swore angrily. "Hey, idiot, go already!"

Skills.

Skills.

"I'm a patrolman," Oliver said.

That brought another round of snickers. Oliver made the mistake of glancing back. It was like looking into a pack of ravening wolves.

"He was a patrolman," one cooed. The guy looked like he'd come straight from a Chicago street gang, with wild, greasy hair. "Maybe you should make him a guard like you, eh? He'd make a pretty one, too. Wouldn't you, princess?" The gangbanger made kissy lips at Oliver.

Oliver quickly faced front again.

Laughter broke out in the room, loud and frightening.

A huge crack echoed as the guard slammed his nightstick on the counter.

"Silence!"

The guard waited until the snickers simmered down before his murderous glare went back to Oliver. "Try to think real hard, inmate R2964E5. What skills do you have? Janitorial? Can you do laundry?" He spat each word with such venom it upped Oliver's anxiety.

What can I do?

What can I do?

Each heartbeat stabbed his ribs. All he could think about is what he had *done*. How many in Carrie's clan would go through this same process? Carrie? Zach and Amber? Old May and CJ Trenton? Their faces made an endless loop of misery in his mind.

"I'm a patrolman," he repeated softly.

The nightstick slammed down again, only across the back of his fingers. Oliver screamed and jerked his hand back.

"You *were* a patrolman," the guard said. "Now you're nothing." Scribbling something on a slip of paper, he said, "Give this to the food service manager and head to that station over there. Next!"

Oliver shook out his hand. He couldn't bend his fingers. They throbbed with red hot pain. But he did as commanded, heading to the next spot, the only station that didn't have a line in front of it.

A guard looked up from behind a table. "What's your number?"

"R2964E," Oliver recited.

The guard typed something in his computer before nodding. "Follow me. Hey, Zinka," the guard called. "I'm going to need you for this one."

Oliver glanced over his shoulder as they led him out of the Commons. He was the only person in orange being taken anywhere else. He'd stood in that last line until his feet ached, but he hadn't seen a single inmate being escorted like he was now.

They led him into a small room where another man sat. The man was dressed differently from the other guards, wearing a simple white lab coat.

"Got one for you," Oliver's guard said.

The man pushed up his glasses. "The first of the day. Lucky him. What's your number, inmate?"

As Oliver recited it, he looked around the small room. Strangely, it resembled a doctor's office with medical equipment hanging from the walls. But there was a distinct smell in the room, almost like something burning.

Oliver's eyes zeroed in on a large metal object on the counter. One end was plugged into the wall. The other end was shaped in a circle with a crossed-out star in the middle.

He stared at that crossed-out star. His heart stopped.

A traitor's seal.

Given to those who committed treason against the government.

"Lift your sleeve," the man said, picking it up. And then to the guards, he added, "Hold him tight. I can't have him flailing around."

ten

"You alright?" Greg said, rushing back to Carrie. She had stopped in his grandparents' doorway, holding the door jamb and blinking a hundred times.

She rubbed her eyes. "Yes. It's just so bright outside. Can you help CJ?"

Greg took his grandpa from her and helped him out onto the porch. Greg and Carrie had come over early to catch his grandparents up on everything. Being the stubborn people they were, they insisted on attending the morning meeting on their front lawn. Greg had already helped his grandma outside, the feebler of the two, shuffling her one tiny step after another. He'd barely gotten her settled down on the front porch step when Carrie stopped. Richard O'Brien brought up the rear, inching gingerly across the living room. A sad group.

"Almost there, Grandpa," Greg said.

Like his frail wife, Greg's grandpa took forever lowering himself onto the cement step. He hadn't been as sick when he started the medicine. Still, his clothes hung on him worse than usual, and his tan Dockers that he wore every day of his life were cinched tight with a frayed belt to keep them from falling. Greg's grandpa had lost weight that he needed to put back on soon. Even his thick, white beard was a tangled mess. But he was back on his feet. That had to be good.

Once Greg got him settled, he went back to Carrie, who leaned against the brick, rubbing her eyes. Light sensitivity seemed an unfair curse for the girl who loved the outdoors more than anybody he knew.

"When I get rich," Greg said, "remind me to buy you a rockin' pair of sunglasses."

Carrie smiled. "Okay."

"Or do you want my hat? I'd be happy to donate my lucky Yankees cap to somebody who looks way better in it than I do."

The memory made her smile, but she shook her head. "No. I'm fine."

Greg surveyed the group congregating in the front yard. Terrell Dixon lay on the grass, Sasha Green sat with the little Kovach boys under the huge oak tree, and Carrie's siblings talked to their friends on the driveway. Braden Ziegler hadn't come because he still felt too miserable. His mom woke with a splitting headache of her own. Ashlee Lyon stayed behind, promising to keep an eye on both of them.

Kristina Ziegler made the eighth person who had caught this G-979 virus. Since she had slept in Carrie's basement with the other "healthy people," they'd probably have more starting soon, making Greg wonder if they'd ever completely contain it.

Sighing, he slid his fingers into Carrie's and pulled her close. That took the edge off his stress. But she wasn't quite close enough. Sliding an arm around her waist, he kissed her forehead, a long lingering kiss that let him enjoy the scent of her soft hair.

"Greg," she whispered, "people can see."

"I know. Why do you think I'm behaving?" He kissed her temple next, planning to make his way down her enticing jawline. She had the softest skin of anybody he knew.

Her cheeks colored. "Greg."

He grinned and traced the blush settling across her summer freckles. "Come on. How am I supposed to resist this?"

Her lashes lowered, heightening her loveliness.

"What in the world?" his grandma said suddenly.

Greg looked over his shoulder. His grandma sat on the porch step, mouth hanging open at the sight of the two of them connected at the hip.

"What's wrong, Grandma?" Greg asked innocently.

"Well...it's just that I thought..." She struggled for a moment before giving up with a harrumph. "Why didn't you tell me you two were an item now? CJ, did you know Carrie is with our Gregory? CJ! Turn around and look."

Greg's grandpa barely glanced back. "Yep."

That only made her scowl. "You should have told me. It would have cured me right up."

Crazy enough, it probably would have. Forget medicine. The woman's entire existence revolved around her family and making sure they got what they needed—or what *she* thought they needed. In Greg's case, that meant a sweet girl like Carrie Ashworth.

Greg's smile faded. His mom would have liked seeing him and Carrie together, too—seeing Greg happy like he was.

"I told you that you two would make a lovely couple." His grandma shook a wrinkled finger at him. "What took you so long?"

"Would you believe it, Grandma, but Carrie wouldn't have me. I chased her for months and months, but she wouldn't give me the time of day. I guess this illness zapped the last of her fight, 'cause she finally caved. Lucky for me, don't you think?"

It was Carrie's turn to gape at him. "What are you doing, Greg?" she whispered, "That's not even close to…You never even…"

With her face so close, he nearly kissed her again. She was so dang cute when she got all flustered. Instead, he pressed a finger to her soft lips.

"Shhh. Let me have a little fun."

"You better be treating her well, Gregory," his grandma continued to rant. She pushed her thick glasses up. "No letting that sharp tongue get away from you either. Are you treating my Carrie well?"

He crossed his heart. "Doin' my best, but it's a big job. Real big."

Carrie poked him, but he could tell she was fighting off a smile. Her beautiful smile was one of the first things he'd noticed about her. He loved provoking it out of her.

A movement out of the corner of his eye caught his attention. Little Jeffrey Kovach was waving at him—or rather, waving at Carrie.

Greg pointed and whispered. "I think your other friend is trying to get your attention."

Carrie looked up. "What?"

Her bad ear. Greg wanted to kick himself. In an effort to save her from more old lady interrogation, he pointed to the three year old across the lawn.

Blinking rapidly, Carrie saw what he had. "I'll be right back, May," Carrie said.

Greg wasn't about to lose her to some kid, not with a matriarchal lecture brewing, so he followed Carrie through the group. Sasha leaned against the massive tree trunk while the two boys played in its shade.

Carrie crouched down by Little Jeffrey, close but not too close. She'd been on the medicine long enough she probably didn't need to be cautious anymore, but she still was. Nobody knew what to do if a little kid caught it. Give half a shot for tiny ones like Little Jeffrey? Not even Ashlee knew.

"Hi, Jeffrey," Carrie said. "What did you find today?"

The kid grinned a big toothy grin. "Look, look!" His dark eyes, so much like Jenna's, watched in amazement as four tiny ants crawled around his arm. Greg's skin crawled at the sight, but Carrie just smiled.

"Wow," she said. "Where did you find those?"

Little Jeffrey dropped to his stomach and parted the grass to reveal a tiny mountain of dirt. Thousands of ants scurried about. "Look!"

With the kid hunched over, Greg saw several more ants crawling around his t-shirt and one even scurrying across his cheek.

"Those are amazing," Carrie said easily. "Which one is your favorite?"

Little Jeffrey thought a minute before pointing at the ant exploring his elbow.

"Oh, yes. I like that one, too," Carrie agreed.

Jonah, the younger of the two boys, kept hitting his stick against the tree trunk until Sasha yanked it from him. "No hitting trees, Jonah." She shook her head at Carrie. "I keep finding sticks and dead bugs all over my house. You can't take any of those ants home, Jeffrey. They have to stay here. Do you understand? Bugs stay outside."

The light vanished from the boy's eyes.

Greg scowled at Sasha. The Kovach boys had lost both of their parents within one day's time. Jenna died, and Jeff had been kicked out for violence against clan members. Sasha could at least be nice.

Carrie had been ten times the babysitter Sasha was, but after the attack, Jeff Kovach worried that Carrie hated him. Since Sasha had never been able to get pregnant—plus she was married and settled while Carrie had Amber and Zach to take care of—Jeff left his boys with her and Dylan. If Jeff ever returned from North Dakota, he'd obviously want his boys back.

Would Sasha miss them as much as Carrie did?

Carrie searched the grass by her own feet. "Look, Jeffrey. There are more ants over here."

That did it. The kid perked back up and sprinted over to her.

Carrie moved back to give him space. In the bright sun, her honey-colored hair glowed almost as much as she did watching him. During Greg's six weeks at the Naperville training facility, Greg had pictured her like that hundreds of times. Carrie, just standing there, glowing in the sun. It helped to pass the endless hours of field drills, marksmanship, and mind-numbing propaganda classes. When his sergeant pounded him with nightsticks, Greg thought about Carrie's peaceful, gentle nature to keep from fighting back. At night, as he lay exhausted in his upper bunk, he used to stare at the dark ceiling and imagine what it would be like to hold Carrie, to kiss her senseless, and to possibly, maybe, if all the stars aligned, come home and win her affection once and for all. Even during his mission with Isabel Ryan, Greg vowed that if he ever made it back to Logan Pond, he would make Carrie laugh like she deserved to. While she didn't find him nearly as funny as he thought he was, he didn't care.

There was plenty of time for that.

Sometimes he wondered what had happened to the others in Naperville, like Burke and Lopez. Were they fighting illegals? Killing rebels? Or had Isabel and Commander McCormick found Kearney and the resistance, or had Kearney listened to Greg and relocated the rebellion? But those moments of wondering were few and far between. Greg happily left his short career as a special op behind. The only thing he cared about now—the only person—stood a few feet from him, smiling at some little kid playing with ants.

Greg had the sudden, overwhelming, and entirely premature thought that he wanted Carrie to be his kids' mother. Someday. Far in the future. Really, really far. Or maybe not so far. He and Carrie were in their twenties. He'd learned the hard way how fragile life was, so why wait to pursue happiness?

The thought intrigued him.

Carrie glanced up and caught him watching her.

He was half-tempted to ask her feelings on the subject but decided it

"What?" she asked. wasn't worth her dropping dead. So he shook out of his thoughts. "I think everybody's here that's coming. You ready?"

Nodding, she ruffled Little Jeffrey's dark curls before following Greg back to the porch.

Twenty minutes later, the clan had a compromise.

Before Jamansky showed up that evening, they would empty the homes and head down a trail behind the pond. There they would wait Jamansky out, staying long into the night if needed. After the supposed raid Friday, they would reassess. Greg had stayed awake half the night, trying to come up with something that would appease everybody in the group. Now his plan paid off. There hadn't been a single argument. Just a simple, quick consensus. Abandon the neighborhood for the evening. Make lasting decisions in two days. Even Carrie had agreed, which surprised him.

"What about my grandparents?" Greg asked the group. "Should they go with us, or are they safe here?"

His grandpa looked at his grandma who had leaned against Carrie on the step sometime during the discussion.

"Normally I would say it's fine for us to stay," CJ said. "But if we end up with a repeat of that raid in March...well, I don't think we're up to that. Grandma and I better go with the rest of you."

"Alrighty then," Greg said. "We leave this afternoon, which means we should start packin' up the houses now. Terrell says the spot is about half a mile from here. Families should bring enough food to keep people happy—maybe somethin' to entertain the kids, too. And bring sleeping stuff in case somethin' goes wrong."

There were groans at that last part but no outright complaints.

"Can I bring the baseball, Greg?" Zach asked. "We could play another game."

"Sounds perfect. Anything else before we start packin'?" he said to the group.

When nobody spoke, Carrie straightened. "As soon as Jamansky leaves, I'll come over and let you know that it's safe to come back."

Greg whirled around. So that's why Carrie hadn't fought his plan.

"When I said everybody behind the pond," he said, "I meant everybody, Carrie. No exceptions."

She gave him a strange look. "But Jamansky's coming to see me."

"And you won't be home."

"Greg..."

"I'm not budging on this," he said firmly. "It's not safe for you to be there."

His grandma patted her hand. "Gregory is right, dear. That man is dangerous."

"But he won't do anything to me," Carrie said. "I have my citizenship now."

"Yeah?" Greg said. "So did we when he cuffed me and killed my mom."

Carrie jerked back as if slapped. Her gaze dropped to her hands, making him regret letting the words come out so sharply. Technically Jamansky hadn't killed his mom—not directly—but Greg would never forget the moment his gun turned on her. She'd fallen to the floor, he'd knocked her over, breaking her hip and aggravating all of her other issues. And yet, Jamansky had scoffed.

"Looks like I'd be doing her a favor."

She died a few hours later.

Carrie knew what had happened that day. She knew what Jamansky was capable of. So why would she risk seeing that creep?

"You know, Greg," Ron Marino said, "Carrie has a point. It will look suspicious if no one is home when this patrol chief comes back. What if he decides to visit Carrie some other time, only this time we won't know he's coming? Or maybe he'll just wait around for her to get home. Either way could cause us major issues."

"Exactly," Carrie said. "I have to stay. I have to find out about Oliver."

Every one of Greg's muscles went rock hard, but in a burst of genius, he said, "Hey, Richard, you woulda done anything for my mom, right? Does that courtesy extend to her son?"

Richard O'Brien looked suspicious. "Possibly. Why?"

"What if you're at Carrie's house instead when Jamansky comes tonight?"

"No!" Carrie said, jumping to her feet.

"Now hold on," Greg said. "Richard has his citizenship, too. What if you let him pretend to be your dad or uncle or whatever? He can just tell Jamansky you're gone, had to step out, or some other reason."

Carrie was shaking her head before he finished. "I need to ask about Oliver."

"Which Richard can do as easily as you," Greg noted.

"But he's coming to make sure I'm feeling better. I'll ask a few questions, and that's it," Carrie said. "I can handle myself just fine."

Like Oliver did?

That time Greg bit back the words, knowing they weren't worth the pain they would cause her. She still hoped Oliver was safe somewhere.

Thankfully, Richard saw the logic of Greg's plan. "I can handle myself, too, except I don't have two siblings counting on me. I have to agree with Greg. I'm the safer choice. So will you do me the honor and allow me to pose as your father?"

"But you're still sick!" she said.

Richard smiled tiredly. "As are you. But I'm afraid this situation isn't safe for you. If this patrol chief really is romantically interested in you…"

"Obsessed," Greg cut in. "Ashlee specifically said Jamansky's *obsessed* with her."

"If that's the case," Richard said, "then—"

"It's not!" Carrie said, face reddening.

"Or if he tries to get revenge on Oliver by lashing out at you," Terrell Dixon added from his spot on the grass. "Either way, Richard's the safer bet. I agree, too."

Desperate, she scanned the group for support. The women seemed unsure, but every man Greg saw nodded emphatically. They got it. They knew enough about David Jamansky—and alpha-types like him—to understand how dangerous he could be to a woman like Carrie.

"All in favor of Richard talking to Jamansky instead?" Greg asked.

Every hand rose. That is, every hand but Carrie's. Greg could feel her eyes boring into the back of his head, a deep laser-like beam that meant he was going to pay for this later.

"Then it's settled," he said. "Everybody but Richard behind the pond tonight. We better start packin' up the houses now if we're gonna be done in time."

As people started for home, he found the courage to turn around. Those deep blue eyes pinned him, expecting an apology. He refused. Carrie's life motto involved sacrificing herself to save others. But he couldn't let her. Not this time. Not even for Oliver.

She broke away first. "I better get home, May. Apparently I have to pack up my house."

Standing, she walked down the sidewalk and past Greg without another glance.

"Want help?" Greg called out.

She didn't answer.

He grunted to himself. He was pretty sure that she'd heard him just fine.

Running a hand through his shaggy hair, he sighed. "Alrighty. Let's get y'all ready."

eleven

The last time the clan played baseball, Amber, Maddie, and Lindsey offered to be cheerleaders. Amber had loved that, especially watching Braden get all sweaty as he killed it on the field. Today she sat with her friends—old and new—on a ratty blanket, watching the game. Braden lay next to her, in and out of consciousness, with Ashlee Lyon acting as a germ barrier to Braden's younger sisters.

Amber studied the slow rise and fall of Braden's hand on his chest. She loved that he still wore the red bracelet she'd made him. He said he wasn't as cold today, but his skin still burned hot and he slept almost nonstop.

Desperate to know how he was doing, she nudged his shoulder. "Hey," she whispered. "Are you awake?"

Braden didn't respond, but Maddie did. Not very nicely, either.

"Leave him alone, Amber," Maddie growled.

Lindsey leaned forward to see down the line. "Is she trying to wake him up again?"

"No, I just thought he moved," Amber said.

"Right," Maddie drawled. "Let him sleep. He's been through enough."

As if Amber didn't know that? She just liked it when he woke up. It reassured her that he was actually improving. For some reason, he was taking longer than the others to bounce back, which worried her.

Sighing, she hugged her knees to watch the stupid game.

The area they were hiding in was bumpy and filled with weeds, so the players spent forever stomping down a spot to play. Then Greg went easy on the batters since they were back to using the rusty pipe and everyone had to catch the ball barehanded. He pitched soft enough even Amber could have hit it. He was the only decent player out there, too. Jeff Kovach was long gone, Terrell was too weak—obviously Braden, too—and Sasha was watching the little boys. Somehow Zach had convinced Carrie to play even though she looked tired. Then again, Zach always got away with murder. Carrie stood over the third base rock, rubbing her bad ear and blinking a million times—two annoying habits she needed to break. Soon.

Everything was irking Amber today, including Ashlee Lyon who, for some reason, was being super quiet.

Leaning over, Amber felt Braden's forehead. Hot, even in the shade. How did anyone think he was improving?

"Hey, Ashlee," she said. "When can I give Braden the next shot?"

Ashlee Lyon scratched a spot on her arm. "Tonight. Before bed."

"I think we should give him an extra one now. He's not doing very well."

"They told us in the township that it would take a day or two for the medicine to kick in. He just needs time."

"Time stinks," Amber muttered. Either it went aggravatingly slow, or it sped by, stealing perfect moments before they had barely started.

She leaned back on her elbows, still keeping her left side pressed against Braden even though it made her hot and sticky.

"Speaking of time," Ashlee Lyon said, glancing up at the sun, "what time do you think it is?"

"No clue. Are you really that worried about your ex and Richard?" Maybe that's why Ashlee was being so quiet.

"Yes. I hope he doesn't bring his dogs." Ashlee Lyon hugged her knees. "If he does, he'll have no problem tracking us down—tracking *me* down."

That kick-started Amber's heart. Ever since she'd woken up in March to patrol dogs barking and searching the neighborhood, she'd had nightmares about them returning.

"Bretton and Felix know me well," Ashlee said. "If David's smart, he could track me from the office to your neighborhood. And then…"

She didn't have to finish.

Amber smacked her leg. "Why are you telling me this? Have you told Greg and Carrie any of this?"

"No. It just occurred to me."

"Well, don't," Amber said firmly. "They're stressed enough. I'm sure it's fine. We'll be fine. We're nowhere near the neighborhood, so we're fine, okay? Stop freaking me out."

A soft moan sounded on the other side of her.

Amber twisted around.

"Braden!" she said excitedly. "You're awake!"

His beautiful, turquoise eyes opened. Barely. Blinking a few times, he found her hovering over him.

"How long was I out…that time?" His voice sounded groggy.

"Forever," she said. "But that's okay. I know you're tired. Sorry. Did I wake you up?"

"Yeah." He licked his dry lips. "Thank you."

Ashlee Lyon stood. "He needs to drink. I'll go get him some water."

As she left, Amber brushed some sandy-blond hair off Braden's warm forehead. "Does your head hurt any less?"

"Some. How's…the game?" he asked.

"Awful. I wish you were playing."

Another weak smile. "Me, too. I think…" He paused for a slow breath. "I think I lost something."

Amber looked around. She hadn't seen him bring anything in the wagon they'd carted him in, and he still wore his bracelet. "What is it?"

His hand moved around on the ragged blanket, tapping and feeling around until it found hers. He brought it on top of his warm chest and clutched it to him. Then he closed his eyes again with a contented sigh.

She didn't mind that time when he drifted back to sleep.

———————◆———————

When Carrie saw Ashlee Lyon heading toward the water bucket, she decided that was excuse enough. Energy drained, she waved at her brother.

"Hey, Zach, I'm going to rest for a bit."

Zach didn't care. He was in baseball heaven. But Greg shot her a worried look. She hadn't felt up to baseball, but Zach begged her to play. Greg had pitched in his usual position, but he'd watched her often, giving her a thumbs up anytime she made a good play—anytime she made *any* play. Groveling from afar. He offered his NY Yankees cap again to shield her eyes, but she insisted she didn't need it. Now he looked amazing in his hat and she had a stabbing headache.

She knew the game. Usually she even enjoyed playing it. But with everything...

Ashlee ladled some water into a small drinking cup.

"Can I join you?" Carrie asked.

Ashlee looked up. "Oh. Sure." The government clerk forced a smile like she had been doing all afternoon, but Carrie could see through the anxieties and worries. That pushed Carrie's own fears back to the surface.

Richard. Jamansky.

Oliver.

"Are you doing okay?" Carrie asked.

Ashlee took a small sip of water. "I'm thinking about going back."

"Oh. Okay. I can take you back once Richard returns."

"Not back to your neighborhood," Ashlee clarified. "Back home. "

Carrie stared at her. "Why?"

"I don't belong here. I'll only cause more issues by staying. And if I can just get access to my computer, I might be able to figure out where Oliver is."

"You're not causing issues," Carrie said. "Seriously. As for going back, it doesn't seem safe. Maybe Jamansky will tell Richard where Oliver is tonight. Hopefully after tonight and the patrol sweep Friday, we'll know more. What if you wait until then?"

Ashlee sighed. "Yeah. I guess."

The game dwindled until it was just Zach, Greg, Tucker, and the Dixon twins tossing the ball around. The boys were running Greg ragged, but he didn't seem to mind. He never did, which was good because the game—even the little she had contributed—had worn out Carrie. She needed to get off her feet. But at least Zach was enjoying himself.

Which reminded her...

"Can I ask you a question?" she said to Ashlee. "I need to get citizenship cards for Amber and Zach. Do you have any suggestions?" Carrie dreaded going into Shelton. In the last six years, she'd only been around real citizens once, and her date with Oliver hadn't exactly turned out well. Case in point, she was sitting in a weed patch instead of her house.

"My partner, Ellen," Ashlee said, "will probably be covering my shifts. She's not exactly the easiest to work with, even before I disappeared, but don't let her scare you. Just tell her what you need and make sure you have all your paperwork. You'll need to have the fee ready and prorated for the year which should be a few hundred dollars for both of them. And you'll need the new currency, but I think Greg already exchanged your money."

"A few hundred dollars?" Carrie said. A small fortune. "I'll have to check with CJ. Our hospital trip used a lot of our money, but I don't know how much. Actually, didn't you give Oliver money to help us?"

Ashlee shrugged. "Some."

Just another way Carrie was indebted to her. "Thank you."

"It's fine." Ashlee waved away a mosquito buzzing around her blonde hair. "I just wish I'd brought the rest of my money with me. I wish I'd done a lot of things before I ran off like a spoiled brat." She ducked away from another bug. "Why am I the only one getting eaten alive? It must be my hairspray." Scratching her scalp, she said, "You'll need Amber and Zach's birth certificates, and any other paperwork you can think of. Ellen shouldn't ask for it, but it's better to be safe than sorry, right?"

Better safe than sorry.

Carrie stole a glance over her shoulder at Greg. His arm was cocked back, ready to pitch another one. But seeing her gaze on him, he straightened. A corner of his mouth quirked up, offering her another tiny, apologetic smile. The hundredth of the day.

Safe.

Sorry.

"Are you sure you don't want me to come with you?" Ashlee asked. "If I returned, I could process their cards for you."

It was a half-hearted offer, like Ashlee really didn't want to go back home, she just didn't know where else to go. "No. I'll be fine. I'll go with them Wednesday and get it all figured out. I don't mind going on my own."

"Goin' where?" Greg said, coming up behind her.

Carrie flinched but didn't turn. "Thanks for your help, Ashlee."

"Sure." Ashlee's gaze flickered to Greg, probably wondering if Carrie would answer him. When Carrie didn't, Ashlee said, "Well, I better give Braden his water before he falls back asleep."

As she left, Carrie picked up her own cup and ladled water into it. Out of the corner of her eye, she saw Greg watching her, waiting for an answer.

"How are your grandparents holding up?" she asked, taking a sip.

"Fine," Greg said pointedly. "And you?"

"Fine."

A soft breeze blew her hair around, acting as a partial shield between them. She watched the game, thinking through the price of citizenship—both literal and theoretical. With Greg gone, the boys had started tossing the ball back and forth, faster and harder to see who could catch it barehanded without flinching. It looked painful.

Greg still watched her.

She shaded her eyes to search across the field. "Are you sure your grandparents are okay? May looks tired, and your grandpa seems to have fallen asleep. I actually need to ask him something. Excuse me."

"Carrie, wait," Greg said. "Are you ever gonna talk to me again?"

"What do you mean? Talk about what?"

"The game. The weather. Where you think you're goin' Wednesday. Why you're mad at me. Why you won't even look at me now." Reaching up, he turned her chin until she met his questioning gaze.

"I'm not mad," she said.

He cocked one bushy, skeptical brow.

Didn't he realize that she could never be mad at him again, not after everything he'd done for her? She owed him too much. She owed him her life. So she wasn't mad at him—could never be again. But her thoughts were too turbulent today, so she politely squirmed free and turned back.

"I'm just worried," she said. "Is Jamansky at my house yet? Will Richard know what to say? How mad will Jamansky be when he finds out I'm avoiding him?" The questions tumbled out of her, but beyond those, how would the clan afford to have three more people paying taxes? What if they ran out of medicine? And Oliver. Always Oliver. She sighed. "I'm just worried, Greg. I'm sorry."

"I know. So am I."

Zach threw a fast ball, trying to mimic Greg's pitch, but it flew too fast for Tucker. The ball sailed straight into the woods.

"What the heck, Zach!" Tucker yelled. "You lost the ball!"

"Why didn't you hit it?" Zach shouted back.

The boys darted into the trees to search for Greg's baseball, yelling and hollering about whose fault it was.

"Carrie," Greg said, ignoring the kid drama, "I'm sure Richard is fine. He'll know what to do. Don't worry about him."

Her insides boiled at those words. Richard would know what to do, but she wouldn't have?

She set her cup aside. "I better help the boys find the ball."

Without further explanation, she headed across the field away from him. As Greg started after her, she changed direction.

"Zach!" she called. "I think the ball went off this way."

Heading into the trees, she scanned the ground for anything white. The boys darted around her, climbing in and through and around the thick underbrush. Twigs and branches tugged her jeans, but she kept searching.

She saw a flash of light blue a ways off–Greg's lucky shirt. Only he wasn't behind her. He was searching further down, pushing branches and foliage back to find the ball he'd had since high school.

Zach found it first.

"Got it!" Zach called, holding the ball up high.

The boys whooped and darted past Greg, heading back to the open field. Carrie wanted to return, too, but Greg had moved over to block the path out.

"Call me crazy here," Greg said, "but I'm pretty sure you're mad at me, so out with it."

Carefully, she stepped over a fallen log and approached him. She would have kept going, but he snagged her arm.

"At least tell me where you think you're goin' Wednesday."

"Into town," she said. "To get Amber and Zach's citizenship cards." Her chin lifted an inch, daring him to disagree.

His mouth dropped before clamping shut. He seemed to search for a response that wouldn't get him in more trouble. He should have thought longer because he said, "You should take Richard with you."

"Really? And how many times did Richard go with *you* into town, Greg?"

"Not enough."

His blunt comment startled her into silence. Could Richard have stopped things from escalating with Greg, Mariah, and Jamansky, or would Richard have ended up as another victim? Was Richard in trouble even now?

"Look, Carrie," Greg said, holding up his hands in surrender, "try to understand where I'm comin' from here, why I might not want you home right now. If situations were reversed, would you want me there?"

She stared at his upheld hand and the ragged pink scar running down his left palm. That scar was her fault from when she'd tried to save Jeff and Jenna's things. *"You taught me a valuable lesson that day,"* he had once said. *"Stay outta Carrie's way when she's tryin' to save the world."* Her gaze dropped to his faded UNC t-shirt, remembering the horrid criss-crossed, whipping scars that covered his back. And beyond those were emotional scars she couldn't begin to comprehend.

"It's not like I want to see David again," she said.

His eyes narrowed. "David?"

"Jamansky," she said, deciding first names sounded too familiar. "Part of me is relieved to not be there right now." And honestly, the young patrol chief sometimes looked at her in a way that made her skin crawl, like he was examining a feast to devour.

So why was she so upset?

It was the lack of control. Oliver was in trouble. The only way she knew how to help him involved David Jamansky.

Her headache tripled.

She grabbed a nearby branch and pulled off a small leaf. "It's just that Richard's never met Jamansky before. Jamansky won't want to tell him anything. I hoped to find out where Oliver is tonight, but now..." She swallowed. "Now..."

Oliver could be dead and we wouldn't know it.

She couldn't bear to say the words.

Greg watched her playing with the leaf. The longer he watched her, the harder the emotions pounded against her.

"Oliver sacrificed six years of his life to protect this clan—and me. I have to do something. But instead I'm playing baseball on a beautiful summer evening. Baseball, Greg." Her voice caught. Eyes burning, she dropped the leaf to the thick foliage below.

Oliver.

"Come here," Greg said, tugging her to him.

In the safety of the trees, he wrapped her up in his arms. She let him, needing his strength around her, supporting her, and assuring her that she was just overreacting. Oliver was fine. Her friend would be back any day, any time.

"Wherever he is," Greg whispered into her hair, "I'm sure he'll find a way to contact us to let us know what's goin' on."

"But that's just it," she said, pulling back. "We don't have phones. We don't get mail. We don't have computers or texts or anything. The only way Oliver can contact us is by coming here or sending someone else for him."

"Somebody like...Jamansky," Greg said slowly as if he finally, *finally* understood.

"Yes! I know you don't think Oliver sent Jamansky, but what if he did? What if he had no other choice? If Oliver had to suddenly leave for Virginia, if they took his car or something, he might not have had time to warn us and had to use his boss as a last resort. I mean, it's a long shot and probably wishful thinking, but what if, Greg? Only Jamansky has never met Richard before. Heck, *Oliver* barely knows Richard. Jamansky will never tell Richard a thing."

Greg tipped his head back and stared up into the thick canopy of trees. When he looked at her again, he sighed. "You're right. Do you wanna go home? Jamansky might not have shown up yet. Just..." He ran a hand down the side of his face. "Do you wanna go back?"

"No," she said.

"No?"

She shook her head, feeling the depression return.

He grunted. "I'll never understand women."

She smiled in spite of everything. "I don't want to go back because, unfortunately, you're probably right. It's not safe."

"I'm sorry," he said.

"Me, too."

She tucked some hair behind her ear. "You know, maybe we can do something else while we're waiting. Something that might get my mind off of everything."

"Yeah?" He looked confused for a second before he broke into a slow smile. "Ah, good thinking. Nobody can see us back here." Sliding forward, he wound an arm around her waist. "I'm sorry for bein' so bossy." Then he leaned down to her.

"Wait," she said, heat rushing to her cheeks. "That's not what I meant."

"You sure?" He traced her lower lip with his thumb. Chills followed his touch, muddling her thoughts, but she nodded. They'd been in the woods longer than the boys. Someone was sure to notice, and while Greg had no problem worrying about what people thought about him, she was too self-conscious. Her relationship with Greg had caused issues in the clan before.

His hand dropped away from her face. "Alrighty. What'd you have in mind?"

"First, I'm going into town with Amber and Zach Wednesday, and I don't want you to fight me on it—or get the clan to vote against me. Please?"

His brows pinched again. "Why now? Why with so much other stuff goin' on?"

"That's just it. Did you wait to get your yellow card? You and your mom went the day after you arrived. My biggest fear since my parents died has been losing Amber and Zach. With all this craziness now, I need to know that, at the very least, they're safe."

Though it seemed to pain him, he nodded. "For the sake of my sanity, will you at least take Richard with you? Pretty, pretty, pretty please?"

"Yes," she relented. "If he's feeling up to it."

"Good enough. But just so you know..." He leaned back in and lowered his voice. "That doesn't exactly affect right *now*."

He gave her a look that dissolved the last of her defenses: part mischievousness, part longing, and all gorgeousness. The shadow from the leaves danced across his face, yet his eyes were light and alive. He might hate his untrimmed hair, but his Yankees hat pushed it down until it brushed the tops of his dark, thick brows, giving him an almost boyish look.

Definitely irresistible.

His arms slid around her waist to lock behind her back. "So..." he whispered with another smile, "what do *you* wanna do right now?"

A million things.

"Actually..." she started, but his face was so close—all of him was—that she struggled to think clearly. At this distance, she could make out every angle of his jaw, every whisker, every dark eyelash in the dappled sunlight. He might be comfortable with this closeness, but it still felt so new to her, so exhilarating, she didn't even know where to put her hands. Resting them on his chest seemed too familiar, but suspended mid-air made her look awkward. It's not like Greg hadn't kissed her before. He had. A few times even, and it had been unbelievable and—

"Actually...?" he prompted.

"Sorry. Actually, I thought we could..." She let her hands drop to his chest. He didn't seem to notice, so she told herself to stop obsessing about touching him. His sculpted muscles. The hours of rigorous training he'd endured, or the heat of his t-shirt from the sun. Why didn't he notice?

"Are you blushing?" He peered down to study her face and grinned. "Oh, man. You are. Wow, this must be good."

"I want to talk to Terrell," she blurted. "Right now. As in, now now."

"Terrell?"

"And Zach. You can come, too," she offered weakly.

"Terrell," he said again, as if trying to digest it.

She nodded. "And Zach."

"Now?" he asked in a whine.

Her head bobbed again, sure that her cheeks, ears, and neck were a splotchy mess of red.

"Fine," he said, arms barely loosening around her. "What exactly do you want to talk to them about?"

"Finding other clans," she said. "If I remember right, the teens meet tonight."

"Oh? Oh." He took a deep breath that she felt beneath her hands, making her self-conscious all over again. "Good thinking. Don't you want to wait to hear how it went with Jamansky first?"

"I don't know. Who knows how long Richard will be, and the teens only meet once a week. I feel like that should take priority." Plus sitting around and waiting for news was driving her crazy with anxiety. "I know Terrell's not feeling well, and Richard's not here, but maybe they won't mind if you and I go without them—if you want to go."

"Oh, I'll go. Alrighty. We can go ask Zach when the teens meet." His arms tightened around her again. "But first, can *I* request somethin'? It's real fast, or rather"—that look returned, that mischievous, irresistible look of his—"mostly fast."

"Um…'' She bit her lip. "What is it?"

Slowly, he tilted her chin up until his nose brushed against hers.

"I was kinda thinkin' that I wanna know what it feels like to fly," he whispered.

"Fly?"

Cradling her face with infinite tenderness, he leaned down the last few inches and closed his eyes. Her stomach flopped as his lips met hers. Then the world fell away.

His kiss was soft, almost careful. But then his fingers wound through her warm hair and he pulled her tighter in. She melted into him as the last of her worries floated away. A few gentle kisses became several longer ones, and she couldn't seem to think about anything except how unbelievably soft his lips were.

When he pulled back, she was definitely flying. And embarrassingly dizzy. And—she gulped—clutching his t-shirt. She opened her fingers and patted his shirt down flat.

Stupid.

She was so stupid.

"That…" he said a little breathless, "was awesome."

Somehow those three words meant more to her than his kiss had. For a long minute the two of them stood, staring at each other, just smiling.

Then he grabbed her hand. "Let's go find some clans."

twelve

David Jamansky's car reeked of Szechuan chicken, making his stomach growl. It had been a long day filled with whiny, wussy patrolmen. Oliver Simmons had only covered a tiny portion of their precinct. He'd been virtually useless, yet Bushing and Portman acted like David had asked them to cover the eastern half of the United States.

But would the feds send a replacement for Simmons? Not with the civil war brewing.

Add to it the mounds of paperwork and the scathing email Mayor Phillips had sent this morning, and David felt ready to snap. He needed this evening. Carrie's health better have improved. She better not look so sickly either. They had things to discuss—things to *do*.

Carrie.

Just picturing her innocent face helped him relax. It was going to be a good night. He'd make sure of it.

Distracted by the evening's possibilities, he took a turn too fast. The brown bag with the bottle of wine tumbled onto the floor. Swearing, he reached down to grab it. The car jolted as he hit a massive pothole, flipping the Chinese bag onto its side. Szechuan juice spilled everywhere. Screeching to a stop, he searched for napkins. When he found none, he pounded the steering wheel.

This day had just been one thing after another.

By the time he reached the Logan Pond subdivision, his nerves were strung tight. But he couldn't afford to be distracted any longer.

His gaze swept back and forth, searching for any illegals wandering the yards or sidewalks. He checked houses and windows, too. This time Carrie's clan knew he was coming. He'd nearly brought Bretton and Felix with him, but he wasn't sure how they would respond to Carrie. His German Shepherds weren't exactly the cuddly type. They'd been trained for precision and intimidation, not strangers, so he'd left them home. Now he scanned house after house. The neighborhood looked as dead as ever. He couldn't decide if that was a good thing.

At some point, he needed to find out how many illegals lived here. Maybe he would weasel that out of Carrie tonight. Plus, if this clan had contact with others in the area, he could score huge.

All these years they'd been fighting against the illegals, hunting them down—which only forced them further into hiding—when all they really had to do was befriend them.

Let them come to him.

At this rate, the feds would promote him to Central. Plus the bonus money would be nice. They paid by the head these days, which was perfect for this clan. Mayor Phillips didn't even know about the group either, so all the money would be David's, and his alone.

He just had to find a way to get Carrie away from her "friends" before he wiped them all out. She hadn't been as thrilled to see him yesterday as he hoped. Tonight, he planned to do better. Turn up the charm.

As he turned onto Woodland Drive, he half-heartedly wondered if Ashlee had come here to hide. He'd checked everywhere else for her, but all the information he'd forced out of her had been useless, blubbering drivel, proving that she knew less about Carrie and this clan than he did.

So where had the lying, backstabbing wench run off to? Ashlee probably went all drama and hung herself.

If only.

He parked in Carrie's crumbling driveway and did a quick check of his hair, polo, and breath. All good. Then he adjusted the pistol tucked inside his belt. He'd brought it because her clan could still ambush him. But why would they? He was their last access to the patrol sweep calendar. They had to think he was on "their side" now—especially since he'd restored Carrie's power. Still, he felt better with his Glock hidden.

Grabbing the bottle of wine and bag of Chinese food, he hopped out of the car, pasted on his best smile, and strode up Carrie's sidewalk. He was looking forward to her overwhelming gratitude. Being without power for six years would make her putty in his hands.

Knocking on her peeling front door, he stood back. To his surprise, an older gentleman answered.

"Hello," the man said. "Can I help you?"

"Who are you?" David said more brusquely than intended.

"I'm Richard O'Brien." The man extended a hand.

"O'Brien?" The guy was twice Carrie's age with a graying ponytail and sickly, pale skin that made it look like he'd caught the virus from Carrie.

Her father?

Not with that last name.

O'Brien. That name rang familiar to him, but he wasn't sure how.

Unaccustomed to shaking hands with illegals—especially sick ones—he ignored the germ-infested, outstretched hand and said, "I'm Chief Jamansky from the Kane County district. I need to speak with Carrie. Please," he added as an afterthought.

Mr. O'Brien eyed the wine bottle and the bag with a dark Szechuan stain down the side. "I'm afraid Carrie's not home right now."

"Not home?"

"No. I'm sorry."

A twinge of nervousness shot through David. Something was definitely off. He could feel it. He'd specifically told Carrie he was coming back tonight with dinner, so where was she?

She was an adult. Her dad had no business keeping her from him.

Then it occurred to him: Oliver wouldn't have deeded a house to Carrie if her dad lived with her. So who was this guy? Illegals tended to bunch together in groups, shoving as many as thirty people under one roof. This guy could be anyone.

"When will she be home?" he asked, growing impatient. "I know she's been sick. I came to check on her."

"I'm not sure, but she's feeling much better today—thankfully. She actually wanted me to ask if you knew anything more about where Oliver Simmons was, her friend."

Hopefully rotting on a smelly prison floor like David had for a month. If Mayor Phillips hadn't sprung him, he would still be there.

"He's in Virginia," he said coolly. "Like I told her."

Richard nodded. "Okay. Thank you. I'll tell her you stopped by."

O'Brien started to shut the door, but David slapped it back open, stopping him.

"Actually," David said, "I'll just wait."

"I'm not sure that's a good idea. It could be quite late. Can I give her a message for you?"

David's patience snapped. He could offer to come back tomorrow, but he wasn't even in Shelton tomorrow. He'd have to wait until Wednesday. He craned his neck to see inside of Carrie's house. It looked empty and dark. Not a single light on.

He glared at the man. "What's going on? Where is Carrie? Who are you really?"

"Oh, my apologies, officer. Here, let me show you."

The older guy reached for something from his back pocket. David's hand flew to his concealed gun, but the man didn't pull out a weapon. He handed over a yellow citizenship card.

Confused, David snatched the ID card and examined it. The man wasn't illegal after all. His card had been issued a few months ago, making him a full citizen. How? David wished he had brought his verifying machine, but he'd left that home along with every weapon he suddenly wanted at his side.

Richard O'Brien, he read.

63 years old.

Then he stared at the address. *1438 Denton Trail.* That wasn't Carrie's address. In fact, if David's memory served him right, that was the same address as the only other legal residents in this neighborhood, CJ and May Trenton.

In a flash, he suddenly remembered how he knew that name.

"O'Brien!" he barked, his whole body tensing at the connection—and the memory. "You're Pierce's dad."

The guy's eyes widened in fear. "What?"

"Gregory Curtis Pierce," David said, spitting out each syllable. "You married his mom and got your citizenship this spring, didn't you?"

He nodded nervously. "Yes, sir."

Greg's stepdad.

David nearly punched him. Greg Pierce had been nothing but trouble since the moment he moved in. His mom, too, who accompanied him into town. She was this guy's wife. Mrs. O'Brien.

Why was Greg's stepdad there at Carrie's, playing watchdog?

"Sorry to hear about Greg's death," David said with a sneer. "We heard it was pretty grizzly, too. Let me think, was it insubordination? Didn't they shoot him for mouthing off or something? That must be rough for you and your wife."

Richard O'Brien's hand tightened into a white-knuckled fist on the door knob, but somehow he managed to answer calmly. "Yes. It has been a trying time for us. Very trying."

Good, David thought. *Let them suffer.*

With all niceties gone, he leaned forward. "Now, let's try this again, shall we? This time without the lies. Where is Carrie?"

"I told you, she's not here. She's...she's with friends for the evening."

"Then I'll wait."

Terror flashed across the man's face. "She might be gone for days."

Like hell she would. Carrie didn't have a car and she'd been illegal until two days ago. She couldn't have gone far.

David's hand slid to his hip, lifting the corner of his polo enough to expose his gun. Richard O'Brien didn't miss the gesture. He backed up a step.

"Why are you keeping her from me?" David said. "I'm here as a friend of Oliver's—a friend of Carrie's. I'm sure she told you I'm going to help your clan now. Did she tell you about the upcoming sweep?"

O'Brien nodded quickly. "Yes. Friday night. We will be ready. Thank you, officer."

He dared to thank him?

David nearly shoved him aside to storm the house. Carrie couldn't be hiding far. Upstairs? The basement? A few real threats, maybe even some physical coercion, and this guy would probably spill it all. David could salvage his night after all. Except...he'd come to earn this clan's trust. He couldn't have them running again. Throwing his weight around would accomplish nothing.

Gritting his teeth, he straightened. This guy wanted to play games.

He could play games.

"Too bad Carrie isn't home," he said. "Oliver phoned today from Virginia with a message for her—actually an urgent message for all of you. Unfortunately, he said that I can *only* give it to Carrie. But I won't be in Shelton tomorrow. So I guess you'll have to wait."

He paused to see if the man would cave and grab Carrie from whichever dark corner he had hidden her. When he didn't, David's eyes bored into him.

"So I will be back Wednesday, late morning. I suggest you have Carrie home then. Do I make myself clear?"

Richard O'Brien paled. "Perfectly."

thirteen

"Zach, don't the teens meet tonight?" Carrie asked.

Her brother's gaze flickered from her to Greg and then back to the ground. "Don't know."

Greg rolled his eyes. The kid was a horrible liar. "Nice try. When do y'all meet?"

Zach kicked a clod of dirt. "After dinner."

The sun had started to lower for the evening, making it around seven o'clock. Carrie looked tired and overwhelmed by the prospect of a long night of walking.

"We can always try next week if you don't feel up to it," Greg offered.

"No," Carrie said. "With this virus spreading and the rebellion, I don't want to wait. Let's go. I know you don't feel well, Terrell, and I'm not trying to leave you out. You're our trading guru after all, but I just…"

"Trading guru? More like Barry's slave," Terrell said, still horizontal on the tattered blanket. He scratched his thick, black beard. "It's not like I volunteered for this assignment anyway, so I'll happily say I'm too sick to wander around for miles on the off chance of meeting people who don't want to trade with us anyway." He closed his eyes and lay back down. "Have fun."

Carrie's big, blue eyes lifted to Greg, suddenly dancing with anticipation. This had been her plan after all, trading seeds, chickens, goats, and anything else with other clans. She claimed to have just tweaked Greg's flower shop idea, but even his idea had been sparked by something she'd said a long time ago. No, this farmers' market idea was all her, and she was practically bouncing to get to it. He could have kissed her again. Instead, he slid his fingers into hers.

"You ready yet?" he teased.

She answered by tugging him forward.

A few steps into their trip, Greg noticed it was just the two of them—which was nice and all, but kind of beside the point. Glancing over his shoulder, he spotted a scrawny, freckled teen trying to sneak away.

"Hey, Zach," Greg called, "where do you think you're goin'?"

Zach flinched. "Don't make me go. They're gonna kill me. Just pretend like you found them by accident."

"Come on, Zach," Carrie said. "We don't know the way, and those teens need to know we're not a threat. Besides…after all your lies and sneaking around, you owe me."

Zach was skittish as they left, scanning the trees and jumping at the slightest sound. He limped heavier than usual, whining about his bad ankle even though he'd played baseball just fine.

For the most part, Greg and Carrie ignored him.

They filled the time talking plans, strategies, and other things—like what her parents had been like, if Greg still missed North Carolina, and funny stories from growing up. Thanks to his grandma, Carrie knew several of his not-so-flattering childhood moments, including his surfing disaster. He quickly set the record straight: no, he wasn't an amazing surfer, and no, the shark hadn't tried to eat him, but he'd face-planted anyway right in front of the girl he was trying to impress.

"Fortunately," he said, "all of my less-than-manly screaming scared the shark away. Unfortunately, it also scared away the girl. Didn't know she could run so fast."

Carrie laughed. "That's a little different from the version your grandma tells. So what kind of shark was it?"

"No clue, but let's call it a bull shark," he said. "A huge one."

She laughed again, a soft sound of delight that made his humiliation worth it. Their clasped hands swung softly between them as they followed Zach.

"So," she said, "is the rotten apple story true?"

Just how many stories had she told Carrie?

"Grandma," he growled. "Why exactly are you friends with her? You two are nothing alike."

88

Carrie smiled fondly. "She and CJ watched over us after my parents passed away. May always made me feel like I mattered. She listened to me and—"

"She actually listens to somebody?"

"Sometimes," Carrie said with a laugh. "The rest of the time, she just talked and talked. She always knew how to fill the silence, even when things were hard and I didn't know what to say. There were some days that..." Her free hand trailed over the long, wispy weeds. When she spoke again, her voice grew soft. "There were days I missed my parents so much I could hardly function. I was so scared of raising Amber and Zach alone, but your grandma never gave me time to dwell on that. She kept telling crazy Greg and Kendra stories until I found a reason to smile again. That got me through some really hard years. I will always love her for that."

If that was the case, he could forgive his grandma for the wild tales.

"It also helps that she absolutely adores me," Carrie added happily.

"That she does. Drove me nuts when I moved in. You were all she could talk about."

The light faded from her eyes.

"Hey, that was a compliment. She loves you." He squeezed Carrie's warm hand. She seemed to be slowing even more than her tired pace. "Wanna take a break for a sec? I can call Zach back."

"No. I'm fine."

"By the way," Greg said, glancing around, "you can get us home from here, right?"

"No," she said. "Can you?"

He stopped abruptly. Normally he paid strict attention to the direction of the sun, major land marks, and such. But Carrie and Zach seemed so confident in where they were heading.

"Sorry," she said with a tired smile. "I shouldn't tease you. I know where we are. That's the highway up there."

Zach limped across weed-filled railroad tracks and headed directly toward the huge highway. His head stayed down, barely looking more than two feet in front of him.

A soft purr in the distance made Greg's heart jolt.

Greg dropped Carrie's hand and raced forward. He sprinted over the abandoned tracks as the sound of the engine grew.

"Zach!"

The kid turned. Fifteen feet from the highway. Greg couldn't see the car coming, but he could hear it.

"Get down!" Greg yelled.

Zach didn't. He turned to see why Greg was freaking out. Greg practically tackled him to the ground. They fell into the tall weeds just as a patrol car came racing down the highway. Weeds and dirt cut into them as they dropped, but Greg clapped a hand over the kid's mouth as he watched.

The patrol car didn't slow. It raced down the road, going an impossible speed.

As soon as it was out of sight, Greg released the kid.

"Do you have a death wish?" Greg brushed himself off. "You've gotta be smarter than that, Zach. Come on."

"I would have heard it," Zach said defensively.

"Not in time."

Greg's gaze swept the area back and forth, up and down, doing the thorough, paranoid sweep of the highway that the kid should have done in the first place. Did any other parents of these teens realize they were out wandering like this? These kids were so stupid.

Zach shook free of Greg's grasp and started off again, climbing over the guard rails and crossing the five-lane highway.

By the time Carrie reached Greg, she looked frightened. "Thank you," she said.

"I'm glad you're gettin' Zach and Amber legal," Greg said. "A herd of elephants could sneak up on your brother right now. My sister was like that. Totally clueless about her surroundings. Used to stress me out like you wouldn't believe."

"I'll try to keep up with him," Carrie said, speeding up.

They headed over double-yellow lines until they were clear on the other side and back in the tall weeds.

"Do I ever remind you of Kendra?" Carrie asked after a minute.

Greg glanced sideways. "You? Not really. Kendra was little-miss-social. Why?"

She didn't answer, but color flooded her sun-kissed cheeks.

Curious, he pulled her to a stop. "Why?"

"Just…when you first came to Illinois, it seemed like you hated me before you even knew me—practically before we'd met." Carrie shrugged. "I just wondered if I reminded you of her."

As they started off again, he listened to the soft swish of their feet, remembering. Meeting Carrie for the first time. Seeing her in his grandma's kitchen.

After everything, she deserved an explanation.

"It was like my mom and grandma were tryin' to replace Kendra," he said. "With you."

He could see her trying to reconcile this. Why he'd refused to shake her hand. Why he'd treated her so abominably. Why he'd kept her from his family.

"When I walked in that first day and saw you laughing in the kitchen with them..." He blew out his breath. "Y'all were havin' a grand old time, and it's like they didn't even miss Kendra. It hadn't even been a year since she'd died. It killed me. It didn't seem fair that you were there and my baby sister wasn't. Kendra loved Grandma's house more than any other place in the world."

"I'm sorry, Greg. I didn't know."

"Geez, don't apologize!" he said. "If I haven't said sorry enough for that day, I apologize again. I was a complete, moronic jerk. I will always be sorry for the way I treated you. It's unforgivable."

She squeezed his hand. "No, it's not."

He nearly pulled her to a stop again, needing to kiss her all over again. But they were already struggling to keep up with Zach. Baseball had worn out Carrie. So Greg clutched her hand and pulled her onward.

"Now your turn," he said. "You owe me five embarrassing stories from growin' up."

"What if I don't have any?" she said, the teasing look returning to her killer blue eyes. "What if I was the perfect child?"

"Regardless, you blush at the drop of a hat. I bet you have a thousand stories. In fact, I could probably make you blush right now without even trying."

That was all it took. Her cheeks turned rosy again. But she just pointed. "I'll tell you later. Look. I think we're here."

An old red barn came into view. Zach had stopped, letting Carrie and Greg catch up to him.

"Impressive, Zach," Greg said. "You found it comin' from a different direction. Nice."

Zach answered with a scowl that basically said, *I hate you.*

Chuckling, Greg clapped him on the back. "How do we get inside?"

Zach limped forward, but not to the huge red doors. Those were padlocked. Instead, he crept around the side, over a fallen fence to a small opening around back. The opening looked tiny, like a dog door. A small, Chihuahua-sized opening that Greg would never fit through.

"You're kiddin', right?" Greg said.

Zach dropped to his stomach and shimmied through the opening.

"I'm never gonna fit through that," Greg said.

"You can wait outside if you'd like," Carrie said.

Fat chance of that.

Carrie wiggled and twisted through the small opening, unscathed. Grunting, Greg dropped to the dirt and tried sliding through head first. His shoulders didn't fit, so he tried feet first. He squeezed, squirmed, and wiggled, scraping the skin from his arms and nearly tearing his sore shoulder from its socket. When he emerged on the other side, his arm stung with new scratches.

"Was that as graceful as it seemed?" he whispered, brushing himself off.

Carrie laughed softly, making the pain worth it.

The barn smelled of old hay and dirt. Only a few slivers of light shone inside, and it took a moment for his eyes to adjust. Once they did, he spotted Zach heading toward an old rickety ladder in the corner. Soft voices drifted down from an upper hay loft. Somebody said something indistinguishable and laughter broke out upstairs. It sounded like a decent-sized group of teens.

Zach grabbed the first ladder rung and started up. Dust and dirt rained down on Carrie who went next. Greg climbed up last, feeling the wood creak with each step.

"Hey," somebody called excitedly as Zach reached the loft. "Freckles came back. Where have you been, Freckles? We thought…" The boy trailed off as Carrie and Greg came into view.

The teens froze, eyes wide. Eight of them sat in a circle in the dark corner. Their looks of shock quickly turned into glares of betrayal aimed at Zach. Zach didn't notice. He was too busy staring at his feet.

"Hi," Carrie said with a nervous wave. "I'm Carrie, Zach's sister. We're wondering if we can talk to you for a minute."

One of the girls folded her arms. "You don't belong here. And after bringing you, neither does Freckles. He's banned."

"Yeah. Banned," others agreed.

Zach's chin lowered further.

"I know we weren't invited," Carrie said quickly. "And normally we wouldn't have come, but these are extenuating circumstances. There are things happening around this area, and we really need your help."

The grumbles grew.

Greg climbed the rest of the way up, only unlike Zach and Carrie, he kept going, crossing the dusty loft to stand right in front of the teens. They looked up, startled by his bold approach. A few even backed up, frightened.

He offered a friendly smile. "Hey, I'm Greg, a friend of Zach's. And here's the thing. We really need to talk to your parents."

That went over as well as him trying to fit through a Chihuahua-sized opening.

"Like Carrie said," Greg went on, "there's some stuff happening in these parts that has us worried for clans in the area. This stuff could kill your friends and family, even you. But instead of being all creepy and following y'all through the backwoods to your homes, we decided to go the friendly route and just ask you straight up. So what do you say? Will you help us help you?"

Eight pairs of unblinking eyes stared up at him.

Greg rubbed his hands together. "Great! Who wants to go first?"

fourteen

In the end, only two kids took Greg's offer: a girl with black braids and a boy with long, scraggly hair. They came from the same clan, the Sprucewood Clan. If Greg and Carrie could prove themselves with these teens, maybe the others would introduce them to their clans next time—assuming the others actually returned to the barn.

"Traitor," Greg heard the boy whisper as he passed Zach.

Zach's head hung lower.

"Hey," Greg said, striding forward to catch up. "Thanks again for your help. What's your name, kid?"

"Crowbar," the teen said.

"Crowbar?" Greg repeated. It sounded like a Harley-driving motorcyclist, not a gangly teen. But at his challenging scowl, Greg amended, "Nice to meet you, Crowbar."

"And I'm Delaney," the girl with the black braids said brightly as she bounced along.

At least one of them wasn't out for war. Delaney had been the first to volunteer and actually seemed excited by the prospect of taking strangers to her clan.

"Well, it's good to meet you, Delaney. Like I said, I'm Greg, and that's Carrie and her brother, Zach."

"Oh, I know Zach," Delaney said, shooting Zach a conspiratorial smile.

Zach turned twenty shades of red. His eyes flickered to Greg to see if he'd noticed. It would have been hard not to. So Delaney was the reason

Zach had been sneaking out all this time. Made sense. Cute girls had a way of making guys do all sorts of crazy, stupid stuff. Maybe Zach was the reason Delaney had volunteered so eagerly.

Crowbar started walking backwards so he could glare at them as he walked. "When are you going to tell us what this is all about?"

"Have any of your people been sick?" Greg asked.

"Every once in a while. Why?"

Relieved, Greg nodded. "If it's alright, we'll tell everybody at the same time. By the way, how many people are in your clan?"

"Forty-four," Delaney said, still all happy and chipper. "It's not much farther."

At that, Crowbar sped up, pushing through the long grasses until he disappeared. Delaney pulled ahead, too, seemingly anxious to get home. Zach hung back by Carrie and Greg, hobbling slower to match Carrie's tired pace.

"Thanks a lot," Zach muttered.

"You know," Greg said, "when we're trading on a weekly basis and you're allowed to see Delaney any old time you want, you'll be thankin' us for real."

"Really?" Zach said, eyes so full of hope Greg nearly laughed. "You think we'll see her every week?"

"That's the plan," Greg said.

With a grin so wide it looked like it hurt, Zach sped up to Delaney, limp suspiciously gone. As soon as he fell into step beside her, Delaney chattered away to him like a bluebird. Anytime Zach said something, Delaney tossed her head back and giggled.

Carrie looked sick. Not just tired and pale, but physically ill as she watched the two of them.

Restraining a smile, Greg said, "Are you alright?"

"But…" She stared at the two teens. "Zach's too young to like girls. He likes baseball, and food, and …"

More of Delaney's giggles floated back to them.

"And girls," Greg finished.

Carrie closed her eyes. "I really can't handle another love-sick sibling."

A few minutes later, they entered a wooded area with huge trees creating a thick canopy high above. The area was so shaded that nothing below could get enough sunlight to grow, making a soft dark floor beneath. Zach and Delaney slowed down to let them catch up. Crowbar was nowhere to be seen. He'd probably run ahead to warn everyone that strangers were coming. For all Greg knew, they could be met with a rifle reception.

He stiffened, but kept going.

Flashes of colors stood out in the shade, small domes set around the giant trees. The soft scent of campfires wafted over to them.

"Y'all live in tents?" Greg asked.

"When it's warm," Delaney said. "It cuts down guarding time. The patrolmen don't bother us here. They're too lazy to walk this far inland. But in the winter, we move back to our houses."

Greg nearly asked where those were but didn't want to press his luck. "Why don't the three of us hang back here while you get your parents." He much preferred his odds if Delaney was the one to make the introduction instead of Crowbar. Plus, this way they weren't walking into someone's territory.

"Sure," Delaney said happily. "It's just me and my mom, but she'll be excited to meet you guys. I'll bring our clan leader, too."

As she bounded off, Zach looked back. "Can I go with her?"

"Not a chance," Carrie answered. "Stay."

Poor kid. He was going to get the fullness of Carrie's wrath later, when she felt up to it.

Zach slumped onto the dark, soft ground.

"Maybe you should sit, too," Greg said.

Carrie shook her head. "I'm fine."

As they waited, Greg studied the small camp in the distance. The tents, the smell of campfire, illegals milling about.

A sudden wave of uneasiness swept over him. The whole thing felt eerily similar to the camp he and Isabel Ryan had invaded. The rebels. Kearney. Commander McCormick had ordered Greg and Isabel to stay as long as it took to find the heart of the resistance, yet only twelve hours later, they'd been caught and exposed. Radios, maps, green cards, and enough supplies to condemn them as government spies.

There was something life-changing about staring death in the face.

Greg had knelt on his knees, gun to his forehead, knowing he'd never make it back to Carrie, his mom, or anybody. Now it was like he had stumbled back into that camp and any second Kearney would leap out with a gun and—

Carrie nudged him. "Are you okay?"

His breaths were coming too fast. His hands felt cold and sweaty. He pulled her in for a tight, all-encompassing embrace. When that wasn't close enough, he pressed her bad ear to his chest, squeezing her so tightly she probably couldn't breathe.

"What is it?" she said into him.

Zach gave them a curious glance before going back to digging through the fallen twigs.

"Nothin'," Greg said, begging the memories to leave. He kissed the top of Carrie's sun-warmed head. This wasn't West Chicago, and he was no longer a spy.

A black-haired girl emerged a few minutes later, as happy as ever. Delaney brought with her four adults, two women and two men—and no Crowbar. The group hadn't brought rifles either.

Greg told himself to relax.

"What's going on?" a man asked, striding forward. For some reason he wore bright yellow swim goggles. "Who are you?"

Normally Greg would have stepped forward and shaken a few hands, but he purposely didn't. The group seemed to feel the same wariness and stopped well before they were to Greg and Carrie.

"I'm Greg," he said, voice tight with nerves. "We're from the Logan Pond Clan. We're reaching out, hoping to make contact with others in the area."

The man with the swim goggles scowled at Delaney before turning back. "You're from where?"

"Logan Pond," Carrie said, sounding much more relaxed than Greg felt. "It's south of here, near the main road into Shelton."

"We were told to steer clear of that subdivision," the goggle guy said. "We heard you have legal citizens living there."

"A few," Greg said. "Actually, as of last weekend, Carrie is one of them. But the majority of us are illegal still, which is why we're anxious to make contact with others in the area. Have any in your group been ill recently?"

For the next few minutes, Greg and Carrie explained the virus, their theories as to its origin—and deadly intent—and how quickly it had spread. The only thing Greg didn't tell them was how many extra doses of the cure they had. People killed others over things like that.

Unfortunately, Delaney's clan was in the same predicament as their clan. Nobody with medical knowledge.

"So…it's like genocide?" Forrest said, the leader with the yellow swim goggles. It took Greg that long to figure out why Forrest wore what he did. Prescription goggles—probably the only prescription glasses the guy had.

"Yeah," Greg said. "For the next while, you might want to avoid making physical contact with anybody outside of your clan. You might also want to warn your kids. This thing is spreading like crazy."

Delaney's mom put an arm around her daughter. "Oh, believe me, Delaney's not going to be wandering off anymore."

Zach shot Greg a dark glare.

"Well," Forrest said, "thanks for the warning."

"How much do you know about the rebellion?" Carrie asked.

"We've seen the fires," Forrest said. "Actually, a few from our clan left to join some group outside of West Chicago. The rest of us, well, we're peaceful people. We're not interested in fighting."

"Neither are we," Greg said. Really not interested. "We just wanted to make sure y'all were aware of what was goin' on. Also to be on high alert. The patrol precinct in town is goin' through some upheaval with everything, so be extra careful."

"Will do," Forrest said.

"There's one last thing." Greg waited a moment for Carrie to take the reins. She looked almost startled that he wanted her to lead out on it, but with his encouraging nod, she started.

"The last reason we came is on a happier note." Clasping her hands in front of her, she said, "We're here to see if your clan would ever be interested in trading with ours."

That brought another round of surprised looks.

Forrest folded his arms. "Why?"

"Each clan in this area probably has things it excels in," she said, "as well as things they're deficient in. For example, our clan has done pretty well growing crops, but there are things we haven't been able to produce, like soap, candles, or flour. We've been trading for those on the black market, but that's not ideal."

"Barry?" Forrest said.

"Yeah," Greg said. "I hear he's a real sweetheart."

Another guy snorted. "Oh, yeah. So compassionate."

"Eventually we're gonna run out of things to trade," Carrie said. "That's why we thought it might be beneficial to open up trading among all of us. We were thinking we could meet up once a week to trade goods, like a farmers' market of sorts. We would meet somewhere in neutral territory so people aren't worried or traveling too far. Would something like that interest your clan?"

Greg could practically see Carrie holding her breath.

Delaney's mom looked at her fellow clansmen before answering. "Possibly, but we'd have to discuss it with everyone first."

It wasn't a *no*, and that seemed good enough for Carrie. She glowed with pleasure. "That's fine. Definitely fine. We just wanted to open a discussion."

"Why don't you give us a few days to discuss," Forrest said.

Greg slid his hand into Carrie's, happy for her as much as he was excited by the business prospect.

"Sounds good," Greg said. "We'll come back in a few days to follow up. How does Friday sound? Maybe midday?"

"Sounds good," Delaney's mom said. "You know, we've kept in partial contact with the Aspen group. I don't know if you've heard of them, but we've traded chickens and things with them over the years. Is it alright if we invite them to come, too?"

Carrie was practically dancing for joy. "That would be perfect."

fifteen

Oliver pushed his tray across the cafeteria roller. He bypassed the mashed potatoes. After peeling potatoes for hours on end, he no longer had the appetite for them. Instead he set an apple and a simple cup of wriggly, red Jell-O on his tray.

"Hey!" a guy barked. "Who do you think you are?"

Oliver glanced over his sore shoulder, wondering if the other inmate was talking to him. He was. And he looked ready to blow a gasket.

The inmate pointed at the red Jell-O on Oliver's tray. "You took the last one."

Before Oliver could apologize or think to put it back, the guy jumped him. He plowed Oliver over.

Oliver fell with a crash onto the hard floor. Pain exploded against his already-tender ribs. He screamed.

Prison guards came running. "What's going on?"

Oliver clutched his chest. Each breath was a stab of agony.

Two guards grabbed the guy and pulled him back. "What did you do to him?"

The inmate's hands flew up defensively. "I barely touched him, I swear."

Oliver couldn't stop moaning. It hurt so badly. He made the mistake of rolling onto his branded shoulder, and more pain shot through him. They'd given him a patch to wear over the burn wound, but that was long gone. Now the tender flesh rubbed against the rough orange jumpsuit.

"Come on." One of the guards took Oliver's arm and helped him to his feet. "Up. Get up. What did he do to you?"

Red-faced and furious, the inmate glared at Oliver, daring him to say a word.

Oliver dropped his gaze. "Nothing. I fell. I just..." He took another agonizing breath and winced. "I cracked my ribs awhile back. That's all."

A gift from Jamansky that kept on giving.

As things dissipated, Oliver bent down to grab his tray. The only thing that survived the ordeal was his apple. One apple for dinner. He didn't even care. He picked up a cup of juice—one of many—from the last spot and found the farthest, most remote table in the corner and sat with his apple.

Someone plopped their tray down next to him with a loud *clank*.

Out of instinct, Oliver cowered, jarring his ribs a second time.

When the pain subsided, he looked sideways and saw Reef, his cellmate, scowling at him. The prison had been designed to house two men per cell, but since the Collapse, they'd packed it with wall-to-wall men. Oliver's 4x9 cell had five men. With a thick mullet and braided beard, Reef was one of them.

The second they'd ushered Oliver into the small, urine-infested cell, Reef made it clear that he ran the place. He ordered Oliver to sleep on the floor. Oliver hadn't argued. He should have, though. The place was revolting. Supposedly they came in once a week and hosed the cement cells down, but he didn't believe it. Oliver had slept on the stained floor, gagging until he passed out from exhaustion.

Unfortunately, Reef didn't seem to care—or take the hint—that Oliver wanted to be left alone now. Reef leaned his wrestler-sized body into Oliver's personal space.

"Look," Reef said, "if you want to survive in here, you've got to learn the rules."

The only rules Oliver knew were the ones the guards had given at his arrival, and none of them mentioned anything about not taking the last Jell-O cup. He'd counted fourteen fist fights and two all-out brawls in the short time he'd been there. It was all the guards could do to keep the men from killing each other.

Whatever rules this place had meant nothing.

Oliver needed to cough, but couldn't risk the pain, so he took a quick sip of juice.

"Did you hear me?" Reef barked.

Oliver nodded.

His eyes flickered to the clock on the wall. Ten more minutes until he could peel again. He massaged his hands and tight knuckles, anxious to hide in that back room they shoved him in. Guards watched him while he peeled, and when he finished each shift he not only had to check the peeler back in with them, but they frisked him quite intrusively to make sure he hadn't somehow stolen it.

Why would anyone steal a potato peeler?

To use as a weapon, of course.

The potatoes he peeled not only fed these brutes, but half went through a food processing facility that eventually fed blue card holders in municipalities as well. Welfare food. After six months of pristine behavior, he could work up to dish duty.

Assuming he could survive that long.

His thoughts wandered to Carrie and what Jamansky had done to her. Ashlee Lyon and what Jamansky had done to *her*. But he quickly steered them back to safer, less-painful places.

Like here.

Now.

"Fine," Reef growled. "You might have a death wish, but I'm going to tell you anyway. First rule: pay attention to your surroundings. That means you shouldn't be sitting with your back to the group."

Oliver nodded again.

Swearing, Reef grabbed his arm, hauled him to his feet, and shoved him around to the other side of the table. Oliver dropped hard, aggravating his ribs all over again.

"Never sit with your back to the group again!" Reef said. "Understood?"

Oliver couldn't stop himself. A cough erupted against his lungs. Desperate, he chugged his juice down. By the time he finished, he could barely move on his small, round seat without pain searing through him.

"Let's test you on rule number one," Reef said. "How many guards are in this room?"

Oliver lifted his eyes. There were probably a hundred or so inmates eating at tables throughout the massive cafeteria. Several guards patrolled the area, tapping nightsticks in their hands. Most guards were male, but not all, making him think about Carrie all over again. Where was she? What horrors was she enduring?

Reef shook his head angrily. "How were *you* ever a patrolman? There are twenty-two guards here. That's down one from yesterday, which tells you what?"

That the inmates had the ability to kill guards, too.

A lovely thought.

Reef stabbed a finger at him. "You really do have a death wish. I guess it doesn't matter then. At least you've already got rule number two down: don't talk too much. Keep it that way. Keep your ears open, too. Listen for anything that's off. Listen between the lines, too, if you know what I mean."

Not talking wouldn't be a problem. Oliver planned to never speak again.

"Don't join any gangs either," Reef went on, picking some food from his teeth. "They'll tell you they're out to protect guys like you, but most gangs in here end up beating their own members more than anyone else for violating one rule or another. So keep to yourself. Understood?"

Gangs.

Of course.

"Fourth...guys in here can sense any trace of fear. So when you talk to someone, always maintain eye contact."

A bead of sweat dripped down Oliver's forehead.

Reef reached across the table and grabbed him by the orange jumpsuit. "I said look me in the eyes. Now!"

The jumpsuit scraped against Oliver's shoulder.

Oliver yelped.

A few tables over, people stopped eating to watch. The inmates looked anxious for another fist fight to break up their monotonous incarceration. A few guards turned on their heels to head toward them. Reef dropped Oliver for a second time—not-too-nicely—but his murderous eyes dared Oliver to look away first.

Heart thundering painfully against his ribs, Oliver forced his gaze to stay on his cellmate's beefy, weathered face.

Maintain eye contact.

"There," Reef said. "Better. One last bit of advice so your scrawny hide doesn't wind up dead. Any free time you get, bulk up. Pushups.

Jumping Jacks. Do them like your life depends on it, 'cause it does. Bulking up might give you a fighting chance—or at least make others think twice before attacking you again. Got it?"

"Why are you helping me?" Oliver whispered, eyes still painfully locked on Reef's face.

"I'm sick of watching guys like you get cut to pieces in here."

Cut.

Another lovely word.

As Reef moved off, Oliver pushed his breakfast away, no longer hungry. *Live free or die,* he thought. Maybe it would come to that after all. But not yet. Not until he took down David Jamansky.

"Wait!" Oliver said with a sudden thought.

Several paces away, Reef turned back.

"Do we ever get computer access?" Oliver asked.

Reef snorted. "Yeah, right."

"What about letters?" Oliver said. "Are we allowed to send letters?"

"Some of us. Those with good behavior," Reef said.

Oliver's pulse jumped. "Are you?"

Reef glared at him for a long moment. "Depends on what you're offering."

———————◆———————

Carrie walked into the Trenton's front room, bracing herself. At Greg's suggestion, they'd headed directly home instead of swinging back by the field. She'd been thrilled with how things had gone in Sprucewood, but now she felt tense and anxious. According to Niels Ziegler, Jamansky had already come and gone.

Richard sat on May's couch, rubbing the back of his neck. The room felt heavier than Carrie's body. A small group gathered to hear the full report. Ashlee stood next to Richard, looking more distraught than the others. She chewed her poor red nails to bits.

Richard's head lifted when he saw Carrie and Greg enter. "How did it go?"

"You first," Greg said.

As Richard recounted the visit and Jamansky's reaction, Carrie's stomach knotted. She looked Richard over to assure herself that Jamansky hadn't hurt him. She couldn't believe that after Jamansky's grand show of friendship yesterday, the patrol chief could have been so combative with the sick, older man. At least he thought Greg was dead. That was the only bit of good news in the whole thing, but Greg looked like he wanted to punch something.

"The guy brought dinner, wine, and a gun," Greg said. "Just what kind of night was he planning?"

Carrie refused to let anyone answer that question—even in their minds—and changed the subject quickly.

"What about Oliver?" she asked. "Were you able to find out anything?"

"Jamansky said Oliver has a message for us," Richard said. At Greg's grunt, he quickly amended, "I'm just relating what he said. Unfortunately, he said the message is for Carrie and Carrie alone, so he's coming back Wednesday to see her." Richard's gaze locked on his stepson. "I'm sorry, but I don't think there's any way around it this time. It's as close as he came to an outright threat. If we want to hear this message, Carrie needs to be home when he comes back."

Greg closed his eyes, anger rolling off him in droves. Ashlee Lyon chewed a few more nails. Carrie hugged herself as she tried to figure out what to say to Jamansky next—or how to give him clearer signals. And boundaries. The guy thought he was coming for a date.

A chill ran through her.

"There is one bright spot, however," Richard went on. He waited until he made sure he had everyone's attention. "I think Oliver might actually be in Virginia."

"What?" Carrie and Ashlee Lyon said in unison.

Richard nodded. "Jamansky claimed that Oliver called him this morning. The way he said it…" He rubbed his goatee. "I don't know. Perhaps I'm reading too much into it, but he seemed so certain, like Oliver actually had called him."

Hope flooded inside of Carrie. She turned to Ashlee. "Is it possible?"

"I…I don't know," Ashlee said. "Technically, there is patrol training in Virginia, but it's mostly for federal patrolmen."

"A few of my fellow trainees were sent there," Greg added.

Oliver might be in Virginia, alive and in one piece. If he had called, if that part was true, what had he wanted to tell Carrie?

She had no idea, but there had to be a way to contact him. Oliver once tried to get Greg a letter while in training. Maybe she could do the same.

For a long minute, everyone in the room tried to piece things together. The shadows slid across the floor, stealing the last bit of daylight until Greg finally pushed away from the wall.

"It's gettin' late," he said. "We better get people settled in the houses before it's full-on dark."

Those staying at Carrie's house started shuffling out the front door. The others staying at May's went to set up their sleeping items.

Carrie stepped over to the couch and gave Richard a brief hug. "Thank you, Richard. I'm sorry Jamansky was so upset."

"Don't be," Richard said. "In fact, I've been thinking that perhaps I should be there again when he returns. Not that he likes me all that much, but at this point, I think the more people we have around the better. What do you think? He said he'd be back late on Wednesday. Would you like me there with you?"

Out of the corner of her eye, she saw Greg watching her, practically begging her on his knees. He didn't have to ask though. With Jamansky so unstable, she would have asked Richard to stay with her anyway.

"Would you mind terribly?" she asked.

"Not at all," Richard said.

"We can come, too," May said from the kitchen. "Right, CJ? We'll make it a big family affair so this patrol chief sees us as a united group."

A family affair.

Carrie loved the sound of that.

"Thank you," she said. "How about I make lunch for everyone? We'll just hang out until he shows up. Maybe we can even play some cards."

She stole a glance at Greg. He scowled deeply, probably because he was the only family member without citizenship—and thus, not invited—but the others seemed to like the plan.

Carrie rubbed her stiff shoulders. "Well, I should probably get home and help get everyone settled. Thanks again, Richard. I'll head into town with Amber and Zach early enough on Wednesday to be back in plenty of time."

She started for the door to follow behind the others staying at her house for the night.

"Hold up, Carrie," Greg said, striding toward her. "What if you go into town tomorrow? Jamansky said he's gone for the day, so he won't be there to pester you. Just take Richard with you."

"Tomorrow?" She thought of her mile-long list of to-dos, everything she hadn't gotten to today. Plus, tonight had worn her out more than she cared to admit.

"I really need to catch up on my laundry and garden and—"

"I'll do it all," Greg cut in. "Laundry. Weeding. Mop your floors. Whatever. I'll do it."

Picturing him scrubbing her clothes made her smile. "Don't you have your own projects? I thought Dylan wanted you to hunt in the morning, and aren't you on guard duty again tomorrow?"

"Not until later," Greg said, "and Dylan can hunt by himself."

His eagerness—and torture—was enough to sway her. Jamansky wasn't in Shelton tomorrow, so she would be. That meant Zach and Amber would be full citizens in just twelve short hours.

Twelve.

She smiled. "Okay. We'll go in the morning, but don't worry about my projects. They can wait."

She looked over her shoulder. Richard looked so exhausted she hated to even ask, but she did anyway.

"Hey, Richard, can I ask one more favor?"

sixteen

As if the heavens popped, the rain poured, hard and heavy. Carrie lowered her head, water streaming down her face as they plodded toward Shelton. She'd had enough foresight to bring her coat, but Amber and Zach had refused to bring anything, insisting the rain would stop. Now they huddled under her coat while she trudged forward, drenched and miserable.

Typical.

"Ah! I can't see!" Amber cried as a gust of wind blew the coat up and sent sheets of rain sideways at them.

"Can't we wait under a tree until it slows down?" Zach said. "My ankle hurts."

Her siblings weren't making the trip into town any easier. Then again, even her mood had grown soggy. The last time she'd been in Downtown Shelton had been in the safety of Oliver's car, admiring the rows of flowering pear trees. Now her mom's blue blouse clung to her and her shoes sloshed in the cold mud, leaving her skin in a constant state of chills.

"Fine," she said. "Let's wait over there."

The three of them sprinted to a thick tree with low enough branches to block the worst of it. They clung together near the tree trunk to warm up as the wind howled.

"This is so stupid," Zach said. "Why did we have to come today?"

Carrie didn't say because he wouldn't understand. Frankly, the wetter she became, the less important Jamansky's absence seemed. Amber and

Zach were going to end up with citizenship pictures worse than hers. Their hair hung in their faces.

"You know what Dad always said," Carrie said, trying to lighten the mood. "Easy come, easy go. This storm will be gone soon."

But the minutes ticked by and the rain wasn't going anywhere. At least under the safety of the low branches they only got a few drops here and there instead of the full torrent.

Carrie was glad Richard hadn't come after all. When she had knocked on the Trenton's front door first thing, no one had answered. She had slipped quietly inside and spotted Richard curled up, snoring on the couch. Richard was a morning person like she was, the reason they had agreed to leave so early, but with the rain, she decided to spare him a long, cold, miserable walk. He needed another day to recover anyway.

"Stop rubbing your ear," Amber said, slapping her hand. "It's annoying."

Carrie hadn't been aware that she'd been doing it. The rain just sounded off, like her ear was clogged after swimming. It made her feel lopsided.

"Can we please focus on the positive?" she said. "Isn't there anything you guys are happy about? What about being legal? How cool is that?"

Zach grunted.

"Hey," Amber said with a sudden smile, "have I told you my theory yet about Ashlee and Oliver?"

Carrie shivered. "What do you mean?"

"I mean…" Amber said, "I think Ashlee Lyon has a crush on our little Oliver."

"What? Why?"

Excitedly, Amber told Carrie about the night she'd come into town with Oliver, and how, when the two of them thought Amber was sleeping, Ashlee Lyon had leaned over and kissed Oliver on the cheek. A thanks of sort for asking for her help. According to Amber, Oliver had blushed like crazy.

"That doesn't mean anything," Carrie said. "Ashlee is a flirty kind of person."

"Sure it does." Amber tossed her dark hair around to dry it out. "You should have seen them together. They're cute."

Carrie tried to picture red-nailed Ashlee and painfully shy Oliver. "But they're so different."

"Oh, nobody cares!" Zach said. "Look. The rain stopped. Let's go!"

They took off, sprinting the rest of the way into town before the rain could start again.

Downtown Shelton came into view with the backs of boarded-up buildings and rain-soaked streets.

When they rounded the corner and saw all the patrol cars in front of the township office, trepidation leapt through Carrie. She wondered if the anxiety would ever leave her completely, regardless of how long she and her siblings were legal. Already she dreaded coming every month for the required check-ins—although they could come when May, CJ, and Richard did. Another group effort.

Amber and Zach cowered behind her as they neared the township office. Carrie pasted on a big smile. Today was a day to celebrate. Six years in the making.

"Come on," she said excitedly. "Let's get you two legal."

She pulled open the glass door and a blast of cold air flew out, causing a new round of goose bumps to ripple across her skin. Air conditioning. She ignored it to focus on the older woman behind a waist-high counter.

Ellen.

The woman looked every bit as grumpy as Ashlee had described. Her eyes lifted, taking in Carrie and her siblings' shabby clothes and drenched hair with a look of disdain.

Ellen held out her hand. "Cards."

Carrie was glad Ashlee had prepared her for this. "Actually, that's why we're here. We recently acquired a home in Shelton. I got my yellow card this last weekend, but my siblings haven't had a chance to get theirs yet."

"What's the last name?" the woman asked.

"Ashworth," Amber said, gaining a little courage.

"This is the deed to our house and their birth certificates." Carrie stepped forward and unfolded the papers she'd stuffed under her mom's blouse. They were slightly damp, but not damaged. As she handed them over, she caught a glimpse of Oliver's signature on the bottom of the first page, giving her a quick pang of sadness.

Ellen took the paperwork to a file cabinet in a corner of the office. Shuffling through several drawers, she found what she was looking for.

She pulled out a small stack and studied the papers side by side. Her eyes narrowed.

"Where is your citizenship card?" she asked, bringing both sets back to the counter.

Carrie handed over her card.

Ellen held it up, comparing Carrie to her horrid picture. Based on the growing frown, Carrie decided to forgo asking to retake her picture. It wasn't important.

Part of her—a small part—wished Ashlee still worked here. She would have been a lot nicer to them.

Once Ellen decided Carrie was indeed the same as the nearly dead woman in the picture, she swiped the yellow card through a small machine. The machine beeped and turned red. Ellen muttered something under her breath and reached over to press a button on the counter.

"Your request for citizenship has been denied," she said.

"Denied?" Carrie stole a quick glance at Amber and Zach. "Why?"

Ellen lifted the two sets of papers. They were identical, a copy of Carrie's deed. But unlike Carrie's version, someone had scribbled red handwriting across the top of the office version. Before Carrie could read the scribbles, Ellen snatched them back.

"This states that your proof of residency has been revoked," Ellen said.

"Revoked?" A twinge of fear crawled up Carrie's spine.

"What the heck does that mean?" Amber snapped.

Carrie shot her a warning look. Getting angry wouldn't help. Taking a slow breath, she forced another smile.

"I'm sorry," Carrie said, "but there must be a mistake. Our home was just purchased. Obviously I have already been issued my card, so maybe the paperwork hasn't been fully processed yet?"

The older woman grunted. "Let me check one more place."

"Thank you."

Gathering up the paperwork, the clerk went searching in a different file cabinet.

Zach leaned over and whispered, "What does this mean, Carrie?"

Her heart pounded in her chest. *Revoked.* Oliver and Ashlee had rushed her paperwork through.

How long did it take to clear?

"Sometimes governments are slow with paperwork. Don't worry," she said, sounding more confident than she felt. "It probably means that we'll have to come back another day." Maybe even when Jamansky was in the office and could vouch for her and her house.

Greg would love that.

"You mean we have to walk all the way back here again?" Zach whined.

Carrie shushed him as three patrolmen entered the lobby from a side hallway. They were dressed in their standard green uniforms and beige ties. Two looked about Carrie's age, but the third was middle-aged, a huge guy who looked as grumpy as Ellen. Carrie tried not to tense at the sight of them. She didn't have to worry anymore. She and her siblings were legal now. Almost.

The patrolmen looked directly at the Ashworths before the huge one turned to the government clerk.

"Hey, Ellen," he said. "You called?"

Ellen shut the drawer. "Yes. Those three there."

The large patrolman eyed Carrie and her siblings. "All three?"

"Yes." Ellen turned to Carrie. "Sorry."

It took Carrie a second to realize what she meant—who she meant. *Those three there.*

Three.

Her stomach lurched.

The patrolmen started heavy-footed towards her at the same time she fit the pieces together. Proof of residency revoked. Her house. Ellen had pushed a button, a light flashed red, and patrolmen had come.

Those three.

Three.

Suddenly Carrie couldn't breathe, couldn't move.

No!

But everything around her screamed, *Yes!*—her yellow card no longer in hand, Ellen's curt apology, and three patrolmen headed their way.

Carrie threw an arm in front of her siblings.

"What's going on?" she demanded in a voice half as loud as it needed to be.

The huge patrolman grabbed her left wrist and pinned it behind her back. "You have the right to remain silent. Anything you say can be…"

His words blurred as he twisted her other wrist painfully behind her. She heard a click of metal as he cuffed her hands behind her.

Carrie gasped for air.

Arrest.

They were arresting her.

Zach screamed as a second patrolman grabbed him. Amber stood wide-eyed, staring as the last one clamped his hand on her arm.

Carrie thrashed. Sheer terror rushed out of her in a shout. "No, wait! Wait!"

"Let's go." The huge officer's fingers dug into her arm as he dragged her toward the glass doors.

Her life was about to be sucked away from her—away from them. Amber and Zach would be taken.

She was being taken.

"Stop!" Carrie screamed, digging in her heels. "Let me explain! Wait!"

A flash of red suddenly darted through her vision. Zach, ducking low, charged forward, fists swinging for Carrie's patrolman. He only made it a few feet before his young patrolman caught him and threw him to the ground.

Zach slammed back on the tile. Air whooshed out of him. The young patrolman ground his knee into Zach's stomach to keep him down.

Zach gasped, choked, and turned red.

"Stop!" Carrie shouted. "You're hurting him! STOP!"

She kicked and flailed against her officer but couldn't find leverage.

They were twelve feet from the doors.

Ten feet.

Eight.

"Zach!"

The last officer held Amber tightly by the arms, leaving her rooted in spot. Amber looked white as a sheet, staring as Carrie's patrolman dragged her away forever.

Forever…

The word seared like a knife.

"Please!" Carrie twisted back to see Ellen, handcuffs digging into her wrists. "You have my card! You know I'm legal. Tell them!"

"Your citizenship has been revoked," Ellen said flatly.

Carrie felt herself going numb. She couldn't think fast enough. She was legal. She had her house. Her feet kept sliding, unable to halt their progression.

Six feet.

Four.

In an act of mercy, they suddenly stopped. Carrie's bus-sized officer halted in front of the glass doors.

"What are you waiting for?" he yelled at his partner holding Amber. "Get them out of here!"

"But, Giordano, sir," the young patrolman started. "What about—"

"Go!" he roared.

Then he shoved Carrie outside. Carrie tried to grab the door, the handle, anything, but it was too late. Rain fell on her.

Petrified, she only cared about two things...

"Amber!" she shrieked back through the glass. "You have to take care of Zach! Amber!"

Carrie couldn't tell if her little sister heard because, faster than should have been possible, the patrolman dragged her out into the rain, away from everything that meant anything to her.

"Amber!" she screamed again.

She tried to lock her feet against something, throwing as much weight to the slick sidewalk as she could. Her knees scraped the wet ground, her hands wrenched behind her, tearing the flesh of her wrists, but it did nothing to stop their furious progress.

"Please!" she begged, a sob ripping through her. "Please let me say goodbye! I'm all they have!"

The patrolman threw her, head first, into the back of a patrol car and slammed the door.

seventeen

Amber couldn't move.

She stayed frozen in the township lobby, staring at the empty doors as Carrie's words repeated in her mind:

You have to take care of Zach.

You have to take care of Zach.

The words kept circling, refusing to stop because as soon as they stopped, she had to think about what they actually meant.

Carrie wasn't coming back.

The young patrolman gripped her arm as he argued with his partner, words too fast to understand.

You have to take care of Zach.

How?

Carrie was like the air, always there. People couldn't live without air. They needed it to survive. As if to prove it, Amber's chest suddenly caved in on itself. She started hyperventilating.

Shallow breaths came faster. She forced her lungs in and out. *Breathe!* With a huge, involuntary gasp, the air unleashed Carrie's plea for the hundredth time.

You have to.

Zach.

Take care.

Zach. The other person imploding in her world.

Blinking slowly, she turned her head.

Where was Zach?

A sudden rush of sound filled her ears in the ever-shrinking lobby. She heard her brother before she found him. He knelt on the floor, half-sobbing, half-shouting Carrie's name. How she hadn't heard him before seemed impossible, because once she heard his wails, she couldn't rid them from her ears.

"Carrie! Carrie!"

Zach's patrolman yanked him to his feet. "Let's go, brat."

"Carrie!" Zach screamed again, voice growing hoarse.

You have to take care of Zach.

You.

An astonishing sense of calm overcame Amber. She could take care of her brother. Somehow. She would grow food, stay home alone at night, wash Zach's nasty clothes, and keep him safe. The clan would help, too. They would. She didn't let herself think much beyond this moment, because right now, she knew her next step.

And it was easy.

Turning, she looked up into the face of the officer who held her. He was younger than she expected him to be, close to Braden's age.

"I'd like to go home now," she said calmly.

"Wouldn't we all," he muttered. Then to his partner, he said, "I'll take Simmons' car. Bushing, you take the other."

Amber's officer started walking her across the lobby toward the doors. The same doors Carrie had been dragged out of.

"Make sure I get my cut!" the old clerk called.

"Yeah, yeah."

The whole thing felt so surreal, like swimming through mud. So it took forever to dawn on Amber: these officers weren't taking them home. They wouldn't return them to Logan Pond or Braden or anything. She and Zach were going to jail—or at least Carrie was. She had no idea where they sent kids. Some place worse. Some place that wasn't home.

Panic seized her.

Her feet turned to cement, stopping her.

"Move!" her patrolman said, yanking on her.

Against her will, she stumbled forward.

"But...but I have to go home," she said.

Zach's red, swollen eyes found her as if he too had just remembered she was still there. His expression mirrored her own horror, but beneath, she saw something more, a glint in his eyes like hardened steel. The same look he had when he and Amber argued, signaling that the fight wasn't done. It had only just begun. A look that meant he was about to—

Zach rammed his shoe into the shin of his patrolman.

The patrolman fell back with a shout. Unprepared for the release, Zach fell and plummeted into a row of metal chairs. He collided, shoulder first, slamming into the corner of the nearest seat. Scrambling up, he grabbed the chair, and hurled it at his patrolman.

"Run!" he yelled at Amber.

The chair bounced before it hit the patrolman's legs. Cursing, the officer picked it up and hurled it back. Zach's arms flew up to shield himself, but the chair smashed into him, sending him back into the next row.

Things fell like dominoes.

Zach.

Chairs.

Zach's officer stormed over, grabbed him by his red t-shirt, and shoved him against the wall. Then he whipped out handcuffs and had Zach locked up in a blur. Once Zach was restrained, he flung another set of handcuffs at Amber. She screamed as they hurtled toward her. Her patrolman snatched them mid-air.

"I don't need them," her patrolman said, tucking them into his belt. "She's not the fighter her siblings are. Let's go."

The room spun around his face—his young face that was strangely covered in white, swirling blotches of light.

She blinked slower and slower.

A dream. This had to be a dream.

"I want to go home," she said in a small, tiny voice.

A flash of guilt flickered across his eyes, but it was the old clerk who answered.

"Oh, you're going home alright, love," she sneered from behind the counter. "Only your new home will have pretty curtains and new friends who won't get you into any more trouble. It'll be a lovely place where your sister can't hurt you ever again."

"Carrie!" Zach shouted again.

He thrashed around, teeth snapping like a wild dog as he tried to sink his teeth into the arm of his officer.

Amber's patrolman stopped. "Want to trade?"

"No," Zach's patrolman said, struggling. "I like this one."

Amber's patrolman gave her one last look. He almost seemed sad. If she didn't have Braden, she might have tried to cheer him up. Somewhere in the back of her mind, a voice screamed, *Spit in his face! Claw his cheeks! Yank out an eyeball!* Yet her head grew unbearably heavy. It began to droop backward.

Through a cloud of haze, she heard the woman behind the counter say something, but more and more Amber was understanding less and less. Her mind grew foggy. The last words she heard were from her own patrolman.

"Don't wait up. This might take a while."

eighteen

Carrie tried begging in the patrol car.

Begging.

Pleading.

She couldn't see the patrolman through her blurred tears. A metal grate separated the front from the back as he drove down a deserted county road. They were headed north, but she didn't know anything more specific.

The patrolman made two phone calls while he drove, muttering low and angrily. As he finished the second call, she forced herself to calm down until the only sounds in the car were the soft rain on the roof and the windshield wipers swishing back and forth.

Once she trusted herself to speak, she tried another avenue.

"Please, sir. Officer Giordano," she said, using the name the other patrolman had used for him, "I know Chief Jamansky." She closed her watery eyes, willing a first name to clarify in her frantic thoughts. "David Jamansky. He's your chief, right? He knows me. He actually came to my house last night. He can tell you that I'm legal. *Please.*"

The huge patrolman didn't answer.

"Can you tell me why my papers were revoked?" she tried. "I have a right to know why I'm being arrested."

Still no answer.

"What's going to happen to my brother and sister? Can they go home?"

It's like Giordano didn't even hear her.

"Will you at least tell me if they'll be allowed to stay together?" Her voice broke on the last word.

His silence was just another blow.

The emotions began to engulf her. "Please," she begged, voice growing raw. "What's going to happen to them? I'm all they have. I'm all they have."

Though the metal meshing separated them, she saw his eyes flicker to the rearview mirror. "Your brother and sister will be taken care of."

Taken care of. So they wouldn't be sent home. They wouldn't be taken in by May and CJ, protected, watched, and fed by people who loved them. They would become wards of the state, raised by those who would turn them against her in a place rumored to be worse than the municipalities.

Her stomach rolled.

How would she even find them, let alone release them?

She struggled to keep hold of herself.

"For..." She took a shuddering breath. "For how long? My sister is sixteen. When can she go on her own?"

"Her eighteenth birthday," he said.

Two years for Amber.

Five years for Zach.

An eternity for Carrie.

Desperation came flooding back. She squirmed, twisting her hands back and forth behind her. The handcuffs squeezed the skin, but her hands were small and petite. If she could just...get free. She twisted harder, collapsing her thumb joints to shrink her hands. Pain stung where her skin scraped off raw. But the harder she twisted, the more her joints swelled. The cuffs were too tight. Too tight. She'd have to break bones, which she was more than willing to do, but she couldn't even make a millimeter of progress.

"Don't waste your energy," Giordano said. "They're not coming off."

She fell back against the seat, defeated. Her chin lowered and she could no longer hold back the torrent of tears.

Jamansky was behind this. She didn't know how or why, but Jamansky had done this to her.

He'd done this to all of them.

120

Why? Why insist she be home tomorrow if he'd planned her arrest today? She hadn't even told him she was going into town. He had no idea she needed to get Zach and Amber legal. How had this happened?

Greg.

His name filled her mind. It was the final blow. What would Greg do when he found out?

A crushing weight squeezed her chest, her ribs, her lungs, like she'd been dropped in a vise that tightened slowly around her, squeezing the life out of her. Her body, damp and cold with rain, began to shake. All-consuming shivers turned her into a mass of trembling limbs.

The drive wasn't long—although it could have been for all she knew. Time had ended.

As the patrol car slowed, she lifted her head to witness the finality of her arrest. A large, gray building was surrounded by endless, high, barbed-wire fences. A sign out front of a smaller building read *Rochelle's Penal Institution for Women.*

Her patrolman parked along the curb and walked around to open her door. She kicked out, trying to get his huge gut, but he was ready. He sidestepped and grabbed her arm, yanked her up and out.

Through the rain, she suddenly remembered something.

"Wait." She dug in her heels. "Wait! I have money. A lot of money. I can pay you if you release me." Her rain-soaked hair hung in her face. She didn't have available hands to push it back, but that didn't matter. Her heart raced with hope. "I have money."

Giordano stopped and eyed her. "How much?"

It took her a moment to recall the number. "Four hundred. I have it with me, but you have to release me first. Just let me go free and you can have all of it."

Greed filled his beady eyes as he glanced at the guard tower. She didn't care. As he considered, she scanned their wet surroundings. The work camp was out in the wide open. No trees. No other buildings to hide behind. But she'd walk—no, sprint—all the way home. She didn't even know the way, but she could figure it out. Then she'd find a way to free Amber and—

Sudden pain sliced through her. The patrolman jerked her arms back as far as they would go.

"Where is it?" he sneered. "Which pocket did you hide the money in?"

She tried to kick him again, but against his three hundred pounds, she was nothing. It only took him a minute of digging through her pockets before he had it.

"Thanks for this, princess," he said, waving CJ's thick wad of cash in front of her. "I really needed this. It's our little secret, eh?"

He grinned.

She kicked him, only that time her foot found purchase. She felt the impact all the way from her toe to her knee. So did he.

Yelling, he swore and, in his distraction, loosened his grip.

It was enough.

She dropped to the sodden gravel. Without her hands and with her already-unsteady balance, she struggled to right herself, feet sliding on the rain-soaked pebbles, but then she was up, running.

She only made it three strides before he caught her and yanked her back. A blur of movement, and pain exploded in her cheek so hard her vision went dark.

"And here I thought we were friends," he hissed.

Her vision swirled. Her ears rang. Her cheek throbbed with every heartbeat. By the time she could think straight, they were to the building and heading inside.

A federal patrolman stood, hands up. "Whoa. We're not taking new prisoners. Sorry, but we're full. Try Crystal Lake."

"Not my problem," Giordano said, still huffing from the exertion. "Commissioner's orders, so deal with it. Her computer work should have already cleared. She's from the Kane County District."

Sighing, the guard pointed. "Fine. Take her down there for processing."

Three guards in black met them down the hallway. They flipped off the TV and grabbed their rifles.

"What's going on?" one asked.

"I've got a new recruit for you." Pulling keys from his pocket, Carrie's large patrolman undid her handcuffs. "Have fun with her, boys. She might not look it, but she's a feisty one."

Giordano shoved her forward.

Her hands were free, but she wasn't prepared for the release. She stumbled straight into one of the guards.

Catching herself, she backed up and rubbed her raw wrists. Hot tears ran down her throbbing cheek. High-pitched ringing filled her bad ear.

Her wet clothes clung to her and her hair was plastered to her face. She didn't even have the presence of mind to be scared. That is, until the first guard spoke.

"Everything off," he said to her. "Strip all the way down."

Her head lifted. "What?"

"We'll dispose of your clothes later. Just leave them on the floor."

She took two steps back and clutched her mom's wet, blue blouse. "No. No!"

The prison guards closed in around her.

"There now," her huge patrolman said, barely restraining a smile. "They've got to make sure you aren't hiding anything under all that...wet stuff. But don't worry. They'll give you a cozy jumpsuit that should fit you quite nicely."

The taller guard glared at him. "You can leave now, Giordano."

"Oh, I'm in no hurry," he said, leaning against the wall.

Another guard advanced on Carrie. "I'm sure you don't want those handcuffs back on, miss, so what's it going to be? Do you want to do this the easy way or the hard way?"

———— ✦ ————

Greg tucked his slingshot back into his pocket and mopped the rain from his face, happy to finally be under the shelter of the porch. He wouldn't have guessed that Illinois could rain as hard as North Carolina could. He felt sorry for Carrie and the others. Even with a coat, it couldn't have been a fun walk into town. Then again, Carrie loved a good storm.

Stomping his feet, he entered Richard's house and started for the stairs, already dreading his long guarding shift.

"Hey," a voice called out. "Is that Greg?"

Greg backed down the stairs and peered into the family room. "Richard? Sorry to barge in without knocking. I didn't expect y'all to be back already. How'd it go in town?"

"We didn't end up going," Richard said, coming into the front entry. He eyed Greg's wet clothing. "Some of us weren't in the mood to get soaked today. How was hunting?"

Greg rubbed his wet arms, trying to work some warmth into his skin. "Useless. It took forever to convince Dylan, the village idiot, that no animal would willingly be out in this—including us."

"Sorry."

"Me, too." Greg braced himself to ask, "When are you headin' into town?"

"I haven't spoken to Carrie yet," Richard said. "Once the storm lets up, I'll track her down and find out."

"Just not tomorrow, alrighty?"

"Most likely not."

Greg looked at him pointedly. "Not tomorrow. Or the next day. Really any day after today Jamansky could be there, so y'all are just gonna have to suck it up and go in the rain. Don't wait too long, either. The township office closes at 5 p.m., whenever the heck that is."

Richard shook his head with a smile. "You have issues. You know that, right? It won't hurt to wait a few days—or even a week—to get Amber and Zach legal. Carrie has been ill most of the last week. If she doesn't feel up to spending the day drenched, I'm not going to force her to go—and neither are you. It's her call."

Richard O'Brien was as close to a father as anybody Greg had known in twenty years, but Greg thought of him more as a friend. An older, usually-wiser friend.

He sighed. "Fine." Hopefully the rain would let up anyway. "Do you have a towel I can use to dry off a little?"

"Upstairs closet," Richard said. "Terrell will be glad you're here early. His headache hasn't cleared up, and he's been grumbling about guarding all morning."

Greg rolled his eyes. *Poor baby.*

As he started up the stairs, Richard called, "How long are you on shift?"

"Until sunset," Greg said, dreading it. Then again, if it was raining this hard, Carrie couldn't weed or do laundry outside. Maybe they could wait out the storm together. Smiling, he leaned over the railing. "Hey, send Carrie over if she's free."

"Sure thing," Richard said.

Greg took the stairs two at a time.

Several long hours passed of him twiddling his thumbs and watching the main road for any sign of danger. He had nothing but his thoughts to entertain him. He planned everything from setting up this farmers' market to how he could keep the vulture, Jamansky, away from Carrie tomorrow. But even those thoughts couldn't occupy him forever.

He was struggling to keep his eyes open by the time he spotted Richard out the window, striding up the wet sidewalk with Dylan Green. The rain had finally stopped after a steady stream all day, leaving the air damp and warm. The sun hadn't quite set yet behind the lingering clouds, but Greg ran out to meet them on the driveway, hoping to finish his shift early.

"Your turn," Greg said to Dylan.

"Hold on," Dylan said. "We're coming to see if Carrie is here."

"I wish," Greg said. "She never stopped by. Why?"

Dylan exchanged a brief look with Richard. "I just dropped Sasha and the boys off at the Ashworth's for the night. No one's home."

"I never found Carrie either," Richard said. "Now it seems as if no one knows where she is."

"Did you check the Watson's house?" Greg said, smiling. Halfway into his shift, he figured she had spent the day with Rhonda and Chuck planning out her new yard. "Carrie was anxious to get her yard started. My guess is she lost track of time."

"Good idea," Dylan said. "I'll check over there and let her know she has a house full of people waiting for her."

Greg grabbed his arm. "Nice try, sly dog. *I* will check with Watsons. *You* will take over here."

Dylan muttered something unintelligible but turned and walked into Richard's two-story home to start the next shift.

Two minutes later Greg stood at the Watson's front door, baffled.

"Sorry, Greg," Rhonda said. "We just figured Carrie got busy today. Do you want us to look for her with you?"

"No. I'll check Ziegler's," he said. "Maybe Amber knows where Carrie went."

As he headed toward the end of the cul-de-sac, he couldn't push away the gnawing feeling that something wasn't right. Carrie wouldn't spend a whole day on anything but her garden, in one form or another. With the rain, where else could she be?

He didn't even make it halfway to Braden's house because a group was gathered on Carrie's driveway, including the Ziegler's entire family. It only took one question for a pit to carve itself in Greg's stomach.

"Hey, Greg," Braden called. "Do you know where any of the Ashworths are?"

nineteen

As word spread, the rest of the clan met on the road in front of Carrie's. It had been roughly twelve hours since anybody had seen any of the Ashworths. Greg had been the last one, giving Carrie a quick kiss as they left her house that morning: him to hunt, and them huddled under Carrie's coat on their way to grab Richard. Nobody had seen them since.

Twelve hours, Greg repeated, sickened.

"They could have stopped off to make contact with another clan," Terrell said. "Maybe Zach remembered another group."

"Or they could have gotten lost," Sasha said. "It's a long way."

Richard shook his head. "Not likely. Carrie knows the area well. I'm sorry, Greg. I never heard them this morning. Are you positive that you saw them heading here?"

Greg couldn't even nod. He'd already tried to comfort himself that they'd just gotten lost, strayed off the beaten path to hide from the storm or pick wild strawberries, but Richard was right. Richard was horrifyingly right. Carrie knew her way around this area better than anybody. She wasn't lost. She wasn't visiting some other clans.

She was gone.

"Jamansky," Greg whispered.

Richard's eyes widened. "What?"

Greg's blood began to boil. "Jamansky has her. He took them."

The entire group fell silent.

His grandpa was the first to venture a question. "Why?"

"Because I kept her from him," Greg said, stomach pitching. "He was coming back to see her, and she wasn't home—because of me—so he took her."

Revenge on Oliver.

Ashlee Lyon covered her mouth. Braden, who had been sitting on the curb, slowly rose to his feet, pallid skin flushed with fury.

"Was it worth it?" Braden asked. "Was it, Greg? They could be in jail, gone forever!"

Richard held up his hands. "Let's not jump to conclusions. We don't know anything yet. Even if Carrie and the others went into town, Jamansky wasn't in Shelton today, remember?"

"That's right," Ashlee said. "David went to Geneva for a big high-up meeting. He wasn't anywhere near Shelton."

Right.

Greg tried to talk himself off the cliff. This might be harmless—some simple reason keeping them away for twelve, long, wet, unexplained hours.

But inside, he knew.

His fists clenched, furious with himself for not following them into town. He'd told Carrie that he and Dylan could hunt anywhere, but she'd brushed it off and said they'd be fine. So he'd let it go—let her go.

"They're probably just waiting out the rain somewhere," Sasha said.

"The rain stopped an hour ago!" Greg snapped suddenly. "Look, I'm not waiting around. I'm headin' into town."

"Are you sure that's wise?" Richard asked. But at Greg's sharp look, he backed down. "You're right. I'll go with you."

Within seconds they had a group prepared to spend all night searching if necessary. Night was closing in fast, and a few grabbed makeshift lanterns. For the most part, it would be a blind search, complicating things. The rest would stay behind to check the immediate area around Logan Pond.

When they reached the edge of the neighborhood, Richard turned back under the flickering light of the lanterns. "If anyone finds them or any sign of them, send up the call. If you reach town before the others, hold back behind the old library. And please stay in groups of at least two or three. I don't need to tell you how nervous it makes me to have all of you out in the open, so stay aware, stay smart, and stay together. Nothing rash," he added with a look aimed at Greg.

Greg ignored the warning because they were taking too long.

Too long!

He turned and started off but only made it a few steps. Somebody grabbed his arm.

"If anything happened to Amber," Braden said, standing nose to nose with Greg, "anything at all, I'm holding you personally responsible."

Greg nodded. He already knew this was his fault.

All of it.

He took off, sprinting for town. The rugged two-mile path into Shelton was nearly invisible under the cloud cover, but that didn't slow him down. Soon the voices calling out behind him faded to nothing.

Once Greg hit the abandoned cornfield, he spotted a packed-down trail through the wet weeds. A few places even held three sets of deep footprints filled with muddy rain water. He should have sent up the call, but his pounding heart refused to let him stop for even a second. Because the Ashworth's tracks only led one direction. They'd gone into town and hadn't returned.

He followed their trail with the speed of a hound dog, each step bringing a new vision of Carrie strapped up, tied up, beaten, bruised, half-dead on the floor of a prison, or worse, at the mercy of David Jamansky. His mind became his enemy. With each new horrid possibility, he sped up until he was a blur in the night.

At one spot, he nearly lost them. The weeds thinned and all footprints had washed away in the storm. After a few minutes of frantic, breathless searching, he found their trail again and took off, muscles and lungs burning. Branches whipped his face, logs and boulders slammed against his shins, but he flew.

Their trail entered town in nearly the same spot he always had, just behind the township office. He searched the exterior of the dark brick building first, then pressed his face up to the glass doors. The small building was dark inside except one emergency fluorescent light. But bright light spilled out of the conjoining building.

The patrol precinct.

Breathless, Greg crept up to the three patrol cars out front. Oliver's car was parked closest with the identifying dent in the side. Greg wasn't surprised to see it there since Jamansky had driven that same car to Carrie's.

Double-checking his surroundings, Greg peered inside the black interior. An empty coffee mug. Useless papers on the passenger seat. Nothing with ties to Oliver.

Greg had ridden in the trunk of that same car not that long ago, clueless about how much could change in such a short time. The other two patrol cars held nothing useful, and neither had "Chief of Patrols" plastered along the side.

Jamansky wasn't at the precinct as far as Greg could tell.

Out of options, Greg scurried up to the lit patrol building and pressed his back against the brick to peer inside. Four patrolmen stood around a desk, talking. Their soft laughter drifted out to him. Greg recognized three of them from the raid on his grandparents' house in March, including the huge, line-backer-sized man.

He nearly charged inside and demanded they tell him what had happened, but he wanted to get the other clansmen's reports first just in case they'd seen something he'd missed.

He headed back behind the old library, hoping against hope. The small group was still gathering. Terrell held Carrie's drenched, abandoned coat, having found it under a huge tree. That told Greg little but solidified it for the others. The Ashworths had come to town. Other than that, nobody had seen anything that Greg hadn't already seen for himself.

"Now what?" Richard asked.

"I'm goin' in," Greg said. His mind went over the speech he'd prepared for those four patrolmen—and Commander McCormick, once he found out.

Richard looked confused for a moment before his head snapped up. "Oh, no. Not a chance, Greg. Your mother would never forgive me, and neither would Carrie. What's option number two?"

"Hold on," Greg said. "The second they know I'm a federal patrolman, they'll be forced to tell me—"

"No, you wait!" Richard rode over him, more forcefully than Greg had ever seen. "I love your mother too much to let you throw your life away on some rash, idiotic decision. Not just her, but your grandparents, too. You're the last family they have. Need I remind you that getting yourself arrested won't do Carrie any good anyway?"

"Maybe it would," Greg countered. And just that fast, his mind tripped over the possibility. Getting arrested. The fastest way to figure out where they'd taken Carrie.

Richard glared at him, his face glowing orange with lantern light. "You wouldn't end up in the same place as her. They house men and women separately—possibly not even in the same county. And even worse, do you think the government, in the chaos it's in now, will simply welcome you back with open arms after what you did? You'll be snagged and court-martialed faster than you can say your name. Military prison will be twenty times worse than anything else we might be facing with the Ashworths, so we will do this rationally or not at all."

"For all we know," Terrell said, "they went a different way home and they're sitting within the warmth of their home right now."

"And if they aren't?" Greg challenged, refusing to let a few little words like *court-martialed* affect him. "What if Jamansky has her, Richard?"

"Then we'll deal with it as a clan just as we've always done. They can handle themselves for one day while we get our bearings."

"One day?" Greg yelled.

Richard laid a hand on Greg's shoulder. "I promise you on my life that we will find them. Right now, though, I'm begging you to trust me. I need your brains and wisdom, but I need you *here*. Don't let me down."

Greg yanked free. "Ditto."

"Now," Richard said, "what's option number two?"

It took Greg a long moment before he could answer. "We split up. Half go back and search the woods again, the other half searches here in town for any other—"

"Whoa, whoa, whoa," Dylan interrupted. "You want *us* to search town? Are you nuts? We can't just be wandering around the open, Greg. It's bad enough we're where we are now."

Greg looked around the small group and, to his disgust, several nodded. He shook his head. "Guess I'm goin' alone after all. Option number one."

"Wait, I'll search town with you," Richard said. "Perhaps to be safe it should just be the two of us anyway."

"Count us in," a woman said, her dark shape coming up the trail. "We'll search in town, too."

Ashlee Lyon held Braden Ziegler around the waist as the two straggled into the group. The second they stopped, Braden dropped to his knees, doubled over for breath.

Greg marched over to them. "What are you doin' here? Neither of you should be here."

"I have to…" Braden said, "to know what happened."

"And I can find out," Ashlee said. "I can, Greg."

Niels Ziegler loomed over his son. "I told you to stay home. Greg is crazy. There's no way I'm letting you search town."

"Try to stop me," Braden said, still on his knees. A pathetic position to insist on being defiant, but he went on. "I'll volunteer as a patrolman if I have to."

As Niels, Richard, and Terrell worked on convincing Braden of the stupidity of that decision, Greg locked eyes with Ashlee, stuck on her words.

"Can you really find out what happened?" he asked her.

"Can you help me break into the office?" Ashlee said in return. "I just need access to my computer. If you can get me inside there, I can figure out if they were—"

Richard spun. "No way! None! The patrol precinct is connected to the township office. Someone is bound to hear, a lot of someones with a lot of guns."

"No worries." Greg still stared at Ashlee, mind racing. "All of my useless military training might not be so useless after all. I can get you in. But…" His voice lost strength. "Can you find her?"

"There's only one way to find out," Ashlee said.

Pulse leaping, Greg looked at Richard. Richard was shaking his head even before he spoke.

"It's better than turnin' myself in," Greg said. "And it's better than risking a group of us wandering around in the dark. So are you in or out? No hard feelings either way."

Richard closed his eyes. "I can't believe I'm doing this."

Close enough.

"Alrighty," Greg said. "You and Ashlee scout out the place. Check every window and door for bars, locks, and such. But don't touch a thing. We don't wanna be settin' off any alarms yet."

"Yet?" Richard echoed.

"Yeah. We gotta figure out what we're up against first." Greg moved toward the dark street. "Meet me back here in five minutes."

"Where are you going?" Ashlee called.

"Carrie's flower shop."

That got a reaction, but he didn't have time to explain. The flower shop had been left in ruins. Hopefully something in there would help him break in. He didn't need much. Something small and metallic to help him get in undetected.

"See you in a few," he said. "Oh, and don't get caught."

Then he made another mad dash in the dark.

twenty

"Are you okay, hon?"

Carrie curled against the painted cinderblock wall, one hand over her nose to block out the worst of the smells, the other covering her good ear to block the sounds. She'd already thrown up twice, adding to the awful smells in her cell, and the thirty percent she could still hear out of her bad ear was plenty. She didn't know which was worse, listening to some crazy woman moaning a few cells down or not listening and being left to her own thoughts. She couldn't handle reliving everything again, but her mind kept taking her back, over and over and over.

The office. The car. The prison.

The office. The car. The prison.

Amber.

Zach.

The guards.

"It'll be okay, hon," someone said, laying a hand on her shoulder. "You get used to it here."

Blinking slowly, Carrie saw a woman kneeling beside her on the hard, cement floor. Carrie tried to pull herself together enough to focus. The woman looked older than Carrie by thirty years, or maybe in the woman's present condition—filthy, with a few missing teeth—she just looked that old. The other women in the shared cell looked to be in worse condition since most didn't have enough social sense to keep their mouths from gaping wide open.

Prison…

Six cement slabs—one above, one below, and four painted walls—closed in around Carrie. A metal bunk bed sat in one corner with thin mattresses and even thinner pillows. A toilet and sink sat in another. Filth permeated everywhere else. But the smells...the sounds coming from places she couldn't even see...

She swallowed the bile rising in her throat.

It took the woman three times of saying, "I'm Donnelle. What's your name, hon?" before Carrie could think straight enough to answer.

"Carrie," she whispered.

Donnelle smiled warmly. "Carrie. What a pretty name. Where are you from, Carrie?"

Shelton.

Logan Pond.

The office. The car. The prison.

Amber. Zach.

Guards.

She curled deeper against the cement wall and begged her mind to shut off.

"Ah, Donnelle," one of the women called. "Give her some time. She's still in shock."

"Aren't we all," another said.

Then they laughed. Every woman in the small cell threw back her head and laughed as if she'd heard the world's greatest joke. It was unthinkable to hear such a happy sound in a place like that, at a time like that.

A hand went on her shoulder again, but she ignored it. For the first time in her life, she had nothing left to give. Not a smile. Not a polite response. Her thoughts rested solely on her two siblings and how she had failed them. And Greg.

And her parents.

Just when she thought she had cried every last drop of moisture...

"It's so soft," a new voice said.

"Leave her alone, Marge," Donnelle warned.

Somewhere in the deep recesses of Carrie's brain it registered that someone was stroking her hair.

"So silky and soft," the woman continued. "I want it."

"Marge!"

The stroking stopped and footsteps retreated.

"Don't mind her," Donnelle said, still crouched beside Carrie. "Marge is…well…I'm sure you can understand. Speaking of which, you should probably sleep with your toothbrush underneath you. But never mind her. Do you want to sleep on the bed, Carrie? It's your first night and all. After that, the bunks go to the elders like Crazy Marge. We do everything that way. The longer you're in, the more privileges you get. Someone like Marge there is goin' on six years, so she's an elder elder, if that makes sense. For tonight, though, you can choose top or bottom bunk." Donnelle tugged on her arm. "Come on. I know it doesn't look like it with all the lights they keep on around the clock, but it's time to sleep."

Carrie squeezed her swollen eyes shut.

Make it stop.

"Oh, give it up, Donnelle," one of the other cellmates called. "She ain't moving."

Donnelle sighed wearily. "Don't worry, hon. You'll see. Things aren't always as bad as they seem."

By the time Greg found what he needed and met back up with Richard and Ashlee, the clock inside the dark office read eleven o'clock, late for people who slept with the sun.

"Your mother will haunt me for this," Richard whispered, continuing his quiet-but-ignored rant. "We're all dead. You know that, right? She will haunt me forever for letting you do this."

While Richard whined, he kept his back to the doors, scanning the dark downtown for any movement.

After all of Richard and Ashlee's sleuthing, Greg had determined the front doors would be easiest to break into. He crouched in front of the lock with his two paper clips, wiggling and bending away.

"Do they keep the security cameras on all night?" Greg whispered.

"Yes," Ashlee said, "but they only check them if something happens."

Greg listened for each click in the lock as he wiggled the paper clips. The second deadbolt was taking longer than the first. He should have listened to that class in Naperville. Finally, three more clicks and he felt the last one release. He twisted the paper clip hard and the second deadbolt opened.

Before he could pull the handle, Ashlee grabbed his hand. "Will you be able to lock these again?" she asked.

"Maybe."

Her eyes widened. "But they'll know someone broke in."

"Or they'll assume your coworker forgot to lock up."

"Ellen never forgets anything," Ashlee hissed. "They'll know, Greg. They're going to know someone broke in, and if they do, they'll check the cameras and they'll see." She swallowed. "He'll see me."

Greg studied her in the muted moonlight. He wished they had brought dark hoodies to hide her bright blonde hair, but he hadn't, nor did he have time to come up with an alternative.

"I can go in alone," he said. "Just tell me where to look. You don't have to do this."

Ashlee sighed. "Yes I do. Let's go."

Inch by painful inch, Greg opened the door. Even though Ashlee claimed the township hadn't been able to afford a working alarm system for years, he still tensed for loud blaring sirens to go off. When none did, he opened the door far enough that all three could slip inside.

They hugged the walls, sliding under the security camera and along the dark lobby. The single emergency light lit the direct center of the office, so they stayed along the dark edges while Greg scanned every inch of the office.

Everything looked peaceful enough. Nothing out of place.

No blood on the floor.

Ashlee stopped at the hallway that led to the patrol precinct. Greg listened a moment to the soft talking and laughing next door.

Another class Greg had endured in the Naperville training facility included which punishments awaited those who turned their backs on their duties—especially those with rank and power. He'd ignored it at the time, assuming he'd never be given either. But now…

Greg wasn't afraid of discipline for going AWOL, but if that discipline landed him in a military prison, it would make things a million times worse. They couldn't afford that kind of complication.

"You know," Ashlee whispered, "Carrie could be in the holding cell."

Greg grabbed her arm. "You didn't tell me you had holding cells here."

"Yes. In the precinct."

Richard nudged them from behind. "Just stick with the plan. First things first."

Ashlee pointed toward the desks behind the counter. Greg could just make out the shape of a computer screen. Richard took up his post next to the hallway, watching and listening for any movement from the patrolmen, while Ashlee and Greg crept behind the counter.

As Ashlee inched up to her desk, Greg leaned close.

"You don't have any weapons stashed in here, do you?" he whispered.

Her eyes widened but she nodded eagerly. With the care of a brain surgeon, she quietly rolled out her desk chair until she could sit. Then she leaned over and opened the bottom drawer. From what Greg could make out, the drawer was filled with regular files, but she pushed them all forward until she extracted a small object from the back. She placed it in Greg's hand.

His fingers closed around the object. He nearly shouted for joy as he held it up in the soft light. A small 9mm pistol. He'd spent half his training perfecting his aim with a similar gun. Ashlee handed him two smaller objects, ammo magazines.

Greg gripped the pistol in both hands, feeling a sudden surge of power. Richard glared at him from across the way. Greg ignored him to check the gun's safety and to make sure the chamber was loaded and ready to go. The pistol was smaller than he preferred, but he didn't care.

As he tested the size and feel of it, Ashlee turned toward the computer. Her hand hovered over the computer's power button, hesitating.

"What's wrong?" he whispered.

"The light," she said.

Greg studied the black computer screen that was about to illuminate the heck out of the front office. Richard pointed to the security cameras aimed their way, but if they only checked them if something was out of place, they'd be fine. Greg had to see what was on that computer.

"It'll be fine," Greg whispered. "Go."

The computer hummed to life. Greg squinted against the blinding light. Ashlee quickly tapped a button to turn down the screen's brightness. It still illuminated her and Greg's faces perfectly.

When the login screen popped up, she typed in her username and password. The screen flashed blue:

ONE FAILED LOGIN ATTEMPT.

She swore softly.

"Try again," Greg whispered.

Same screen, with an additional warning:

TWO FAILED LOGIN ATTEMPTS. PLEASE CONTACT ADMINISTRATOR TO ACCESS ACCOUNT.

Ashlee and Greg stared at the bright screen. They'd blocked her account. Ashlee was locked out.

"Are they gonna know you tried to login?" Greg asked.

She teared up in the soft blue light. "Probably. Especially if they see the doors unlocked or check the cameras...or..."

"I'll find a way to lock the door. Just..." Staring at the warning screen, he rubbed the back of his neck. "What do we do now?"

Richard glared at them with another *I-told-you-this-was-a-bad-idea* look.

Ashlee pushed the power button again, plunging the office back into darkness. She rolled away from the desk. "Let me see if Ellen updated the log book. Don't get your hopes up, Greg. Usually she makes me do it."

Ashlee slid across the floor, silently heading up to the front counter. Slipping the small gun inside his pocket, Greg followed. Ashlee grabbed a tattered binder and flipped through it until she reached the right tab. Her finger ran down the list and stopped.

She looked back at Greg. "I'm sorry. I'm so sorry, Greg."

Greg snatched the binder and lifted it to where the words caught in the emergency overhead light.

Even knowing it might be coming, seeing the name—seeing *her* name—was like a punch to the gut.

Carrie Lynne Ashworth
Time of Arrest: 8:12 a.m.
Note: Two minors taken into custody; one male, one female

He gripped the binder, breathing speeding up.

Carrie.

It took him a full minute to find his voice. "Why was she arrested? She had her yellow card."

"Not according to that," Ashlee said.

Greg bent over the binder again. Below the other lines it read:

Reason for Arrest: Unable to produce valid documentation.

"Didn't she take her card?" Ashlee whispered.

His thoughts raced, trying to remember. He'd stood with Carrie in her kitchen that morning when she had checked and double-checked that she had everything in order: citizenship card, money, deed to her house, Zach and Amber's birth certificates.

"Yes, I know she did. She wouldn't have been that careless. Knowin' her, she probably checked and rechecked it five times before coming into this office."

"Then let me check something else," Ashlee said.

She tiptoed away from the counter and back into the darkened corner of the office. A file cabinet squeaked as she slid open a drawer. Scowling, Richard put a finger to his lips.

While she searched, Greg stared at the log book.

Carrie Lynne Ashworth
Arrested: 8:12 a.m.
Note: Two minors taken into custody; one male, one female
Reason for Arrest: Unable to produce valid documentation
Arresting Officer: Bruce Giordano

Giordano. Greg knew that name. That was the huge patrolman who had attacked Greg at his grandparents' house in March. While Jamansky had searched the house, Giordano backed them into a corner and grilled them with questions. He'd been a brute. When Greg tried to calm his mom and grandma down, Giordano clubbed his shoulder. Yes, Greg knew Giordano well.

Giordano had arrested Carrie.

Not Jamansky.

Greg pinched his eyes shut. This couldn't be happening. This couldn't be.

Feeling time ticking, he forced himself to remain present and aware. He searched the log for anything else—where Giordano had taken her—why Carrie hadn't produced valid documentation. When he found nothing, he kept rereading those words.

Carrie Lynne Ashworth. 8:12 a.m.
Carrie Lynne
Carrie

"Greg," Ashlee whispered urgently. "You need to see this."

He shut the binder and dragged himself to the back of the office. Ashlee handed him several papers stapled together. Again, he had to lift them close to make out the words. When he did, he jerked back. The deed to Carrie's house.

"Look," she said, pointing to the top.

Somebody had scribbled across the top of the deed.

Home purchased with illegal funds.

"Illegal funds?" Greg repeated.

"I don't know what it means," Ashlee whispered.

Greg stared at it, trying to piece it together. Carrie's home wasn't valid anymore which would revoke her citizenship. She'd come. She'd been taken. His eyes lifted to the open lobby, single fluorescent light shining over the place she would have stood, unprepared.

Unaware.

He should have been there.

"The holding cell?" he whispered suddenly. "Is there any way—"

"No," Ashlee cut in. "I already checked the other log. She's not there."

"Then where is she?"

"Probably Crystal Lake. Or maybe Rockford." Ashlee shook her head. "I'm not sure. It depends on where they have room. If I could have just gotten into the computer...I'm so sorry, Greg."

Crystal Lake. Rockford. He didn't know Illinois geography, but both sounded a million miles away.

He stared at the ground, no longer seeing anything. "I should have been here. I shoulda just come."

140

"And done what?" Ashlee whispered. "Tried to stop the arrest?"

"Not *tried*."

Ashlee put a hand on his arm. "There's no way you could have stopped it. If you had tried, you would just be locked up with her. In reality, you wouldn't even be *with* her. You would just be locked up or dead."

"Anything is better than this."

"No, it's not. Now you can help them."

"How? How!"

Richard whirled around. "Shhh!"

The only sound in the office was the soft conversation that carried from the patrol precinct next door.

Greg tried to work through everything, specifically how Jamansky fit into the picture. Jamansky hadn't even been the arresting officer, but he'd obviously been behind it all.

Greg looked up suddenly. "How far back did you check in the log book?"

"Just today," Ashlee said. "Why?"

He studied the deed, rereading the red scribbles—*Home purchased with illegal funds*—before his eyes slid down to the signature at the bottom. In careful script was a man's name, the person who had bought Carrie's house.

Jumping to his feet, Greg stormed back to the front counter. Richard shot him a warning look, and Greg tried to quiet his steps. Ashlee followed. Greg flipped through the binder, ignoring the page with Carrie's information and flipping back two days earlier. His finger ran down the names and events, until he found it.

Oliver Gerard Simmons
Arrested: 6:07 p.m.
Reason for Arrest: Treason
Arresting Officer: Chief David Jamansky

Greg's fist slammed down on the counter, making the tattered binder jump. "I knew it. I knew it!"

Ashlee's hand flew to her mouth. "Oh, Oliver."

"Still think Jamansky wasn't behind Carrie's arrest?" Greg hissed.

Before she could answer, Greg noticed a frantic movement. Richard was freaking out by the hallway, waving his hands toward the doors.

"Go!" Richard whispered. "GO!"

Freezing, Greg listened.

The conversation had stopped next door.

"Did you hear something?" he heard somebody say.

Greg shut the binder and grabbed Ashlee's sleeve. Richard was already opening the glass doors by the time they reached it. The three of them slipped out into the dark night and took off down the street. They raced around the corner of the building and through the dark woods.

"Greg, wait!" Richard said, struggling to keep up. "Let's gather everyone back to the clan so we can have a meeting and figure out what to do."

Greg didn't need a meeting. He already knew what had to happen. Picking up speed, he crossed the street and sprinted back the way they'd come.

As he passed the library, a dark shape stepped out in front of him. He pulled up short, heart jumping out of his chest, but it was just Braden.

"What did you find out?" Braden asked, tense expression barely visible in the soft moonlight. "Do you know where they are?"

"Yes," Richard said, catching up. He looked at Greg, but Greg stared down at the ground. So did Ashlee.

Braden's head bounced back and forth between them. When the silence stretched and none could bring themselves to answer, Braden fell back a step. "What happened?"

Richard sighed. "Carrie has been arrested, and…" His eyes flickered to Greg. "And Amber and Zach have been taken as well. It seems as if Jamansky is behind this after all."

"No," Braden said, shaking his head. "No!"

"I'm sorry, Braden," Richard said. "But they're gone."

Braden locked eyes with Greg. His nostrils flared in the moonlight. Then he cocked his arm back, took a step forward, and punched Greg squarely in the jaw.

twenty-one

Two lonely candles lit the Trenton's front room, adding to the somber mood. Greg leaned against a wall, arms folded tightly to keep from pounding something. His jaw ached, his head throbbed, but they were nothing compared to the crushing weight in his chest.

He kept picturing Giordano grabbing Carrie, hauling her away from Amber and Zach, checking her into prison. Thinking of her spending her first night there was torture.

"You have no idea where they're being held?" Jada Dixon asked. "Not even a guess?"

Ashlee, who had done most of the explaining, just shrugged. "My best guess is that they took Carrie to Crystal Lake or Rockford's facility. Possibly even Rochelle. They're having major overcrowding issues, so she could be in a half a dozen places. Amber and Zach are easier. Amber is either in Bristol or Campton Hills. And Zach will probably be in Montgomery or DeKalb. There's another boys' home somewhere, I just can't remember where. I'm sorry."

"Wait," Sasha Green said. "Zach and Amber aren't together?"

Greg squeezed his eyes shut. He already knew the answer.

"No," Ashlee said. "They have separate facilities for boys and girls. The only person I'm pretty sure on is Oliver." She paused, blinking rapidly. "I'm guessing they sent him to JSP, I mean the Joliet State Penitentiary. That's where they usually send dissidents."

"Then what do we do?" Terrell asked.

Go to Crystal Lake, Greg thought to himself. *Or Rockford.* Except if Carrie could be in half a dozen places and none were close to each other—or Shelton—it could take forever. Especially on foot. That was unacceptable.

Braden stood in the candle-lit kitchen, studying a map with his dad, already making plans to get to Amber. And yet Greg had nothing on Carrie.

Nothing!

Ashlee's voice cut through his thoughts. Greg hadn't even heard the question she was answering.

"Yes, but I have to warn you," she said, "there is a long waiting list to visit people. Even once your name is on the list, it still takes weeks to get a visitation slot."

Weeks.

As people kept discussing options in unproductive circles, Greg was finally able to solidify one thing in his mind. When there was a break in the conversation, he straightened.

"For all we don't know, there's somethin' we do. Jamansky was behind Oliver and Carrie's arrests. He knows we're here, he knows about our clan, so he'll be comin' for us next." Greg paused. "I think it's time to abandon Logan Pond."

The room fell silent.

"Where should we go?" Ron Marino asked.

"Ferris," Greg said. He'd thought about trying that clan Sprucewood, but he knew so little about them that he didn't dare risk it. Ferris was the only logical choice. "It's been abandoned for years. Even the patrolmen know it's empty. There's plenty of room for everybody there. Plus, it puts us close enough to here that we can check back on things." He turned to his grandpa. "What do you think?"

His grandpa stroked his bushy, white beard a moment. Then he nodded. "All things considered, it's probably for the best. Safety first. All in favor of leaving Logan Pond?"

Slowly, every hand rose in the dim candlelight.

"Alright," his grandpa said with a sigh. "That will give us some peace of mind about everyone else while we work on getting Carrie and her siblings back. I suppose we need to decide if we evacuate now or in the morning?"

"Now," Greg said. "Definitely now."

"Right now?" Sasha said. "In the dark? But it's the middle of the night. I can't even find my way to Ferris in the full light of day. And what about the little boys?"

"I know the way," Terrell said. "I'll lead out and get everyone there safely, including all the little ones."

Several people were frowning, but no one objected outright.

"Then let's do it quickly and quietly," Richard said. "Gather up your families and as much of your belongings as you can carry. Meet back here as soon as possible, as in under twenty minutes. We'll leave then. Any things we can't take tonight, we'll come back for in the morning."

As people began filing out of the Trenton's home, Richard approached Greg.

"What do you think about your grandparents?" Richard asked. "Should they come with the rest of us?"

For the umpteenth time, Greg wished he'd checked the deed to his grandparents' home. He had no idea if their citizenship had been revoked along with Carrie's.

"Yeah," he said. "Even if they still own this home—which isn't a given anymore—I don't like the idea of them being left behind. Who knows what could go wrong next? They need to be with everyone else, especially now that Grandma has gone to pieces again." The second she had heard about her beloved Carrie, she'd started wailing. She hadn't stopped since. Even now, Greg could hear her in her bedroom, crying over another loved one lost. It was enough to tear his heart out.

Richard nodded. "I'll tell CJ."

"Richard?" Greg called before he got very far.

"Yes?"

"Do you need my help tonight? I was hopin' to head back into town and keep an eye out for Jamansky."

Richard stiffened. "Not a good idea, Greg."

"You've gotta help the clan," Greg said tiredly, "and I can't sit around and move bags through the woods while Carrie rots on a prison floor. I've gotta do something. Jamansky knows where she is. I know he's behind this, but…" He held up a hand before Richard could interrupt. "I won't approach him. Not tonight. I just wanna see where he is and what he's up to. But I won't do a thing without talkin' to you first. You've got my word."

"Fine. Do what you need to." Richard took a step towards him, eyes beseeching. "But please, *please* control yourself. I already have more people to break out of prison than I can handle right now."

"Understood." Greg needed to be helping Carrie, not making things worse.

With that settled, Richard turned and made his way over to CJ. Greg overheard him discussing the best way to tell May that, after losing Carrie and her siblings, she also had to abandon her home of thirty years.

Greg looked around his grandparents' front room, barely visible in the flickering candlelight. Sixteen hours ago, his life had been nearly perfect. He and Carrie had eaten breakfast, laughed, held hands, and discussed trading with other clans. The future had been bright with possibility. And now...

He refused to finish that thought.

"Greg," Ashlee said, approaching him. "I have a quick question."

"You can come with us," he said tiredly. "To Ferris. We'll find a place for you."

"Oh, I know. I mean, thank you. That's not what I meant. I, um..." Her eyes avoided looking at him directly. "Do you know who all still needs shots? With Amber gone, I thought I better take over."

He looked at her blankly. Amber had been giving people shots twice a day.

Amber was gone.

"Right. Uh..." He rubbed his burning eyes, struggling to think. "My grandparents, Richard, Terrell Dixon, and Braden. Then there's Rhonda Watson, Kristina Ziegler, and..." He stopped, knowing he was forgetting somebody. Eight people needed shots. He'd only listed seven. So he ran through them again.

The second he figured out the eighth person, his whole body went cold.

Ashlee noticed the change. "What?

"Carrie," he said.

Carrie had been on the medicine for three days. Only three.

He looked up. "How long are they supposed to get shots?"

"Five days," Ashlee said. "How long did Carrie...?"

"Three."

"Only three?" She caught herself and said, "I mean, maybe three is enough. It might be."

Greg's mind raced. Carrie's illness could return with a vengeance. Would they treat people in the prisons? Not a chance. The whole reason President Rigsby created this virus was to wipe out those who had sided against him. Illegals. Rebels. The very people crowding the prisons.

He slowly sank down to the floor, fingers pulling out his hair.

Three days.

Carrie had received six doses instead of ten.

Was it enough?

"I'll go do the other shots," Ashlee said quietly. "I'm sorry, Greg."

A few minutes later, Greg realized somebody stood over him. Braden. Greg forced himself back to his feet, but he had no energy to duck out of the way. He didn't even want to. Braden was the only person holding him responsible for this—which he should. Greg had hidden Carrie from Jamansky. Jamansky would have the last laugh now.

Greg stood directly in front of Braden where he was fully available for the next blow. But Braden looked contrite. He ran a hand over his tousled hair.

"Greg," Braden said. "Hey, look. I…I'm sorry about before."

Greg's jaw throbbed in an even, steady rhythm. "Don't be. I would've punched myself if I knew how. In fact, feel free to do it again."

"It's just that…I just can't imagine what it's like for them. But that was no reason to take it out on you."

Unable to tolerate any more visions of Carrie or her siblings, Greg put a hand on Braden's shoulder. "Tell you what. You figure out how to get Amber and Zach back so I can focus all my energy on Carrie. Deal?"

"Deal."

Greg took a deep, painful breath. "Alrighty. I'll come over to Ferris first thing in the morning. We'll discuss options then."

Braden gave him a strange look. "Where are you going?"

"Back into town. There's somebody I need to see."

———◆———

"Are you feeling any better this morning, hon?"

Carrie nodded at the woman with a few missing teeth—Donnelle, if she remembered right. Carrie's neck and back felt cranked from sleeping propped against a cement wall, her arms were stiff from the patrolman wrenching them behind her back, and her wrists felt cut and swollen. But with the new morning came clear thinking. And with clear thinking came a rush of reality. If this was her new reality, she had to do something about it.

Breakfast came in the form of mushy oatmeal delivered right to their cell. Carrie couldn't make herself eat. She'd never be able to keep it down. So she offered it to the oldest-looking cellmate who, for some reason, kept wanting to stroke Carrie's hair. The woman—Crazy Marge—quickly ate both helpings of oatmeal with her dirty hands.

Within a few minutes of breakfast, a guard stood by their cell door. He held out seven wet rags. Carrie's cellmates took the rags into the various corners of their small cell and started washing up. With only four corners and seven women, that left her and three other "young'uns" with nothing but wall.

Carrie used the cool rag to wipe her salt-dried tears while the others did a more thorough cleaning, unzipping their orange suits freely as if their pride and dignity had been stolen along with everything else.

"We get clean uniforms on Mondays," Donnelle explained from her corner. "Thursday is shower day, and there's no air conditioning in the buildings, so these morning washings are heaven sent."

Carrie couldn't bring herself to nod, but her other cellmates jumped in, discussing which cell block housed the stinkiest women. They decided Block 12.

The guard returned and pounded his nightstick against the bars with loud *clanks*, signaling the end of the "baths." Each woman handed back their rags and lined up at the door. Carrie did, too, even though she didn't know why.

"Time to work," Donnelle said. At Carrie's surprised look, she continued, "We sew lousy clothes for lousy people who stoop to the lousy government. It's great fun," she added with a wide grin.

The woman was as crazy as her teeth. Carrie nearly asked if they would train her how to sew but decided it didn't matter.

The guard unlocked their cell, and Carrie followed the line past several others identical to her own. She was surprised to be up on a second floor of wall-to-wall cells. She hadn't remembered coming up stairs yesterday. The guard led them outside and across to another building.

As she followed, she wondered what Amber and Zach were doing. Would they be given an education, or would they be in work camps like she was? In pain like she was? Terrified like she was, dying a little more with each step? And what about Greg?

Before the questions could overwhelm her, she told herself that, no matter what they were up against, Greg would be fine, and Amber and Zach would watch out for each other. Amber had watched Zach while Carrie was in the hospital. She would just have to do it again.

Donnelle snagged Carrie's arm, pulling her back a step in line. "We're in the material preparation room for the month of July. I'll get you a spot by me, okay?"

Donnelle seemed to have seniority of some kind, because when she asked the guard to have Carrie work alongside her, the guard agreed.

Carrie was grateful.

In a dark, warehouse-like building, Donnelle showed her what to do. Standing at long tables, she and Donnelle started marking fabrics in three spots before passing it to the next person—Ariella—who folded the fabrics in a certain way. Marking. Passing. Marking. Passing. Somehow Carrie's fingers knew what to do without any use of her brain, like they had detached themselves and were working independently. The material was blue, thick, and rough like Carrie's orange, tent-like uniform. Maybe someone in some blue card municipality would be excited to get a new outfit.

Donnelle talked nonstop while they worked. Sometimes Carrie answered, or at least she meant to. It didn't seem to bother Donnelle when she didn't.

"Did you grow up in Illinois?" Donnelle asked.

Carrie nodded.

"Not me. I grew up in the South." Donnelle slid a pile of material to Ariella. "You ever been to South Carolina, Carrie?"

It wasn't even the same state as Greg's, but it was close enough to knock the air from her lungs momentarily.

For the next hour, Donnelle chattered away about moving to Illinois, meeting her husband, a lengthy divorce, and winding up as a waitress working double shifts with a boss who made her life miserable. Carrie tried to listen. She really did. But her thoughts always seemed to circle back to everyone and everything she'd lost.

"You married, Carrie?"

She shook her head.

Though I could have been, she thought curiously.

When Greg had proposed months ago, she had been floored. "It's for business purposes only," he had said. "A sheet of paper, nothin' more. A way to get you legal." He would just tack her onto the family, pay her taxes, and call it a day. Even though it could have gotten her a flower shop and made money for the clan, the whole idea of a fake marriage had been offensive. He'd hated her back then—or so she thought. Maybe if she had been less emotional about it, a little more practical like he always was, she could be married to Greg now.

What a strangely wonderful thought.

Donnelle lowered the blue material. "Why, Carrie, you're smiling?"

Carrie reached up to feel her face. She was smiling. Even more amazing, she was almost on the verge of laughter. And suddenly she understood how people could laugh under such circumstances. Laughter was just one small tweak from hysteria.

"You have a lovely smile, Carrie. Real beautiful." Donnelle nudged her. "You obviously have someone special to make you smile like that. Tell me about him."

"Greg." That was all Carrie could manage. Not that he was from the South, too, or that he had a smile a hundred times better than her own. She couldn't describe his uncanny ability to blurt out the truth, or how he spent his days trying to solve the world's problems. All she could get out was his name. Even then, Donnelle was nearly dancing, pleased Carrie had shared that much.

A prison guard slammed his nightstick down on the table, making Carrie flinch.

"Keep working!" he yelled.

Heart racing, Carrie picked up the next piece of blue and spread it flat on the table to mark her three spots. Sweat trickled down her neck, making her wish they would open a window or something to create a breeze.

As the guard moved off, Donnelle leaned close and whispered excitedly, "Greg. That's wonderful. But y'all aren't married?"

Carrie shook her head, but once again found herself smiling as she pictured Greg pacing back and forth in front of her, words spilling out of him as he excitedly told her about his flower shop idea.

Greg.

That one word, the same one that made her smile before, pushed her over the edge. With one small tweak, she was falling, drowning in the hysteria of it all. He would never grab her hand again or tell her how beautiful she was. He would never hold her close and assure her that things would work out. He couldn't even take care of Amber and Zach, like she knew he would, because they were gone, too.

And Greg would be angry, so very angry when he found out she'd been arrested. And that scared her, too. Another person lost. Another one stolen from him. How many new walls would he build around his shattered heart? Would life ever stop beating him down?

Hot tears slipped down her cheeks. The material in front of her blurred into a giant smear of blue.

She would never know if Amber, Zach, Greg, May, or anyone lived, died, breathed, or found a way to move on without her.

She knew nothing.

She would *always* know nothing.

"I'm sure Greg is a wonderful guy," Donnelle said. "In fact, I bet he's thinkin' about you right now."

They stopped briefly for lunch. Lunch looked less appetizing than breakfast, and Carrie passed once again. Her stomach felt like it had been left behind in Shelton, so she offered her food to Crazy Marge who snatched it right up.

Donnelle continued nonstop through the endless hours of work. School, old jobs, her aunt in Kentucky, and the three teeth she'd lost since incarceration. She reminded Carrie of a younger version of May, only more talkative, if possible. Donnelle hardly took a breath as she rolled from one subject to the next.

Carrie's fingers started to ache from the long hours. She could feel hot blisters forming on her fingertips, but she kept marking piece after piece.

The only breaks they received were for counts, when the guards lined them up long enough to confirm the number of inmates. That was it.

After the last head count, Carrie noticed Donnelle taking short breaks to rub her head or neck.

"Are you...?" Carrie paused, checking for a guard. She lowered her voice. "Are you okay?"

Donnelle dropped her hand. "I'm fine. Just starting a headache because it's so blasted hot in here, and I didn't sleep real well last night."

A headache. Carrie's illness had started as a headache, too. Then again, lots of people got headaches. It meant nothing. But the way Donnelle rubbed the back of her neck, the pinch between her brows.

"Have other women here had headaches lately?" Carrie asked. "Bad ones?

Donnelle stopped working. "Yeah. Why do you ask?"

Carrie couldn't hold her gaze. She studied the small piece of chalk in her hands. What could she say? "Nothing. Never mind."

"You know somethin', don't you?"

Carrie grabbed the next piece of blue and spread it flat. "Maybe. What do you know?"

Donnelle let it all out in a rush. How the previous Friday, a woman on the line, Ravia, started complaining of a headache. Next day, she had a fever and chills, could hardly stand up straight to work. The guards kept yelling at her to keep up. When she started to cry, they just shouted louder. The next day, Ravia wasn't there. She disappeared, but others started the exact same thing. Headache, fever, fatigue, and then they would disappear. Donnelle kept her voice low. With Carrie's hearing struggles, she had to lean close to make out anything.

"People are dropping like flies," Donnelle whispered. "What is it?"

"If it's the same thing I had," Carrie said, which it sounded to be, "it's like meningitis, only far more..." Powerful, potent, deadly. She didn't know how to finish.

Donnelle's face paled. "Oh."

"Do they have a medical unit in here? Have the guards been giving out any shots of any kind?" Carrie asked desperately.

Donnelle rubbed her neck again. "We're lucky to get a washrag each morning."

Then it had to be something different. Except...according to Greg and Oliver, President Rigsby himself had engineered this disease to wipe out those who had gone against him.

What better place to test its potency than prison?

As the afternoon wore on, folding and marking, Donnelle's pace slowed until Carrie started helping her, just to keep things moving. A few times Donnelle stopped to lean against the table, which earned her a stiff rebuke from the guard. Even more disconcerting, Donnelle stopped talking. For a full ten minutes, it was just the sound of other conversations around them.

"Sorry," Donnelle said finally. "I'm really out of it today. Have you got kids, Carrie?"

"Yes." Carrie's gaze flickered to Donnelle again, measuring the coloring of her skin, the pinch of her brows, the place she rubbed her head. How could Carrie help her if this was the same thing?

Worse, would Amber and Zach get sick, too? Or would the president deem them worthy enough to receive the treatment? They were wards of the state, not prisoners. Would that be enough?

"Lovely," Donnelle said. "What are their ages?"

"Sixteen and thirteen," Carrie said softly.

Although other people around them had caught the virus, even though they had very little contact, Amber and Zach hadn't. Greg had a theory that the illness had been manipulated to skip children somehow. Now Carrie hoped—she prayed—for him to be right.

Donnelle gave her a curious look. "Aren't you a little young to have teenagers?"

"Sorry. They're my brother and sister."

Her survival instincts stopped her from explaining how they were taken, too, ripped from her arms. Instead, she turned the question back to safer waters. "How old are your kids?"

Donnelle lit up, looking a little livelier. "One's eleven. The other is nine. I love 'em to pieces. They visit me when they can, but it's tough. There's quite the waitin' list to get in and visit. Plus my mom isn't in the best shape anymore. It's pretty hard for her to get them here."

"They're with your mom?" A wild burst of jealousy shot through Carrie.

"Yeah. Praise all that's good and holy for that. I can't even imagine what I'd do if they'd been taken." Her voice dropped to a conspiratorial whisper. "Those places for kids are prisons of their own, only it's a prison of the mind, if you know what I mean. They pump them full of nonsense, brainwashing them into government-loving robots. Kimber from Block 6 says they've started sending the older ones out to fight, even before they're eighteen. Can you believe it? Sending sixteen-year-olds out to fight rebels?"

Carrie's hands froze over the fabric.

Clueless, Donnelle went on. "I suppose my boys would be too young anyhow. But they're also forcing the younger kids to rat out any illegals they know, including their own parents. My boys are awful at keeping secrets. They'd probably divulge our whole clan the first day. Ah, well. Tashina, that tall lady from 7, says they work the kids every bit as hard as they work us here. Even the girls' homes are rumored to be just as brutal as the boys'. So needless to say, I'm beyond relieved that my boys weren't taken."

The dizziness came back with a vengeance. Carrie gripped the table to keep from falling.

"They…" Carrie struggled to find air. "Boys and girls aren't together?"

Donnelle snorted, which earned her a glare from a guard. "Would you put teenage boys and girls together in one place?" she said softly. "I don't even think they keep them in the same cities."

They weren't together.

Amber and Zach.

Carrie had envisioned Amber taking care of Zach, the two of them eating lunch together in a quiet corner of a crowded cafeteria, going to class together, working a field together, or whatever they were forced to do. A support for each other. And yet they were alone. Entirely, completely, and utterly alone.

Because of her.

Carrie's ears started to ring as she replayed Donnelle's words. Every aspect. Every horror. Alone.

"Are you alright, hon?" Donnelle put a hand on her arm. "You don't look so…"

The table with the blue material began to disappear in a collapsing tunnel of vision. Carrie blinked rapidly, but it was too late.

Everything went black.

twenty-two

Amber Ashworth looked down at her school uniform. Blue. Everything in her new life was blue. Including the suit of the woman who was lecturing her behind the desk. Including the skin around the eye of the girl who had offered Amber a pity hug earlier. Including the room they had locked Amber in afterward and in which she now sat, wrists strapped to a chair. The only thing that wasn't blue was the bright red bracelet around her wrist, the one that matched Braden's. They would have to kill her before she took that off.

"Miss Ashworth? I'm speaking to you."

Amber studied the blue sky out the window behind the woman's head. The window didn't look as thick as other windows in the building. Possibly with a chair or something bigger, Amber could break it. They were up two stories, but what were a few broken bones compared to a shattered heart?

"She's not the fighter her siblings are." That patrolman couldn't have uttered more painful words. She was a fighter. She would show the entire world how much she could fight.

She twisted her wrists, testing the strength of the rope.

When she had sat in the cafeteria, she made the mistake of thinking about her family: Zach, if he was as miserable and lonely as she was; Carrie, if she was still alive. Carrie had asked Amber to do one thing— just one!—and Amber had failed that, too, because that's what she was. A failure. She couldn't take care of Zach. She couldn't even take care of herself.

She hadn't even realized she was crying in the cafeteria until Natalia, a stupid, prissy girl who thought she knew everything about everything, put an arm around her shoulders and told her that everything would be all right.

Amber had elbowed Natalia in the face.

The girl's perfect nose had gushed blood. It had taken two caregivers to pull Amber off of her. Amber just turned her wrath on them instead, kicking, screaming, and biting.

"Miss Ashworth, I asked you a question. Miss Ashworth!"

Amber's eyes went back across the blue desk to the blue-suited woman with the glaring blue eyes. Amber didn't bother responding. She hadn't said a word since arriving and she wasn't about to start now. They could force her to package soap all day, they could even force her to eat, but they wouldn't get a word out of her.

Not one.

She twisted her wrists again. They'd tied the rope to the chairs ridiculously tightly.

The woman clasped her hands on the desk, forming a tight steeple. "I understand more than you think, Miss Ashworth. I know it's rough, especially for you teenagers when you first come here to Bristol's Academy for Girls. But you'll see soon enough, the girls like it here. They're happy." She forced a smile to reiterate her words. Amber wondered if she knew how fake it looked. "You can be happy here, too. We'll keep you busy this summer, and come fall, you'll have ample opportunity to catch up on all of the schooling you've missed these years. But first," her voice hardened, "you will stop causing trouble for everyone. Do you understand? Anymore of this violence, and we'll have to confine you permanently to a…"

As the blue-suited woman droned on, Amber's gaze went back to the window. They were restraining her now, but if she could get back in here another time, maybe after another black eye or two, it just might be possible.

———◆———

Zach's hands felt raw and blistered as he climbed into the hot, stuffy bus. He hadn't seen a mirror yet, but he was sure his freckled face had burnt to a crisp after the long day in the sun.

When that jerk of a patrolman had dumped him in this place, the headmaster said, *"Oh, don't worry. We'll keep him busy. Busy boys stay out of trouble."*

That seemed to be the home's motto.

The older teens tried to scare Zach, saying they made them dig zombie graves all day. He wasn't stupid enough to fall for that, but still, he had hoped the work involved something he understood like weeding cornfields or even working in a chicken factory like Greg once had.

No such luck.

That morning they packed all the boys onto four busses, heading out to "refresh the streets"—which was code for cleaning up the rubble. Apparently they took the boys to a new location each day. Anything the illegals burned, any windows smashed, walls vandalized, or fences torn, the boys got to clean up while armed guards kept watch.

Today they worked on a municipality building in DeKalb that had been burned to the ground.

Zach spent the morning sweeping glass. That hadn't been horrible. He heard boys whispering while they worked, talking about how anxious they were to turn sixteen and start training to fight. Zach still had three years before then, so he hadn't listened much.

Then they switched him to the rubble crew.

Some of the blackened ashes had still been smoking as he dumped them into the bins. Because he was the new kid, he didn't get shovels or wheelbarrows. He had nothing but his hands and arms to gather up the piles and trek them to the dumpsters. Three separate times he'd burned himself thinking he'd finally learned how to tell which piles were still hot. Now he couldn't even grab the railing into the bus without pain flaring.

Straggling down the aisle, he searched for an open spot to sit on the hot bus. Several boys glared at him, so he picked an empty spot near the back.

Zach turned his palms over and studied the two blisters that had split open. The red, gaping wounds killed. Not only that, but they were filthy from the blackened ashes. He didn't know how to fix blisters—especially dirty ones. He didn't even know how to heal sunburns. Carrie always told him what to do.

How was he supposed to fix his blisters by tomorrow when he'd be back doing the same thing?

Cold water?

Soap?

Heat built behind his eyes.

Blinking rapidly, he pretended to rub his eyes as if he'd gotten something in them before the others could see.

It was probably safer to not think about Carrie or Amber or what was happening to them. Instead, he decided to act like Greg. Greg liked to solve problems. Zach had a problem—several big ones, actually. His hands weren't going to survive this kind of work. Maybe when he made it back to the boys' home, he would plunge them into cold water and hope that cleaned them well enough. Carrie used cold water when she burned herself cooking over the fire. Tomorrow he would wrap his hands in something while he worked, a rag or something.

If they'd even give him one.

As he entered the tall boys' home, ready to head straight for the bathrooms, an adult shouted at him.

"Hey, you!" the headmaster called. "New kid. Come over here!"

After the long, grueling day in the sun, Zach had to drag himself over to the headmaster's office. The headmaster stood inside with another man in a dark suit.

As soon as Zach entered, he felt cold air blowing from somewhere. Air conditioning. It felt amazing.

"Did you see that?" the headmaster said to the man. "Look at how he walks."

The man turned to Zach. "What's wrong with your ankle, son?"

"I...I don't know," Zach said, looking down. He'd been limping for years, but didn't think about it often. Of course a few boys there had started calling him "Peg leg," which he didn't love.

"Sit there," the man said. "Right up on Mr. Cartwright's desk. Let me take a look at that leg."

Zach winced as he used his blistered hands to push himself up onto the desk. But instead of inspecting his hands, the man—a doctor—rolled up Zach's pant leg and started feeling around his ankle.

"You broke it?" the doctor asked.

"I fell out of a tree a few years ago," Zach said. "My mom's friend tried to fix it, but it didn't set right. It doesn't bother me, though."

The doctor shook his head. "This is why illegals shouldn't be allowed to raise children. It's appalling." He turned back to the headmaster. "If

158

you want him to be useful in the future, Mr. Cartwright, I need to reset his bone."

"But he broke it years ago," Mr. Cartwright said. "Can you still fix it?"

"Yes, but it will require surgery." The doctor rubbed his jaw. "If it's healed like I think it has—of course I'll be doing x-rays to double-check—I'm guessing the bones have knit together and probably calcified. I'll have to go in and cut the bone to realign it, basically sawing it in half."

Saw.

His bone.

"No!" Zach said. "You can't!"

The doctor looked at him. "It's not as bad as it sounds, son. I'll put a metal plate and screws in to stabilize it." Back to the headmaster, he added, "He'll be in a cast for weeks at the very least, and it might be several months before he's functioning normally again, but once it heals, he'll be as good as new."

"Several months? Never mind then," Mr. Cartwright said. "I can't have him out that long."

Zach heaved a sigh of relief.

But the slimy doctor wouldn't let it go. "Think of it as an investment, Mr. Cartwright. A few months' sacrifice now, and he'll be fully functional later. He looks like a healthy kid. Skinny, but healthy. He'll recover quickly, and then you can use him how you want down the road. But if he's allowed to grow another six to eight inches on this ankle, he'll be useless to you for the rest of his life. It needs to be fixed, preferably before he hits his growth spurt."

Mr. Cartwright pulled on his bottom lip. "Then I suppose we should do it. How soon?"

"Wait!" Zach jumped off the desk. "I walk just fine. I can even run. Look, I'll show you how fast I can run."

Mr. Cartwright grabbed his arm sharply. "You will stay where you are, young man."

Zach froze. The man's fingers dug into his bicep until he trusted Zach to stay put. Then he circled around him like a vulture.

"I think Dr. Wheeler is right. We better fix you up so you can become a good, strong soldier some day. Would you like to become a soldier, maybe even a patrolman? You can shoot guns and arrest people."

"No!" Zach wanted to get out of there. Now. "You can't make me."

Mr. Cartwright grabbed his arm again. "I can make you do whatever I want, and you better watch your tongue, boy. Talking back will only get you time in the basement."

Zach swallowed. He didn't know what the basement was, but from the few whispers he'd heard, it sounded bad.

"That's better." Mr. Cartwright turned back to the doctor. "How soon?"

twenty-three

"Is that you, Richard?" his grandma called.

Greg shut the door to the Harrison's home. Of all the homes his grandparents could have picked, he wished they hadn't chosen Gayle Harrison's, but it was in the back of the sub, and it used to be nice. Greg wondered if Carrie was in the same work camp as her mom's best friend.

"Hello?" his grandma called again.

"No, Grandma," Greg said, "Just me. I'm back. Guess you don't know where Richard is?"

She came into the dusty entry way. "He was helping Sasha and the boys. Any word in town?"

Greg shook his head. Each hour of hiding in the shadows had only plunged him further into despair. His thoughts had swayed violently from starting bold revolutions to pitiful suicide, from storming prisons to kidnapping mayors. Nothing useful. Nothing logical. When the sun rose over the tall trees, he had given up and started back.

His grandma covered her face and broke down. "Oh, my sweet Carrie."

"She's gonna be okay, Grandma," he said, patting her back. "I'm sure she's just fine."

"How?" she cried. "Do you really think she's *fine*?"

No, I don't. Not a bit.

"Think about it," he said. "This is Carrie we're talkin' about. She'll probably find a way to spruce up the prison. I bet she has flowers by her bed and new curtains on the windows."

And slashes across her back. And bruises on her face.

Greg squeezed his eyes closed to clear the images.

"She's a wonderful girl, isn't she?" His grandma wiped her cheeks. "The way she finds happiness in the middle of everything. But she's so tender and sweet. How will"—the water faucet turned back on—"how will she survive, Gregory? How can she with such horrible, awful people?" She was really losing it now. "They're probably all murderers...and fornicators...and, and, and they'll kill her!" Her eyes widened with horror. "Or worse!"

Now their thoughts were on the same page. He could think of plenty of things worse than death.

"I'm sure she's fine," he said quickly. Anything to stop the tears that amplified his self-loathing by the second. "Real fine. Just really, very *fine*."

"And how are *you* doing without her?" his grandma asked, voice quavering.

The question caught him off guard. Suddenly the lie wasn't available. He was the furthest from *fine* that he'd ever been.

A lump swelled in his throat.

"I'm, uh..." He rubbed his jaw and had to grit his teeth to keep from turning into the same emotional mess she was. "Well, I'm..." He swallowed.

She patted his hand. "I know. I know."

As the two fell into silence, Greg's mind became his enemy, flashing from image to image, like a slide show from his demented imagination: Carrie on a small cot in prison, feverish with the returning virus; or her beaten and dying on a cold cement floor, clothing savagely ripped from her by patrolmen who didn't have a shred of human decency. Sometimes all of the images combined into one giant possibility that loomed in his mind like a tsunami offshore.

There were definitely things worse than dying.

"It wouldn't be right for you to be okay without her," his grandma said. "And because of that, I know you'll get her back for me."

"I will," he promised softly.

At all costs, he promised himself.

"I better find Richard," he said, straightening.

He meant to give her a parting wave, but when he glanced back at her, he noticed something he never had before, a resemblance that caught him by surprise. Her eye shape. The pointed chin. The high curve of her cheekbones. His grandma looked like his mom—or rather, the other way around.

How had he never noticed before?

As he stood there, on the verge of losing everything, it wasn't his grandma that stared back at him. It was his mom, with all the love, compassion, and empathy a mother feels for a child in pain.

On impulse, Greg crossed the dusty home and swept his grandma up in a hug that was sure to squeeze the last few years out of her.

She patted his back gently. "Carrie will be fine," she soothed. "She will be just fine. And before you know it, we'll all be back together."

The front door swung open. "Any luck in town?" Richard called. Then he stopped, seeing them. "Oh, sorry."

Greg released his grandma and took a quick breath to gather himself again. "No sign of Jamansky in town. Only four patrol cars came and went all night. None his."

Richard seemed relieved by that answer, but he was kind enough not to rub it in Greg's face.

"How'd it go last night?" Greg asked.

"We're still trying to get people settled," Richard said. "Moving in the middle of the night was…"

"Madness," his grandma finished for him. "Pure madness."

Richard nodded tiredly. "There's nothing quite like fleeing through the pitch black woods with crying children and whiny adults, all the while knowing that when you get to your dark destination, you have no idea where to put everyone."

"That good?" Greg said.

Richard chuckled. "People have emptied most of their homes, but we still have to clean out CJ's garage."

"I can help."

Both Richard and his grandma looked at him.

"You're not heading back into town?" Richard said.

Greg would have loved to hunt Jamansky down, but he feared that a confrontation in his current state of mind would end badly—very badly on either side—and he'd never find out where Carrie was.

"Not until I come up with a better plan," he said. "Right now, I'd love somethin' to occupy my thoughts."

An hour later, Greg stood in front of his grandparents' abandoned home in Logan Pond. Their house looked exactly like it had a few days ago—at least the exterior did—but now it *felt* abandoned. The whole neighborhood did.

He'd volunteered to pack up every last box from the garage into Old Rusty, Terrell's giant wagon contraption. He volunteered to do it alone, too, giving him solitude. He needed time to think, to figure out what to do next.

What he didn't need, and what he hadn't anticipated, were the memories.

The second he walked into the garage, the past hit him. He and Carrie, rummaging through boxes, looking for chains and tires for bikes that were half as big as Greg needed. She'd torn through the boxes like a maniac, trying to help him find transportation home. And now…how would he get *her* home?

Clenching his fists, he told himself to stop sitting around moaning. *Do something.* But all he felt like doing was curling up on Carrie's mattress and waiting for her to magically walk back through her front door.

Maybe if he contacted McCormick directly. Greg might be able to craft his story in a way that might help him avoid a court-martial.

Sighing, he forced himself to move. Instead of packing up the garage, he decided to check out the size of Old Rusty so he knew how much he could fit in each load.

Leaving the garage, he walked around the side of the house, through the wooden gate, and into his grandparents' backyard. Before he knew what he was doing, he had passed up Old Rusty and started wandering the long rows of crops.

Up and down, back and forth Greg walked the massive garden. Supposedly the Marinos had picked all the ripe vegetables that morning, but Greg still saw plenty—plus all the work that needed to be done: weedy carrots, out-of-control cucumber plants, pea vines that somebody would want cleared out. Only that somebody wasn't there.

He stopped at a single plant in the middle of it all.

Carrie's tomato plant.

It stood three feet tall, healthy, and completely out of place in the rows of dead peas. She'd saved it from the raid in March, babying it like only she could until he told her to plant it, like the arrogant jerk he was, well before tomatoes go in the ground. Now it stood taller than the others. Little yellow flowers ducked out beneath the leaves.

Kneeling in the soil, Greg started weeding around the stem. He plucked big weeds, even the tiny ones, careful to keep from disturbing the plant's roots.

Carrie was a fighter. Wherever she was, whatever nightmare she was experiencing, she could survive this. She had to.

Except...his mom hadn't.

And his mom had been every bit the fighter Carrie was.

Lost in thought, he barely heard the sound. Stopping, he held his breath to listen. Then his head jerked up. It sounded far away at first, but was unmistakable, and growing louder. The hum of an engine in the neighborhood.

A patrolman.

Greg jumped to his feet and ran to the fence in time to see a patrol car pulling down the street in front of his grandparents' house at a leisurely pace. When he saw the driver, he nearly knocked over the fence.

David Jamansky.

Wild, violent thoughts ran through Greg's mind. Carrie's arrest was just the final straw in a long line of offenses. And now Greg would make Jamansky talk just like Jamansky had forced Ashlee to. Greg would find out exactly what had happened to Carrie and her siblings.

He watched through the fence slats, hardly able to focus with the fury coursing through him. A single thought tugged in the corner of his mind.

Why had Jamansky come?

Alone, too.

Even stranger, Jamansky pulled into Carrie's driveway, got out of the car, and sauntered up her sidewalk with a smile on his face. A smile. He wore jeans, a button-down shirt, and a smile?

Once Jamansky reached Carrie's porch, he disappeared behind the brick and out of Greg's view.

Greg saw his chance.

He threw open the gate and sprinted down his grandparents' yard, across Denton Trail, and over two more yards. He stayed close to the houses in case Jamansky reappeared. The whole time he cursed himself for leaving his gun with the others. He needed that 9mm, tiny as it was. Although with the rage burning through him, he felt armed enough.

As he reached Carrie's yard, he slowed. He couldn't see anything, but he heard Jamansky pounding on the front door.

"Carrie, open up! O'Brien, enough games! Open this door!" More pounding combined with a lot of cursing. "Carrie!"

Greg stopped dead in his tracks.

Carrie? Why was Jamansky calling for Carrie? He'd been behind her arrest!

Unless...

...he hadn't been.

But that didn't make sense.

Greg's mind raced. Today was Wednesday. Jamansky said he would come back Wednesday to give Carrie some message from Oliver who obviously wasn't in Virginia. Wednesday. Today was Wednesday.

Was it possible...? Did Jamansky not know?

Greg looked around. A tall tree stood in Carrie's front yard. The trunk wasn't wide enough to fully hide him, but it would protect his organs well enough—at least the vital ones.

He crept up behind the tree trunk. Jamansky was too preoccupied, pounding and yelling, to notice him.

The patrol chief pounded two more times and then gave up. Swearing loudly, he kicked the door. Then he glanced around. Greg slimmed himself behind the tree trunk. Somehow, distracted as he was, Jamansky missed him.

Peering back around, Greg saw the tall patrolman grab the handle of Carrie's door and slowly push it open. The guy was going to search her house.

Over Greg's dead body.

"What are you doin'?" Greg barked, stepping out into the open.

Jamansky whirled around.

twenty-four

Jamansky whipped out his gun.

"I wouldn't do that if I were you!" Greg called, ducking back behind the too-skinny tree trunk. "You have two rifles trained on you right now, so I suggest you drop your gun. Now. Drop it!"

Jamansky froze, eyes darting around.

"You've got three seconds before my buddies start shooting!" Greg yelled. "So unless you want a hole through that tiny brain of yours, you better drop it. Three...two..."

His gun clanked to Carrie's cement porch.

"Now kick it out of the way," Greg ordered, knowing confidence and command was the only way to pull this off.

Jamansky squinted in the bright sun, trying to see who was speaking, but he obeyed, sending his gun skittering off the porch. If Greg had been any closer, he would have snatched it, but he wasn't stupid enough to think that the gun was Jamansky's only weapon.

"Now hands up," Greg ordered. "Up high where we can see them. Up now!"

Veins bulging with rage, Jamansky's hands slowly lifted.

Greg nodded, breathing a little easier. "Why are you here?"

"I'll tell you as soon as you show yourself." Jamansky said, scanning every inch of Carrie's tree. "Show yourself, coward!"

Greg stepped out into full view.

For five full seconds, Jamansky couldn't have looked more shocked if Greg had dropped a nuclear warhead on him. Then his expression turned to murder.

"Pierce!"

Jamansky started to reach for another weapon, but Greg shouted, "You gotta death wish? My best shooter can hit a soda can from half a mile away, so go ahead. Believe me, I want you dead a thousand times more than you want me dead."

Jamansky's hands rose obediently again while his eyes swept the area, trying to figure out where the shooters were.

"Why are you here?" Greg asked again.

"I could ask you the same thing," Jamansky shot back. "I guess you're not so dead after all. What did you do, go AWOL? Or did they kick you out? I can't wait to report to the feds that you're hiding out with a bunch of illegals. They're going to love that."

"8A374B1552M," Greg said.

Jamansky's eyes narrowed. "What?"

Greg took a slow breath. It wasn't too late to back out. It wasn't. But he needed answers, and Carrie and her siblings didn't have time for him to sort everything out into perfectly gift-wrapped boxes. If he rattled off the numbers, Jamansky wouldn't need to check Greg's green card—a card he no longer had.

"With your right hand," Greg said, "slowly grab your authorizing device and punch in the following code. No funny business either. I'd hate to soil that nice porch with your corrupt blood."

As commanded, Jamansky reached one-handed for his authorizing device. Greg repeated his numbers one by one, wondering how long it would take to alert Commander McCormick. Minutes? Seconds? Then again, the code alone might not alert the Special Patrols Unit at all.

A pointless hope.

Greg knew the second his face popped up on the screen because Jamansky started shaking his head. Hopefully he noticed that Greg now outranked him.

"This says you're dead," Jamansky said.

"Obviously it's a cover. I'm on a special mission that requires certain people in certain places to assume certain things that may or may not be true. Now," Greg said, "slide your device back away and tell me why in the blazes you're here at this house."

"I came to see Carrie Ashworth," Jamansky said easily. "I assume you know your cute little neighbor. Obviously you do because first your stepdad kept her from me, and now you are. Where is she, and why are all of you playing bodyguard?"

Greg's breathing sped up. "What do you mean, where's Carrie? What kinda game are *you* playin'? Carrie's in prison! She was arrested yesterday."

"What?"

It was like Greg had dropped another bomb. Jamansky's mouth gaped open. Then suddenly his face reddened with rage.

"You idiot!" Jamansky yelled. "She's legal now! Why did you arrest her? I needed her. I had this whole plan worked out, and you've ruined everything. Didn't you do a single ounce of homework before you came charging through here?"

Every sentence out of the guy's mouth confused Greg more.

"I didn't arrest her!" Greg shouted back. "She was taken yesterday in Shelton's township office by *your* guy, Giordano."

Jamansky's eyes twitched. "I don't believe you. Why would he arrest her?"

Greg just stared at him, stunned. Even the most gifted liar couldn't have pulled off that kind of response. Jamansky legitimately didn't know about Carrie. He didn't know. Which meant...he didn't know where she was.

Greg's hopes plummeted. His voice lost some of its strength.

"What happened?" he asked. "Why did they take her?"

"How am I supposed to know?" Jamansky said. "She was legal!"

As Jamansky swore up a storm, Greg felt himself going numb. His insides. His mind. But he couldn't shut down, not yet. Gritting his teeth, he let the anger charge him forward again.

"You will find out what happened to her," he said, low and deadly. "That's an order."

"An order?" Jamansky scoffed. "Who do you think you are?"

Greg pointed to the small device. "A special op with the Special Patrols Unit, so find out where she is. You've got one day to report back to me."

For a moment, the air between them was charged. Then Jamansky's expression morphed from fury into curiosity.

"Hold on. Why do *you* care where Carrie is? What's she to you? Obviously you're involved with this illegal clan somehow, something I'll be happy to report to your superiors. But why do you care where Carrie is?"

Greg's nostrils flared. He refused to answer.

Jamansky nodded slowly. "Interesting. Are you making a play for Oliver's girlfriend? Wasn't Ashlee enough for you? Now you've got to steal Oliver's girl? And while he's away at training, too. That's heartless. Maybe I should let him know what you're—"

"Who's the one makin' a play for Carrie?" Greg snarled.

Jamansky didn't even bother restraining a smile. He brushed down his crisp button-down shirt. "So what if I am? I've got my reasons. Carrie seems like a nice, sweet girl, don't you think? Truth be told, she's quite taken with me, too."

Blood pulsed through Greg, hot and violent, but one wrong misstep and he'd lose any possibility of getting her back.

So he redirected.

"You and I both know Oliver Simmons isn't in training," he said, "so cut the lies. What'd you do to him?"

In an instant, Jamansky was seething again. "Exactly what that traitor deserved. We caught him involved in illegal activity for six years. I hope he dies in JSP."

As a special op and government employee, Greg needed to agree. Oliver had disobeyed the law—a lot of laws—and he needed to be punished. Greg couldn't worry about Oliver. Not yet.

Jamansky's eyes scanned the houses again.

"They're gone," Greg said.

"Who?"

"Everybody. The illegal clan. My grandparents. They all packed up and moved out after Carrie's arrest. They left for good."

"What?" Jamansky's head whipped around. "Why?"

Not the best of poker players. In that split second reaction, Greg saw a glimpse of the patrol chief's plan. Get close to Carrie and her clan, then arrest the full lot of them.

Disgusted, Greg shook his head. "I watched them pack up and move out last night. They didn't all leave together, though. They left in small groups, some in the middle of the night, the rest this morning. My best guess is they've disbanded because of her arrest."

Jamansky's eyes narrowed skeptically. "Disbanded? And supposedly you had nothing to do with that?"

"They weren't my concern," Greg said. "As I said, I'm on a special mission."

"Or so you claim." Jamansky glared at him across the yard. "No worries. I had a lot of money riding on them. I'll round them up soon enough."

Not if Greg had anything to do with it.

"So, Mr. Special Op," Jamansky said, "why don't you figure out where Carrie is? If you are who you say you are, you have access to more information than I do."

Good point.

Thinking quickly, Greg said, "I'm stuck here until I've completed this assignment. I can't be seen, but I *can* give you a direct order. You will find out where Carrie and her siblings are, and you will report back to me tomorrow."

"Her siblings?"

"They were taken at the same time. Amber, 16. Zach, 13. Find out where they are."

Jamansky studied him across the twenty feet that separated them. "What's in it for me?"

Greg's jaw clenched. "Not dying."

The patrol chief's gaze swept the area again, stopping on Greg's home across the street—which, if Greg had actual shooters, would have been where he'd stashed them. For all Jamansky knew, Greg had a whole squad of federal patrolmen on this assignment with him.

"What if I can't find out by tomorrow?" Jamansky said evenly. "It could take days to track them all down."

"Carrie doesn't have days!"

"Why?"

A knot twisted in Greg's gut. "You think they give prisoners medicine?"

That caught Jamansky's attention. His brows shot up. Jamansky had visited Carrie at her house. He'd seen what condition she'd been in. Greg felt himself plummeting again. He clung to the rage to keep his head above water.

"Find them and report back to me tomorrow," Greg said. "Same time. Same place."

He was taking a huge gamble. Commander McCormick could have already been alerted and federal patrolmen could be swarming the neighborhood within the hour, looking for Greg. But he narrowed his eyes.

"If you find out sooner," Greg said, "come anyway. I'll have one of my guys watching for you. Oh, and for your own sake, come alone tomorrow. That's an order."

twenty-five

Jamansky was still steaming. Sitting in his office, he had run circles around the whole thing. Carrie, arrested. Greg Pierce, the Special Op. Logan Pond Clan, gone.

It hadn't taken long to find Carrie. With a few strokes of the computer, he'd tracked her information down and which prison Giordano had taken her to. A few more strokes, and he'd pieced together what had happened to land her there in the first place.

His initial response had been to fire his entire staff—regardless of the fact that they'd just followed protocol. But they'd sent his entire plans up in flames. Carrie gone. The clan gone—supposedly. And yet…he was a smart guy. He could adapt. With effort, he even schemed up a way to work this whole debacle in his favor.

Once he had that settled, he stared at his phone, debating. Finally he picked it up and dialed the number listed on the bottom of his verifying machine.

A woman answered. "Yes?"

"This is Chief David Jamansky from the Kane County Unit."

"Yes. How can I help you?"

He scowled at the picture on his small screen before plunging in. "I have a question about one of your federal patrolmen. He's supposedly a special operative in your unit. Gregory Curtis Pierce."

A slight pause before she said, "What about him?"

"My verifying machine says he's dead."

"That's correct. Killed the end of June."

"That's what this says, too. Only…he approached me today. At least, I think it was him." Jamansky held the picture close. Just the sight of Pierce's smug face made him want to hurl the device across the room. "Yes, it was definitely him."

A longer pause. Long enough Jamansky thought he'd lost the connection. But then the woman said, "Where exactly did you run into him?"

"Near his home in Shelton. He said he's on some special mission and gave me his authorization numbers. When I saw that he was listed dead, I decided to call in and verify."

"I see," she said evenly. "And he gave you this phone number to call?"

"No. It's listed below his information. He just gave me his authorizing numbers and said he was *dead* as part of his secret assignment."

"Why?"

"I don't know why," Jamansky snapped, tired of her pointless questions. But his instincts had served him well. Something was off about Pierce's story. He could hear it in her voice. "He gave me a direct order to help him. He wants me to assist him with a…" He caught himself, deciding he didn't want the feds sniffing around this whole Carrie-arrest mess. "…a local matter. Am I under obligation to assist him?"

"Of course."

Jamansky glared at the phone. "But he's dead."

"Obviously not," the woman said curtly. "When you see him again, tell him that he is to contact me at once. If he doesn't have access to a phone, provide one for him. Tell him to call this number. And under no circumstances are you to speak about this—or about him—to anyone else. Am I understood?"

Jamansky felt like a school boy who had been chastised. "Yes, ma'am."

"Lieutenant," she corrected.

"Yes, Lieutenant," he said. "May I have your name so he knows who to contact?"

"He'll know who this is," the woman said, then she clicked off.

For a long time, Jamansky clutched the phone and glared at Pierce's cocky face. The only thing that made the call worth it was that it sounded like Gregory Pierce might be in trouble with his superiors.

———— ✦ ————

Carrie woke up disoriented, with a pounding headache. Something large hovered a few feet over her, but it wasn't until she breathed in through her nose and caught a whiff of the all-encompassing stench that she remembered where she was. Locked up. For some reason she was lying on the bottom bunk. As a newbie, she wasn't supposed to get that privilege. She had no idea how long she had been asleep. She didn't even remember falling asleep. And then suddenly she did.

It hit her all over again.

Zach and Amber.

Alone.

Curling into a tiny ball, she begged herself to return to a state of unconsciousness, but a loud grunt sounded behind her. Twisting around, she saw a guard outside of the cell.

"Eat!" he ordered. He pointed to a plate of mush at the foot of the metal bunk bed. In actuality it was a plate of noodles—maybe spaghetti—but it might as well have been mush for all she wanted it.

Tears pooled in her swollen eyes. She shook her head, trying to warn him that eating wasn't a good idea. Not with the state of her stomach.

"Your supervisor said you passed out because you haven't eaten all day, so eat now. Next time we won't be so forgiving."

That wasn't why she'd passed out, but she doubted he cared. He watched her, waiting.

Grabbing the plate, she began eating the spaghetti with her hands. With each bite of mushy noodles, her stomach felt worse instead of better. It rolled and sent acid climbing her throat. She could barely swallow it down. Thankfully, the guard only stayed to witness the first few bites. As soon as he left, she shoved the plate aside and curled back up on the bed.

It was hot in the cell and oppressively stuffy. Still, she pulled the blanket over her and pressed her good ear to the pillow. Then she covered her bad ear to block out the thirty percent it could hear. She craved the kind of sleep that would take her away forever. She never wanted to think or feel or remember again. She wanted—she needed—to block it all out.

When she woke again, the disorientation hit her afresh. For the space of five seconds, she felt blissfully happy. A lingering dream left her feeling the deep kind of contentment that made her smile for no reason. She had been laughing with her dad and Greg—which was impossible because they'd never even met. As soon as she realized that, the dream vanished and reality slapped her all over again.

A metal bunk bed still hung over her, and the lights were on in the cell—although that didn't tell her much. It felt like a lot of time had passed. Lifting her head, she saw her cellmates sleeping in their various spots around the cell.

Then she felt something heavy on her feet.

Black hair spilled out at the bottom of the mattress. Donnelle. Carrie's foot tingled with pain, having fallen asleep under Donnelle's weight. Carefully, she extracted it. Donnelle rolled over and cracked a sleepy eye open. When she saw Carrie awake, she bolted up and hit her head on the upper metal bunk.

"Ow," Donnelle groaned, rubbing her head. "Ow."

"Sorry," Carrie said. "I'm so sorry. Are you okay?"

"Yes, but are you?" Donnelle kept rubbing. "Are you sick? Do you black out often? Please tell me it's not your head. I mean, you haven't been here long enough to catch anything from the rest of us, but I've been so worried that—"

"I'm fine," Carrie said, breaking in. Technically her head throbbed, but she was fine. At least physically. "I'm sorry I passed out."

"It's my fault." Donnelle teared up. "I didn't put two and two together until they dragged your body out. So I guess your brother and sister were taken? I had no idea. All that stuff I said, Carrie, you have to know that it's just hearsay. Your brother and sister could be fine. You said they were teenagers, right? Teenagers know how to fend for themselves. They'll know how to…to…" Her head dropped and she covered her face.

"It's okay," Carrie said. "Please don't feel bad."

Donnelle's cries picked up to loud sobs.

"Hey, keep it down!" a lady yelled from some cell unseen.

Donnelle buried her face in the scratchy blanket which muffled the sound.

Carrie rubbed her arm, hoping to ease her worries, but heat emanated from Donnelle's skin, distracting her. It wasn't the hot and sweaty kind of heat. Donnelle felt feverish.

"How is your head?" Carrie asked softly.

"Awful," Donnelle wailed.

Carrie tried to assess Donnelle's coloring, but too much of her was buried in the blanket.

A guard circled past their cell, sparing them a warning glare.

Donnelle wiped her eyes and looked up. "Tell me your parents weren't arrested, too."

Carrie shook her head slowly. "They weren't."

"Well that's good news then." Donnelle sniffed back a smile. "I'm sure they'll have you out of here in no time. Your brother and sister, too. Just give your mom and dad time to get things in order. You'll see. They'll get you out of this godforsaken place."

Even though Carrie blinked twenty times, even though she begged herself to hold it together, her eyes still filled. She couldn't handle anymore crying, and neither could Donnelle.

"Oh, no," Donnelle moaned. "Not your parents, too. I just can't say anything right. Maybe I should shut up."

"Maybe you should!" Crazy Marge said from the upper bunk. "Some of us are trying to sleep here."

"Yeah. Shut your trap!" someone else yelled.

Silence descended over the prison until the guard reappeared. He wrapped his nightstick against the metal bars, loud and intrusive in the quiet prison.

The wakeup call.

With groans, her cellmates started to move. Some sat up. A few rubbed their eyes. One headed for the open toilet in the corner. As Carrie averted her eyes, she noticed Donnelle rubbing the back of her head again.

Carrie moved over to feel her forehead.

"You're burning up," Carrie said. "I can try to talk to the guard. See if he'll let you rest today."

"No. No, I'm fine. They won't let me rest anyway." Donnelle rolled off the mattress and landed on her knees. She just knelt there, looking too tired to stand.

Carrie felt the same. Her body had grown heavy overnight and her energy felt zapped in a way that worried her. And her head. That spot behind her ear started stabbing again. Maybe it was just a sympathy headache. She'd had three days of medicine, but what if that wasn't enough?

"Carrie Lynne Ashworth?" a guard called.

She turned too quickly, an old, careless gesture that made the small, cement cell spin. Regaining her balance, she saw a different guard, the one from last night, had returned. Only this time he held a large rifle.

"Yes?" she answered weakly.

"Come with me," he said.

All of the women in the cell turned to stare at her.

Carrie felt the blood drain from her face. She looked at Donnelle. "Where is he taking me?"

"I...I don't know," Donnelle said. "None of us have ever left by ourselves. Maybe they're takin' you to a doctor? You hit your head real hard last night."

"I did?" Carrie felt around and found a large, tender goose egg near the base of her skull. Maybe that was the source of her headache. Maybe she wasn't getting sick again.

The officer rammed his rifle against the metal bars. "Come now!"

Carrie flinched and shuffled across the small cell to him.

"Hands in front of you," he said.

She obeyed.

He clicked handcuffs around her still-raw wrists. They burned. She hadn't seen another soul handcuffed since she'd entered. Of course, she hadn't seen any guards carrying guns either.

With a loud scraping of metal, he opened the cell door and motioned for her to follow. Petrified, she stared at his rifle. As bad as prison was, at least she was alive. If she was truly being taken to a doctor, then why had they waited so long? And why her, when Donnelle needed it more? If it wasn't a doctor, then what?

Interrogation?

Torture?

How many illegals were depending on her ability to withstand an interrogation? Not just her own clan, but Delaney's now, too.

The fear of the unknown was almost worse than the fear of death because it held so much terrifying potential.

With one last nervous glance back at Donnelle, she left her small cell. He led her down the brightly lit causeway, passing dozens of gray cells identical to her own before heading down the set of metal stairs. Women hung by their bars, watching her pass. Some even shouted out catcalls which the guard ignored.

In the third from the last cell, Carrie found the origins of the wailing she'd been hearing since she arrived. A tiny ball of a woman huddled in a far corner, rocking back and forth. Maybe that woman had been interrogated. Maybe she was crying for all the names she had betrayed.

Carrie's insides started to shake.

Greg. May and CJ. Sasha, Jada, Terrell, and Little Jeffrey. She desperately needed to wipe their names from her mind.

As they left the cells behind, they passed through a series of doors and hallways. Carrie gritted her teeth. She wouldn't betray her clansmen. Even if it was the last thing she did, she would protect their names.

The patrolman used his card each time to grant them access until he led her down a narrow hallway. The hallway was cold, air conditioned, sending goose bumps up and down her arms.

He stopped outside of a solid white door. "If you give me any trouble," he said, "you'll spend the remainder of your sentence scrubbing the toilets of every single cell. Do you understand?"

Even more terrified, she nodded.

He opened the door and ushered her inside a small, white room. Someone stood as she entered. A man. It wasn't a doctor, though, or an interrogator. It was a patrolman in a green uniform and beige tie.

Carrie's heart stopped.

David Jamansky.

twenty-six

Carrie's knees buckled. She dropped to the floor, slamming her handcuffed hands against the hard cement.

"You've got ten minutes," the guard said.

"I understand," Jamansky said.

Carrie pressed her forehead to the cold cement to keep the small white room from whirling like a tornado. David Jamansky was there. Why? To rub it in? To see how much he'd broken her?

She should have screamed at him, begged for an explanation, or at least clawed his face. Yet all she could do was kneel, forehead to the floor, to keep from passing out again.

His arm went around her waist to help her up, but before she could scream, *Don't touch me!* the guard's voice boomed behind her.

"I said no contact!"

"Right." Jamansky's hands lifted away. He pulled out the nearest chair for Carrie and then grabbed the other for himself.

Carrie struggled to sit. Her legs shook. The rest of her felt detached and unsteady. Jamansky sat directly in front of her, elbows on his knees, hands clasped as he studied her. His blond hair was perfectly combed, his uniform perfectly ironed. She could barely stand to look at him, the man who had destroyed everything.

"Are you okay?" he asked.

The question was so absurd, so disturbing, it took her a moment to find her voice.

"You took them." A sudden sob tore through her. "You did this. You took my brother and sister."

"Whoa. Hold on, Carrie. You can't think that *I* did this to you. I'm your friend, remember?"

Her eyes burned. "You took them," she whispered.

"Come on. You've got to believe me. I had no idea what happened to you until I went to your house. They told me you'd been arrested. That's the first I'd heard of it. I wasn't even near Shelton when you were taken. I was in some stupid meeting in Geneva."

How can you deny it? she wanted to shout. *You're the Chief of Patrols!* But she was stuck on the first half of what he said.

They.

"You went to my house?" she said. "You...talked to someone?"

His face tightened, but he just rubbed a spot on his uniform. "Yeah. That guy I met earlier, the older man, O'Brien. He told me you had been arrested. That was the first I heard about it."

Richard knew she'd been arrested. Which meant...

...Greg knew.

Hot tears slipped down her cheeks. In vain she tried to wipe them with her bound hands. She couldn't allow herself to think about Greg's reaction or how angry he would be that she'd gone without Richard. Nor could she bear to think of what he might risk to get her out.

Jamansky leaned forward. "Why did they arrest you? Didn't you have your papers with you?"

"I had my papers. I had everything! But your clerk said they had been revoked. Then patrolmen came." Her throat constricted. "They came and...they didn't even let me say goodbye. They just..." Her words were cut off in another strangled cry of grief as she pictured Zach and Amber's faces, white, frozen, and terrified.

"I will get to the bottom of this. You have my word. But first..." He bent down to examine her. "You look pale. Are you still sick? Did you tell them that you recently had G-979? They need to get you medicine, today if possible."

Medicine? Had he not looked around or noticed her filthy jumpsuit? Sick people meant fewer mouths to feed, more beds for the healthy. Sick people disappeared in here.

His voice rose, only aimed over her head. "Don't you medicate your prisoners?" he yelled at the guard. "Can't you see that she's ill?"

"Six minutes," the guard said back.

Seething, Jamansky scrutinized Carrie with his ice-blue eyes. She had enough presence of mind to be humiliated. Her heavy orange tent-like uniform. Her swollen wrists, torn and raw. Her hair hanging in her face. The way he looked at her reminded her of the patrolman who had arrested her, stolen her money, and then sat back while the other guards searched her. He worked for Chief David Jamansky.

"Your guy," she said, willing some strength into her voice. "The one who arrested me. He..." She felt sick all over again. "He stole my money."

Jamansky looked confused.

"I had four hundred dollars when he arrested me. He stole it all before he brought me inside here. I want it back."

An insane request, but she wanted to do her own scrutinizing. Jamansky claimed he had nothing to do with her arrest. Let him prove it.

"Who was it?" he said, keeping his face even. "I will make sure he is punished."

She pictured the large man close to her. Her breathing sped up. "I...I can't remember his name. A big man."

"Giordano. Not surprising. He can be quite the brute. Did he..." He paused. "Did he hurt you?"

Another wall of tears hit her. She blinked them back, hating herself for being so weak, feeling like her eyes were constantly swelling shut. She had cried more in the last day than she had in the last six years, but she couldn't control the tears any more than she could control her surroundings.

She was a slave to them both.

Jamansky's fists clenched. "He will be punished severely, and I'll make sure you get your money back. You seem to keep forgetting that I'm your friend, Carrie. I'm on your side."

Friend.

Holding onto the anger, she decided to call his bluff.

"If you're my *friend,* then tell me where Oliver is. Where is he really?"

His brows lowered, mouth twitching a moment before any words came out. "I already told you. He's in Virginia for training."

"Then will you give him a message?" she asked.

His eyes narrowed. "Why?"

Because if there was any chance, any way at all that Oliver was actually in some harmless government training, she had to let him know what had happened. He could help. No, he *would* help them find a way out. But he couldn't help what he didn't know.

"I need to talk to him," she said.

Jamansky sat back, regarding her. "I'm not sure how to put this, Carrie, but Oliver is not…exactly…"

Her stomach clenched. "What?"

"Oliver has requested a transfer. He no longer works in my unit." He let that sink in a second before adding, "He won't be coming back from Virginia. Ever again."

She blinked slowly, trying to dissect each word. "Why?"

"Rumor around the precinct is that some girl broke his heart. I'm assuming…" He waved a hand in her direction.

Anger flashed. "You're lying."

"I wish I was. Look, I don't know what happened between you and Oliver, or how much you hurt him. When I talked to him about Virginia, he sounded relieved about the opportunity. I assumed he would only be gone a few months, so that's what I told you. But now he's vowed to never return. I'm sorry to be the one to have to break the news. I'm sorry he wasn't man enough to tell you himself."

Lies. Lies. Lies! she wanted to scream.

The last she'd seen Oliver Simmons had been in her yard when he dropped her and Greg off. Oliver said he would come back to check on her, but then he had disappeared and Jamansky had appeared, and everything had erupted into chaos.

"I know it's none of my business," Jamansky said, leaning forward, "but the guys at the station said he left because his girlfriend had been unfaithful. Is it true? Did you…cheat on him?"

The word felt like a slap.

Stung, she looked up.

Jamansky nodded as if that was answer enough. "Not that I blame you. Who's the other guy? Anyone I know?"

She glared at him, breaths quickening.

"Ah, so I *do* know him," he said, interpreting her response how he wanted. "I hope it's not that Pierce guy, the one who lives in your neighborhood. Because that guy is a snake. You should see how he hits on my clerk in town. Total womanizer. Tell me a nice girl like you didn't fall for his bait."

Her fists clenched in her handcuffs. She was done with David Jamansky. She was done with the lies. But he kept talking.

"Wow, Carrie. I thought you were smarter than that." He shook his head in disgust. "Although…that might explain something." His eyes widened suddenly. He shot to his feet and started pacing the small white room in front of her. "Oh, man. I can't believe he's this vindictive!"

"Who?" she said coldly.

He stopped in front of her. "Oliver Simmons. Look at what he's done to you—look what he did to your family, Carrie! All because you fell for some other guy? How could he do this?"

Carrie jerked back. "Oliver didn't do this."

"How else do you explain everything? I knew you were legal. Everyone in my precinct did. I specifically gave them orders not to touch you or your house, and yet here you are. Oliver must have called Ellen and Giordano himself and bribed them somehow, just to get his revenge for cheating on him."

"Oliver Simmons wouldn't hurt a fly!" she yelled. "He wouldn't do this to me, Amber, *or* Zach! Never in a million years!"

"How can you defend him? I bet he's behind your new lover's arrest, too."

She froze. "What?"

"That O'Brien guy—Richard, right?—isn't he Pierce's stepdad?"

She couldn't even nod. The cold room dropped a few more degrees. *New lover's arrest. New lover's arrest.* The words sent ice through her.

Jamansky grabbed his chair and sat again, leaning forward. "When I went to your house today, Richard O'Brien told me that you and your siblings weren't the only ones who had been arrested. Apparently a swarm of federal patrolmen surrounded Pierce's house this morning. They took him for no reason. Just slapped him in handcuffs and dragged him away. He's a special op, right? But they took him, so I couldn't understand. But now I do. Oliver did it."

The blood hammered through her veins.

Two thoughts cut through everything. First, how did Jamansky know that Greg had been made a special operative? And more importantly, how did Jamansky even know that Greg was alive? Only two days ago,

Jamansky had been shoving Greg's death in Richard's face like some victory.

And now...

Her breathing sped up. Why would Jamansky invent a story like that, that Greg was not only alive but arrested? If the government knew Greg wasn't dead as reported, they would definitely send federal patrolmen after him. Her stomach rolled, threatening to heave up the mushy spaghetti. No. It couldn't be true. Not Greg.

Not Greg!

She begged for another explanation for how Jamansky knew about Greg, a reason that didn't end with Greg's arrest.

The cold room spun violently.

"Look, Carrie. Don't think about Oliver anymore," Jamansky said. "The guy is a total traitor. He deserves to hang for what he did to you and your family. And I'll make sure Giordano and Ellen pay for their hand in this. But I'm here now, and I'm going to help you get out of here, okay?"

She looked down at her orange uniform, at the dirt and the cuts on her wrists, imagining ten times worse for Greg. He'd been beaten so many times during military training, and that was before he had run.

What would they do to him?

For a second time, Jamansky's words were sluggish to register in her thoughts.

Her watery gaze rose. "What did you say?"

He smiled. "I can get you out of here. Just give me a few days to get things in order."

"But..." Words failed her. Jamansky would free her.

He reached out and rubbed her leg. "You'll see. Everything will be as it should be, okay?"

"Times up!" the guard barked.

Jamansky glared up at him. "That wasn't ten minutes."

The guard grabbed Carrie's arm and yanked her up to standing. He pushed her out of the room.

"I'll be back in a couple of days," Jamansky called after her. "Just give me a few days and everything will be as it should be."

twenty–seven

Greg lowered Carrie's weather journal. He'd reread every entry four times. Tracking her life, even if only through the weather, somehow brought her closer. But he stopped to listen. Then he leapt up to the window.

A dark green patrol car pulled up the main road.

He dropped the journal and ran.

"He's here!" he called, flying down the stairs. Greg sprinted out the front door, across Richard's driveway, and into the middle of the street.

Just in time.

Jamansky slammed on his brakes, bringing his car to a screeching halt. Greg didn't even flinch as the car stopped two feet from him. The patrol chief let out a furious stream of profanities that carried through the thick windshield.

"That's far enough," Greg said back.

The patrol chief threw open his door. "Are you insane?"

Greg might have answered, but he heard something that caused his muscles to seize. He leaned sideways to see around Jamansky. Two huge dogs barked wildly in the backseat, teeth snapping.

"I told you to come alone," Greg said.

Jamansky's chest heaved in and out. "Oh, don't worry. My friends can't betray any of your…secrets."

Greg eyed the German Shepherds. Patrol dogs—*trained* patrol dogs.

"Dogs can be shot as easily as you can," he said.

Understanding, Jamansky scanned the houses on each side of them. The nose of a rifle poked out of an upstairs window. Richard kept his face hidden as planned, but Greg wanted the gun to make its show early on. Terrell hid across the street in another house, hopefully not asleep. His window remained empty. Stupid Terrell. Thankfully, the one gun had the desired effect.

Jamansky's hands lifted. "Hey, I just brought my dogs along for the company. I actually think they're going to like you, Pierce. Here. Let's find out."

Before Greg knew what he was doing, Jamansky opened the back door and released his two dogs. They ran straight for Greg, barking and snarling.

Greg fell back a step.

He waited for Richard to start shooting, but Richard didn't. Of course Richard didn't. Greg cursed his stepdad and his supposed morals. Sometime overnight, the 9mm pistol had disappeared from under his pillow. Richard claimed innocence, but the guy couldn't lie to save his life. What Greg would have given to have it tucked inside his shirt now.

Jamansky let his dogs snarl at Greg's feet before he called out, "Bretton, Felix, *sitz!*"

The dogs dropped to their haunches in front of Greg. Breathing heavily, Greg took another step back just to be safe. Their teeth might have been put back in their proper places, but he preferred to have a few feet—or a football field—between him and those fangs.

"I found her," Jamansky said.

In Greg's distracted state, it took a second to understand. Then his head lifted.

Carrie.

"Where?" Greg said a little too anxiously.

"Ah, yes. That would be something you'd like to know. But first..." Jamansky's eyes flickered back to the rifle hanging out the upper window of Richard's home. "We have some bargaining to do."

Greg folded his arms. "I thought I made it perfectly clear that your payment is spending the remainder of your days alive and *outside* of iron bars."

"Yes, but then I spoke to someone. A woman—sorry, a Lieutenant. We had a nice chat yesterday, and you want to know something? The whole conversation struck me as odd. She'd like you to call her, by the

way. Told me to provide a phone for you. What do you think?"
Jamansky moved as if to reach inside of his car. "Should I get my
phone?"

Greg didn't move.

Isabel Ryan.

Jamansky had called Isabel.

If that was the case, why hadn't anybody shown up to haul him away?
Richard had nearly flown through the roof when Greg admitted to what
had happened yesterday with Jamansky. Ever since, Greg had been
hesitant to return to Logan Pond, figuring his old unit would be camped
out, searching for him. But this morning, the neighborhood had been as
dead as ever. Like the fool he was, he thought McCormick hadn't been
alerted. Nobody knew a thing.

Obviously not.

He gritted his teeth, debating whether or not to call his former partner.
He'd spent last night working through a cover story that might save him
from a court-martial. But...McCormick would demand that he come in
and report immediately. Then what? Even if they bought his story, they'd
expect him to return to active duty.

He needed time to find Carrie.

"Something tells me you don't want to call in," Jamansky said. "In
fact, it occurred to me that you should have just asked for my phone and
called in yourself yesterday. Your buddies in the Special Patrols Unit
would have more information on Carrie than I do. Yet you're choosing to
deal with me. Why?" He paused, waiting for an answer Greg refused to
give. "It makes me wonder if your commanding officers aren't...fully
aware of your mission right now—at least not entirely. Am I right?"

Greg's nostrils flared. "Where is Carrie?"

"Make the call first," Jamansky countered.

Greg took a slow, deep, composing breath. Then he lifted two fingers
high in the air.

The signal.

A single shot rang out. Asphalt and gravel puffed up a few feet from
Jamansky's feet.

Jamansky jumped back with a shout, hands flying into the air.

Unfortunately, Jamansky wasn't the only one startled. The dogs leapt
up, barking and snapping at Greg again. The one on the left looked
particularly hungry. Greg cursed them and Richard who should have shot

them long ago. Commander McCormick's unit had used signals on the training grounds to alert one another. Greg had given Richard and Terrell three for today. One finger: show the guns. Two fingers: give a warning shot. Three fingers: shoot Jamansky. He shouldn't have had to give a fourth: shoot anything else that threatened Greg's life. That should have been a given.

Richard!

When Greg figured out that the beasts wouldn't attack him without an actual command, he shifted his focus back to Jamansky.

"You've got exactly five seconds to tell me where Carrie is," Greg said. "Five...four..."

"Rockford!" Jamansky growled, hands still high. "Carrie's in the women's camp in Rockford."

Rockford.

Ashlee had mentioned that one as a possibility. If Greg remembered right, the city was twenty-five miles northwest. Far, but he could make it by morning. Richard had agreed to go with him to be spokesman. If they could just see Carrie, see where she was being held, Greg could figure out what to do from there. He might even be able to find a way to bribe the guards and sneak in some medicine.

Keeping his voice even, he said, "And her siblings?"

"Still working on it," Jamansky said. "As you know, the government doesn't always keep great records."

Greg didn't know, but he nodded. "Fine. I'm out on assignment for the next day or two. Leave any information you find there, posted on that doorway of that house." He pointed to Richard's home. "I'll expect to see something when I return. For now, you're dismissed. And you better call off the dogs before I have them shot."

Jamansky looked ready to strangle something, but he whistled loudly. His dogs turned and trotted back to him. He let them into the back seat and shut the door.

Before he got in, he said, "I can get her, you know. Carrie. I can have her released. Can you?"

Greg blinked. *What?*

Jamansky smiled darkly. "I didn't think so." Slamming his door shut, he walked back. "Tell you what, Pierce. You want Carrie released, and I need a favor. So let's strike a bargain."

Greg stiffened, sensing a trap.

"I need you to testify against Oliver Simmons," Jamansky said. "He stands trial in two weeks for several offenses including aiding and harboring fugitives, embezzling government funds, and working the black market—plus whatever else I can dig up on him before then. I need you to rip him to shreds and show what a lying, conniving traitor he is. That's my price. You agree, and I'll get Carrie out."

Greg couldn't mask the shock that shot through him. Not just the demand, but the payment.

Carrie.

He saw a flicker of movement out of the corner of his eye. Richard stood in plain view in that upper window, waving his arms vigorously. The conversation had carried easily in the empty neighborhood.

Testifying against Oliver.

"I trust you can finish whatever *mission* you're on by then so you can reappear in public," Jamansky went on. "Because to pull this off, you'll need to be all dressed up in a shiny uniform, special operative status and all."

"What about her siblings?" Greg said evenly. "You'd have to release them as well."

A pause before Jamansky said, "Done."

"And her house?"

Jamansky's eyes narrowed. "What about it?"

"I'd expect a full restoration of her ownership," Greg said, "and along with it, her citizenship."

"Wow, aren't you the greedy one. That will be more difficult. The feds are claiming that Simmons bought her house with illegal funds."

Greg nodded slowly, digesting that. If Jamansky said Oliver had been embezzling money, then anything Oliver had purchased with that money—including homes—would have been confiscated. Without a place to live, Carrie should have moved to a blue card municipality and begged for mercy and refuge, but she hadn't.

Citizenship revoked.

"Well," Greg sneered, "you've got plenty of experience bendin' the law. I'm sure you'll figure somethin' out."

Jamansky chuckled. "You've found yourself in quite the predicament, Pierce. Totally and completely dependent on someone you totally and completely despise. So do we have a deal or not?"

Out of his peripheral vision, Greg saw Richard giving the clear *Don't even think about it!* signal.

Greg took a few slow, measured breaths, counting the cost. Oliver in exchange for Carrie and her siblings. Oliver didn't deserve to be sacrificed like that, not after all he'd done. Then again, Greg knew Oliver well enough to know what Oliver would want him to do if situations were reversed. If Greg was in prison and Oliver stood there instead, bargaining for Carrie's life, Greg knew what Oliver would want him to say.

Then again, what would Carrie want?

The slime ball of a patrol chief smiled. He already knew he'd won.

Insides twisting with something dark, Greg nodded. "Fine. How soon will I have Carrie back?"

"You mean, how soon will Carrie be out of prison? You're assuming Carrie even wants to come back here."

Greg's fists clenched. "This deal is only valid if you return her to me."

"Oh, I'll ask her if she wants to come back, but it's my duty to lay out all of her choices for her. Make sure she knows that she has more"— Jamansky's smile grew—"favorable options."

"If that's the case," Greg said, voice rising, "then I'll only testify against Officer Simmons *after* she and her siblings are safely returned to me. That includes the deed to her home and her citizenship restored."

Game was up and Jamansky knew it.

He glared at Greg. "You do your part, Pierce. I'll do mine. I'll have her out by the trial. Now here's what you need to do."

twenty-eight

Oliver paced his small cell. It had only been a few days, obviously not enough time for his letter to arrive, but he couldn't help wonder what the fallout would be, if any.

Would the feds believe him?

Would it even make a difference?

For all he knew, Reef had botched up the whole letter and no one would get anything.

Worse than being locked up, worse than the lack of food, hygiene, soft mattresses, clean clothes, showers, medicine, entertainment, air conditioning, private toilets, or any of the other things prison deprived him of, was the not knowing. That was what killed him. He knew nothing happening in the outside world. His letter. His friends. His precinct. Even the revolution. Not knowing. That was the real punishment of prison.

It was enough to drive him mad.

"Tell me again how you worded that letter," Oliver said.

Reef clasped both hands behind his head, sprawled out on the bed, one leg kicking lazily over the side. "Just like you said."

Oliver told himself to calm down. It would work.

It had to.

He paced another moment. Normally this new government turned a blind eye to corruption among their own. President Rigsby's entire cabinet reeked of corruption to the highest levels. Normally they wouldn't care one bit if their local leaders were fattening their own pockets with under-the-table deals. But when those local leaders started stealing from them, cutting into *their* profits?

Oliver hoped it was enough.

It had to be.

His ulcers flared. He rubbed his stomach, missing his antacids. Maybe he could give his plan a little nudge.

"Any chance you would be willing to send another letter?" he asked.

"You know," Reef said with a pointed look, "you're rather gutsy for a scrawny guy. I'm only allowed two letters a week. What makes you think you get both of them?"

"This one is equally important, life or death."

"Correct me if I'm wrong here," Reef said, "but you don't exactly have much left to offer."

Oliver couldn't argue with that. The first letter cost him every other meal. He couldn't offer to do Reef's work detail because they didn't even work in the same areas. Plus the guards didn't let inmates help other inmates.

Figuring he could survive on one meal a day, Oliver said, "What do you want?"

"Hmmm. What do I want? I'll figure out the price later. First, who is this next letter for? It better be some hot babe, because I'm not wasting another letter on another lame government agency."

"No," Oliver said. "This letter is for a friend." If he could even call her that after what he'd done.

"Boring." Reef closed his eyes as if to go back to sleep.

"She's female."

The second Oliver said it, he regretted it. Prison created lonely men desperate for any kind of entertainment, even if it came in the form of stories. Female encounters and past escapades seemed to be a favorite topic, especially with Reef. The tales Oliver had heard made him want to scrub his ears out with bleach. Most of the stories were revolting, disgusting, and greatly exaggerated.

Reef lifted his head. "Is she hot?"

With a sigh, Oliver nodded. Ashlee Lyon was pretty. Very pretty. Even she knew it.

It was a one in a million chance he wasn't too late, one in a million chance she would even get a letter from him. But he had to try. No one else he knew received mail—at least, no one that he could trust. Plus, he had been the one who dragged Ashlee into his nightmare. She had just been an innocent bystander, someone trying to help out a friend—or rather, a coworker. Now he had to help her, warn her somehow. Assuming it wasn't too late.

Reef rubbed his hands together. "A nice, hot babe. Alright. Let's talk price."

———— ◆ ————

Ashlee Lyon pulled the borrowed t-shirt up over her nose. Stinky goat smell still seeped through.

"I've been to Bristol's Home for Girls," she said through the shirt's fabric, "so I can definitely get us to that one. But I've never been to the one in Campton Hills. Sorry, Braden."

"No, it's okay," Braden said. "This is good. Are you sure you want to go with us to find Amber and Zach—I mean, when Richard is ready?"

Ashlee wasn't, but she nodded anyway. She knew how to get to two of the four places. She had to help.

The goat suddenly jumped and tried to back-kick Braden. He grabbed her hind leg and gently set it on the ground.

"I know it's different here in Ferris," he said, stroking the goat's caramel-colored back. "But you'll get used to it. Just give it time."

Ashlee wondered if he was talking to her or the goat.

The whole clan had squished into three homes in this Ferris place. She'd been put in with May and CJ Trenton's group, which she liked. The older couple had been very nice to her. The goats and chickens roamed the yard behind. They seemed happy enough, but what did she know?

Once Butterscotch settled down, Braden started milking her. In perfect rhythm, milk squirted into the empty bucket. Ashlee watched in amazement, wondering how Oliver had ever befriended these people.

She'd always pictured illegals to be hairy, homeless vagrants who wandered the backwoods with filthy faces and no shoes while their kids ran wild and unsupervised. True, these clansmen had beards and longer hair than most men she associated with, but they were also highly-educated, hardworking, relatively-clean people. They were former lawyers, college professors, and financial analysts who refused to yield to President Rigsby's overbearing, overreaching emergency laws. They'd lost their homes in the Collapse. They'd stayed anyway, squatting illegally on government property ever since.

Because they had fought to survive together, these neighbors had a bond she'd never seen before—or experienced herself. Sure, her parents loved her like parents did, but she lived her life, and they lived hers. For all she knew, they didn't even know she was missing yet. Would they stage a state-wide search for her like these people were for the Ashworths? The clansmen weren't even related to Carrie or her siblings, yet they'd turned their lives upside down to find them.

The whole thing left her in awe.

The only part that irked her was that she hadn't heard much about helping Oliver. Maybe because he wasn't officially part of their clan. But Oliver had been hiding their clan for years, protecting them in a way they couldn't protect themselves.

Didn't his freedom matter to anyone?

Oliver had always seemed like a quiet, awkward guy. But the more she learned about him and what he'd been doing, the more she admired his courage and selflessness. Didn't those qualities count for anything? Why didn't they care that he was rotting away in JSP because of what he'd done for them?

If only she'd been able to get into her computer. She and Oliver had started a file on the main network, throwing everything in there that might expose David Jamansky and Mayor Phillips for the lying, corrupt scoundrels they were. If she could just figure out how to access that file and send it along to the feds...

"What's the building like in Bristol?" Braden asked.

Ashlee might not know anything about goats, chopping wood, or washing clothes by hand, but she liked being the clan's new informer. In her own unique way, she was helping these people, too.

"I only visited Bristol's Home for Girls once, a long time ago," she said. "My cousin was staying there when it was still a regular girls' school." Ashlee's mom had tried to get her to transfer, but Ashlee had made the cheerleading team at Shelton High, propelling her to the top of the social food chain—a spot she refused to give up. "From what I remember, it's three stories tall with large gardens around it."

"Was it fenced?" Braden asked.

"I don't remember, but I'm sure it is now." Ashlee pulled her blonde hair off her hot, sweaty neck. "This place might not be a prison technically, Braden, but it might as well be. The government knows they've stolen people's kids. Richard might be able to get in to see Amber—if we're lucky. But it's going to be almost impossible to get her out. I'm sorry."

"As long as it's *almost* and not completely, I can live with that." Braden sat back and wiped his damp brow. "I just wish Richard was available. I know he has to help Greg. I know Carrie's sick, so that takes priority. It's just hard waiting."

Ashlee smiled sadly. She liked Braden.

"I wish I had my green card with me," she said. "A green card is one level higher than Richard's yellow one. Being a government employee might even be enough to get me in to see Amber."

Braden turned. "Is your card still valid?"

She put a hand on her hip, temper flaring. "David might have locked me out of my computer, but he better not have revoked my citizenship."

He shot to his feet, nearly toppling the bucket of milk. "Then let's get it. Where is it?"

"In my purse. I looked for it when Greg and I broke into the office, but it was gone. David probably took it—jerk. But come to think of it, I have a spare card at my house." Her eyes suddenly widened. "And my house is on the way to Bristol."

"Yes! How far is your house from here?"

These people kept wanting her to give them distances in miles. She only knew times. "Ten minutes of driving."

While she was home, maybe she could grab a few of her things, like decent clothes and makeup. Maybe some chocolate.

"And Bristol is past that?" he said. "You don't have a car, do you?"

"No. David usually gave me a lift to work. Him or one of the other—"

"Where's Ashlee?" she heard someone call. "Where is she?"

Twisting back, Ashlee saw Greg running around the side of the home with Richard close behind.

"Right here," she called with a wave.

"Rockford," Greg said, breathlessly reaching them. "Carrie's in Rockford. How do we get there?"

Ashlee's eyes darted between Greg and Richard. "David came back?"

"Yeah," Greg said, "but I've no clue where the women's camp is. Do you know?"

He handed her CJ's small map of Illinois. She stared at it, wracking her brain. Unlike Bristol, she'd never been to Rockford before.

Her stomach clenched but she tried to smile. "That's great news. You know where Carrie is. That's really, really…" She trailed off.

David had returned.

She had wanted to follow Greg to Logan Pond today. Not that she wanted to talk to her ex-boyfriend—ever again. Her bruises were barely healed. But for some reason, she felt desperate to catch a glimpse of him. She couldn't figure out why he was so obsessed with Carrie. Through the years, she'd put up with him chasing lots of women, but Carrie wasn't even his type.

"Hey." Greg tugged on the corner of her sleeve. "Where'd you get this? This is Carrie's shirt."

Ashlee glanced down. The stained, faded yellow t-shirt fit her ten times better than those ugly sweats had. "Sasha said I could borrow it since I don't—"

"Find somethin' else," Greg said stiffly.

"Oh, sorry," she shot back angrily. "I didn't have time to pack before I fled for my life. What would you have me wear anyway? I refuse to put that green uniform back on."

"Greg," Richard said. "Carrie wouldn't mind."

Greg looked like he still minded—especially as his eyes narrowed on her bright, red lips.

"Don't even think about it," Ashlee said before he could comment. "The lipstick is all mine. I grabbed it when we broke into the office." At least her emergency stash had been where she'd left it. She rubbed her lips together, loving the smoothness. The bright red color made her feel like herself again. Maybe that's why Greg hated it. He'd never liked her much—her fault for flirting with him way back when—but even this was over-the-top rude for him. "It happens to be the only thing in this place that is actually *mine*, so deal with it."

His brows rose, but then he nodded. "You're right. Sorry. I'm just stressed."

Everybody was.

"Did Jamansky tell you where Amber and Zach are?" Braden asked anxiously.

"Not yet," Greg said. "But he'll post it on Richard's door when he finds out. Terrell's gonna check back every day to see while we're gone to Rockford."

"Or I can," Braden said eagerly. "And you think Richard can get in to see Carrie?"

"That's the hope," Richard said. "At the very least, a visit and a plea for medicine. I should probably warn CJ that we'll be gone for a few days."

Braden's expression fell. "You'll be gone that long?"

"At least," Greg said. "We've gotta assess the situation and see if there's a way to break Carrie out. I don't wanna have to wait two weeks for her release."

Ashlee's head jerked up. "Two weeks? How will Carrie be released in two weeks?"

Greg's mouth opened but snapped shut again.

Richard folded his arms. "Go ahead, Greg. Tell them what bargain you struck with Jamansky."

Ashlee's stomach plummeted. "You made a deal with David?"

Greg and Richard glowered at each other. Obviously the two men didn't agree, which meant it was bad. Really bad.

"It's...complicated." Greg said to her. "So do you know where in Rockford this place is?"

Ashlee wasn't about to be sidetracked. Her voice rose. "What bargain did you strike with Jamansky? Does it have to do with me?" Her throat thickened. "Are you exchanging prisoners?"

Greg rolled his eyes. "No. He doesn't even know you're with us."

"Then what is it?" she said.

Guilt flashed across his tanned face. He kicked the grass softly. "I, uh, might have to testify against Oliver."

It took a second for Ashlee to understand.

"What? No!" she cried. "You can't do that!"

"Don't you have a problem with that, Greg?" Braden said. "Don't you think Carrie will have a problem with you testifying against Oliver?"

"Yeah." Greg scrubbed a hand down the side of his face. "In her mind, it'll be unpardonable. But what else can I do?"

"Something else—*anything* else," Richard said. "Oliver has done a lot for Carrie. A lot for us."

Greg whirled. "Exactly. And what would he have told me to do? If Oliver was right here, right now, would he have left Carrie in prison to save himself? No, not even save himself. Just to have one less testimony against him?"

Ashlee dropped her gaze to the grass. Would Oliver really sacrifice himself like that for Carrie?

"That's irrelevant," Richard said. "You can't stab Oliver in the back and expect Carrie to forgive you for it. Not even for Amber and Zach."

"What?" Braden said. "Amber and Zach, too?"

Greg nodded soberly. "Jamansky agreed to return all three of them. Plus they get their house and citizenship back as well. We could get all of them back, Braden."

Braden looked floored. Hopeful. "All of them?"

"Everyone except Oliver," Ashlee pointed out angrily. "I thought you people were better than the others. Better than Mayor Phillips and David. But you're not. You're just as selfish." Her eyes felt hotter than her sun-cooked skin. "How can you use Oliver like that? If you testify against him, you'll ensure he never leaves prison. How can you be so cruel?"

"Hold up," Greg said, shooting her a dark look. "Before you throw us all under the bus, I wasn't done. As part of the deal, Jamansky agreed to let me meet with Oliver, face to face."

That took a second to sink in. Her eyes widened. "When?"

"A week from today," Greg said. "When I'm there, I'll see if there's any way to break him out."

"I don't understand," she said, shaking her head.

"We know where Carrie is," Greg said. "Tomorrow we'll know where Zach and Amber are. That gives us a week to break them all out. Then next Wednesday, I'll head to JSP and meet with Oliver, see how I can get him out as well. Then it won't matter what Jamansky thinks I've agreed to."

"You can meet with Oliver but not the others?" Braden said. "Why?"

"Jamansky only arrested Oliver," Greg said. "He doesn't have the same kind of access to the others."

Ashlee studied Greg, trying to give him the benefit of the doubt. The guy was obsessed about finding Carrie, but he wouldn't forget Oliver. They'd find a way to get all of them out.

Somehow.

But how?

"What about Carrie's house and citizenship?" Ashlee asked, still leery. "If you don't testify, Jamansky won't give them to you."

Greg nodded softly. "I know. But I'd rather get Oliver out. It's what Carrie would want anyway."

Ashlee took this all in. It sounded good.

A little too good.

"No offense, Greg," Ashlee said, "but you're not the first person who wanted to break their loved one out of prison. You'll never pull it off."

"Yeah, but how many of them have been through special op training?" he said. "Surely they taught me somethin' useful in Naperville. And if that doesn't work, I'll just barge in and rattle off my numbers. Isabel's already been alerted that I'm back, so I'll just march in as if I'm on assignment and demand they release all of them."

Richard grunted under his breath.

"What?" Greg said defensively. "It could work."

Ashlee watched Richard. The gentle, older man looked stiff and angry still. He didn't trust this plan of Greg's. Honestly, the longer Greg talked, the crazier it sounded to her. Crazy. Desperate. They weren't that different. His plan had too many holes, too much potential for failure. He couldn't expect to work with someone like David Jamansky and have it go well. It would be like picking up a ticking bomb and expecting it to wait to go off until the one who threw it at you decided to defuse it.

"What if it doesn't work, Greg?" Ashlee pressed. "What if you can't break all four out in time?"

Greg's shoulders fell. "We just have to. For now, we've gotta get to Rockford. Richard will try to get in and see Carrie, get her medicine, while I scope out the place."

"And if you can't get her out?" Ashlee said, growing frustrated.

Greg looked back at Richard.

Richard shook his head.

And Ashlee knew. Greg would do it. He'd do anything he could to get Carrie and her siblings free. Even if it meant helping David Jamansky. Even if it meant Carrie couldn't forgive him for it.

Even if it meant testifying against Oliver Simmons.

"I thought you were better than this, Greg," Ashlee said. Her throat burned. "I'm disappointed in you."

"I really don't care," he said tiredly. "With luck, I'll be back in two days with Carrie. So how do we get to Rockford?"

twenty-nine

"How much farther?" Greg asked.

"That last sign…" Richard said, huffing with their brisk pace, "said four miles. That was…ten stomach growls ago."

"Then we should be close," Greg said.

He wiped the sweat from his face. Poor Richard's t-shirt was drenched, front and back, even though it was still early in the day. They'd have to find a stream soon before they dropped of dehydration.

They'd traveled late into the night last night and started off early again this morning, only stopping for a few hours. The work camp wouldn't allow visitors in the middle of the night anyway.

Greg had counted seventeen different fires on the twenty-mile journey, mostly to the west of them. One sent up huge plumes of black smoke. He hoped that meant the rebellion was still going strong and Kearney's band had grown in size and power. Maybe someday they would have the manpower to launch an all-out assault on President Rigsby. Until then, they were just annoying the heck out of the government.

Which pleased him.

"When are you…going to tell me your newest plan?" Richard said.

Greg considered his choices to the beat of their footsteps. There weren't many, none good.

"My first idea is the least complicated. It involves convincing the prison guards—or judge or whoever—that you and Carrie are married."

"That's your *least* complicated?" Richard said. "I'm old enough to be her father."

"That's the next plan," Greg said.

Richard shot him a sideways glare. "I see that three hours of sleep did nothing to enhance your brain cells."

"Or I can turn myself in right off the bat," Greg said. "Just walk into the prison and demand they release Carrie. It might work."

"Sure. Right after they clap you in handcuffs. What else?"

Greg frowned. It wasn't until yesterday that anybody, including him, realized Carrie had taken the bulk of the clan's money with her. That left them nearly broke. Richard held the rest, less than one hundred dollars. It would never be enough to bribe any guard to do anything.

"If they believe my special op status, maybe I'll just convince them that Carrie and I are married. Although I'm not sure who will be harder to convince. The guards..." Greg's chest constricted. "Or Carrie."

Richard pulled him to a stop. "Carrie still loves you."

"No, Carrie *loved* me before she lost her two siblings because of me."

"It wasn't your fault, son."

The familiar term surprised Greg. Technically, Richard had only been his stepdad for six weeks, a short time before Greg's mom passed away.

Son.

"There are a lot of powers at play here," Richard went on, "that have nothing to do with you *or* Carrie. It wasn't anyone's fault but the corrupt system we live in."

Greg ran a hand over his hot, shaggy hair, wanting to believe it but not quite able. "I should've been there, Richard. I coulda stopped this."

"It would have just been you instead of her."

"Exactly! Me instead of them. I deserve to be behind bars. But they can't...and she won't be able to..." More disturbing images popped in his mind. Starving. Beaten. Abused. Dead. "Not Carrie. Not her."

Richard's expression softened. "Don't underestimate her. I watched her take care of her siblings after her parents died. She did it on her own, day after day, fighting to survive. She has been everything those two kids needed, so don't underestimate her. She's stronger than you think."

Greg couldn't even nod. He knew Carrie was strong, but so were his mom, Kendra, Carrie's parents, and millions of others.

A few minutes later, their wooded trail ended. Nothing but open space sprawled between them and the Rockford Women's Penal Institution. It stood, broad, gray, and impossibly large, enclosed by two separate barbed-wire fences. All trees and bushes had been cleared around the building for half a mile in every direction, which meant every person coming and going could easily be spotted by one of the guard towers.

"Any message you want me to relay to Carrie," Richard said, "should I happen to get in and see her?"

"Should you happen?" Greg turned, panicked. "You gotta get in. She's gotta know we're tryin' to get her out."

"I will if I can."

Greg held out his hand. "Give me the medicine. I'll go myself."

"Listen," Richard said, holding the small white box strong, "I will use every power within my means to see Carrie. Now, what message would you like me to give her?"

"First, get her the medicine. That's a must. Then tell her that I'm sorry, and we're tryin' to get her out, and we've got plans in the works, but she's gotta hold on a bit longer—she's gotta keep fightin' until we can get her out. And tell her that we're lookin' for Zach and Amber, too. And Oliver. We'll have them all back in no time."

His mind was a torrent, trying to remember everything.

"Tell her that I'm here and I'll stay here the whole time until she's released if she wants. But whatever you do, don't tell her about Jamansky or any of what I've agreed to." He couldn't bear for her to know about his backup plan.

Mercifully Richard didn't add commentary. He just nodded. "Anything else?"

A thousand more things, but Greg handed him the small box of syringes, enough to treat Carrie for another five days should she need it.

"Hurry," Greg said.

As Richard started for the building, the slideshow in Greg's mind started again. Starving, beaten, abused, dead. Greg had been in the government's claws before. He knew what it was like. And just in case he might have forgotten, they left him with a back and shoulder covered in scars.

No matter how much he wanted to believe Richard about Carrie being strong enough, Greg knew he was wrong. Carrie was everything his grandma said about her: a gentle soul living in a harsh world. She was delicate, tender, and very, very breakable. They all were.

Richard entered through the front doors of the looming, gray fortress, clasping his citizenship card. It was a sign of his stepson's frantic state that he hadn't wondered if Richard's citizenship had been revoked along with the others. Richard was worried, though. Who knew what Oliver's arrest had set in motion?

Nervously he strode up to the front desk and to the guard dressed in black.

"I'm here to visit a prisoner," Richard said, trying to sound as if he'd done this a dozen times.

"Card," the guard said, holding out a hand.

Richard slid his yellow card across to him. The guard examined it first, eyes darting from Richard's face to the card again, before swiping it through his verifying machine. When the little light turned green, Richard nearly shouted for joy.

First hurdle cleared.

The guard picked up a binder. "When is your appointment?"

"I actually don't have one," Richard said, "but I—"

The guard slammed the binder shut. "No appointment, no visit."

"My apologies, sir. I wasn't aware that I needed an appointment. But I don't need a long time with the prisoner. Just a few minutes will do."

"No exceptions. Come back when you have an appointment."

"Please, sir," Richard said. "I've come a long way. I can wait all day if you can squeeze me in somewhere. Even if it's later today or tomorrow, I just really need to speak with her."

The officer glared at him. It was the kind of look that said, *I dare you to ask me one more time.*

Richard blew out his breath. "Fine. May I schedule an appointment, please?"

The guard handed him a small slip of paper. "Call this number."

But I'm right here! Richard wanted to yell. "Yes. Thank you. However, I don't have a working phone."

"Not my problem." The guard went back to his book.

The government and their stupid red tape.

Dreading Greg's reaction should he reappear empty-handed, Richard decided to be pushy.

"Officer Baron," he said, reading the man's name tag, "I really have come a long way. I don't have access to a phone, and since I'm already here, could you possibly make an exception, just this once?"

The guard reached below his desk, and grabbed out an awfully large rifle. He pointed it at Richard.

"Come back when you have an appointment. *Capisce?*"

Heart thundering, Richard stared into the end of the rifle. He didn't have any children of his own. Greg was the closest thing he had. But beyond that, Carrie was the orphaned daughter of Richard's old friend, Tom Ashworth. Carrie didn't have a father here to speak for her.

So he had to.

Slowly, Richard reached into his back pocket and felt around for a red, crisp bill. With the care of a soldier disarming a grenade, he slid the new currency across the counter.

"Please, sir, I'd really like to set up an appointment. Now."

The guard's face reddened. "You think you can bribe me with twenty dollars?"

"Sorry." Richard fumbled for another bill. He placed a fifty on top of the first.

The patrolman's eyes widened before darting around the room. Fast as a cobra, the money disappeared.

"What's the inmate's name?" he asked.

thirty

Carrie knelt next to Donnelle and felt her forehead. Inhumanely hot.

"Ha!" Crazy Marge said over Carrie's shoulder. "She's not going to make it either." She fingered Donnelle's black, frizzy hair. "I'll keep this for my collection."

"Marge," Carrie said, waving her off. "Leave her alone. Please."

Thankfully, Marge backed off.

The other women still slept around the cell. It seemed like the morning wakeup call should have already come, but maybe it just felt like morning already because she'd spent all night fretting over Donnelle.

Donnelle had declined rapidly the day before. Working alongside her, Carrie noticed Donnelle growing quieter and quieter until she stopped talking altogether. A definite warning sign.

Guards kept yelling at Donnelle to keep up. Anytime they caught Carrie helping, they shouted at her instead, threatening her with "punishment" if she didn't go back to her own station. By the end of the shift, Donnelle looked like an old woman, pale and hunched over. She'd even started shivering even though the workspace was hot enough to cook eggs.

Sadly, Carrie wasn't far behind.

Her energy was gone, and she could no longer ignore her migraine. For the first hours after Jamansky left, she'd felt hopeful. He could help her. He could do it. But the more people she talked to and the longer she thought about it, the more she realized the impossibility of ever leaving this place. Donnelle didn't know a soul who had been released—and Donnelle knew everyone. The only people who left were in body bags. And Jamansky wasn't exactly known to be a man of his word.

More empty promises. More lies. No medicine had come, and knowing none would sapped her strength faster than the illness itself. If this virus followed the same path as last time, she would start a fever overnight and then…

She rubbed her neck and the back of her skull, hating how stiff she felt.

There had to be a way to get medicine. Next time the guards returned, she would ask—no, beg—for help. Someone would have compassion. They would see Donnell and know.

Until then, Carrie had to stop the progression of the virus.

Crazy Marge climbed back onto the top bunk where she perched on a corner like a vulture waiting to strike.

Carrie stood and stretched her back, impossibly achy from sleeping propped up against the metal bed frame.

The sink in their cell had, at best, a small trickle of water at any given time. Carrie didn't have anything to soak, so she wet her hands and went back to Donnelle, wiping her cool hands across Donnelle's brow to cool it down.

Donnelle didn't budge even though Carrie repeated the process every few minutes.

Her thoughts wandered to where she should have been today. Back in Delaney's clan, discussing trading. Would Greg go without her? She hoped he would move on and press the clan forward. The farmers' market had become his dream as much as hers. At least one of them should achieve it. But she worried about him. When he lost his sister, he'd shut down. When he lost his mom, he nearly had again.

She wished she could beg him to not shut down again. To not become bitter or hate the world.

Her heart ached from missing him so much.

Kneeling next to Donnelle again, she closed her heavy eyes, trying to envision Greg free, safe, and meeting with the Sprucewood leaders. Would they meet on a Tuesday? Would they meet in the woods?

Would he find a way to be happy again?

Would he find her siblings?

Would he find her?

Even if he did, would she live long enough to find out?

Her eyes filled. The grief washed over her as she leaned against the thin, smelly mattress. Questions continued to tumble around with no answers or consolation.

Two minutes.

Her entire life had been destroyed in a matter of two minutes. She'd walked out her front door that morning, holding Greg's hand, her siblings following. They had been happy. She had been heading into town for liberty for Amber and Zach, to make them safe from the clutches of the government.

How could a life, a family, a couple be destroyed in a matter of *two* minutes?

"Is Donnelle any better?" someone asked.

Sniffing, Carrie looked up too quickly. Pain stabbed her temples. Lisbeth stood above her, another cellmate. With oily brown hair and a high, quiet voice, Lisbeth seemed too young to be incarcerated.

Carrie wiped her eyes. "No."

"Me neither. I've started a headache. How…" Lisbeth twisted her hands in front of her. "How long do I have, Carrie?"

Those words knotted Carrie's stomach.

Yesterday, before Donnelle took a turn for the worse, she admitted that Carrie had only joined their particular cell because there had been a vacancy. Their cellmate, Sherry, had died the day before with the same symptoms. They'd taken her body out a few hours before Carrie arrived.

How many people had Sherry spread the illness to?

"I don't know," Carrie said honestly.

"Maybe it's a blessing," Lisbeth whispered. "Live free or die, right?"

No! Carrie wanted to shout. She'd seen too many deaths already. Her parents. Jenna and Mariah. How many people would she kneel beside as they slipped away? How long before it was her?

People needed to fight this. They needed to beat it somehow.

A sharp *clank* sounded in the cell as the guard came by, hitting his nightstick against the bars. The wakeup call, finally.

Donnelle still didn't stir.

"No work duty today, ladies," he said. "The prison is on lockdown until further notice."

"Really?" Lisbeth said.

Carrie's shoulders lowered in relief. No work. A blessing for Donnelle. She wanted to ask if lockdowns were normal but didn't have the energy.

Taking her morning washrag from the guard, she went to the sink and wet it as much as she could. Then she laid the cold rag across Donnelle's forehead. Trying to stop this virus from progressing felt like trying to stop a typhoon with an umbrella.

"Sir," Carrie called suddenly. Pushing herself up, she went to the bars and tried to peer down to where he handed out more washrags. Carrie's cellmates liked that particular guard. Supposedly he was nicer than the others. His name was Eddie, but they usually called him Headie Eddie because of his dark, shaved head.

"Eddie," Carrie said more loudly, "my friend is really sick. Can you help her? Or is there a doctor who can? Look at her on our bottom bunk. She's really sick."

"She's not the only one," Headie Eddie said, handing washcloths through the next set of bars. "Why do you think we're on lockdown?"

Carrie glanced around to what she could see of the prison, cell after cell of women trapped behind bars. Lockdown would have been a good idea if they were treating the sick ones—or at least quarantining them from their cellmates.

Carrie flipped Donnelle's washrag over on her forehead. Donnelle looked so pale, so lifeless.

When Headie Eddie circled back a few minutes later, collecting the washrags, Carrie ran back to the bars.

"Please," she said, "My friend is not doing well. Can she get medicine? Can you at least ask around. There has to be something you can do."

"She'll be better tomorrow." He turned. "Marge, don't make me fight you for your rag today. Do you want breakfast or not?"

Crazy Marge stuck her tongue out at him. Apparently she didn't trust anyone without hair.

"Come on, Marge," he said.

With a glare, Marge extracted her rag from inside her orange uniform and handed it over. With that, Headie Eddie started off.

"Wait!" Carrie called through the bars. "This isn't just some flu or strep throat. This is the G-979 virus, I know it is. If she doesn't get help, she'll die."

He held the collection bucket to the next group of women.

"Do you want her to die?" Carrie said, growing frustrated. "Do you want them all to die?"

"Probably," Lisbeth said, behind her. "More open beds."

Fire shot through Carrie's veins.

"So that's your job?" she yelled at him. "Lock us in here like caged animals until we die? We live on government property because we're too poor to afford anything else, and suddenly that's a death sentence?"

From around the prison, women started yelling. "Yeah, animals!" "Let us out!" Their shouts echoed off the cement walls. "Give us meds!" "Let us out!"

Headie Eddie whirled around and stormed back to Carrie with such fury, she fell back a step. He swung, slamming his nightstick against the metal bars. The force of it left her ears ringing.

"Silence!" he yelled. "Before I have to silence you."

So much for being the nice guard.

Carrie's eyes stung. "She's going to die. This isn't something you can just recover from. We're all going to die unless you help us."

Something changed in his dark eyes. A flash of guilt. But he walked off and left them alone, locked inside of their cells.

"You're going to kill us all," Carrie whispered.

———— ♦ ————

Greg jumped to his feet. He watched Richard stride out the front prison doors in a hurry. Richard had only been inside for maybe five minutes, *way* too fast to have seen Carrie.

Greg's heart pounded with a mixture of disappointment and rage. He knew Richard couldn't pull this off.

He knew it!

He wanted to sprint out to meet him but didn't dare risk being seen out in the open, so he waited, pacing back and forth in the woods while his insides felt ready to burst.

"What happened?" Greg said the second Richard was within hearing distance.

Richard just kept walking. Even when he was close enough to explain, he kept going, passing up Greg and heading back the direction they'd come.

"Let's go," Richard said.

Greg snagged his arm, stopping him. "No way. If you can't get in to see her, then I will."

"No need."

"Why? What happened? I told you to get in no matter what!"

"Carrie's not here!" Richard snapped.

That pulled Greg up short. "What?"

Richard's jaw tightened under his gray goatee. "They have no inmate by the name of Carrie Ashworth at this location. In fact, they haven't had a single prisoner here from Shelton in over a month."

"What? No. That can't be," Greg said.

"I saw the list of inmates myself," Richard said. "They're closed to new prisoners because of overcrowding. Carrie is not here, Greg. I'm sorry."

"But Jamansky said she was in Rockford!" His mind raced. "Is there another work camp in—"

"Not for women. The guard told us to try one of these places."

Richard handed Greg a slip of paper. Greg recognized several of the places because Ashlee had already mentioned them. All six of them. In six entirely different cities.

The weight of it hit him, full force.

Carrie wasn't here.

Greg's gaze dropped to the box of medicine Richard held. No cure. No release. Greg couldn't even bully his way inside because Carrie wasn't here.

"No," he said. "It's gotta be a mistake. We just came twenty miles. How did this happen?"

"You really have to ask?" Richard said darkly.

Understanding slammed into Greg like a ton of bricks.

Richard nodded. "I'd bet my last dollar that Chief Jamansky sent us on a goose chase."

thirty-one

Jamansky walked into the station. Fat, old Giordano looked up from his desk.

"You seem happy, chief," Giordano said.

Jamansky loosened his tie. "Yeah. It's been a good week. A great week, actually."

"That's a change," Giordano said.

True. Every since his arrest in the spring, it had been one problem after another. But now things seemed to be falling into place. Finally.

Giordano stapled some papers together and pushed away from his desk. "Anything you need from me? I'm heading out on patrols for the night."

"No. Actually, yes." Jamansky turned. "You're on northern Shelton tonight, aren't you?"

"Yeah. Why?"

"There's a subdivision on the western outskirts, one of Simmons' old areas. It's called Logan Pond, not very large. As of a few days ago, twenty or more illegals lived there, but a little bird told me they've abandoned it. But I don't believe him. Leave the dogs behind and take Portman, Bushing, and whoever else you need to do a full, silent sweep."

"Will do."

"Good. Oh, and Giordano?" Jamansky said.

"Yes, chief?"

David Jamansky smiled again. He'd nearly fired Giordano and Ellen for their hand in everything, almost ruining Jamansky's perfect plan. But now that things had shifted and he had Pierce in the palm of his hands...

"I'm giving you a raise," he said.

Giordano's brows lifted on his beefy forehead. "Wow. Thanks, boss."

Whistling, Jamansky left him and walked back to his office. He sat in his plush, leather chair and kicked his feet up on his desk. It had been crazy putting everything into place. He probably needed to take notes on all he'd done—and promised—just to keep track.

Rockford.

He was still congratulating himself on that quick thinking.

Pierce had given him a day to figure out where Amber and Zach were. Jamansky didn't need a day. He already knew, but he posted a note on that house that said, *"Still working on Amber and Zach's whereabouts. Hope to hear back soon. –J."*

Easy.

Not so easy had been yelling at the idiotic Rochelle prison guard, demanding that they give Carrie medicine. He couldn't have her dying on him. Not now. It would ruin all his plans. He lost a pretty penny bribing the guard, but again, task completed.

The only thing that irked was Ashlee. Every time he even thought his girlfriend's name, he wanted to rip her home to shreds. Not even her parents knew where she'd gone. How had Oliver Simmons turned Ashlee against him so quickly, so completely? He didn't know, but with luck, they'd find her body washed up on some lake shore.

As long as he ignored that aspect of things, he felt pretty good. It had been a very busy, very good week. And if things went well in the next few days, it would only get better.

Ellen knocked softly on his door.

"Enter," he said.

"Chief, sir," Ellen said, "two federal patrolmen delivered this for you today."

He looked up. "What is it?"

"Not sure, but I told them you were out."

She handed him a letter-sized envelope. He set it on the corner of his desk and sat back again, hands behind his head. His next step needed to be even more careful and calculated. One wrong misstep, and it could all blow up in his face.

"Um...sir?" Ellen said, still in the doorway. "I believe that letter is important. You might want to take a look."

His eyes narrowed. "Have you been reading my mail again?"

"No." She gulped. "No, of course not."

Liar. He hated that woman. Ashlee Lyon might be a lousy clerk—and even lousier girlfriend—but at least she knew her place.

Sighing, he grabbed the envelope and read the return address.

"Department of Investigations?" he read, perplexed. He'd never received a letter from them before. Of course, he hadn't been Chief of Patrols all that long either.

Tearing it open, he slipped out several typed sheets of paper.

He read the cover letter, hardly understanding what it meant. So he read it again. And then again.

His blood began to simmer. At first, he thought Greg Pierce had been behind it, but Pierce couldn't have known any of the things listed. But someone else did.

Two someones did.

Jamansky thought back to the whispered conversation he'd overheard in the township office, how Ashlee and Oliver Simmons had huddled close, thinking nobody knew of their treachery and deceit. Accomplices in his demise.

His hand slammed down on his desk with a sudden *thwack.*

"I'll kill him!" he roared. "I swear I will kill them both!"

Ellen jumped back. "Sir?"

"Get my keys!"

———◆———

"Wait," Oliver said. "You wrote what to her?"

Reef slapped him on the back. "You're welcome."

Oliver pictured Ashlee Lyon reading that letter—Reef's bold words. The floor dropped out from under him. "No, no, no. You don't understand. She and I aren't...We're not..." He huffed angrily. "We're coworkers!"

"Maybe not anymore."

Reef winked at him.

Oliver couldn't worry about Ashlee's reaction. So what if she thought he was a total fool. Nothing new there. He had to focus on what he could: getting Ashlee the message.

The guards came around and told them to clear out. Lunch break was over. But Oliver continued to fret about it. Served him right for trusting a guy like Reef.

He was halfway through potato number two hundred and twenty-seven when a guard approached.

"Follow me," the guard said, motioning to him. "Someone wants to see you."

Oliver didn't like the sound of that. His ulcers knotted in his empty stomach.

The guard led him through halls and doors he'd never seen while he tried to figure out who it could be.

Stopping at a door, the guard swiped his card across a scanner. He ushered Oliver into a small, narrow room with stools lining each side in long rows. Each stool faced a Plexiglass partition with dividers and a phone on each side of the glass. Three other inmates sat on different stools down the line. Each of them talked on a corded phone to people on the other side of the glass.

A visitor's room.

Oliver could think of a handful of people who might visit him, but only two or three he actually *wanted* a visit from.

"Station number six," the guard said, pointing.

Curious and somewhat frightened, Oliver sat on the small stool. The other side of his partition was empty. He didn't want to get his hopes up on who the visitor might be. It couldn't be Ashlee. Not yet. Unless she had come on her own, but why would she? It had to be someone else. Hopefully not his uncle. Not that his Uncle Gerard was a horrible person, but the drunken judge only talked to Oliver when he needed money—which Oliver no longer had. Maybe someone from Logan Pond? Carrie or Greg? Could he be that lucky?

His leg bounced nervously under the small counter. The summer heat had baked the building, sending sweat trickling down his back.

When the door finally opened on the other side, Oliver's leg stopped bouncing. His heart stopped, too.

A patrolman stormed in, tall, blond, and searching for the right station. When he spotted number six with Oliver behind the Plexiglass, his face reddened with rage.

Jamansky stormed right up to the glass and slammed a piece of paper against it.

"What is this?" he shouted, loud enough that the three other inmates turned.

Terror seized Oliver for the space of two seconds until he realized what the paper was, who it was from, and what it meant. Then suddenly he was smiling. He couldn't help it. Being in a maximum security facility had its advantages. The thick, bulletproof glass separated them. Jamansky couldn't do anything to Oliver that he hadn't already done.

Oliver read the letter smashed up against the glass.

TO: CHIEF OF PATROLS, DAVID ARTHUR JAMANSKY,

Allegations have been drawn and an investigation has been reopened into potential illegal activity involving yourself and Mayor Lucas Phillips. You have been placed on probation pending further review.

Please send in the following files:

Even better than Oliver had hoped. They'd put Jamansky on probation. The mayor, too. Oliver practically grinned as he kept reading.

The letter listed seventeen different incidents spanning the last two years, suspicious activities that Jamansky had been involved with. Each had a date and a request for information. Some Oliver recognized, like number eleven:

11) List of items procured during March 31 sweep of Logan Pond Subdivision, Shelton Township. Along with list, send in patrol logs and payments sent.

That one felt good—incredibly good since the raid on Logan Pond had haunted Oliver long enough. With the help of Greg, he'd been able to turn it back around on Jamansky. The guy even spent a few weeks in prison until he got Mayor Phillips to spring him. Now, tides had turned again.

But other incidents Oliver had never heard of, some from years ago. Which could only mean one thing. When Reef wrote to the Department of Investigations, Oliver told him to mention the file Ashlee had set up on the main network. It held every allegation and bit of evidence they needed to pin Jamansky down. Oliver hadn't been given the chance to follow up with Ashlee, but obviously she'd done more digging on her own.

But how had they opened an investigation so quickly? Reef had only sent the letter earlier that week. Had Ashlee contacted the feds even before that?

Oliver's smile widened.

Seventeen full incidents. Ashlee was brilliant. Hopefully Jamansky never put two and two together that she'd been involved.

Suddenly Oliver hoped that Reef hadn't sent Ashlee's letter yet. Oliver needed to change it. He had to warn her, beg her to run or find somewhere to hide out until this blew over—maybe even until they yanked Jamansky from office, however long that took.

"I will rip you to shreds!" Jamansky yelled. "I will cut you to pieces!"

The glass muffled the shouting, but the guard grabbed Jamansky's arm and ordered him to sit and use the phone.

Jamansky's murderous glare stayed on Oliver, probation letter still smashed to the glass for a full minute, until he finally dropped onto the stool and grabbed the side phone.

Oliver almost didn't pick up his own phone. What could Jamansky have to say that already hadn't been said? Then again, Oliver had a thousand questions of his own. Had Jamansky gone to Carrie's house? Had he arrested the whole clan? Had he gone after Ashlee, who was scared of her abusive boyfriend even before all of this?

Jamansky's scowl deepened, waiting.

The second Oliver picked up the receiver, Jamansky yelled, "Drop the charges! Now!"

Oliver held the plastic phone away from his ear until the shouting stopped. Then he calmly—and somewhat smugly—said, "I don't know what you're talking about. As you can see, I'm stuck in here. Sorry. My hands are tied."

As he said the words, his whole body filled with exultation. Even his cracked ribs seemed to repair themselves at the sight of their inflictor's distress. Not only were the feds investigating Jamansky, but Mayor Phillips, too. Oliver couldn't have been more thrilled.

"Are you sure?" Jamansky said. Then he rammed something else against the glass, a different paper, smaller in size. No, not a paper.

A picture.

Oliver squinted to make out the somewhat-blurry photo. It had been taken from an upper angle, from a low-quality security camera in the upper corner of a room. It showed two people in a small white room sitting directly across from one another. One was Jamansky, hands clasped in front of him. The other was a woman in an orange prison jumpsuit.

Oliver's gut dropped to the floor.

No, no, no!

He stared at the woman's honey-colored hair, limp and hanging in her face, the slump of her slender shoulders, her petite nose, soft lips, and curved chin. He would know that profile anywhere.

He felt like he'd been pierced by a bullet.

"Carrie looks good in orange," Jamansky sneered. "Doesn't she?"

Oliver gripped the phone so tightly his knuckles strained. "What did you do to her?"

Suddenly, it was Jamansky doing all the smiling. "Oh, that's the best part. I didn't do this. *You* did. The second the government found out about your illegal activity, they confiscated all of your assets, including Carrie's house."

Jamansky pulled the photo back and stroked it, as if stroking Carrie's hair. "Imagine her horror when she and her siblings waltzed into town and got the surprise of a lifetime. She thought she was getting their citizenship cards worked up. But, no. All three of them taken in one fell swoop. Isn't that something?"

Oliver went numb. "Amber and Zach, too?"

His eyes darted around the floor, searching for a way to help. A letter? But to where? Which work camp had they sent Carrie to? And how could a letter help anyway? If Carrie's house had been repossessed, how could he get her legal again when he, himself, would spend the rest of his life locked away?

"Let me see it," Oliver hissed into the receiver. For all he knew, the picture wasn't really of Carrie at all, but was just another of Jamansky's tricks, an edited photo.

Jamansky was perfectly happy to comply. He pushed the photo back against the glass.

No matter how Oliver tried to blur his eyes, it was definitely Carrie. Only she looked so defeated, so broken. He dropped back onto his stool. Everything he'd experienced the last week flashed through his mind, only worse for her.

He thought not knowing was the worst thing.

He was wrong.

"How do you think she likes sleeping on the floor?" Jamansky asked. "It's a little colder than they warn you about, isn't it? Smellier, too. I really hope she doesn't run across any prison gangs either. They're brutal."

Oliver ignored the taunts, still studying the picture.

Then he squinted at the other person in the photo. Jamansky had sat across from her in that small room, hands clasped, talking to her. Unlike Oliver's prison, Carrie's facility had different visiting rights. Either that or, as Chief of Patrols, Jamansky had special visitation rights. He sat close enough he could have touched her.

Fury clouded Oliver's vision. "What did you say to her?"

"Oh, I just made sure she knew who was to blame for her arrest. As you can see, she didn't take the news too well. To your credit, she didn't believe me at first. She defended you quite nobly—at least for a time. But now she knows the truth. She knows what you did to her."

Oliver's mouth worked for a moment.

Nothing came out.

"You know," Jamansky said in a sudden conversational tone, "she's not looking too hot. Her coloring is a little off, don't you think? Her eyes are sunken, too. Say, did she have time to finish that round of medicine? Because I think she might be getting sick again. I'd hate for her to...die or something."

The knot tightened in Oliver's gut.

He leaned forward to see if she looked sick, but before he could see anything, Jamansky's fist closed around the security photo and crumpled it into a tiny wad of nothing. He tossed it over his shoulder.

"Drop the charges against me," Jamansky said into the phone. "Drop them, or she dies."

So that was it.

Why he had come.

Oliver closed his eyes. If Carrie was getting sick again, she would die anyway.

"Clear my record," Jamansky continued, "and I might even have her released. I can, you know. I can get her out, get her the medicine she needs. Shouldn't be too hard. A few signatures here, a few misunderstandings to clear up there, and she and her siblings could be free by tomorrow."

Oliver's eyes went wide. *Tomorrow?*

Jamansky waited.

"What…" Oliver cleared his suddenly dry throat. "What do you want me to do? I'm locked up in here. I can't do anything." Even if Reef wrote another letter to the Department of Investigations, how could Oliver rescind anything—especially because that file told the feds exactly where to find proof of everything Jamansky had stolen from them?

"Oh, don't worry," Jamansky said. "I've drawn up an Affidavit on your behalf. Sign it, and I'll send it in for you, because that's just the kind of nice guy that I am. It explains how you fabricated every one of those lies out of spite. And don't worry. It includes every lie that"—his jaw stiffened—"Ashlee fed you."

Oliver tried to not react. He begged his face to stay neutral at Ashlee's name, but inside he was screaming with horror.

What had Jamansky done to her?

Jamansky smelled blood and sat forward. "Where is that wench? Where did you hide her? Tell me!"

Ashlee was gone?

"I don't know," Oliver said. "I…I swear I don't know where she is."

"Well, when I find her, I'll be dealing with her next."

"I'll sign it!" Oliver blurted. "I'll do it. Just tell me what to do."

Jamansky shook his head. "Good. I will *not* be returning to prison. That's where you belong. So you better pray this works, because if a single charge, insinuation, accusation, or even a stupid parking ticket is left on my record, Carrie will be dead by the end of the week. Maybe Ashlee, too, just for fun. Am I clear?"

Oliver nodded blankly. "Perfectly."

thirty-two

Donnelle died.

Carrie tried to convince herself that she didn't know the wild-haired woman very well, so it shouldn't devastate her. Less than a week. That's all they'd spent together. Yet Donnelle had saved her those first days.

As Headie Eddie carried Donnelle's body out, Lisbeth, who wasn't far behind the same fate, whispered four quiet words.

"Live free or die."

Carrie closed her eyes against those words. She never wanted to hear them again.

Enough dying.

It was time for people to just live free.

———————◆———————

Greg had the twenty-mile trip home to figure out what to say—or rather, what to do—to the patrol chief. Obviously Jamansky hadn't thought Greg would visit Carrie.

Greg couldn't wait to pound the truth out of him.

He just needed to find Ashlee's pistol first. Unfortunately, Richard refused to tell Greg where he'd hidden the gun. He wouldn't even admit to stealing it.

When the two men reached Logan Pond, Greg stormed up to Richard's front door and grabbed the note tacked there.

"Still working on Amber and Zach's whereabouts. Hope to hear back soon. –J."

Greg's fist closed over the paper. "I'll kill him. I swear I will."

"Let's just get back to Ferris," Richard said. "Maybe the others will have come up with something."

But as they rounded the corner, Greg saw somebody sitting on his grandparents' porch: a dark-haired, curvy woman.

He stopped, blood running cold. Although he shouldn't have been surprised to see her there. Frankly, he couldn't believe it had taken her that long to show up. But he felt his life—and Carrie's—slipping through his fingers.

"Is that who I think it is?" Richard said.

Before Greg's former partner could see them, he hauled Richard behind a tree.

"Go," Greg said to his stepdad. "Head to Ferris. Tell them what happened."

"I'm not leaving without you," Richard said. "And you don't need to be here either. She hasn't seen us yet. Come with me to Ferris."

Greg's jaw clenched. "I need her help."

"She's not here to help. I can guarantee that much."

"Just go!"

Richard dug in his feet. "You stay, I stay. We're in this together."

"So you'll go down with the ship?" Greg asked angrily.

Richard smiled sadly. "It's the only way to go down."

Greg should have fought him, but he had no fight left in him. The two strode out into the open, walking directly down the street toward his grandparents' home.

Lieutenant Isabel Ryan stood as they approached, her arms folded, expression rock hard.

"Pierce," she said coldly.

"Isabel," he said back.

But the second they reached the front sidewalk, Greg stopped dead in his tracks. Isabel's favorite black pistol—the one with the little pink trigger—had appeared out of nowhere. It rose to the level of his face.

Richard's hands shot into the air. Greg's hands lifted, too, though more slowly.

"Explain," Isabel said.

Greg waited for her to lower her gun. She didn't. Not even a millimeter. His blood pressure spiked. During training, he and Isabel had spent a full day in the shooting range together. He'd never seen anybody shoot like Isabel Ryan—not even Jeff Kovach who had been the clan's best hunter. Her accuracy was off the chart. And now her favorite gun was aimed right between his eyes.

Suddenly his temper snapped. He didn't have time for Isabel's theatrics. The exhaustion and defeat from the last few days—the last few weeks—had soured his mood beyond repair. He glared right back at her.

"You first," he said.

The silence between them was charged with fury. Neither of them were willing to bend.

Richard, ever the diplomat, spoke instead. "Um...hello. I'm Richard O'Brien. You must be Greg's former partner, Isabel."

And fake wife, Greg thought darkly. So much for a, *Nice to see you again, hon.*

Isabel's death glare didn't leave him, as if Richard hadn't even spoken.

"You know," Greg muttered out of the side of his mouth, "that pistol woulda come in handy right about now."

"Sorry," Richard whispered, hands still high. Then he spoke loudly again. "You're not here to arrest Greg, are you?"

"I'm thinking about it," she said. "I'm thinking about taking both of you in, actually. But first, I'm waiting for Pierce to explain."

Greg didn't like this side of Isabel, the cold, bitter side. The two of them had been oil and water during their short time as partners. Still, he thought they'd ended on good terms. He'd saved her life. She saved his. They'd been friends.

Or so he thought.

"Why are you here?" Greg called angrily. "Does McCormick know I'm alive?"

"Yes," she said.

He wanted to kick something.

"So he sent you to bring me in?" he said.

Her grip tightened on her pretty little gun, a little too tight for his comfort. "Yes. Now your turn, Pierce. Explain to me why some jerk called me out of the blue and said he'd had a nice chat with you. He said you started bossing him around like you were still some special op." Her dark eyes narrowed. "Did he tell you to call me like I ordered him to?"

Greg was tempted to lie and let Jamansky rot, but he nodded. "Yes."

"I see. Only guess what? I've heard *nothing.*" She spat the word. "After all I did for you, covering your sorry hide, doesn't that seem a little unfair? What happened, Pierce? I told you not to resurrect yourself unless something—"

"Carrie's gone," he interrupted.

Her dark brows shot up. "What do you mean?"

"Carrie was arrested. Taken. And I can't…I can't…" The emotions hit him all over again. He swallowed. After all the miles and days of searching, his whole body wanted to collapse and never get back up. He took a slow breath until he trusted his voice to work properly. "I can't find her."

The gun lowered a fraction.

"And your mom?" Isabel asked.

The question caught him off guard. Even Richard stiffened next to him. The last time Greg had seen Isabel, he'd been desperate to get home before his mom lost her battle with cancer. As it turned out, he was too late anyway. Six weeks too late.

"She's dead," Greg said. "Died before I got home."

"I'm sorry, Greg," she said. It looked like she actually meant it.

He should have been stressed about what she and McCormick were planning for him—more spying or a lifetime behind bars—but he couldn't help but think about all the access she had. Things Jamansky didn't. And if she hadn't brought the whole squad to arrest him—yet—he still had time.

"Listen," he said. "I need your help. You gotta help me find Carrie."

Her dark glare returned. "Isn't that interesting? Because McCormick wants you to help him find someone, too."

"Maybe if he scratches my back, I'll scratch his."

Her gun straightened. "You've always been a gutsy one, haven't you? Here I come to bring you in, threaten arrest, and somehow you end up asking *me* for help?"

"Fine," he said. "Take me to McCormick. I'll do whatever he wants. I'll spy on whoever he orders me to. But first…find Carrie and release her. That's my deal."

She huffed in frustration. "Look, Greg, I would love to help your precious Carrie, I really would, but I can't. Not anymore."

"Bull! You have a level nine clearance. If that weasel Jamansky can get her out, so can you—probably even today."

Today.

The possibility filled his mind.

"No, it's not that. I'm not in the best position to help you right now, Greg. Neither is McCormick."

Today. The word kept echoing, making him dizzy with anticipation. He could have Carrie and her siblings back by the end of the day.

Desperate, he said, "I swear I'll do whatever you want, just help me first. Carrie's in trouble. She's runnin' out of time 'cause she's sick. This Jamansky guy, the one you talked to, he's as corrupt as"—he nearly said President Rigsby, but remembered who he was talking to—"anybody I know. He deserves to hang. So take Jamansky out, get Carrie and her siblings released, and I'll do anything Commander McCormick wants. No fighting. No attitude. You have my word."

Not a great deal, but a thousand times better than betraying Oliver.

Isabel watched him with a long, grave face, but for some reason, Richard spoke first.

"Greg," Richard said slowly, "I don't think she's in a position to help you right now."

"Yes she is! President Rigsby gave McCormick free reign to do whatever he wants. He could probably march into Carrie's prison and release every single person there."

"Greg," Isabel started, voice suddenly pleading. "Uncle Charlie is, uh…" She blinked. "Commander McCormick, he's not…"

His gut clenched. "He's not what?"

Isabel's gun lowered. "Commander McCormick is no longer head of the Special Patrols Unit. He resigned on Tuesday." She paused before finishing. "And so did I."

thirty-three

Greg and Isabel took turns explaining all that had happened since he'd run from Kearney's camp.

"Uncle Charlie and I were actually thinking about tracking you down," Isabel said. "Once he resigned, I told him where you really were and what had happened in Kearney's camp. And then I got that strange call. I'd forgotten that I'd placed my personal phone number in your records. It felt like fate had brought you back to us."

Greg sat on his grandparents' front porch, head in his hands. McCormick quit his job. He didn't have power or special access to anything. Neither did Isabel. They couldn't take down Jamansky. They couldn't find Carrie.

They couldn't do anything.

"Why did he quit?" he said, voice strained.

"His wife, my aunt Ashira," Isabel said, "caught this G-979 virus. Only when they went to give her the cure, she had an allergic reaction. She asphyxiated. Couldn't breathe. Aunt Ashira passed away before the end of the day. Now Uncle Charlie is…well…" She ran a hand over her eyes. "I'm sure you can imagine. He wants revenge."

Greg looked up. "Revenge?"

"He knows President Rigsby is behind this virus. He knows what it's intended to do—we all do. Based on the reports coming in, it's bad, Greg. Horrific. And not just illegals either. I don't think even Rigsby could have anticipated how fast it's spread." She shrugged. "McCormick can't forgive the president for his wife's death, so he quit his job. He needs help, and he thinks you're the one to do it."

Richard folded his arms. "Help with what?"

"He needs someone to get him on the inside." She hesitated. "He wants Greg to introduce him to Kearney and the rebels."

"Kearney?" Greg said with a mirthless laugh. "The guy who nearly blew off my head?"

"I told him what you said to Kearney," Isabel said. "How you told Kearney the government's plans to spy and infiltrate the rebel groups. I told him how Kearney reacted, how he listened to you and moved the camp."

"The guy almost killed me!"

She smiled. "But he didn't."

Shaking his head, Greg stood. "This is ridiculous. I don't have time for this."

"You can use my phone," Isabel said quickly. "Call any place you want to find Carrie. And when we're done, I'll drive you anywhere you want."

"Anywhere?" he challenged.

"Yes."

"If I help you break into the rebellion?"

"Yes."

Greg looked at Richard, trying to read his thoughts. Richard scratched his graying goatee, looking lost. Greg wouldn't be resurrected. No green card restored or obligatory military service required. He wouldn't be forced to betray his fellow illegals again. In fact, he would be helping them fight President Rigsby, the ultimate enemy. The man who had started everything.

That is, if Greg understood correctly.

He turned back to Isabel. "Just to be sure, why does McCormick want to meet with Kearney and the rebel leaders?"

"Because they have the fire and he has the means."

"The means?" he echoed.

"Yes." Isabel's large, dark eyes locked on his. "McCormick plans to assassinate the president."

By the time Headie Eddie returned, Carrie had it all planned.

A guard had come the night before and summoned Carrie to the metal bars. Before Carrie knew what he was doing, he lifted her sleeve and gave her a shot. The cure. When a female guard returned in the morning for the same routine, Carrie had begged her to give the shot to Lisbeth instead—or Ariella who had started a fever in the middle of the night.

The guard refused.

Carrie didn't know why she had been singled out to receive the cure—whether Greg had weaseled it in, or Jamansky had—but it felt wrong. She was stronger than the others. She'd already received her doses. Now she needed to help them. Strangely, the women in her cell disagreed.

"Don't fight it," Ariella had said. "Be happy, Carrie. This means you'll survive."

But when Headie Eddie showed up after dinner, earlier than the next dose should have been administered, Carrie was ready.

"Carrie Lynne Ashworth?" he called.

She stood, planning out how to grab the syringe and run it to Lisbeth before Eddie could stop her. A ludicrous plan, but Lisbeth was declining more rapidly than Carrie was. Carrie could beg forgiveness later.

But Eddie wasn't holding a syringe. He held a rifle and handcuffs. That had only happened one other time—when Jamansky had visited her.

"Hold out your hands," he ordered.

Confused, Carrie obeyed.

Headie Eddie clapped handcuffs on her and then rattled his keys as he unlocked their cell door for the first time in thirty-six hours.

"Hey, Baldy," Crazy Marge called. "Where are you taking the golden-haired one?"

"Away," Eddie said.

"Away?" Carrie repeated.

His eyes went to her and he flashed her the tiniest smile. "I believe you're going home."

Carrie's knees gave way. She grabbed the bars with her bound hands. "What?"

"She's going home?" Crazy Marge said.

It didn't seem possible, yet her hopes flared anyway. But the second she glanced over her shoulder, guilt replaced any hope she'd felt. Her cellmates watched her with long, empty faces. Lisbeth lay on the bed Donnelle had occupied before, pale and drawn.

"Don't come back," Ariella said with a tiny wave goodbye.

Carrie could have said something to her cellmates—should have said anything—but everything felt inadequate.

Silently, she followed Headie Eddie past the rows of cells. Women hung out of the bars, watching them, probably wondering why the two-day lockdown didn't apply to her.

Carrie's thoughts were too preoccupied to notice much.

Who had come for her?

Her heart beat so quickly it hurt. She wanted it to be Greg, wanted to see him more than anything in the world, wanted to believe he wasn't locked up in a prison of his own, but Jamansky told her that he would be back for her.

Still.

They left the main area and headed down a hallway. The hallway looked different than the one in which Jamansky had visited. A sign above the last door read, *Exit.* For some reason, that solidified it.

She was leaving.

She was going home.

Suddenly, she had a new goal, more pressing than saving her new friends or her own survival. She had to free Amber and Zach—the only thing that would make leaving the others behind bearable.

They went through a last secured door, and David Jamansky came into view.

Jamansky. Not Greg. The euphoria of leaving kept her disappointment at bay. She would see Greg soon. Hopefully.

Glancing their direction, Jamansky gave Carrie no greeting, physical or verbal, as if he had come as patrol chief only and not the "friend" he claimed to be. If anything, he looked angry as he stood at the same counter Carrie had when she'd first arrived, talking to the same guard who claimed they didn't have room for her. He signed paper after paper—her paperwork—while she and Headie Eddie waited in the lobby.

The world spun. She had to lean against the nearest wall to keep from falling.

She was going home.

Why her? Why, when his precinct had arrested thousands of others, had he saved *her*?

Carrie's throat burned.

Her gaze went to the glass doors that led to the outside world. Soon she would be reunited with May and CJ, Terrell, Dylan, Sasha, and everyone else. Well, not everyone. Not Amber and Zach, and maybe not even...

She closed her eyes, willing Greg to be the first one she saw. Jamansky had lied about Greg's arrest. He was wrong. She needed Greg's help to free her siblings. She needed him to hold her and tell her it would all be okay, that he'd already come up with a plan.

Greg.

Jamansky chatted easily with the guard as he signed a dozen papers. Carrie studied the three gold bands on his arm signifying his upper rank. Maybe he could help her free Amber and Zach, too. Though she didn't know how to ask. Already she was indebted to him beyond belief.

With a last paper signed, Jamansky turned and gave Headie Eddie the signal. Eddie pulled out his keys and released her handcuffs.

"Do I get my clothes back?" she asked the guard, rubbing her wrists.

"They burn inmates' clothes upon arrival," Headie Eddie said. "This uniform is your souvenir."

He smiled.

She didn't.

Her blue blouse, her *mom's* blue blouse—and Greg's favorite—burned. She told herself it didn't matter, but she loved the way Greg looked at her when she wore it. After everything, a stupid blouse didn't matter one bit. And yet it was just another piece of her mother—and Greg—gone.

"I'll take her from here," Jamansky said, striding toward them. He took Carrie's arm roughly and said, "Let's go."

His cold greeting startled her, but she moved toward him.

"Good luck," Headie Eddie called.

Fear spread through her as Jamansky marched her toward the glass doors. For all she knew, the tall blond could be taking her some place worse, a prison of his own if he wanted. His hand gripped her upper arm painfully. For the first time, he looked like what he was: her enemy.

They stepped outside into the blinding sun. She blinked a dozen times, desperate to see where he was taking her.

"Play along," he whispered out of the side of his mouth. "I'll release you once we get to my car."

Her gaze flickered sideways as they crossed the parking lot. He needed her to look scared. She told herself to relax. Maybe he'd told them he was transferring her to another prison. Still, she couldn't help but feel like an animal being dragged away to the slaughter house.

When they neared his car, his grip loosened on her arm. "Sorry about that. You're illegal again now, so I had to make a good show."

Her arm throbbed from where he'd gripped her, but she nodded.

"Your coloring is better today," he said, studying her face in the bright sun. "You had me worried there before. Did they give you the medicine I sent in?"

"You sent it?" she asked softly.

"Of course."

Her emotions swirled inside. Donnelle, Lisbeth, and countless others would never walk back out of that work camp.

"David," she said, "I'm not sure what to say or how to thank you for—"

"No need. You don't deserve what Oliver did to you. Let's get you out of here."

He opened the passenger door for her, but she hesitated to get in. The interior of his car looked so clean and nice. Not only was she *not* clean, but the stench of her prison cell had surely attached itself to her uniform, skin, and hair. At least he was offering the seat in front of the metal grate. But she still hesitated.

"What's wrong?" he said.

"Nothing."

Gingerly she sat, trying to keep as much of herself off the seat as possible. When he turned on the car and the cold, air-conditioned air blew on her, she pointed it away to keep her smell from blowing around. Then she stared down at her dirty hands, letting the full reality of everything sink in. She was leaving. She was free. Within the hour, she would be home.

"By the way," he said as he pulled out of the parking lot, "I found out where they put your sister and brother."

Her breath caught. "You did?"

"Yeah. Amber is in Bristol, and they put Zachary in DeKalb."

That pushed her over the edge. She hadn't even asked him to look or told him they'd been taken or anything.

Tears welled up in her eyes. Now she knew where to find them. It still pained her that they weren't together, but the fact that she knew where they were solved her first hurdle. Being their sister and guardian, they would have to let her visit them, wouldn't they? Then again, she wasn't legal anymore, plunging her back into a life of hiding in the shadows. Unless she wanted to wind up back in Rochelle, she would have to find another way.

And her house…

She dreaded how lonely and empty it would be without them. No Zach hogging the bathroom. No Amber yelling at the door. The house across the street might be just as empty, and where was the remedy for that?

A deep ache spread through her for those she'd lost and for those she'd left behind. She lay back against the seat, no longer caring about spreading the smell.

Amber was in Bristol.

Zach was in DeKalb.

And Greg…was somewhere.

She nearly challenged Jamansky about Greg's arrest, but she couldn't trust anything Jamansky said anyway. So she decided to go to Greg's house first, even before her own. If he was gone, if he truly had been arrested, she would find Richard and find out how it had happened. It couldn't be Oliver's revenge. Obviously that had been a lie. But the feds could have easily found out Greg was alive and hiding. Or maybe Greg had gone looking for her and had been caught. That would give her three people to free. An overwhelming prospect.

No, she insisted. Greg was home.

He had to be.

The two of them would free Zach and Amber—somehow—and this whole thing would be a distant nightmare. Within the warmth of Greg's arms, she would forget every sight, every smell, and every horror of Rochelle.

Amber, Bristol.

Zach, DeKalb.

Greg, home.

She was only half paying attention to the road when she saw a sign for Highway 47. Sitting up, she looked around. It had been six years since she had driven on Highway 47, but she knew it well enough to know that Jamansky was going the wrong way.

"Where are we going?" she said. "Shelton is north of here."

He glanced over at her. "My house."

"What?"

He nodded. "Yeah. You're staying with me for a few days while I get everything settled."

Carrie's heart stopped.

thirty-four

"I...I thought you were taking me home," Carrie stuttered.

"Oh, I will," Jamansky said. "Eventually. But my house is closer to where Zach and Amber are being held. You can stay with me until I free them."

So much was packed into those few words that it took her a stunned second to catch the most important ones.

"You're going to free Amber and Zach?" she asked.

"Of course. What did you think I would do? Leave them to rot?" He shook his head in disgust. "Oliver might be that cruel, but I'm not. I've already started their paperwork. I should have them out in two or three days."

Two or three days. Her breathing sped up. They would all be together again in two or three days.

He laid his hand on hers. "I told you, Carrie. Give me a few days and everything will be as it should be."

She should have thanked him again, but his hand closed around hers, warm and oppressive.

Politely, she slipped free and stared out the window. A few days felt like an eternity still, and yet it was eternally better than never seeing Amber and Zach again.

It all sounded so wonderful—too wonderful, if she was being honest.

Why was Jamansky helping her?

It couldn't be out of the goodness of his heart because she barely knew him—and he'd never even met her siblings. Plus his heart didn't exactly have a reputation for generosity.

Trees and boarded-up buildings flew by, reminding her that, with each passing mile, they drove farther from Shelton.

From home.

"David," she said, "I can't even express how thankful I am for your help. It's just that…"

"You're welcome," he said easily.

He was taking her to his house where she would stay with him for two days. Two or three.

Panic filled her.

"My friends will be worried about me and my siblings. I need to let them know what has happened. Not to mention, I'd feel more comfortable in my own home." The understatement of the century. "So I think…I think you should take me home."

"You lost your home, remember?"

"I know, but I can still—"

"Look, Carrie, I'm taking personal time to do this for you. You probably don't know how expensive fuel is right now, but the feds won't cover these miles. I'm not even scheduled to be in Shelton until later this week, so taking you to my house will simplify everything. It will save me from driving unnecessary and expensive miles. Don't you want to be there when your siblings are released?"

"Yes, but…" More of Illinois raced by. "Maybe my grandparents can pay you for the extra fuel."

"Grandparents?" He turned. "The Trentons are your grandparents?"

Hearing the name of another loved one on his tongue made her cringe.

"No. They're…well, they're…" *Broke,* she realized. CJ couldn't reimburse Jamansky for the extra miles because Giordano had slid his greedy hand into her pocket and stolen their money. "They're just friends, but I'd feel so much better if—"

"A few days won't kill anyone, Carrie. Besides…" His ice-blue eyes flickered to her. "I have your medicine at my house. You're due for another dose in an hour, so just clean up and rest while I figure out how to get your siblings out. Then I'll return the three of you together, happy and healthy. No need to make your friends worry about your brother and sister when I have everything under control."

"But—"

"It's done, Carrie," he said firmly. "And don't feel like you're putting me out either. I have plenty of room at my house." He smiled. "My bed is plenty big for the both of us."

She felt the blood drain from her face. "What?"

He laughed, a jarring sound to her tensed bones. "Geez, you look like you've seen a ghost. Obviously, I'll take the couch. You can have my bed. Come on, it will be fine."

The car started to squeeze in around her, suffocating her. Her gaze went to the speedometer. He was pushing sixty miles an hour, too fast for her to jump.

"David…" Her throat constricted. "I need to go home. Please."

His hands tightened on the steering wheel. "Tell you what. If I have time tomorrow, I'll drive to your neighborhood and let that Richard guy know you're okay. I'm scheduled to make rounds farther north, but I'll stop by at the end of my shift. That way the fuel is covered, and they'll know you're safe."

Clasping her hands tightly in her lap, she decided that was good enough. If he told Richard what was happening, they could stop worrying about them. Or Greg would come charging after her.

Either way.

"Okay," she whispered.

The world passed by at an alarming speed until he finally slowed. He turned down a side street and into a neighborhood that looked like someone had taken a white, one-story home and stamped it forty times down the street. Home after home, exactly the same. She watched them pass, wondering which cloned house was Oliver's. She missed her quiet, loyal, honest friend.

"Here's the deal," Jamansky said. "You're still illegal, and everyone in this neighborhood works for the government. I shouldn't have to tell you to stay out of sight. I won't be able to get you out of prison a second time."

Nodding, she crouched down a little in her seat. The neighborhood looked dead, but it was the middle of the day. Everyone was probably working.

Deep within the neighborhood, Jamansky pulled into a driveway. He pushed a button to open his garage. Once inside, he shut it again before turning off the car. The cold air stopped. The whir of the engine silenced.

Everything went still as she stared at the inside of his garage. It was dark, and crowded with piles of things.

Jamansky walked around the car and opened her door. She still couldn't bring herself to leave. Not only was she physically and emotionally drained, but this home hadn't been part of her plan. Not even a remote possibility.

For Amber and Zach, she told herself. *Just a few days.*

He held out a hand to her. "Need help standing?"

Pretending not to see his offered hand, she dragged herself out of the car and followed him inside of his home. Even before she reached the door, she heard loud barking on the other side.

"Hope you like dogs," Jamansky said.

The second he opened the door, two large dogs climbed up him. German Shepherds. Carrie stopped cold, realizing what those dogs were.

Patrol dogs.

Those dogs raided people's homes and dragged them from their beds.

"Sitz," Jamansky ordered. "Let her come inside and then you can meet her. *Sitz,* you little brats. Come on."

Both dropped to their haunches but continued to bark like crazy.

Carrie shrank back into the garage.

He grabbed their collars and dragged them a few feet away from the door. "That's enough, boys. Quiet down. There you go. Come on in, Carrie."

With great effort, she entered Jamansky's home.

"This is Bretton and Felix," he said, patting their massive brown and black backs. "Best dogs in the world. Best friends, too. Here. Give me your hand and I'll introduce you. Don't be scared. They're just a bunch of big babies."

Definitely big. Not so much babies.

They continued to snarl at her.

Jamansky grabbed her hand and held it out to his huge beasts like a dinner offering.

"Freund," he said to them. *"Freund."*

Her heart pounded as both dogs sniffed her palm with their wet muzzles. Their tails wagged like crazy, and not in the happy way. They seemed agitated, probably remembering her smell from their years of hunting her. She tried to retract her hand, but Jamansky held tight.

"Freund," he kept saying.

Their inch-long fangs could break skin and crush bones. She braced herself for it, but after an agonizing minute both dogs sat back, no longer anxious to rip her arms off.

"There." Jamansky straightened. "Now you're friends. Let's get you some food, boys. Did you miss me?"

Jumping up, his dogs followed him into his kitchen. He flipped on light switches as he went as if it was the most natural thing to do. While he cared for his dogs, Carrie stayed rooted inside the door, taking it all in.

Jamansky's house looked strange, almost foreign. A black leather couch sat positioned in front of a large TV. Beautifully bound books lined tall bookshelves. Pictures dotted the room in various metal frames. Rugs. Curtains. Lamps and tables. Nothing strange in and of itself except for the fact that Jamansky had things, like Carrie's family once had before the Collapse—like *everyone* had before the Collapse. His home wasn't large. Hers was probably triple its size, but hers stood virtually empty. That difference left her feeling claustrophobic.

"Want something to drink?" Jamansky called from the kitchen.

She shook her head.

The odd, eerie feeling went beyond the number of items because his things didn't match. One lamp was tall and ornately carved. Another was short and modern in design. The black leather sofa sat next to a brown fabric recliner. Maybe he'd had all those things before the Collapse. But from where she stood, it seemed like he'd benefited handsomely from the hundreds of raids he'd performed over the years. This room—his entire house—felt like a shrine to the downfall of Illinois.

Jamansky came back to her, holding a mug of coffee. "Here you go."

She stared at the coffee, yet another foreign thing.

"It's decaf. Or I have soda or milk, if you prefer. Or..." he added when she still hadn't touched it, "a glass of wine? What sounds good?"

"I'm fine," she said softly. "Thank you."

Her gaze fell on an elaborate Chinese vase in the corner of the room, at least two and a half feet tall. A blue dragon snaked its way in and around the intricate carvings. It was gorgeous, the kind of vase that probably cost thousands of dollars for some world traveler to ship home. As she stared at it, she wondered if Jamansky had been the one who stole her great-great-grandmother's porcelain doll that no longer sat beside her mattress.

His eyes narrowed. "What's wrong?"

Flushing, she said, "You have a nice house."

"Yeah, it's alright. Now that I'm patrol chief, they're supposed to give me a bigger house, but you know how the government works. Slow and stupid. By the way, that's my sister. She's...well..." He ran a hand over his short, blond hair. "She's my sister."

Carrie refocused to where he thought she'd been looking. A large frame sat on one of the end tables next to the vase. Jamansky had his arm around a beautiful blonde, but Carrie knew that it wasn't his sister. It was his girlfriend.

Ashlee Lyon.

The photo seemed to have been taken at some kind of party. Jamansky held a drink in one hand and had his other hand on the small of Ashlee's back in a very un-brotherly way. Carrie hated how easily the lies rolled off his tongue, but she didn't challenge him on it. She wasn't even supposed to know Ashlee.

"She's beautiful," she said. *And surprisingly happy,* she thought, studying Ashlee's face. A far cry from the red splotches she'd had when she had shown up on Carrie's porch.

His jaw clenched. He hadn't liked that comment, but he shook it off and motioned to the couch. "Have a seat. You must be exhausted."

"No thanks."

"Right. You probably want to clean up first."

"No, I'm fine. Thank you, though."

He bent down to peer at her. "Carrie, take a breather. Relax. You've been through a huge, traumatic event, but it's over. You're safe now."

That depended on his definition of *safe.* Then again, she couldn't exactly stay two feet inside of his home, cemented there for the next forty-eight hours.

"Sorry," she said. "I just..."

His eyes softened. "I know. How about a hot shower? You'll feel a hundred times better after a nice, hot shower. My house is yours now, so whatever you need, just ask. Speaking of which, I have some stuff for you."

He left her to retrieve a small bundle from the table. "Here. Hope they fit."

He held a pile of clothing toward her. A hot pink tank top sat on top of beige shorts. A bright blue spaghetti strap poked out of somewhere in the middle, along with other unmentionables. At the bottom were folded-up items of deep red satin. Red satin pajamas? Suddenly she loved her orange uniform. She wanted nothing more than to spend the rest of her life in her putrid, ugly, orange tent.

"Come on," he said. "They're yours now. Take them."

She pawed through the pile lamely. The clothes were nothing like her own style—if she even had a style—but the bright, flashy colors screamed of someone else. Ashlee's face flashed in Carrie's mind once again. Jamansky had stolen her clothes.

Carrie suddenly felt like little Jonah Kovach, on the verge of a toddler meltdown. She wanted her mom's blue blouse back and her dad's ratty old sweats for pajamas. She wanted her un-lit house with its ripped couch and empty floors. She wanted her siblings back. She wanted Greg back.

She just wanted to go home.

"You'll definitely feel better after a hot shower," he said. "Come on. I'll show you where the bathroom is."

Reluctantly, she followed.

His bathroom was filled with more mismatched items. He opened the closet and cupboards, showing her things as he went. "Towels are here, along with shampoo and razors. Use whatever you want. I have plenty."

When he finished, he flashed her another smile. "Enjoy."

Then he shut the door behind him.

She locked the door and stood there for a long minute, trying to come to grips with it all. Two or three days, and then she would have everyone back that she loved.

Dropping Ashlee's clothes on the counter, she slid down to the floor and wrapped her arms around her legs.

thirty-five

"I'm coming with you and Isabel," Richard said, trying to keep up with Greg as he grabbed things from his bedroom.

"Not this time," Greg said.

Greg peeled off his lucky UNC shirt—a lot of luck it had given him—and tossed it in the corner. Then he searched for his work shirt in the "to wash" pile. He usually reserved that one for digging wells. It was stained and stiff with mud which made it perfect for where he was headed. He hadn't shaved in two days which wasn't long enough to complete the homeless rebel ensemble, but his long, shaggy hair would have to—

Richard gasped.

"What?" Greg said, looking over his shoulder.

Underneath his goatee, Richard's mouth had fallen into a silent, horrified, "Oh."

Greg's back.

In his haste, he had forgotten to turn away.

"I'm, uh…" Richard looked a little sick. "I'm glad your mother never saw those scars."

Greg, too.

"What's that one?" Richard said, pointing to his shoulder. "Is that a star?"

Greg looked over the side of his shoulder to where a single star was crossed out in the middle of a circle. "Crossed-out star. A traitor's brand. It hurt a lot more than the ones on my back."

Ironically, it had become the symbol of the rebellion. He'd seen huge paintings of it on a few buildings on the way to Rockford. But even more disturbing was that Isabel had an identical brand on her shoulder, only hers was self-inflicted so she could "blend-in" with the rebels. Which only proved how crazy she and McCormick were. And Greg had just agreed to help them.

He pulled on his work shirt and grabbed Carrie's weather journal, shoving it into his back pocket, along with a few syringes of medicine he could fit, should she need them.

"Where's that pistol?" he asked.

"Back in Ferris." Richard rubbed his jaw, still dazed. "CJ has it."

Figured.

"Keep it," Greg said. "Tell everybody what happened, then work on finding Amber and Zach from your end. I'll call every place I can. Oh, and if you see Jamansky, shoot him."

He started for the stairs but double backed to grab one last thing. His slingshot. Then he flew down the stairs two at a time.

"When will you be back?" Richard called.

"Not until I have Carrie."

Isabel had originally parked near the front of the subdivision to keep from scaring anybody. Little did she know that there weren't any people left to scare. By the time he burst out of his house, she was waiting in her car in Greg's driveway.

Instead of heading to the passenger's side, he opened the driver's door.

Startled, she looked up. "What are you doing?"

"I'll drive," he said.

"What?"

Unlike all the patrol cars he'd seen—dark green and boring—Isabel drove a bright red sports car that was as ostentatious as she was. Besides his itch to drive again, to feel the power of a machine beneath him, he doubted Isabel would test this car's limits. He could be to McCormick, Kearney, *and* the women's camp in an hour's time.

"Out," he said. "I'm drivin'."

Her dark brows lowered. "Nice try. Did you bring something to sit on? Man, you're disgusting. Uncle Charlie won't want you sitting on his nice seats. "

"It's his car? Then I'm definitely driving."

"Just get in," she growled. "You're wasting time."

Greg ran around and slid into the air-conditioned car. His thoughts raced as they left the neighborhood, yet Isabel pulled onto the main road going a nice, leisurely, Sunday-driver pace.

"You're killin' me here," Greg said. "Speed up."

She smiled. "I've missed you, Pierce."

"I bet. Where's your phone?"

Greg started at the top of the list. Isabel didn't have any numbers for the prisons. Apparently, basic women's work camps were below the level of criminals she dealt with. So for each place, he had to call information, get the number, then run through the red tape to talk to the person with the list of inmates. It took an aggravatingly long time. The only upside was that Isabel's caller ID must have still shown up as something official—and intimidating—since nobody questioned Greg or why he needed the information.

Crystal Lake. Montgomery. Rochelle. Aurora. Sycamore. When all of those turned up empty, Isabel helped him brainstorm more places. Wheaton. Even Joliet. With each place, Greg's anxiety upped. He even called Rockford just in case Richard had been wrong before.

Nothing.

He had two women's camps left when Isabel said, "I need the phone for a minute."

"Hold on," Greg said. "I've got two more."

She yanked it from him. "Just let me tell McCormick that we're close. Besides, you're getting belligerent. That last guy sounded close to tears by the time you were done with him. It's not nice to yell at strangers, you know."

Greg took several calming breaths as Isabel called McCormick. He still had two more chances. But when Isabel finished, those came up empty as well. Out of ideas, he did the only thing he could think of.

He called David Jamansky.

A woman answered. "Kane County Patrol Offices. Can I help you?"

"I need to speak with Chief Jamansky," Greg said. "Now."

"May I tell him who's calling?"

Greg had several snide responses, but Isabel chimed up first. "This is Lieutenant Ryan," she said from her side of the car.

"And Greg Pierce," Greg added for good measure.

Let Jamansky stew on that.

"Yes. Of course," the woman said. "One moment."

The line went quiet for a few minutes. When it clicked back on, it was the woman again.

"I'm sorry, but Chief Jamansky isn't available right now. He's out for the evening. May I take a message?"

Greg's blood pressure shot through the roof. "Sure. You tell that low-life scumbag that—"

Isabel grabbed the phone from him, cutting him off. "What's your name?" She paused. "Fine. When will Chief Jamansky be available, Ellen?" She listened another moment and shot Greg a worried look. "Is that so? For how long?"

Greg wanted to pound something.

"Well, how about this, Ellen," Isabel said. "I don't care what kind of vacation he's supposedly on, but you will find a way to get ahold of him. Tell him that the information he gave Mr. Pierce about Rockford is inaccurate. If he doesn't correct that information by the end of tomorrow, his career—and yours—are over. Is that clear, Ellen dearest?"

"Tomorrow?" Greg snapped.

Isabel held up a finger. "Yes, just have him call this number."

When she clicked off, she gave Greg a pitying look. "It's already seven o'clock. Today's almost over. Supposedly Jamansky is scheduled to be out of the office for the next week. But he'll call tomorrow and then you'll know."

"Right," Greg muttered. "Tomorrow. When he'll feed me the next lie."

"Maybe McCormick will have ideas. There are other ways to find Carrie. Don't worry."

Easy for her to say.

As they reached Naperville, Isabel pulled into a neighborhood that looked like Greg had stepped back seven years in time: large, beautiful homes, manicured lawns, even cars—normal cars—dotted the driveways. President Rigsby paid his cronies well.

For the briefest second, Greg wished he'd stayed in his position. Maybe then none of this would have happened.

McCormick stood on his front porch, arms folded, waiting for them. Greg had never seen the commander wear anything but his all-black uniform littered with medals. Now that he'd quit his job, he wore jeans and a button-down shirt. Starting down the sidewalk, the middle-aged man them in the driveway.

As Greg stepped out of the car, McCormick held out a hand to shake.

"It appears that you aren't as dead as I was led to believe, Pierce. It's good to see you again."

Greg didn't return the sentiment. Instead, he said, "Sorry to hear about your wife, sir."

That seemed to diminish the commander's good spirits. "So am I. Let's get to it. What has Lieutenant Ryan told you?"

"Not much."

"Then we have lots to cover. Come on inside."

thirty-six

Carrie couldn't bring herself to take a hot shower. Oddly, she craved her bucket of freezing water at home. So she settled on a cold shower. It soothed her as much as anything could.

Once clean, she fumbled through Ashlee's clothes for something that would cover her up. It seemed like Jamansky had picked the skankiest of Ashlee's clothing. The hot pink tank top dipped too low. The beige shorts rode too high. Sadly, the red satin pajamas covered her best. That convinced her to wash her orange tent in the tub. She had nothing but shampoo to clean the heavy, ugly fabric, but she scrubbed away, taking her time. Then she rung her uniform out and hung it up to dry. Regardless of what Jamansky had "scrounged up" for her, she would be wearing orange tomorrow.

Once the bathtub finished draining, she heard a muffled conversation in the other room. It jumpstarted her heart until she realized Jamansky was just watching television. Out of ways to stall, she opened the door and slipped silently out.

He had changed out of his green patrol uniform into jeans and a white t-shirt. On the black, leather couch, he sat with one arm propped up on the back, watching a movie with his dogs sprawled out next to him. The second she opened the door, their heads lifted and they stared her down.

Jamansky lifted the remote and paused the show.

"Wow, Carrie, you look…" His eyes roamed over her: wet hair, red satin whatever, bare legs. "You look great. I bet you feel a hundred times better."

I did, she thought, skin crawling.

"You know, you don't have to turn off the water in between washing up. I have plenty of water here, so just leave it running while you shower, okay?"

He had listened to her shower?

His house felt smaller.

"Here." Swatting his dogs out of the way, he patted the empty spot. "I was just starting a movie. Curl up and relax. It might help you get your mind on"—he smiled—"something else."

"Actually," she said, tucking a wet lock behind her ear, "I think I'll turn in for the night, if you don't mind."

"It's barely eight."

She looked out the back window. The sun still had another hour before setting. "I know, but I've slept on a hard cement floor the last four days. I'm exhausted. I wouldn't be able to stay awake through a movie. I'd probably fall asleep in the first five minutes."

"I won't mind. In fact, I'll tell you how the movie ends right now. The guy gets the girl. Big surprise, right?"

Every word out of his mouth made it worse.

"Seriously," she pressed. "I'm just tired. Really, very, incredibly tired. I'm sorry."

Sighing, he set the remote aside and joined her near the bathroom door, standing close enough for his potent aftershave to assault her nostrils.

"You'll like my bed," he said. "It's super soft."

"No, David. I don't want to kick you out of your room. I can sleep on"—she was about to say the couch, but he seemed dead-set on his movie—"the floor."

He rolled his eyes. "It's either my bed or the couch, and if you crash on the couch, I'll just carry you back to my bed anyway, so you might as well give in. Unless you want to change your mind about the movie…?"

Begrudgingly she followed him through the dark hallway.

He stopped in his bedroom door, blocking it. "I bet you're starving," he said suddenly. "I can make my famous beef stroganoff in less than twenty minutes. Then you can sleep on a full stomach."

"No. I ate earlier."

Plus, she had no appetite.

"How about a massage then? You're so tense."

Before she could decline, his hands were on her shoulders, rubbing away. She twisted out of his grasp, ready to lock herself in the bathroom again.

"No," she squeaked. "All I need is sleep." And maybe a crowbar. Possibly a gun. "But thank you."

"Oh. We forgot your shot. Wait here."

He came back with a small syringe. "Which arm?" he asked.

"I can do it."

"No. Allow me."

Taking an alcohol swab, he pushed up her red, satin sleeve and began wiping her upper arm with slow, gentle circles. His eyes kept flickering to her with a smile.

Heat crept up her neck. Why was he acting like this? She was nothing like Ashlee—who seemed more his type. She barely knew him. She kept giving him hints that she wanted nothing to do with him, yet he wouldn't back off.

Finally he pushed the needle in. A bite of pain stabbed the injection site, but she rubbed it away.

"Great. Thank you. Goodnight, David."

"Goodnight," he said. "By the way, I work bright and early, so I'll be gone most of the day. I'll pop back here throughout to check on you. Keep the curtains drawn and don't go out. We can't have anyone seeing you."

She nodded, trying to mask her relief that he would be gone.

"I'll check on your siblings after my last meeting," he said. "Make sure everything is in place to get them out. I should be back by six-ish, and *then* I will make some stroganoff that you'll never forget."

"And you'll stop by Logan Pond?" she asked. At his confused look, she added, "You said you would let my friends know where I am."

"Yes. Of course. Tomorrow afternoon."

She stared at him. He wasn't going to stop by. They wouldn't know where she was or what had happened.

"Can I come with you?" she asked suddenly. "I know you have to work, but I could wait in the car or—"

"Not a good idea, Carrie."

"But nobody will see me. I can stay out of sight."

He gave her a condescending look. "You're illegal now, Carrie. It's too risky."

248

"But—"

"I said no!" he barked. As soon as he said it, he seemed to back down. "Sorry. I know you're anxious to see your brother and sister, but we can't get careless now. However…that gives me an idea." He strode into the front room and came back with a small camera. "What if we show your siblings a picture of you and I together so they know they can trust me? Here."

His arm went around her shoulders and pulled her tight against him. Nestling his chin in her wet hair, he whispered something that—even with her bad ear—sounded like, "You smell amazing."

Cringing, Carrie tried to pull back, needing space, but he cinched her close, held the camera far enough out to capture both of them, and said, "Smile!"

Her smile didn't come easily, but she tried for Zach and Amber's sake. They needed to see that Jamansky could do it.

He could free them all.

As he checked the picture, he nodded, pleased. "Yes. This will do perfectly."

Before he could come up with another excuse to keep her, she told him goodnight and shut the door. His bedroom didn't have a lock, so she sank down on the other side, sliding easily in her red silk, and pressed her back against the door.

His room looked like the rest of his house—full, mismatched, and claustrophobic. His bed was massive with a gold and blue comforter that looked anything but welcoming. That convinced her to sleep in the position she'd become accustomed to in prison: on the floor, leaned against a wall.

Two or three days. She just had to get through two or three days.

———◆———

Well after midnight, Greg rubbed his eyes. Hours of talking, and yet all he could think was that Isabel and McCormick had lost their minds.

"They'll never listen to you," Greg insisted. "These rebel groups have been meeting for months tryin' to defeat Rigsby—and *you*, I might add—and now y'all are just gonna waltz in there, tell them you're sorry and you're on their side now? With all due respect, sir, you're nuts."

McCormick sat back on his kitchen chair, looking equally tired. His graying hair lay flat against his head from how many times he'd ran his hand over it.

"They'll listen to you," McCormick said.

"They barely know me," Greg said in exasperation. "Look, I get what you're tryin' to do here, and I wish y'all the best, but"—he stood—"I just can't get involved right now."

Isabel grabbed his arm and yanked him back down. "President Rigsby is going to be here for this rally in five days. We aren't going to have an opportunity like this again, Greg. I know you can get us in to Kearney and the rebels. We need their help to pull this off."

Greg rubbed his forehead, going over it all again.

Only a few people knew about the president's surprise visit to the troops in Naperville's training facility, and all of those were high-ups like Commander McCormick. Apparently, President Rigsby wanted to motivate his new "army" and turn the tide back in their favor. Because the rally was at the training grounds, on McCormick's turf, the commander felt confident they could take him out.

It might work. It could.

If they had months to plan and Kearney agreed to help.

Then again, hundreds of innocent trainees—many younger than Greg—would be within striking distance.

"You can only target Rigsby and his advisors," Greg said. "Nobody else."

"Obviously," McCormick said sourly. "Those are *my* troops out there, not his. We'll strike before the rally ever starts, before Rigsby reaches the stage. I have home court advantage here. I know exactly where they'll bring the president in, who's on security detail, and where to hit."

"It's a good plan, sir," Greg relented. "Except it'll take you three days just to convince Kearney to listen. Then what?"

"We don't have that long!" McCormick snapped.

"Notice how he used the word *we*," Isabel added with a pointed look. "You should start using it, too."

Greg stared down at the fancy kitchen table, feeling the exhaustion wearing him down.

"Look, Pierce," McCormick said, "I don't want to threaten you, but I will if I have to. Every day we wait, people are dying. We need your help to stop Rigsby, and we don't have time to deal with your bull."

So they would turn him in after all, tell the government he'd run from his post. McCormick and Isabel hadn't run. They'd quit their jobs.

He wanted to fight back, but after dealing with Jamansky, he understood the power of desperation.

He scanned McCormick's spacious home. Pictures of his late wife dotted every corner. Even the furnishings and cheerful yellow paint spoke of a woman's touch—a woman who no longer lived because of a single man, the president of the United States.

Greg sat back, thinking about Oliver and Carrie. Amber and Zach. Desperation and despair. He needed to help them.

But...

What about the rest? The millions of Americans who had been turned into virtual slaves because of Rigsby's "emergency laws"? Who was watching out for them, trying to release *them* before they ended up in graves?

People were dying every day.

How was it fair for him to limit his circle of concern to the four people who mattered most to him? By helping McCormick, Greg could possibly save *a lot* more people. Thousands more, maybe millions. Even if he only saved one hundred people, or a dozen, at what point would it be worth it?

He stared out the nearest dark window.

Carrie would tell him to do the right thing. Big blue eyes looking up at him, she would say, *"Doing the right thing is always the right thing to do, regardless of the consequences."*

But he didn't want to.

He wanted to find her.

Even if McCormick's plan worked and they somehow convinced Kearney to help them take down Rigsby's regime, it wouldn't be fast enough. Carrie needed medicine, and she needed it now. After ten failed calls, he would have to visit each work camp and demand to see the list of inmates himself. Carrie hadn't just disappeared. If anything, Isabel and McCormick should be helping him. It had been five days since her arrest. *Five!*

It might already be too late.

His stomach clenched, and his insides turned to stone. That would explain the calls. Nobody could find Carrie because it was already too late.

But he had to know. Because even if it was too late, he had to save her siblings. He owed her that much. That was what she would want him to do. Amber and Zach. *And* Oliver.

No. It wasn't what she would want.

Not fully.

"It's the right thing to do, Greg." He could practically hear her gentle voice whisper it to him, a woman who never put her own wants above another. Regardless of the consequences.

His shoulders slumped. He knew he had to help McCormick—and in turn, what he could of America. The faster he did, the faster he could search for Carrie.

That still didn't solve their first huge, insurmountable hurdle—how to convince Kearney and the rebel leaders to trust Greg a second time. Not just trust him, but trust the two people who had sent him into the heart of the rebellion to destroy it.

He ran both hands over his scruffy hair, feeling brain dead.

"Who's runnin' the show in the Special Patrols Unit now?" he asked.

"No one yet," McCormick said. "But I'm guessing Rigsby will appoint a new commander when he comes. Probably Steiner—a hothead, with little military experience. Steiner has been kissing up to Rigsby for a while, posturing for a position like this. The guy has no morals whatsoever."

"He and the president should get along well," Isabel noted dryly.

"To be frank," McCormick said, "part of why we need to move quickly on this is because Rigsby will be gunning for my head once he shows up. I've tried to keep my resignation quiet, but he's going to find out soon—if he hasn't already. People don't leave his organization without..."

"Punishment?" Greg guessed.

Based on McCormick's expression, it would be a stiff one.

"Just tell him, Uncle Charlie," Isabel said.

McCormick clasped his hands on the table. "They've scheduled an execution as part of Rigsby's speech. Traitors and enemies of the state will be tried and executed for committing high treason against America."

Greg went cold. "He's having an execution?"

"A public one," Isabel said. "Broadcast around the whole country— maybe beyond. Isn't that lovely?"

Greg felt sick, though he shouldn't have been surprised. Typical Rigsby strategy. Kill those who oppose him. Might as well do it publicly and scare a few more million people into submission.

"Call me crazy," McCormick said, "but I'd rather not end up on that list."

If President Rigsby was executing all who went against him, there would be nobody left for him to rule over.

Greg's head snapped up with a sudden idea. "The cure."

McCormick gave him a strange look. "What do you mean?"

"Sir," Greg said, sitting forward, "what does every illegal want right now? Where is Rigsby hitting us hardest? Whenever people get in his way, he kills them off." Greg pulled out one of the syringes he'd saved for Carrie. "What if you take the cure to the rebels? What if you take loads of it—trucks full of it? Show that you're on their side and you want to save them from Rigsby. That'll get you into Kearney's group faster than anything I can do."

Isabel took the small syringe from him, fingering it in her hands. "How do we even know the virus has spread to the rebellion?"

"A week ago, I sat in a hospital so full they were practically putting patients in janitors' closets. And those were the legals. I can guarantee this has spread to West Chicago and beyond. So the real question..." Greg looked between the two of them. "Can you get this cure, and if so, how much?"

McCormick and Isabel glanced at each other, holding a silent conversation.

"It will take time," Isabel said.

"That's something we don't have," McCormick said. "Make the call."

"Now?" Isabel glanced at her watch. "It's after midnight. And how much do you even want?"

"Enough to treat two hundred people," Greg said. "Maybe more."

They both turned in shock.

"Don't tell me you don't have the money for it." Greg waved a hand around McCormick's fancy kitchen. "If two hundred isn't enough, promise Kearney you'll get more."

McCormick chewed his lip, considering. Then he nodded at Isabel. "Make the call."

Setting the syringe down, she grabbed her phone and left the room.

For a time, McCormick and Greg just sat there, thinking, strategizing, and eventually staring at the small, lonely syringe, as if too tired to move. Moving meant implementation, a daunting task.

McCormick finally straightened. "You look like you haven't slept in a month, Pierce. Go crash upstairs while Isabel and I get things in place. Take the bedroom on the right."

Giving in, Greg rose from the table and started for the stairs.

"Hey, Pierce," McCormick called.

Greg turned back.

"Thank you. For the first time," McCormick said, "I feel like we have a real shot at this."

Greg nodded. "The cure alone should be enough to convince Kearney's group to listen to you. Technically y'all don't need me anymore."

It was worth a shot, but his former commander's scowl returned quickly.

"We still need you. *We,* remember? Because if this works, it won't just be the rebels we help. You, your friends, and family." His eyes blazed with intensity. "This could be the catalyst for a return to a civilized society. Don't you want to be a part of it?"

In theory, sure. But in practice, it meant sacrificing his loved ones, possibly forever. That was an awfully high price to pay for an uncertain outcome.

Isabel poked her head in from the hallway. "I bet Uncle Charlie would make a few calls for you, Greg. Maybe he'll even restore your citizenship."

"Citizenship?" Greg said bitterly. "The only citizenship I want back is the real kind. The kind without cards and check-ins."

"That's what we're going for," McCormick said. "So...what will it take for you to stick this out?"

Greg slid his paper onto the kitchen table. "Call these prisons. Ask about Carrie Ashworth. Somebody's not givin' me the full story, and I intend to find out who it is."

thirty-seven

Soft scratching woke up Carrie, something scratching a door.

She rolled over in bed with a long, lazy stretch and caught a whiff of David Jamansky.

She jerked back from the fluffy, white pillow. It reeked of his aftershave. She couldn't even remember lying on his pillow—or his bed, for that matter. Backing up farther, she looked around. She'd fallen asleep next to the door, not tucked under his king-sized, blue and gold comforter.

She jumped out of bed quickly—too quickly—and fell back to let the blood return to her brain. How had she gotten in bed?

Something kept pawing the bedroom door, dogs wanting to be let inside. Other than that, Jamansky's house sounded silent. He said he had to work bright and early, whatever that meant. The clock beside the bed read 6:14 a.m.

Quietly, she made his bed. Black paws appeared beneath the door, trying to reach her. The dogs whined softly, but she didn't let them in.

The sun shone brilliantly through Jamansky's bedroom window, casting a soft glow over his room. She had missed the sun and its promise of something warm and happy ahead. She hoped that, wherever Greg, Amber, and Zach were—and even Crazy Marge—they had a little piece of sunshine, too.

Twenty minutes passed with her staring blankly around his bedroom.

Jamansky's house stayed silent, so she decided to risk it.

Slowly cracking open the door, she slipped out of his room. The dogs met her, tails wagging a thousand miles a minute.

She held a nervous hand out to them. *"Freund,"* she whispered. "Don't eat me. *Freund.*"

Each dog sniffed her hand and thankfully seemed to accept her as something other than breakfast. They followed her down the short hallway.

Peeking around the corner, she saw Jamansky sleeping on the leather couch, mouth wide open in a snore. Still home. She nearly turned back around but decided to grab her orange tent first. Anything to get out of the red satin that belonged to Ashlee and now smelled like Jamansky's aftershave.

But when she entered the bathroom, her orange prison uniform no longer hung over the shower rack. She searched every inch of the small bathroom, behind the door, in the cupboards, even under the sink. Nowhere. Had he washed it? Stolen it? Either way, she had to find something to wear other than—

"Good morning," he said, directly behind her.

Carrie cried out, nearly slipping on the cold tile. "David!" She laid a hand over her racing heart. "You're awake."

"Barely." Yawning, he rubbed his droopy eyes. "I take it you're a morning person. I should have guessed. I bet you always return your shopping cart and send thank you notes, too. So…" He leaned against the bathroom door. "What exactly are you looking for?"

"My uniform," she said, adrenaline still coursing through her veins. "Do you know where it is?"

"I threw it out. That thing was nasty." Without giving her time to protest, he cocked his head and examined her in the red satin pajamas. "Is there a reason you were sleeping on my floor? Something wrong with my bed? You were so exhausted you didn't even stir when I moved you."

She stared at him. Not only had Jamansky checked on her while she slept—which was creepy enough—he'd moved her. Into his bed. She felt like a snake had slithered down her spine.

It was time to set up some boundaries with him. She was a woman who needed clear boundaries. Big, huge, all-encompassing boundaries.

She backed up and ran into a towel rack.

His light eyes locked on her with a smile. "You, Carrie Ashworth, are unlike any other woman I know."

Probably because she wasn't fawning all over him. How many single women did he know anyway?

Two?

The towel rack dug into her shoulder.

Someone else might consider him attractive, but she never could. Not after he'd attacked Mariah, Ashlee, Greg, and probably Oliver. She didn't know why he was helping her, or flirting, or whatever he thought he was doing, but being around him made her feel like she was walking along the edge of a steep cliff. Any moment he could change his mind and push her off.

He reached up and brushed a lock of hair away from her cheek. Feeling his hot fingers made the snake sensation multiply.

"Want some breakfast?" he asked.

"No." She wanted a baseball bat. Even a rusty old pipe would work. "I'm fine."

"Carrie, Carrie, Carrie. What am I going to do with you? Force you to eat, I guess. Come on." As he started for the kitchen, he called, "Pancakes, waffles, or eggs? Choose one or I'll make you eat all three."

"Eggs," she said, picking something familiar.

"Good. Come on in here and keep me company."

Normally she would have offered to help, but she awkwardly leaned against his kitchen counter and watched him work.

He pulled a carton of milk out of the refrigerator—the *refrigerated* refrigerator—and added egg after perfectly white egg to a bowl, different from the muddy-brown eggs Zach's chickens laid. In the same amount of time it took him to find the electric beater with all the attachments, hook the mixer to the electrical socket, and turn it on, she could have beaten the eggs with a fork. But then he turned a knob on the stove, which took far less time than it took to drag in Jeff Kovach's chopped wood— usually green and smoky—try to light it five times with cheap, old government matches, and wait for the fire to burn hot enough to cook.

While he worked, he chatted away about his car, his job, and even himself. She nodded here and there, pretending to listen as his dogs flitted around her. But her thoughts revolved around the twisted turn of events that had landed her in his air-conditioned, over-furnished home.

The unfairness of it sliced like a knife.

How did she deserve to be safe and free instead of Amber and Zach, or Greg and all the women in Rochelle? If she'd just listened to Greg—

or even Jeff Kovach months ago—none of this would have happened. She could have prevented this nightmare. How would Amber and Zach ever forgive her?

How would Greg?

Careless Carrie yet again, but what was her reward? Omelets and a king-sized bed?

"What's wrong?" Jamansky said, glancing over his shoulder.

Her eyes filled, turning him into a watery blur. Because while she felt responsible for so much, some of the blame—or rather, *most* of the blame—rested on him. Clear back with that raid in March, he'd set their clan on a path of destruction. Like dominoes on a table, things kept toppling one after another until there was nothing left.

How dare he make her breakfast? How dare he smile and pretend to care about her after he'd destroyed everything that mattered to her?

How many David Jamansky's were there in the world, destroying people's lives? Who trained them? Why did they get to decide who lived and who died, who could be happy, and who had to live in a hell-like state for the rest of their lives?

"Hey, whoa." He set down the spatula and came to her. "Carrie, hold on. No tears today. Come on."

He reached up to wipe her cheeks, but she flinched back before he could touch her again.

"No tears," he repeated softly. "Because I have good news. I did a little digging last night, and guess what? I can definitely get Zachary out tomorrow morning."

Her watery eyes lifted. "What?"

He smiled. "Tomorrow morning you'll have your brother. Isn't that great?"

It was beyond great. She wiped her cheeks. "And Amber?"

"The place Amber is staying is giving me some grief, but don't worry. We'll have her back soon."

Soon.

She clung to that word. "Thank you, David."

He cocked his head, regarding her with those ice-blue eyes. "Why are you always so surprised when I help you?"

He wouldn't like her answer, so she didn't bother.

"Can I ask you something?" he said, seeming to lean towards her. "Why weren't you home when I came back to see you? "

One of her shoulders lifted.

He stepped closer to her. She backed up into the counter.

"I wanted to make sure you were okay," he said. "I even brought you some Chinese food, but you weren't there. Why? Were you scared of me?"

Her entire clan was. They'd voted against her seeing him. What would he think of that?

Voice lowering to a whisper, he leaned forward another inch. "Are you…still scared of me?"

Her stomach flopped. Definitely scared, but for a new reason. His eyes had a glazed over, dopey kind of look. The kind Greg got sometimes. Right before he kissed her.

"Don't be scared," he whispered. In a motion slow enough to match the speed of her brain, he started to lean down.

"David!" she yelled, twisting out of his reach.

"Carrie," he purred back. Then he moved again. Instead of letting him back her into another corner, she spun into the wide open kitchen.

"David, stop."

"What's wrong?"

"I'm not interested," she said, borrowing Greg's blunt line.

"Interested in what?" He might have pulled off the innocent response if the skin around his eyes hadn't tightened.

He understood well enough.

"I…I'm sorry," she said, "but I'm already involved with someone."

"So am I. Wow, Carrie, you didn't think…" He straightened to his full height. "I'm just trying to help you out. I know you're with that Pierce guy now, right? The one in prison? I'm dating someone, too. Really, Carrie. We're just friends." He smiled again, though it no longer held any kindness.

Before she could respond, he walked back to the stove. "Let's get you some food before you pass out on me."

The second breakfast was over, he left. With a quick shower, he headed out, leaving Carrie alone in his claustrophobic house—or not so alone since he left his dogs with her to keep guard.

She couldn't stand to watch television like he suggested, nor could she bear to read a book. But free time meant thinking, and thinking meant torture. Too many people hurting with no way to help.

So she decided to snoop.

Jamansky kept the curtains drawn in the front room, but through a small crack, she could see his driveway. As long as she could see that crack, she felt comfortable exploring, trying to find out everything she could about David Jamansky.

At first she opened a few cupboards. Then desk drawers. Soon she was digging through anything she could find, checking that crack in the curtain every five seconds. She didn't even know what she was looking for.

She stopped on a small map in his study. It was more than just a map, though. It was a directory of his neighborhood. The front showed every street and home within the government housing, spanning six streets. But the true gold mine lay on the back. Numerically by house number, the directory listed every person in every housing unit with corresponding phone numbers.

She ran her finger down until she found the two she wanted:

Ashlee Lyon.

Oliver Simmons.

Carrie glanced out the crack again. Driveway still empty.

Her pulse raced. Jamansky's dogs didn't care about her snooping around, and apparently Jamansky wasn't in the mood to check on her. She wasn't daring enough to leave and search Oliver or Ashlee's homes, especially since they lived a few streets over, but she was brave enough to try something else.

Crossing the kitchen, she picked up the phone and heard a dial tone for the first time in six years. Another check of the window, and she started dialing. One number after the next.

If Oliver really had moved to Virginia and requested a permanent transfer, he would have taken everything with him. There would be definite signs that he wasn't coming back.

An answering machine came on, and with it, her friend's quiet, nervous voice.

"Hello. This...this is Oliver Simmons. I'm not available right now, but...leave me a message and I'll call back. Uh, thanks."

Heart sinking, she clutched the phone. "Oh, Oliver. What did he do to you?"

With that, she went back to digging, even more desperate to find out everything she could about David Jamansky.

thirty-eight

Jamansky tried to push Carrie's rejection from his mind. Gutsy of her, considering her compromised citizenship. He could end her life with the flick of his wrist.

"I'm not interested." What kind of response was that? Especially because it wasn't true. He could have forced the moment—and almost had—but he enjoyed the chase. She would give in eventually. Her being scared of him just heightened the intrigue. Maybe tonight—or tomorrow after he returned her brother. Her big, blue eyes would overflow with gratitude.

"Oh, thank you for saving my brother, David," she would say, falling into his arms. *"Thank you, thank you!"*

Heading into a meeting with Mayor Phillips didn't improve his mood any. He pushed his way into the mayor's office, clutching the letter with the requested information.

"What are we going to do?" Jamansky asked by way of hello.

Mayor Phillips looked up from sharpening his pencil. "About what?"

"I've been gathering paperwork for two days, and it's not even close. Too many holes." Jamansky dropped into the nearest chair. "Now they're claiming Simmons' affidavit is null and void because of his status. Do you have any idea how much I owe?"

"I'm not sure why you're having issues. They already cleared my list."

"You sent your list already? Why didn't you tell me?"

The mayor inspected the tip of his pin-sharp pencil. "My list was far less substantial than yours. Apparently…I owe nothing."

"Nothing?" He shot to his feet. "I owe an entire year's salary and you owe *nothing*? You backstabbing liar! I said we'd submit together."

The mayor's small, beady eyes lifted. "This whole scheme was your idea. You assured me that every precinct was running things this way and the commissioner wouldn't care. *You* were the one who made the acquisitions and finagled the department transactions, so now it's only fair that you sort it out."

"I see." And Jamansky did. He saw the mayor's whole sordid plan, making his blood pump with fury. "Let's get something straight here, Lucas. You will not throw me under the bus on this one. Am I clear?"

Mayor Phillips set his pencil aside. "Don't forget who sprung who from prison."

"After leaving me rotting in there for a month! You will *not* stab me in the back to save your own skin. If I go down, I'm taking you with me!"

"Off your meds again, are you?"

That did it.

Jamansky stormed around the desk and yanked the mayor up by the collar. He grabbed out his gun and rammed it against the guy's chin.

"Wait!" Mayor Phillips said, hands flying up. "Just wait. Obviously, I'm not dropping the ball. You're better at deciphering the information, that's all. But I'll do whatever digging you want. Actually, I have some good news. I just got a call from Naperville."

Chest heaving, Jamansky glared at him. "What about?"

"Put me down, and I'll tell you."

Jamansky dropped him back onto his chair, but he didn't park his gun. He wanted Mayor Phillips to remember who ran this precinct.

"We're having a special visitor to these parts," the mayor said. "President Rigsby himself is coming to rally the trainees."

"And I care because…?"

"Because he wants a demonstration. He's wanting local convicts sympathetic to the rebel cause. They called asking if I had any ideas—if I knew of any recent arrestees who were traitors of the state."

Jamansky's eyes widened in understanding.

"That's not even the best part," the mayor went on. "They're looking for people to join the firing squad." Smiling, Mayor Phillips nodded. "You're welcome."

As David Jamansky drove to Joliet, he unbuttoned his shirt pocket and pulled out a picture. He set it on his dashboard as he drove.

All was not lost.

Not yet.

The feds had given him two weeks before they would suspend him— or worse. But it might be enough time. And with this newest possibility, he felt like things might work out after all. He couldn't wait to share the good news.

Even before he sat down on his side of the partition, he pressed the newest picture up to the glass.

"Carrie wanted to say hello," he said.

The color drained from Oliver's already-pale face. Personally, Jamansky loved seeing his own arm around Carrie's shoulders, her tucked into his side like she already belonged to him. But the terrified look in her eyes was a nice touch.

In another world, a kinder one maybe, Carrie and Oliver Simmons might have been happy. They were both quiet and reserved. Easy to manipulate. Obviously Greg Pierce had seen those qualities in Carrie, too, and moved in fast.

Jamansky wanted to tack up the same picture in Logan Pond, just to rub it in Pierce's face, but he didn't need the guy breathing down his throat more than he already was. Pierce would be out for blood if he knew where Carrie really was—something Jamansky didn't need. He'd paid the Rochelle guards handsomely to leave his name off of her release forms. Even if Pierce went searching, he couldn't trace her to him.

In three days, Pierce would finish off Oliver Simmons anyway, so there wasn't any point in tormenting him. Once Pierce signed those papers, Oliver would end up in front of a firing squad. Sadly, this picture with Carrie would have to be for Oliver's eyes alone.

Maybe he'd send Pierce the other one—the picture of Carrie in orange. *"Oh, did I say Rockford? I meant Rochelle. No sign of her in Rochelle either? Well, you know how it goes. The government has misplaced another prisoner. I'll keep looking. Don't worry. I'll have her out by the trial."*

263

He had both men right where he wanted them thanks to the lovely—but infuriating—Carrie Ashworth.

Oliver Simmons seemed to shrink on his small stool. He'd started his sentence out as a gangly, balding man. Now he looked shorter, more bent at the shoulders, and he'd lost twenty pounds he didn't have to lose.

Jamansky knew all too well how that felt. The hunger that never ended. The paralyzing defeat of prison.

He couldn't wait for Simmons' execution. A public one, too. Rigsby wanted to make a statement, and statement he would. Jamansky just had to make sure he stood in front of the right prisoner when they handed him the gun.

"Isn't Carrie a vision in red?" he said into the phone. "The satin slides along her soft skin, covering just enough to keep things interesting."

Ignoring that, Oliver squinted to see better. "Where was this taken?"

"That right there"—Jamansky pointed—"is my bed. She's an angel when she sleeps, an absolute vision with her golden hair spilled out over my pillow. Do you even know what she looks like when she sleeps, Simmons?"

Oliver clutched his phone so hard his knuckles turned white. "I thought she was in prison!"

"I got her out. I told you I would. And now she's my little pet." Jamansky stroked her face.

"Why are you doing this?" Oliver whispered.

"The feds called, demanding the first payment. Care to guess how much?" Jamansky's gut clenched. "You should know since you submitted the totals to them."

"What am I supposed to do?" Oliver said. "I signed your affidavit."

"Which is void because of your sentence!"

"Then get me out of here," Oliver said. "I'll do whatever you want, but I can't do anything when I'm stuck in here."

"Oh, yes you can. How much money do you have?"

Oliver's eyes widened. "None. I used all of it to buy Carrie's house."

"Liar!" Jamansky roared. "You have two days to scrounge up some money, or I will personally slit Carrie's throat while she sleeps. Sleep on that tonight, Simmons. I'll be back tomorrow."

thirty-nine

Zach looked down the long row of bunk beds. He'd already counted them twice, but he quickly counted them again. Twelve beds on one side of him. Thirty-four on the other. Counting his own bunk, that made forty-eight beds in his row. The spacious room held three rows which made—he quickly calculated—one hundred-forty-four beds in all. Carrie would be proud of his math. One hundred forty-four beds with one hundred forty-four boys, one hundred forty-three of whom were asleep.

Or so it seemed.

Zach had decided that he would never sleep again. He didn't know how he'd do it or what the Guinness World Record was for going without sleep, but he figured he could make it a good week before he dozed off. Even then, he'd only take ten-minute catnaps in the middle of the night when all the others were sleeping anyway.

If only I'd been this smart the first night, he thought as he stared up at the ceiling. Maybe then he wouldn't have woken up to a pillow damp with tears or a room full of laughing boys. One loud redhead said he'd cried like a girl.

That was all the motivation Zach needed.

He couldn't control their laughing, he couldn't control the nightmares, but he could control the tears. He'd stay awake for the rest of his life if he had to, because the dreams tonight were sure to be ten times worse.

His surgery was scheduled for the morning.

He'd put it off, faking sick earlier in the week. After they did the x-rays, Dr. Wheeler scheduled the surgery for the next day, wanting to get it done as quickly as possible. Being the smart kid Zach was, he woke up the next morning groaning and clutching the back of his head. That perplexed Dr. Wheeler, who claimed he was too young to get the virus. But it worked. They postponed things. Unfortunately, they just started him on the shots instead—something he hadn't anticipated. They hadn't even let him miss work. Finally he gave up the charade.

His days of postponing were over.

Dr. Wheeler promised it wouldn't hurt. He said Zach wouldn't feel a thing—at least during the surgery. But how could it not hurt to have your ankle sawn in half and bolted back together?

Zach lay flat on his back, squeezing out the tears he refused to cry, until he realized what a bad idea it was to close his eyes. They were getting harder to open. So he started again down the long rows, that time counting by twos.

Two, four, s i x…, e i…g…h……t……

When he woke once again to tear-stained cheeks and one hundred and forty-three boys laughing, that was the last number he could remember counting.

———————◆———————

Amber's neck and shoulders ached from her long shift. It was time to make a move.

She wasn't sure how to communicate without words—that was the hardest part of this little plan of hers. But it was either swallow her pride or break her pact to speak.

Pride swallowed, she started doing a little potty dance.

Crystal, next to her, noticed and motioned to the guard. "I think Amber needs to use the restroom."

Amber nodded vigorously.

"Not until the end of her shift," the guard said.

One benefit of mutehood was people stopped speaking directly to Amber, as if she couldn't hear either. Normally she liked that side benefit, but now it irked her. The guard hadn't even spoken to her.

Amber gave a few grunts and upped the dance.

Crystal shot her a disgusted look. "I think she really has to go."

"Fine." The guard pointed to another girl. "You, there. Accompany her to the restroom."

Natalia? Amber grunted angrily. She'd purposely worked beside Crystal because Crystal was a ditzy pushover. Natalia was a prissy snob.

Natalia wouldn't even look at Amber as they left the hot factory floor. The poor girl still had bruises from their last encounter.

As soon as they cleared the area, Amber whispered, "Unless you want another broken nose, I suggest you turn right back around."

Natalia gasped. "You can talk?"

"Of course I can, idiot," Amber snapped. "And I don't need an escort to the bathroom either. So if you know what's good for you and that crooked nose of yours, I suggest you turn right back around."

Natalia didn't need to be told twice.

She fled out of sight.

Amber kept heading toward the bathroom, eyes sweeping the area. Mrs. Karlsson was sitting in her office, talking on the phone. Distracted, she didn't even notice Amber pass. One hurdle down. The bigger hurdle stood next to the stairs.

The stairs' guard was big, bald, and mean. The girls called him Mr. Clean. Amber didn't know why because he didn't clean a thing, but he didn't look like he was in a good mood today—not that he ever did. As she approached him, his arms folded tightly across his massive chest.

"I left my time card in my room," Amber said. "They said if I don't grab it, I won't get dinner tonight."

"No girls allowed upstairs," he said.

"Please don't make me go back without my card." With very little effort, Amber turned on the waterworks and started to cry. "This huge guard already yelled at me on the floor, and…and…" She sniffed. "I hate it when they yell at me. They're so mean and loud and big. Oh, please. Let me get my time card. Or will you get it for me? It's next to my bed, in the small drawer, hidden under all my secret girlie—"

"Fine," he said, waving a hand. "Go get it. But go straight to your room and right back."

Amber raced up the first flight of stairs and didn't even hesitate before heading up the next one. Mrs. Karlsson had two offices: one downstairs, and one on the third floor.

It will work. She kept telling herself this as she raced down the third floor hallway.

When she reached the door that said "Mrs. Karlsson, Headmistress," she stopped. The hallway in both directions looked dead.

She cracked open Mrs. Karlsson's office door slowly, checked inside, and closed the door behind her. No lock on the door handle, so she pushed the chair she had been strapped to not that long ago up underneath the handle. That wouldn't keep Mr. Clean out for long, but it made her feel more protected.

Racing across the room, she grabbed the only other chair—Mrs. Karlsson's desk chair—and hefted it up. It was heavier than she expected.

No time for hesitation.

She threw it against the window.

The chair bounced off without even so much as a crack.

"What?" she said in frustration. "No!"

Then she realized something that made her feel like a bigger loser than Natalia. The window had locks.

Dropping her chair, she opened the locks and slid the window up slowly.

A hot summer breeze blew in, the smell of freedom in the air. Her heart pumped a million times a second.

Don't look down. Don't look down. Just do it.

She climbed out onto the ledge, one leg at a time. A wave of dizziness hit her as she caught sight of the ground below, so much farther down than she anticipated. An ugly tree grew directly below her. Maybe it would break her fall. Either that, or break every bone in her body.

Suddenly her plan seemed really, *really* stupid.

She heard footsteps racing down the hallway. Mr. Clean had figured her out already. She was out of time.

Don't look. Don't look!

She shimmied around, twisting backwards until she hung by her waist. Then, gripping the window sill with everything she had, she lowered herself until she hung by nothing but hands.

Her arms burned with exertion. Her fingers started to slip.

"Hey!" Mr. Clean yelled. The office door handle shook. "Hey, what are you doing? Open this door!"

Something rammed into the door. It shook under his fury. The hinges groaned with his bulk. In another second he would break through, but by then it would be too late.

I am a fighter.

With that, Amber dropped.

forty

It took Isabel a full day to scrounge up the cure from whatever sources she had. Black market or legit, Greg didn't ask. McCormick insisted that all three of them wear bulletproof vests. That seemed pointless considering Greg had plenty of mortal-woundable places still showing. But again, whatever. He just wanted to get this over with.

Last night, Isabel had received a phone message from Jamansky's secretary, basically saying what Greg expected. *"Sorry about the Rockford mix-up. Chief Jamansky meant to say that your friend is actually in Rochelle. He'll be in touch as soon as he has more information."*

Only Carrie wasn't in Rochelle. Greg had called back, just to confirm. As far as he could tell, Carrie wasn't anywhere. Which could only mean one thing:

Carrie was dead.

"Hey." Isabel waved a hand in front of Greg's face. "Are you in there?"

"Yeah. Sorry," Greg said, refocusing.

Isabel gave him a pitying look before she leaned back over the map. "Last report we received, Kearney's group was camped in a forest preserve near West Chicago." She pointed to a spot. "Right around there."

"That should make them easier to track down," Greg said. "Let's dump the car in Winfield."

"That far?" McCormick said. "Walking means time wasted."

"A risk we'll have to take," Greg said. "Kearney will have guards on every road in the area. So we'll go in the back way."

McCormick nodded tiredly. "Let's move out."

As they drove to Winfield, Greg stared out the window at the cloud-covered, gloomy day. The humidity was high, the temperature around an eight on Carrie's scale. Yet he didn't update her weather journal like he had been doing. Instead, he pulled out the single syringe in his pocket.

What had happened to Carrie? Would the work camps have told him if she'd died? Why hadn't he asked?

Heaviness engulfed him. People died all the time. It happened. Just because he loved Carrie, didn't mean she couldn't die, too. The possibility was unbearable, so he shoved the syringe back in his pocket and redirected his thoughts. One aspect of the Kearney plan still needed tweaking.

McCormick parked his shiny red car behind an old grocery store. The three of them got out to start unloading the trunk. Greg watched Isabel and her uncle another minute. The fifty-something McCormick had just lost his wife and was still grieving. Isabel had been held hostage by Kearney the last time. She had a lot going for her—which was more than Greg had.

That solidified it.

"Hold up," Greg said as McCormick went to grab his bag. "Change of plans."

"What?" McCormick said.

"I'm goin' in alone." That brought a round of protests, but Greg hurried on. "I work better alone—somethin' that should be painfully obvious by now. Plus if things don't go well and I happen to die, the two of you can find a different way to take out Rigsby."

"Greg," Isabel started to say, but he overrode her again.

"Look, we did it your way last time," he said firmly, "and both of us nearly died. This time I go alone. Sneaking three people in is gonna be next to impossible, but I can get in undiscovered."

McCormick regarded him for a moment before nodding. "Fine."

"Thank you, sir," Greg said. "If and when Kearney agrees to this, I'll come back and get both of you. Until then, stay out of sight. I plan on goin' slow, so if you haven't heard from me by morning, don't come charging in with guns swinging. Give me a few days before you look for my body. Actually, if I'm not back in a few days, you'll be out of time anyway. You'll have to go after Rigsby on your own."

Isabel rolled her dark eyes. "Drama boy."

"Just bein' realistic."

They rearranged a few supplies, passing food and water from one bag to the next. Greg double-checked that he still had Carrie's weather notebook in his back pocket before he hefted the heaviest bag onto his shoulder.

"How many doses did we end up with?" he asked.

"Enough to treat two hundred," Isabel said, handing him a lighter bag. "I don't have to tell you to be careful with this, right? People will kill to get their hands on these, so use good judgment."

"You say that like you think I've actually got some," he said.

She smiled. "Good point. Gun?"

"No." Another memory he preferred to not repeat. He picked up the two bags, one heavy and one light. "This is plenty. Hopefully I'll be back tonight with good news."

Greg started off but only made it a few steps before Isabel ran after him.

"Greg, wait," Isabel said. "I have something for you."

"As long as it's not too big. I don't have much room."

"It's not for your bag." She reached into her pocket and pulled out a watch. She stared at it a long moment before handing it to him. "Since your wrist isn't great at giving you the time."

Surprised, he took it from her. The brown leather straps felt worn but sturdy, and the watch face had a vintage, classy look. The second hand ticked around the Roman numerals second by wonderful second, mesmerizing him. It had taken him years to get used to never knowing the time.

"Wow. Thanks," he said. "I'm not sure what to say."

She shrugged. "Knowing what a planner you are, I figured you like knowing the exact time. In case you're wondering, it's synced to Greenwich Mean Time, right down to the second. Maybe now you can make all your crazy plans with more accuracy."

He slid the watch around his wrist and cinched it snug. It fit perfectly. He couldn't stop admiring it: the style, the worn out look—especially the worn look.

"This is really great. But...uh..." He scratched his head.

"Why the gift?" Her smile faded into sadness. "It was Pete's."

His brows rose. Pete had been the love of her life who, unfortunately, had been on the opposite side of the law. When the feds came to arrest his rebel group, Isabel tried to warn him, but he hadn't listened. She had watched him shot down.

Pete had died—something Greg knew before, but now with Carrie, it felt particularly awful. That was the reality of life. Boyfriends, wives, children, parents, and best friends died every day, but nobody gave it much thought until it was their loved one.

Carrie could die, too.

How long would he carry her little journal around before he gave it up?

"No." He started loosening the watch strap. "I can't take this. You keep it."

"I want you to have it, Greg," she said, putting a hand on his arm. "You remind me of Pete–bossy and a little rough, but deep-down caring about those you love. You two might have even been friends."

Greg nodded soberly. "He'd be proud of what you're doin' here, helping these people—or, if things go well, helping all of America. He'd be real proud."

Her dark eyes glistened. "I hope so. Thanks for helping me see which path I should be on."

"You woulda got there eventually."

"I'm not so sure." She gave him a soft smile. "You know, Carrie will be proud of you, too. Don't lose hope. She's still out there somewhere."

Don't lose hope. As if he could control that.

"Time's ticking!" McCormick called. "Time to move out."

Greg took off.

He ran the first few miles, staying near roads and open fields to speed things up. But as soon as he neared the area, he headed for the woods, slowing to a virtual crawl. The woods hid a person well, but the slightest movement made sound. In the heart of summer, the underbrush became a thick tangle of twigs, stones, holes, or logs that could easily trip up a nice guy like him. He wanted to hurry, but he had to tread carefully. Being hasty cost them last time. So for the next two hours and fourteen minutes, he was in and out of the river, in and out of the trees, and constantly on the watch. Somewhere along the way, he ditched the heavy, inconspicuous bulletproof vest. He would apologize to McCormick later.

Don't lose hope. He kept chanting it to himself to keep from freefalling into despair. Carrie was somewhere.

Around noon, he spotted the first signs of life. Old fire pits. Packed down brush and grasses. By one o'clock, he smelled them, catching the subtle scent of campfire.

He grabbed a handful of small stones and started climbing.

Traveling from North Carolina, he'd found high posts made the best guarding spots—the higher the better. Not only could he see farther, but most people didn't think to look up, especially not as high as he liked to climb.

Dropping his bags, he walked to a large tree with good, sturdy branches and started climbing. Every twenty minutes, he climbed another tree, a little closer, a little farther. Then he listened to the woods speak to him. Birds, animals, the buzz of insects. They knew when people were intruding in their forest. In five minute increments, he dropped a stone in the slingshot pouch and fired off a few shots. If all stayed calm, he moved north and found another tree to climb.

The humidity won out and a soft misting rain fell.

In between shooting off stones, he rubbed the small scar on his palm, the one that would forever remind him of Carrie and her fierce way of saving those she loved.

At 1:42 p.m., he got a response. He aimed his slingshot farther inland from the river. A muddled reply echoed back to him. Definitely human. At 1:47, he tried another in the same area. That time, he heard a distinct voice.

"There it was again," somebody said. "Did you hear that?"

Greg scanned the woods until he spotted a flash of green that didn't match nature.

Bingo.

Climbing down, he pulled out his smaller pack and grabbed the trowel. He dug a hole deep enough to bury both bags. Once they were secure and he spread branches over the top, he picked a tree closer to those guards and climbed again. His arms were scratched up and his legs were weary from scaling trees, but his heart beat strong and ready.

Humans always thought they were more cunning than they were. The rebels stood out against the quiet woods: the vibrant colors from the tents and clothes, the sounds of movement and laughing. This camp looked to be at least double the size of Kearney's. He couldn't even see the end of it. He saw mostly adults, which was a good sign. Isabel gauged what kind of group she stumbled into based on the adult-to-kid ratio. Plus this group carried an unusually high number of guns. Definitely part of the rebellion.

He couldn't believe they'd talked him into this again.

The branch he clung to swayed softly in the breeze as he watched for a specific guy, late forties, medium build, with a dark beard. Kearney. Unfortunately, that described a lot of the guys he saw.

When a guard passed under him for the third time, taking the same basic route, Greg decided to make a move.

He pulled out his slingshot and fired off a rock to the right. Instantly alert, the guard gripped his rifle. Greg fired off three more stones in the same basic area, trying to make them sound like footsteps. It worked. The guard motioned to his buddy, and the two of them crept off to investigate.

Greg climbed down and inched toward the camp.

He hid behind a large, gray tent on the outskirts of the sprawling camp. Several bundles of wood sat off to his left, which could work as a prop once an opportunity presented itself. First, he needed another distraction.

Four minutes later, the distraction came.

A woman tripped. She had been carrying an armful of pots. Food and water spilled everywhere. Food must have been scarce in the camp, because one guy went off, yelling at her for being so careless. People turned to see what was happening.

Greg moved.

He darted left, grabbed a bundle of wood, and hefted it up on his shoulder. With an easy gait, he strode forward as if he had a specific destination in mind. He didn't allow himself to look left or right, nor did he search each spot for potential problems.

"Act like you belong," McCormick had said during training, *"and people will assume that you do. Act like you're a spy, and people will assume that you are."*

People in camps didn't glance at every passing face or tent, so he didn't allow himself to either. He got a few strange looks, but not many.

The camp seemed to never end—more like several camps connected in a long string. He even passed several corralled horses. That shocked him. These rebels had mastered two of the biggest hurdles in any revolution: communication and transportation. A good sign.

As Greg passed a young teen, and he still had no clue where Kearney was, he decided to try his luck and ask. "Hey, kid, have you seen Kearney anywhere?"

It was a huge gamble. For all Greg knew, this wasn't Kearney's camp, or Kearney might not even be alive still.

The teen gave Greg a full once over. "Was Kearney in our camp today?"

"That's what they told me." Greg forced a sigh. "Great. Where is he?"

The teen shrugged. "Last I heard, he was in the Grains with the other leaders. Maybe they know where he went."

"Guess I'll check there. Thanks."

The Grains. The Grains. Where was that? At least Kearney was alive, and if people—including teens—knew his name and his general whereabouts, he probably had enough leadership to get Commander McCormick what he needed.

Greg readjusted the bundle of wood on his shoulder and kept going. *The Grains.* Was that code for some kind of silo? Maybe a grain factory? Abandoned cornfield?

"Hey, hold on!" somebody said. A woman waved at Greg. "Wait. Don't I know you?"

Greg's heart kick-started. He pretended not to hear and changed trajectories. He headed around a large, blue tent.

Footsteps came up behind him. "Hey, you!" the woman shouted. "Stop!"

Greg did, though he wasn't happy about it. When he turned around, he came face to face with a middle-aged woman who looked vaguely familiar. He knew the second she put his face to her memory. Terror flashed in her eyes. Her gaze flickered around as if she didn't know whether to run or hold him captive.

She did neither.

"Leonard!" she yelled. "Leonard, quick! The spy is back! Leonard!"

Frantic, Greg dropped the wood and held up both hands in a show of peace. "Wait. I'm unarmed. I'm not here to cause any trouble. I've just got a message for Kearney. No need to alert the whole camp."

Too late.

People came running, guns out in an all-too-familiar show of force. Greg backed up, regretting his choice to forego the bulletproof vest.

"Go ahead and frisk me," Greg said before the group could get out of hand. "I'm unarmed. Then take me to Kearney fast. There's somethin' he needs to know."

forty-one

They led Greg for a while. Kearney's camp had grown significantly since Greg had left. He didn't recognize anybody other than the woman who had spotted him and two guys with rifles bringing up the rear. They passed lots of people sitting on logs or camp chairs, watching them pass with long, drawn faces. Some even had blankets wrapped around their shoulders in spite of the hot, moist day.

"People are gettin' sick, aren't they?" Greg said.

"Don't talk," a guy at his back said, shoving the rifle into Greg's ribs. "Walk faster."

A man in heavy overalls led the way. When they seemed to reach a new group of tents, he broke out ahead, springing forward until he reached a large, gray tent. Greg looked around and spotted a tall silo and group of barns behind it. The Grains.

Overall-guy rapped on the canvas walls. Then he opened the zipper and entered.

Greg could hear bits and pieces of a conversation inside. Something about the spy returning. "No, just the guy," Overall-guy said. "He's alone—or I think he is. We sent guards out to find the girl."

More conversation before the overall-guy reemerged. Then he motioned Greg forward.

"Go on in. Kearney wants to talk to you."

Muscles tensed, Greg entered the small tent, ready for an attack. He couldn't see much in the darker tent, and he blinked like mad to make his eyes adjust.

Where was Kearney?

"Come to finish the job, spy?" Kearney said in a soft voice.

Greg found the rebel leader below, lying on a small cot in the corner, arm over his forehead. The guy looked pale and weak. Sick.

"You're the one," Kearney said tiredly. "You brought this killer disease to us, didn't you? And now…you've come to gloat."

Guilt spread through Greg. He couldn't bring himself to ask how many people had died. "If I brought this virus to your camp, I didn't know it. I didn't even know it existed until later."

"Sure, sure." With great effort, Kearney picked up something from the side of his cot. A small pistol. Pointing it at Greg seemed to take all his energy, but he managed anyway. "Why are you back?"

Greg stared at the gun, too tired to even be bothered by its presence. "To help you win the war."

Kearney gave a low, mirthless laugh. "And why should I believe you?"

"Because I'm gonna save your life."

Moving slowly, Greg pulled out a single syringe from his pocket. "Do you know what this is?"

Through squinting, pained eyes, Kearney studied it. "How did you know I was sick?"

"I didn't. I just figured most everybody is."

Kearney lay back, gun resting on his chest, arm covering his forehead again. "I should blow your head off, spy."

"Kill me some other time. If you do it now, you'll lose access to President Rigsby. He's comin' to Illinois, and I can tell you exactly where he'll be in three days, plus how to reach him."

"Why should I believe you?" Kearney said. "Last time I saw you, you—"

"—Saved your camp," Greg said, reminding him. "I told you exactly what was goin' down and how the government was onto your game. I told you to pack up camp, which you've done, so you're welcome. I didn't send the feds after you once I was free either. You're welcome again. If that's not answer enough, I don't know what is."

Kearney tried to glare at him. It looked like it hurt.

"Look," Greg said, "President Rigsby's gonna be here in three days, and I'm guessin' you got a lot of people dyin'. I brought enough to treat two hundred people."

Greg heard low murmurs outside of the tent. Apparently a decent-sized group was listening in.

Kearney gave a choking cough. "I see. You're bribing me. I help you with whatever scheme you've got up your sleeve, and you'll give us the cure?"

"You get the cure either way," Greg said. "It's buried outside of your camp. I'm just hopin' you're smart enough to see that I'm offering you a chance to do what you've wanted to do all along: take down Rigsby."

Kearney squinted at him. "I'm listening."

"Put the gun away first. Then there's somebody I think you should meet. Technically, two somebodies. Although I suppose you already know the one. She's understandably nervous to see you again since you held her hostage last time, so be nice."

"Tell me you didn't bring your pretend wife. I nearly lost my spot in the council for letting her escape. They're going to kill me. Maybe I should just die now."

At that word *die,* Greg's gaze dropped to the syringe in his hand. The one meant for Carrie.

"Before I grab them," Greg said, "I should probably give you this first."

He uncapped the syringe, exposing the metal-sharp needle. A cold sweat broke out on his forehead. He thought about waiting for Isabel to administer the shot for him, but it could take two hours to get her and McCormick. Kearney needed medicine now.

Be a man, he told himself. *Just slide it into the skin.*

Slide.

Still an awful word.

His whole body trembled with ice as he asked, "Which arm?"

Carrie had begged to accompany Jamansky that morning. He promised that he was getting Zach out first thing, but it was already past two o'clock, and no sign of either of them.

She was losing hope of ever seeing anyone again.

Last night, Jamansky claimed that he had visited Logan Pond and told Richard everything: where Carrie was, getting her siblings out, the whole thing. Supposedly Richard had been beside himself with relief, which would have been sweet if Carrie had believed a single word. Jamansky hadn't gone to Logan Pond, and if her hunches were right, he never would.

If he didn't show up soon with her siblings, she would have to find a way to escape and free Amber and Zach—and maybe even Greg—on her own. It just wasn't safe to stay anymore. Not only did Jamansky keep making passes at her, but he was getting more agitated each time she turned away.

Even more disturbing was that after she went to bed early last night, practically locking herself in his bedroom, she had heard him. She hadn't been tired, so hours later she heard him on the phone, talking to someone. Only it hadn't been talking. He had been yelling and swearing, trying to keep his voice down to keep from waking her, but failing. She cracked open the bedroom door and listened. Even with his office door shut, she heard him arguing with someone about money.

Now today, since he wasn't back with Zach yet, she decided to do more digging.

Checking the crack in the curtains, she grabbed a wire hanger and straightened the end. After last night, Jamansky had locked up his office. Bretton and Felix stood beside her, curious as she slid the wire hanger into the lock.

The door slid open.

Heart racing, she saw papers scattered across his desk that hadn't been there before. She didn't dare touch them for fear he would notice, but she saw bank statements and what looked like inventory for a storage unit.

One paper caught her eye. It was partially folded up but looked official from some place called the Department of Investigations.

Memorizing its exact position—and making sure the street and driveway stayed empty—she picked it up and read.

Her mouth slowly dropped.

The letter mentioned an investigation that had been opened against him and the mayor, illegal activity including embezzling money and stealing from the government. They'd placed him on probation and given him two weeks to prove otherwise and return the requested money, or he would be arrested. It was the amount that staggered her: $20,000. She didn't know how money worked these days, but even before the Collapse, that had been a huge sum. Now she guessed it was an impossibility—hence all the shouting.

Her stomach clenched.

If Jamansky was on probation, could he even get her siblings out?

One more day. That was all she dared to stay at his house, and then one way or another, she was gone.

"I've come for one of your boys," Jamansky said to the DeKalb man in the front office. "My unit was behind his acquisition, and now I need him restored. I called two days ago, so his papers should be in order."

The man adjusted his glasses and searched through his computer. "Oh, yes. Zachary Ashworth. I see that you called, officer. Let's see here. Uh…" He looked up. "My deepest apologies, sir, but we can't release him at this time. The young Mr. Ashworth is undergoing a medical procedure as we speak."

"He what?" Jamansky said.

"He's in surgery. I'm afraid he'll be down for a while." The man squinted at the screen. "This says three weeks. You should be able to reacquire him at that time."

Jamansky slammed a hand on the table, making the man jump. "That is unacceptable! No one mentioned anything to me about any surgery."

"Yes, well, his ankle is—"

"An ankle?" Jamansky shouted. "No. You bring him to me now, or I'll write up this establishment and send it into the commissioner himself."

The man looked taken aback. "Yes, sir. Let me make a quick call."

This better work, Jamansky seethed. Because Carrie was getting antsy. He needed this kid to anchor her down.

Maybe he should have let her rot in prison a while longer.

Jamansky kept his glare pinned on the man so he didn't forget who wore a uniform and who didn't. The guy broke out in a sweat as he spoke into the phone. He nodded a few times and then hung up.

"Yes, chief. It seems, uh…that the teen hasn't gone into surgery quite yet, but he's already in the prep room. I'm afraid they've just put him under anesthesia. The doctor apologizes for the misunderstanding and says he'll write a letter to the commissioner himself explaining the situation."

"Anesthesia?" Jamansky said. "But they haven't started the actual surgery?"

"No, but—"

"Then bring him to me."

The man's eyes widened. "But, sir, that would be dangerous to pull him out."

Jamansky lunged. He stormed around the desk, grabbed the man by the shirt collar, and threw him against the wall. Arm to the guy's throat, he pinned him there.

"You will bring that kid to me now," Jamansky hissed in his face. "You have exactly three minutes."

The guy gasped, face turning red. When Jamansky released him, he took off, sprinting down the hall.

They wheeled Zachary Ashworth out a few minutes later. The young teen was lying on a gurney, arm bandaged from the IV, and totally unconscious. A doctor trailed him, swearing up a storm.

"Who do you think you are, barging in here, stealing my patients?" the doctor yelled. "You can't just take him. We're in the middle of a procedure!"

"You're lucky I came when I did," Jamansky said, "or I would have had every one of you fired." He motioned to the nurse. "My car is by the curb. Put him in the front seat."

The doctor was still swearing as Jamansky followed the gurney outside.

forty-two

The kid didn't budge the entire drive. His mouth hung open and he looked paler than a ghost. When Jamansky got to his house, he didn't even pull into the garage. Too hard to get Zach out with how crowded it was. So he parked in the driveway and ran around to grab the kid.

The teen was only thirteen but still had enough weight to make him a pain to carry. Jamansky hefted him into his arms and struggled up the sidewalk. When he reached the front door, he kicked it hard.

"Carrie," he called. "Open up."

He waited, arms straining.

"Carrie!"

Maybe he shouldn't have scared her so badly about avoiding the front door at all costs. The thing was deadbolted, and his house keys buried. Bretton and Felix barked on the other side of the door. Carrie must have fallen asleep. All she did was sleep. Stupid, useless woman. His arms were about to fall off.

He kicked harder. "Carrie! It's me!"

Finally he heard her footsteps approach.

When she cracked open the front door, her eyes widened. "Zach?" She took in the state of her brother—arms and legs flopped to the side, unresponsive to the point that he looked dead—and lost all color in her cheeks. "Oh, please no. Zach!"

"He's fine," Jamansky said, struggling. "Just sedated. Help me to the couch."

As he dropped Zach on the couch, Carrie knelt next to him.

"Zach?" she said, stroking his face. "Zach?"

The kid looked grotesque. His freckled skin was pale, but also badly sunburned in several spots. Splotches of skin peeled off his nose. Chapped, cracked lips. Blisters and scrapes running down his arms.

Turning, Carrie looked at David. "What happened to him?"

"They were about to operate on him when I got there," he said, wiping his brow. "They'd already administered the anesthesia. Who knows how long he'll be out?"

"Operate? On what?"

He shrugged. "Thankfully, I got there in time."

Carrie's deep, blue eyes filled with tears as she studied her brother. Then her head dropped onto his arm, crying softly.

Finally, a reaction David could handle.

Stepping close, he rubbed her shoulder. "It will be okay. I really did get there in the nick of time. I didn't even think they were going to give him to me, but he's here and he's safe. Don't worry. He'll wake up soon."

She nodded against her brother's arm.

Jamansky continued to rub her shoulder, waiting for the inevitable, *"Thank you, David. Thank you for saving his life! How can I ever repay you?"* Then she would throw herself at him in overwhelming gratitude. After all the garbage he'd endured, he deserved it.

The longer the boy sleeps, he thought, *the better.*

But when Carrie finally spoke, she said something entirely different.

"How can you stand it?" she said.

"Stand what?" he said, confused.

She turned her brother's hand over, exposing more scratches, blisters, and burns. "How can you be part of this?"

"What are you talking about? I had nothing to do with this." His temper kicked in. "I didn't even arrest your brother. In fact, I just saved him for you."

"Yes." Her red-rimmed eyes lifted to him. "But how many other families have you ripped apart? How many women are dying in prisons because you put them there?"

"Hey!" he snapped. "I'm just doing my job. I arrest people who break the law!"

"What law, David? The one President Rigsby created so he could stay in power? So he could turn innocent children into slaves? What right does Rigsby have to tell us where to live and how to live? To rip our kids away from us? How many *laws* did he break to create this new society?"

Jamansky's chest heaved in and out. "You better be careful there, sweetheart. I've arrested people for less."

"Yes," she whispered. "I know."

Turning back, she brushed the hair away from her brother's peeling forehead. "President Rigsby is killing people, David. He's murdering his *own* people. These laws, the virus, the raids on our homes, stealing our stuff. How can you be part of it?"

His veins filled with indignation. He pointed at the kid, half dead. "Do you want me to take him back? Do you want me to take you both back? Because I will!"

"So we can die, too?" Her shoulders lifted. "I don't know. I don't know anything anymore except that this is wrong. All of it is very, very wrong." Her forehead fell onto her brother's arm again. "I just want to go home."

"You have no home!"

She whirled, blue eyes blazing for the first time. "Whether or not you, the president, or anyone else acknowledges it, Logan Pond will always be my home."

"Logan Pond?" he scoffed. "There's no one left in Logan Pond. Your people left you, Carrie. That's right. They're gone. I lied to you yesterday. Richard O'Brien wasn't home. Not a single, illegal, traitorous clansman is left. O'Brien told me last week that they were packing up and leaving. The place was deserted yesterday. I just didn't have the heart to tell you."

"Just because you can't see them doesn't mean they're not there."

"You think I'm wrong? You think I don't know? Fine," he said. "I'll prove it to you."

He stormed over to the couch, grabbed her brother's arms, and threw the kid over his shoulder. Then he started for the front door.

"What are you doing?" Carrie jumped to her feet and ran after him. "Where are you going? David, I'm sorry. I didn't mean to upset you. Please put Zach down. David!"

"Get in the car," he said, huffing with the weight of the kid. "Bretton, Felix, *kommen*! We're going for a drive."

———— ◆ ————

Even before they turned into the north entrance of the Logan Pond subdivision, Carrie was searching every crack, corner, and tree for signs of life. Zach lay passed out against his back window, wearing that awful blue uniform, with two massive dogs sitting beside him.

Jamansky didn't say a single word as he sped toward Shelton, but his entire body was rigid with fury. Carrie didn't speak either for fear of losing Amber. She shouldn't have angered him like that. Not now. Not with so much at stake. Now, pulling into her neighborhood, she felt like she was about to lose more than she already had.

Greg. She just needed Greg to see her now.

The second they reached Denton Trail, Jamansky slowed to a crawl. They crept past the Watson's home and past the Trenton's empty yard.

"See," he said. "They're gone."

She refused to believe it even though her senses told her otherwise—the neighborhood felt dead. Her clansmen had perfected the art of survival. Surviving meant hiding. If they were posting guards, they would have spotted the patrol car on the main road and sounded the alarm. They would have headed to May's—or even the woods. Greg would have led them to safety.

Carrie rolled down the window and stuck her head out in the soft drizzle so they could see her.

Please, she begged. *It's me. Just look and see me.*

"Carrie," Jamansky said in frustration. "My car."

She rolled up the damp window but continued searching down Denton Trail and onto Woodland Drive, past her house and around the wet, empty cul-de-sac.

Suddenly her hands flew to her mouth. Sensing something had changed, Jamansky stopped in the middle of the road. He'd already passed Carrie's house for a second time and now faced May and CJ's directly.

The back gate was open. Butterscotch's rope hung empty. In all the years of hiding, they'd never taken the goats outside of the fence. Not once. Not even for government raids.

"I need to get out," she said, barely projecting her voice past a whisper. "I need to see for myself."

He gripped the steering wheel. "No way. We shouldn't even be here right now. It's time to go home."

Soft mist rolled down the windows, as if the car was mourning with her.

"I *am* home," she said stubbornly.

And with that, she yanked on the door handle. Nothing happened. The handle moved, but the door didn't. Locked. She searched for a way to unlock her door, but couldn't find how.

Understanding slowly dawned on her. She turned back to stare at Jamansky.

"I really am your prisoner," she said, horrified. Even if she wanted to leave or run, she couldn't. He'd locked her in. Worse, a metal grate separated the front seat from the back, blocking her from reaching her brother.

"There's a world out there that you don't understand," he said, looking straight ahead. "A world where a woman like you could end up dead in seconds. For your own sake, you're safer here with me."

Her pulse sped up. "You have no right to keep me against—"

"I have every right!" he rode over her. "You're an illegal citizen of the United States of America. If I say sit, you sit. If I say stay, you stay! Do you understand?"

Her heartbeat thundered in her bad ear. She wanted to lash back at him, but instead she felt fear, legitimate, blinding fear that Amber and Zach might slip through her fingers again. Until they were both safe, she had to tread carefully.

Lowering her eyes, she nodded softly.

"Look, Carrie," he said, backing down some, "I don't want to fight. I know this is hard on you, seeing yourself abandoned, but Zach will wake up soon. We need to get him home. I'm sure you understand."

She glanced back at Zach through the metal mesh, his neck bent awkwardly as he slept against the window. Then her gaze went to May's empty, abandoned yard.

Her throat burned. They'd left. Not hid. Left.

Without them.

"Do you?" she whispered.

"Do I what?" he said.

She swallowed. "Do you understand what we've been through? My siblings and I have lost everything and everyone that ever meant anything to us. Our parents. Our friends." She thought about Greg and the possibility of never seeing him again. Greg, May and CJ, Little Jeffrey. "I know you have concerns, David, but I need to get out and see for myself. If you can't understand that, then take me back to prison. I'd rather be there than locked up by you."

The words tumbled out, reckless and unplanned. She didn't want to go back to Rochelle, nor could she bear the thought of Zach being sent back. But something deep inside of her refused to recall her words.

Live free. Live free. It had become her only desire for her and those she loved.

His expression turned dark and turbulent.

"Two homes," he said. "You can search two homes. I shouldn't even let you do that much. You have no idea how dangerous this is." He reached down and pulled out his gun. "Which ones?"

forty-three

The choice was easy. Carrie picked the Trenton's house and her own. Clutching his gun, Jamansky opened his dogs' door first and grabbed their leashes. Then he opened Carrie's door, releasing her from her new prison.

Stomach clenched, Carrie watched Bretton and Felix sniff around May and CJ's driveway. What would she do if the dogs found her friends? What would she do if they didn't? Jamansky's eyes darted back and forth, looking more agitated than his dogs. All the while, his gun stayed up and ready.

"The dogs and I go in first," Jamansky said.

Without knocking, he pushed open May's front door. For a second, all of them stood outside looking in. May's home looked dark and silent. Even worse, it felt empty.

Her gaze stopped on a jar of withered forsythia branches on the kitchen table, the same ones she'd brought May two weeks ago. Now they were dead. Dried leaves and petals lay beneath. May would have never left them out like that if—

Barking erupted.

The dogs jerked forward against their leashes, dragging Jamansky toward the hallway and bedrooms.

Panic surged through Carrie as she questioned the wisdom of searching the homes.

This could end very badly.

Gun high, Jamansky gave her a sign to stay put, but she couldn't. As he started for the dark hallway, she followed past Greg and Mariah's old rooms and straight for the back bedroom. May's bedroom door was shut, but the dogs were going wild at the door.

"May?" Carrie called. Hope burst inside her. May and CJ hadn't left. "May, it's—"

Suddenly she was thrown against the wall. Her head slammed back, hard. Pain shot down her back. Jamansky grabbed her and pinned her to the wall, clamping a hand over her mouth.

"Do you want to get us killed?" he hissed.

She couldn't breathe. Could hardly think. He held her so tightly she couldn't even shake her head.

Gun inches from her face, he released her and glared at his barking dogs.

"Sitz," he ordered.

The dogs dropped, falling silent.

Pressing a finger to his lips, Jamansky slowly backed against May's bedroom door. "This is Chief Jamansky! From the Kane County Patrols. I'm coming in."

The second he cracked open the door, the dogs shot inside May's room. Jamansky peered around the corner.

Time seemed to slow.

Carrie watched him tense. The muscles in his face, arm, and body stiffened. He took one step back, lifted his gun, and fired.

Sound exploded through the bedroom.

One shot, then two, blasted in an ear-splitting, gut-wrenching sound.

Carrie screamed and lurched forward.

"No! Stop!"

By the time she grabbed his arm, Jamansky was laughing. "It was just a raccoon. Look." He opened the door wide. Bretton and Felix stood over a furry, now-dead heap. "The poor guy was trapped in here."

Carrie was simultaneously soaring and sinking. Jamansky hadn't shot anyone, but that was because there wasn't anyone to shoot. May's sheets, mattress, and pillows were gone. The dresser stood in one corner, but she had the feeling the drawers were empty. Even the closet door was open, revealing that May and CJ had packed up and moved out. That was better than arrest. But still…they were gone. Long enough that a raccoon had moved in.

Loss after loss hit her.

She stared at the empty closet and yet saw nothing. Where had they gone? Not government housing. May would rather die than submit to President Rigsby's rule. But maybe they met up with that Sprucewood Clan. Somewhere else? Either way, they had left.

Without me? she questioned.

But of course they would. Who would have ever thought she'd see the light of day again?

Heat built behind her eyes.

Jamansky, still celebrating the raccoon's demise, finally realized she was falling apart behind him.

"I'm sorry, Carrie. I knew we shouldn't have come. Come on. Let's get Zach home. With luck, we'll have Amber tomorrow, and then you can start over. This isn't the end of the world. I can get you a job with the government so you could get your legality back. You can build a comfortable life for your siblings in Sugar Grove."

When she couldn't summon a response to such an unthinkable notion, he continued.

"In a way, this is good. Now you don't have to live in shambles. No more fear. Let's go."

Every word dissolved the shock and replaced it with anger. "You said two homes. I will see two homes."

His glare returned. "Fine. Torture yourself."

Escorting her back outside, they drove through the damp street and parked in her driveway. Her house, yard, and everything looked exactly as they had when she'd left that awful morning.

"I'm going in first," Jamansky said. "You stay here with Zach until we check it out."

She didn't argue, needing time away from him.

Jamansky and his dogs ran up her wet sidewalk and disappeared inside. Even if she wanted to make a run for it, he left her locked inside the car with her unconscious brother.

"Zach," she said. Turning, she wanted to reach back and shake his knee, but a metal grate separated the front seat from the back. "Zach, please wake up. We're home. Talk to me, Zach. What happened?"

A small moan escaped his lips.

"Please wake up," she tried. "I don't want to be alone anymore. Zach?"

His eyes stayed closed.

Giving up, she turned back and told herself that he would wake up soon. Then she would find out what had happened to him—even though she was scared to know. His burns, his scratches. Could he ever forgive her for everything? Could she ever forgive herself?

Eyes closed, she lay back on her seat.

Where would she bring Zach and Amber to? Back here to live and survive alone? No. They had to find the rest of the clan, but she didn't know where to start. And if Greg really had been arrested...

Two minutes.

Since those fateful two minutes in the township office, all she had wanted was to come home. Now that she was here, she felt just as lost and alone.

Carrie rubbed the emotions from her tear-worn eyes. She was tired of crying, tired of everything. More than anything, she wanted to fall into Greg's arms and just forget the world.

Her car door opened.

"Your house is clear," Jamansky said, "but I don't think you should go in. You look pretty shaken up."

"No," she said. "I need to get clothes for Zach and Amber."

A few steps up the sidewalk, she stopped with a sudden idea. "Can I have a few minutes alone inside, David?"

He shook his blond head. "No way."

"You just checked it out. The dogs found nothing. Besides, you'll be out here if there are any problems." *Holding Zach hostage,* she almost added bitterly. "I just need a few minutes alone in my house to come to grips with everything. Please."

Jamansky peered down at his watch. "Five minutes. Not a second more. We shouldn't even be here."

She ran inside her hot, stuffy house. Shutting the door tightly behind her, she held her breath on the off chance, the one chance in a million...

"Greg?" she called softly.

She checked every counter and wall in her kitchen for a note or something. Another shot in the dark. Another disappointment.

Refusing to give up, she glanced out the front window. Jamansky was putting his dogs in the backseat next to Zach. He got in and shut the doors, enjoying the air conditioning.

In a sudden burst of insanity, she ran to the front door and locked it. Then she dashed across her kitchen and opened her back, sliding glass door. Silently, she slipped out onto her deck. Adrenaline and the exhilaration of freedom pushed her down the old, wooden deck stairs. She passed up the hedge and glanced around the brick corner of her house.

Empty.

Taking a single, quick breath, she sprinted across her yard to the next home. But she didn't stop. She kept running, crossing Dylan and Sasha's yard as well, to be safe.

Once clear, she turned left and ran along the bushes until she reached the next brick corner. Jamansky's patrol car sat two houses down from her.

It's now or never, she told herself.

Praying that he and his dogs wouldn't notice, she took the biggest risk yet. She dashed across the street, pushing her lungs and legs at full force. She raced behind the next empty home and doubled over, gulping for air. Then she checked again. Jamansky's car hadn't budged. All the doors remained closed.

She smiled in exultation.

She had done it.

Taking off again, she ran behind that house and through the next wild backyard, heading back for the home that sat directly across the street from her own.

Greg's.

She bolted inside of Greg's kitchen and looked around. His home's emptiness pressed in around her, but she was still desperate enough to call out.

"Greg?"

She scrambled up his stairs, but at the top, she stopped, realizing she didn't even know which room he slept in.

She found it easily enough.

Unlike May and CJ's home, all of Greg's things were still there: a pillow and blanket tossed haphazardly in one corner, his clothes piled in another.

Her legs buckled.

She grabbed the wall.

Greg hadn't packed up and left. He hadn't gone with his grandparents somewhere. He'd been ripped away from his life—from *their* life. Arrested. Like she had been.

She didn't have time to collapse or cry. Instead, she scavenged his room, rifling through his clothing like a mad woman to figure out what he'd been wearing at the time of arrest. His Yankees hat was gone. Work shirt, too. But something else caught her eye.

Lunging, she grabbed his light blue UNC shirt—his lucky shirt. She pressed it to her face and inhaled the scent of him lingering in the fabric: something woodsy. A man who belonged in the trees.

She wanted to scoop up everything of his and take it with her, but that wasn't feasible. Jamansky would be suspicious enough. So she stuffed Greg's lucky shirt under the one she wore of Ashlee's and ran back down the way she'd come. Outside and through his backyard.

As she rounded the next house she saw Jamansky opening his car door.

She had taken too long.

Pushing her legs past their intended use, she flew across the next yard, dashed across the street, and then fled back toward her own. One house. Two houses. The faster she ran, the blurrier her vision got. She wasn't fast enough.

She scrambled up her wet deck stairs, nearly slipping on the second one, and then rushed inside the back door in time to hear him pounding on her front door.

"Carrie, open up now!" Jamansky yelled. "Carrie!"

There was no time to recover. No time to explain why she was breathless and her shirt damp with misty rain. She ran to the front door and threw it open, begging the tears to start.

It wasn't hard.

She buried her head in her hands, and hid her breathlessness in fake sobs.

"They're gone," she cried. "They're all gone."

Jamansky looked stunned for a moment. Then he seemed to melt. "I know."

Parking his gun, he pulled her toward him with the other. His arm encircled her, but for once she didn't push him away. She needed to catch her breath, to distract him from the fact that Greg's shirt was shoved in between them.

294

After a minute, he pushed her back and glared at her. "Why did you lock me out?"

"I...um...Sorry. It's a habit."

An outright lie, but he bought it.

His brows lowered. "Why did you take so long?"

"I meant to gather Zach and Amber's things, but I was just so overwhelmed." She took a few shuddering breaths. "I didn't even grab anything yet. I just need one more minute."

He growled, but before he could stop her, she ran upstairs and grabbed the only clothes her siblings had left. Zach's old, ripped t-shirt would replace the blue uniform he wore. Amber would have to wear her too-small burgundy dress. Carrie slid Greg's lucky shirt in between the two, hoping David wouldn't notice.

He was standing at the bottom of the stairs, gun drawn, expression tense by the time she finished.

"I'm ready," she said.

A mile out of the subdivision, she realized that she had forgotten to grab any of her own clothes. Not her ratty sweats or drab yellow work shirt.

She hugged the pile of clothing close, catching the scent of the backwoods again. Then she settled in for the long ride back.

forty-four

Greg did little talking once Isabel and McCormick entered camp. By then, Kearney had gathered all the major players to hear the plan. Some woman named Coral took charge of the medicine distribution. Kearney sent two armed guards with her to make sure there wasn't a stampede.

Once that was taken care of, the strategy began. The rebel leaders listened, discussed, argued, and eventually huddled around the map McCormick had brought of the Naperville training facility. Greg knew the moment Kearney's group realized they were in the presence of the real deal because the tenor of the conversation changed. Instead of defensively fielding questions, Isabel and McCormick were leading the discussion.

In many ways, Greg felt like an actor who had stumbled onto the wrong movie set. He paced around the group, kicking dirt, stepping over large logs, and picking up bits and pieces of the plan. But he offered nothing to the discussion. Build wells, consolidate a neighborhood, or block off a south entrance, and he was all over it. But war strategy? Planning a tyrant's assassination?

Oddly, this meeting had come about because McCormick lost his wife to the virus. Sure, the SPU commander hadn't liked Rigsby's way of keeping power, but until it struck McCormick's own home, he hadn't seen things for what they truly were.

What would McCormick do once he got his revenge—*if* he got his revenge? Right now, this was pushing him through the grief of losing his beloved wife. What would happen when he no longer had anything to occupy his thoughts? How would he survive without her?

Isabel left the group and wandered over to Greg. "You haven't said much."

"I already told you my one stipulation," Greg said.

From the lawn chair where they'd propped him, Kearney turned his head. Even that seemed to take effort. "What stipulation, Pierce?"

Greg looked at Isabel.

"Go ahead," she said. "It's a valid point."

But before he could answer, a ringing sounded in the group.

One man jumped back and grabbed his pistol. "What the heck is that?"

The others looked around to find the source of the ringing, too.

"My apologies," McCormick said, pulling out his phone. "Not everyone knows I've quit my job yet. I'll just be a minute."

As McCormick stepped away, one of the men shook his head with a smile. "Are you sure you're ready to return to civilized living, Brett? A little phone, and you look like someone set off a nuke."

The group laughed, releasing the tension in the tent.

"So...?" Kearney said back to Greg. "What's your stipulation, spy?"

The rest of the group quieted down, looking curious to hear from the guy who had brought them all together but now had nothing to say.

Greg folded his arms. "No civilians hurt. The people bein' trained, those in Naperville who might be wearin' a uniform, are mostly there by force. They'd rather be on our side, but they can't. So leave them out of the fighting. Focus on Rigsby and his cronies. Do that, and I don't care what else you do."

Kearney studied him with tired, narrowed eyes. "You know, Pierce, I can't figure you out."

"Join the club," Isabel quipped.

"I take it you two aren't married after all," Kearney said dryly. "Let me guess, no baby on the way either?"

"Ah," Isabel said. "Let's not focus on the past when the future looks so bright. Don't you agree, boys?"

She didn't get quite the response she was looking for. Most of Kearney's group still had legitimate concerns—mostly centered on timing. Rigsby would be there in three days. How could they pull anything together fast enough?

"Rochelle!" McCormick said, breaking back into the group.

As one, they all turned, but McCormick was heading straight for Greg.

"Your lady friend actually was in Rochelle's work camp," McCormick said breathlessly.

Greg stared at the phone in his hand. "What?"

"Rochelle?" Isabel repeated. "But Greg called Rochelle—twice. Carrie wasn't there."

McCormick smiled. "I said she *was* in Rochelle. They released her Saturday. That's why she wasn't on the list when you called. They apologized profusely for the mix-up."

Greg couldn't move. The whole world seemed to freeze.

"Carrie's free?" he asked softly.

Not dead. Free.

"Yes," McCormick said, looking thoroughly pleased to share such happy news. "Maybe now you can breathe a little easier. Your girlfriend should be home safe and sound soon."

Soon.

Greg's eyes darted around the camp. He couldn't remember how far Shelton was from Rochelle, but Carrie had a good sense of direction. She would make it fine. She had been free for two days. She could already be home.

He looked up, baffled by one thing. "Why did they release her?"

"They didn't say," McCormick said. "Maybe they figured out she didn't deserve to be there."

"Few people do," Kearney noted dryly.

Murmurs of angry agreements rippled through the group.

They were right. Those work camps were filled with women who didn't deserve to be there. More likely, Greg and Isabel had scared Jamansky into releasing Carrie early. But why wouldn't Jamansky have said so in his message?

Greg didn't care.

A smile tugged at the corners of his mouth. Carrie wasn't just free, but she was alive enough to be freed. He glanced over his shoulder towards the western sky, as if he could catch a glimpse of her.

"She could be home," Isabel said, dark eyes dancing. "I bet we just missed her."

"Or in Ferris," he said. Did Carrie even know to look for them in Ferris? He should have left a note or something at her house, but he'd never dreamed this would happen. Either way, Terrell was checking in on Logan Pond every day. He would spot her.

Greg spun back around to McCormick. "What about Amber and Zach? Were they released, too? Or Oliver Simmons?" At McCormick's confused look, Greg shook his head. "Never mind." Rochelle wouldn't know any of that.

"Hey, Uncle Charlie," Isabel said. "Don't you think we've used and abused Pierce long enough? He's given us his two cents on this Rigsby plan—and even that wasn't worth two cents. What do you say we send him home?"

"Home?" McCormick and Kearney said at the same time.

Isabel nodded.

McCormick glanced over the group of rebels. They didn't care what Greg did. Not even Kearney would miss him. So McCormick reached into his pocket and pulled out his car keys.

"Fair enough," McCormick said. "Enjoy the ride, Pierce. Just have it back to us by tomorrow night."

Greg stared at the keys. "Thank you, sir, but by the time I run back to your car, I can be halfway to Shelton." And once he was with Carrie, he wouldn't want to leave. Ever again. Already his mind was racing with how to find Amber, Zach, and Oliver Simmons. Driving a pretty red car would have to wait. "I'm fine goin' on foot. Thanks for lettin' me go."

McCormick stepped forward and shook his hand. "Good luck to you, Pierce. Thank you for your contribution. I hope we cross paths again."

"I'd like that," Greg said, meaning it. "I hope your plan works."

"So do I."

Then he smiled again, unable to believe it.

Carrie was free.

Things were going to be okay.

"Hey, spy," Kearney called, "thanks for the cure."

"Thanks for not killing me," Greg shot back.

That brought another round of laughs.

Isabel came over to him, eyes going soft. "Good luck, Greg. If you change your mind and decide you want to join the fun, meet us in Naperville. Even if you just want to watch it all go down, I'll save a spot for you."

"Thanks, but revolutions aren't really my thing," he said.

"So you keep saying, but I don't believe you." Grinning, she gave him a quick hug. "Tell Carrie I said hello. One of these days, I might actually get to meet this girl of yours."

"Well, you're welcome in Logan Pond any time," he said. "In fact, if you're ever lookin' for a place to settle, I'll save a house for you."

"You know," she said, "I just might take you up on that."

———◆———

Greg sprinted through the Ferris neighborhood, straight for the home his grandparents were staying in. He burst inside and looked around.

"Where's Carrie?" he asked.

"Gregory, you're back?" his grandma called, coming in from the kitchen.

"Yeah. Is Carrie here?" he said breathlessly.

His grandpa set his book down. "Was she released?"

That was all the answer Greg needed. Huffing, he spun back around and took off for the front door.

"Wait," his grandma said, rushing to follow him. "Where are you going? Did you find my Carrie?"

"Not yet," he said. "I've gotta run to Logan Pond. She's probably sittin' in her house, wonderin' where everybody disappeared to." Grinning, he gave his grandma a quick hug. "I'll be back soon."

"Hold on," his grandpa said. "Didn't Jeff Kovach say something about seeing Carrie in Logan Pond, May?"

Greg skidded to a stop. Of all the people his grandpa could have mentioned, Jeff Kovach was the last one he expected.

"Jeff's back?" Greg asked.

His grandma pushed up her thick glasses. "Oh, Gregory, you've missed so much. Jeff Kovach is back. I almost didn't let him return, but he sounded so sorry for—"

"Wait," Greg interrupted. "Jeff saw Carrie? Jeff's here?"

He couldn't keep up.

"Come," his grandpa said. "Let's go find him."

They found Jeff in the temporary home Sasha and Dylan were staying in. Jeff's large, burly body seemed to take up the whole doorway as he strode outside.

"Hey," Greg said. "You're back."

Jeff shook his hand heartily. "Yeah. I returned two days ago. I spent a full day wandering around the neighborhood, wondering where everyone went. I thought I'd never see my boys again."

He glanced over his shoulder at Sasha Green, who carried Jeff's youngest outside. Jonah was clutching Sasha's neck as if he wasn't so thrilled by his father's surprise return. Little Jeffrey followed, taking everything in with his large, dark eyes. Both kids looked lost. Sasha gripped them as if she might not let go. She was going to be childless again.

"Guess things have been a little crazy around here." Jeff frowned at Greg. "Sorry to hear about the Ashworths."

"How was...everything?" Greg asked for lack of a better word. The last he'd seen Jeff Kovach had been after Jenna's death. Greg had given him tips on how to travel on foot, staying out of sight. "Did you make it to North Dakota?"

"Yeah. I found my parents." He smiled through his thick, wild beard. "In fact...where did Mitch go? Mitch?" Jeff called.

Another man emerged from the house, less brawny than Jeff, but with obvious sibling similarities.

"This is my brother, Mitch," Jeff said. "He came with me to get the boys."

"You're leaving again?" Greg said, struggling to keep up.

"My parents have a good setup in North Dakota. The laws aren't quite as strict there." Jeff shrugged. "I figure the boys and I should be around my family, you know? Everyone else can come, too, if they want."

Sasha's eyes filled. She squeezed Little Jonah harder.

"Wow," Greg said. "I'm glad you found your family."

His grandpa spoke up. "Greg said Carrie was released from prison two days ago. He thinks she should be to Logan Pond by now."

Jeff's eyes widened. "Then it was Carrie. I knew it!"

In a quick, hurried tone, Jeff Kovach explained how he'd been in his house yesterday when he heard a patrol car drive through. He and Mitch had hid. The car stopped at Greg's grandparents' house first. It was far enough away, they couldn't see much, but then it went to Carrie's, a few houses closer.

"We heard dogs," Jeff said, "but it didn't seem like a raid. Then a woman got out of the patrol car."

"Carrie?" Greg said, stomach clenching. "What did the patrolman look like?"

Jeff looked at his brother. "It wasn't Oliver."

Greg's stomach clenched. "Tall? Lean? Blond hair?"

"Yeah, but here's the weird thing. A few minutes later, we saw Carrie dash across the street. Not by her house, but farther down by Sasha and Dylan's."

"She just booked it across the street," Mitch said, "like she was running from something. But then she ran back a few minutes later."

"Last we saw," Jeff said, "she and that patrolman drove away. When Terrell found us later, he said we'd seen wrong. It couldn't be Carrie because she was in prison. But now...I guess she's free. That's great!"

Jeff smiled.

Greg didn't.

"What kind of patrol car?" Greg said, feeling himself go numb. "Did it have *Chief of Patrols* written across the side?"

"Yeah," Mitch said. "How did you know?"

Greg stared down at his feet. If Jamansky had driven her home after her release, why hadn't she stayed?

"Maybe she's back now," Greg said.

Greg's grandpa shook his head. "Terrell checked just a while ago, to be sure. She's not there. Sorry, Greg."

Why wouldn't she have stayed? Even if she couldn't find any of them, she would have stayed home. He could only think of one reason why she would have left with Jamansky.

She had no choice.

"Oh, I'll ask her if she wants to come back," Jamansky had said when he planned to release her at Oliver's tribunal. *"But it's my duty to lay out all of her choices for her. Make sure she knows that she has...more favorable options."*

Greg started backing up. "Where's Ashlee? I need Ashlee."

"She already left," Dylan said. "She left with Braden and Richard to find Amber and Zach."

Greg looked around. "I gotta go."

"Where?" his grandma said. "Gregory, you can't leave. You just got here. Where are you going?"

He couldn't even think straight to answer. He took off.

forty-five

Ashlee pulled out her hidden key from inside her fence post. She unlocked her back door and waved Richard and Braden inside. Richard held her small pistol in front of him—the one Greg had taken—ready for an attack, but no attack came. Her house was dark and empty.

Flipping on a few lights, she headed straight for the kitchen. She found her spare green card right away in her junk drawer.

"I thought it was in your purse," Braden said.

"I have a few cards."

Richard gave her a strange look. "Is that allowed?"

She shrugged. "If you know the right people." Namely David Jamansky. "Now to find out if it's valid. I wish I had an IDV machine. I bet David has one at his house. Should I sneak in and check? I bet he's working."

"Not worth the risk," Richard said. "Just bring it with us. I still think I should be able to get inside to see the kids. If that doesn't work, we can decide what to do from there."

She nodded and looked around her empty house. Little had changed—same over-sized chairs, and white, airy décor—but it felt different, like she'd been gone for months.

Her gaze went to one room she'd missed more than any other: the bathroom. "Maybe I'll shower really quick before we go. I'll be fast. Do you guys want to take quick showers before we go? I bet it's been ages since you've had hot showers."

"No!" Braden said. At his sharp response, she turned. He looked a little embarrassed, but said, "I'm sorry. We really don't have time."

Richard smiled. "I think he's a little anxious."

"Fine," Ashlee said. "At least grab some food."

Ashlee opened her fridge. "Ew," she said, waving a hand in front of her face. "Ew, ew, ew. Maybe food isn't such a good idea."

"It can't all be bad," Richard said, eying what food she had with obvious hunger.

"Help yourself," she said. "I'm going to grab a few things."

As she walked into her hallway, she heard Richard say, "Carrots still look good. Oranges, too. Goodness, when was the last time I had an orange?"

"Oooh," Braden crowed. "She has Cheerios."

Ashlee smiled. The small pleasures of life. "Hey," she called, "if you see any rotten eggs, save them for me."

"Why?" Braden asked.

"So I can egg David's house," she said. "Oh, and get my secret stash of chocolate. Upper cabinet, next to the sink." With everything happening, she was going to need every last bit of chocolate.

While they raided her fridge, she raided her bathroom. Grabbing a bag under the sink, she shoved in lipstick, makeup, shampoo, hairbrushes, and her beloved toothbrush.

As she turned to leave, she caught a quick glimpse of herself in the mirror. A woman she hardly recognized stared back at her. Her blonde hair was a disaster. Ratty, frizzy ends, with dark roots showing through. She rubbed her cheeks and the skin under her eyes. She looked thinner. That wasn't so bad. Her skin had grown tan, too—another benefit. Leaning forward, she spotted a smudge of dirt on her forehead. Strangely, she didn't mind that either. In fact, she looked stronger than before—maybe even a little wild—and she kind of liked it.

But not enough to leave her beauty supplies behind.

She rushed into her room to grab clothes next but stopped. Someone had opened her drawers and strewn things about. *David!* she growled. He'd been digging through her clothes, through every single drawer. *Pervert.* What did he think he'd find? A map to her secret hideout? She dug through what was left and picked a few of her favorites.

By the time she came back out, Richard and Braden were hunched over deli sandwiches.

"Men," she said, shaking her head with a broad smile. "Offer them a shower, and they turn it down. But offer them food…"

"Sorry," Richard said, mid-chew.

She laughed. "Don't be."

As they snarfed down what they could, she shuffled through the things on her counter. Scattered mail. Papers David had obviously searched, trying to find her. She reached over to check her answering machine.

No messages.

Thanks a lot, Mom and Dad, she thought bitterly.

"Don't you want to be careful moving things around?" Braden said in between bites. "Jamansky will know you were here."

"This is *my* house!" she snapped. "I hope he knows I came home. Maybe I should leave him a note. Tell him to go…"

Her voice trailed away as her eye caught hold of something. In her moving things around, a letter had slipped out between the rest of her mail. It looked like the usual, official, boring drivel she got, except it had been addressed to her in a man's handwriting, and he had misspelled her name.

Ashley Lion.

It was the misspelling that caught her eye. Nothing official was ever misspelled. They always sent everything through a computer, linking it to her citizenship record.

Curious, she pulled the letter out of the pile. Then she gasped. In the upper left corner it said, "Joliet State Penitentiary."

JSP.

Her eyes widened. "You guys, come look! Hurry. I think this is from Oliver."

She nearly squealed as she opened it.

To Ashley Lion,

I'm writing for a friend. Well, he's kind of a friend. He's my cellie (that's code for cellmate), but he's not allowed to send letters, so I'm sending this for him. We're not even sure if you'll get this, so he asked me to be vague. He's kind of a nervous guy, but I bet you already know that. *wink, wink

I apologize if this is lengthy. We don't get a lot of social interaction here, so I'm going to take my time and enjoy writing to a gorgeous babe. (Technically, I don't know if you're gorgeous. My buddy won't tell me what you look like. But based on how he was acting, I'm guessing he thinks you're totally hot. In fact, you should send us a picture.)

"What in the world?" Richard said, reading over her shoulder.

"It doesn't even make sense," Braden said.

Braden was right. This guy couldn't be talking about Oliver because even if quiet, reserved Oliver Simmons thought she was attractive—which was a huge *if*—he wouldn't use the word *hot* to describe her *or* any other woman. Not without dropping dead first.

Even more curious, she kept reading.

So, hey. How are ya? My friend seems sad, but that's to be expected. He's learning the ropes here, and I'm keeping an eye out for him. (You're welcome.) But he's really, really, <u>REALLY</u> worried about you. So I'm supposed to ask:

Are you okay? Are you hurt? He wouldn't tell me why, but he said he put you in some kind of "grave" danger. Because of that, he said to tell you to beware of certain things and certain people because those certain people know certain things about some certain project you and he were working on.

Ashlee stopped.

Of course David already knew about their project. He'd squeezed the information out of her. Would David have arrested Oliver if it wasn't for her? Guilt flooded her veins. How much had he known before she squealed like the coward she was?

Richard gave her a strange look. "What project?"

She stared at the words. "Oliver and I were trying to nail down Jamansky's illegal activity. Trying to prove it on paper. David and the mayor have been embezzling money for years. They sell most of what we acquire on the black market. But it's not exactly like the black market gives receipts. So we were trying to prove it from our end, showing everything that had come into the office, and then prove that only a third of it—or less—had been reported to the government."

Braden's eyes widened. "Wow."

Even more desperate, Ashlee kept reading.

If you're able, my friend has a file of itemized logs in his house that should help prove things. His spare key is in his garage under the rock. (He said "the rock" which makes me think there's only one.) The file is in his file cabinet under the false heading of "Mileage." He's hoping you can send it in for him. Just make sure to put his name on it, and he'll take all the blame. He was adamant that you LEAVE YOUR NAME OFF. (He told me specifically to underline and put that in capital letters.)

Hopefully that all makes sense to you. Like I said, he's pretty stressed about you.

*But enough about all that. Let me tell you about me. I have dark hair, perfect eyes, and a killer body. I work out all the time in here to stay sane. I've been in JSP for fifteen years, serving one and a half life sentences—don't ask—but I'd give it all up for just one glimpse of you. *wink, wink*

I think you should send us a nice long letter in return. In it, confess that you're madly in love with both of us, and it's not fair that we're making you choose between us. In fact, you're completely torn up over the decision.

A guard is tapping on the glass. I'm out of time, sweetheart. Hope I remembered everything. Hugs and big wet kisses from your two favorite inmates.

Reef and You Know Who

PS) Don't forget to send a picture.

PPS) I know you can't send a letter—or picture. They don't allow any letters to come in, so I guess you'll just have to come visit ~~us~~ me.

"What does it all mean?" Braden said.

"I…I don't know," Ashlee said.

"Look." Richard grabbed another envelope from the stack. "I think this is another one."

Sure enough, one more buried envelope had the guy's same handwriting—and misspelling of her name. When she pulled out the next letter, it was a third of the length and written in a scrawled, hurried script.

Dear Miss Lion,

Forget everything I said before. Your boyfriend (I didn't realize you had a boyfriend; that would have been nice to know) visited my buddy and threatened him pretty bad. Now my friend wants you to forget everything and hide. Yep. Hide. He says to make it somewhere your boyfriend can't find you since he threatened to go after you and some chick named Carrie. He wants to hurt both of you real bad. I guess the feds already got ahold of whatever you had in that file. They put your boyfriend and the mayor on probation, and now he's out for blood.

"Probation?" Ashlee repeated. "David's on probation?"

I suggested you go to the cops, but apparently that's a bad idea. Now we're both super stressed that it's too late and you won't get this letter in time. If you get this, please find a place to hide.

Reef and You Know Who

Ashlee put a hand on her cheek, reading it all over again to figure out what it all meant. Then her jaw clenched tight. She threw both letters down on the counter.

"I'll be back," she said.

"Where are you going?" Richard asked.

"To Oliver's house. I have to find that file."

"But he said to forget it," Braden said. "Jamansky threatened you and Carrie."

"Carrie's in prison, and I'm already hidden," Ashlee said. "David can't touch either of us, so I say let him hang. Are you guys coming or not?"

forty-six

There was indeed only one rock in Oliver's garage. Still, Ashlee felt
weird breaking into Oliver's home—even with his permission. It felt too
private. But the three of them entered through his back door.

Darkness filled his home. She flipped on a few lights. Even though his
house was identical to hers, it looked different. He had very little
furniture, and no pictures. Not even cozy curtains. Just lonely, closed
blinds.

Walking around, she made little kissy noises.

"What are you doing?" Richard said.

"Seeing if he has a cat." At Richard's strange look, she said, "Hey,
Oliver could be a cat guy. You never know."

But no cat came.

Probably because it had starved to death. Poor kitty.

Ashlee still wasn't sure how she hadn't paid much attention to Oliver
Simmons over the years. They lived a few streets apart and worked even
closer in the same precinct. But he was the kind of guy who became
invisible.

She found his small desk in his office. She opened the bottom drawer
and smiled sadly. Not only had he organized his files perfectly, with tiny,
uniform, handwritten letters, but they were alphabetical.

Oliver.

She had no problem finding the one titled "Mileage," and flipped it
open. Oliver had placed several small papers inside, paper-clipped into

sections. Some were logs from the Kane County official registers. Others were small notes Oliver had written.

She held up one.

"Hey," she said to the others, "look at this one."

"Check out Ferris raid, two years ago, October."

Braden nodded. "Weird coincidence. Does all of that mean anything to you?"

"Yes. It means a lot of work, unfortunately."

Every time she came across a handwritten note, she paused, reading his notes, reading his thoughts. One was a note to himself to investigate boxes in the back shed—something he'd never had time to get to.

Because she'd spilled everything.

She had told David, and now Oliver was rotting in prison because of her.

Her throat clogged. Her eyes started to burn. Of all the people in the world who deserved incarceration, he was the last.

She looked up at Braden and Richard. "I know you're in a hurry to see Amber, but I have to send these in. I have to finish what Oliver started, and it's going to take me some time. I'm not even sure what all he has here. I'm sorry to bail on you, but Richard should be able to get in and visit—maybe. I'll try to catch up later. Somehow."

Richard looked at Braden.

For a long time, Braden just stared at the file. Then his shoulders lowered. Looking around, he found a chair and pulled it up beside her. "If we help, you can go faster."

She smiled a slow smile. "Good. Look around and find some envelopes."

Amber lay on her blue cot, staring at the ceiling twenty feet above. The pain was bearable. The humiliation, tolerable. But the defeat was paralyzing, even more than the broken leg.

Tears leaked down the sides of her face.

"I'm supposed to help you get to lunch," a girl said. "Do you know how to use your crutches?" She was younger than Amber. Intrusive. Inconsequential.

Amber remained on her cot, staring up at her ceiling.

"I can help you with the crutches if you need," the girl said. "I had a cast once, too."

She waited for Amber to respond or move, but Amber did neither.

"Stupid mute," the girl muttered. "I don't know why they bother with you."

Neither did Amber.

The girl left the communal room. Her retreating footsteps mocked Amber's ability to get up and leave. Her leg throbbed so badly tears continued to flow freely down her hot cheeks. She squeezed her eyes shut, hating herself for being so stupid.

Her plan had failed on many levels: height, yard guards, and fence. How had she not noticed the fence? And now she was a cripple. She'd heard the bone crack in her leg when she hit the ground. Even if she hadn't busted her leg, the yard guards had reached her before she could even attempt to stand.

I'll have to stop eating, she decided. It would be ten times harder than not speaking because she loved food, especially the variety they gave the girls there.

"Miss Ashworth?"

A different voice approached her, adult, soon to be intrusive, and yet still inconsequential.

Just leave me alone! Amber wanted to yell.

"Miss Ashworth?" Mrs. Karlsson repeated, hovering until Amber looked at her. "Natalia informed us that you're perfectly capable of speaking, so speak."

"Why? So you can kill me?" The words felt strange in her throat after so long in silence.

"Ah," Mrs. Karlsson said. "Good. Now we won't have to force the words out of you."

As if they could.

Clasping her hands tightly, the headmistress said, "All of your behavior since your arrival has convinced me of your former status. You weren't just any illegal, were you, Miss Ashworth? You belonged to a rebel group."

Amber laughed darkly. "Yep. That's me. Quite the rebel."

"That's what I thought." Mrs. Karlsson motioned to a man who had come in behind her. "Go ahead. Use whatever means you need to get the information."

Information? Amber jerked back. The move jarred her leg, shooting pain up and down her.

A man sat beside her bed. He looked like a nerdy librarian from fifty years ago, sweater vest and all. He even had a pocket protector with several pens. He grabbed one out and tapped a small notebook.

"How's the leg?" he asked, almost sounding like he cared.

"Drop dead," she said.

Rolling onto her side, she pulled the scratchy blanket up and over her head.

"Well, this should be fun," the man said. "Let me explain how it works, Miss Ashworth. Every name you give me gets you time off for good behavior. Mrs. Karlsson told me that you hate working the floor. Perhaps with this injury you'd like a break from your duties?"

Names.

They wanted names of rebels they thought she knew. Amber panicked.

She flipped over, facing him. "Wait. I'm not a rebel. My clan was peaceful. I don't even know anyone in the rebellion."

He smiled condescendingly. "Tell you what. You obviously don't like pain, and I don't like inflicting it." In a flash, he reached out and grabbed her cast, twisting it just enough to make her yelp in pain. "So let's make this easy on ourselves. Start with ten names. Just ten. That shouldn't be too hard. And if you'd rather give me places instead..." He twisted a little harder. "That works, too."

———— ◆ ————

Greg crouched behind Carrie's flower shop, *Buds 'N Roses,* unable to take his eyes off the patrol car parked down the street. "Chief of Patrols" was painted across the side of it. Carrie had been inside that same car not long ago. Where did Jamansky have her now?

Oliver's tribunal was still a week away. Supposedly Jamansky would return Carrie then, but Greg couldn't even trust that anymore.

Jamansky was holding Carrie hostage.

If Greg confronted him, attacked, or even threatened him, he could lose the chance to find Carrie. There had to be another way that wouldn't jeopardize her safety more than it already was.

Frantic, Greg kept going over every incident from the past: Jamansky attacking him, attacking his mom, attacking Ashlee, attacking Oliver. The guy had pulled a gun on his injured, aged mom without flinching. *"Looks like I'd be doing her a favor,"* he'd taunted.

Greg squeezed his eyes shut and refocused. The Chief of Patrols might have stashed Carrie in one of the precinct's holding cells, but that didn't seem his style. Jamansky would keep her out of sight, and from more than just Greg.

He eyed that patrol car again, deciding it was his best option. Who knew when Jamansky would disappear on him again?

A few regular-looking citizens strolled down the sidewalk toward the township office. He backed out of sight until they were safely inside, and then he dashed across the street. Making a wide, careful circle around the offices, he ended up on the far side of Jamansky's vehicle.

Crouching low, he opened the driver's side door and popped the trunk. Dark and stuffy inside. Sadly, Greg already knew that he fit inside of a patrol car's trunk.

Checking the precinct one last time, he hoisted himself up and inside.

forty-seven

Greg slept off and on over the next few hours. The heat in the trunk was unbearable, the smell of his own sweat, even worse, but as the day progressed, the heat abated, his nose acclimated, and he did his best to sleep out Jamansky's shift. A few times he heard voices and cars coming and going, but they were never Jamansky.

Finally, he woke with a start, hearing footsteps approaching. Voices accompanied the footsteps, louder than before.

A car door opened, and the voices amplified as two men got in. Jamansky was in the middle of a conversation with another man, a voice Greg vaguely recognized. If Jamansky decided to throw something in his trunk, Greg was a dead man. But Jamansky got in, continuing the conversation.

Two car doors shut.

As the engine started up and the car began moving, Greg tried to track the movements. Reverse. Left. Left. Straight for a while, speeding up. He'd never used conventional roads to get to Shelton, and it didn't take long for him to feel lost, which would make finding his way back interesting. Hopefully, he would have Carrie to help him get back home.

No, not hopefully. This time he wouldn't return home until he had her.

The conversation in the front seat faded in and out of coherency. Lying on the dark, itchy trunk's interior, Greg only caught about half of what the men were saying. Mostly it sounded like two guys shooting the breeze. The one guy invited Jamansky over for drinks after work, but

Jamansky turned him down. Then the other guy said something that made Greg's ears perk up.

"How long are you going to hole up with this new girl of yours?"

Greg tensed.

There was a long pause in which Jamansky must have responded nonverbally because the other guy spoke again.

"You think I don't know about her?" the guy said. "You disappear for a few days, keep your curtains drawn, and act all weird and secretive. Sorry, boss, but I caught a glimpse of her last night when I was out."

Jamansky swore.

So did Greg.

Jamansky was keeping Carrie at his house?

"So who is she?" the guy asked.

"None of your business," Jamansky said.

The other guy laughed.

Greg jolted, suddenly placing the voice. It was the dark laugh of a big man. Giordano. Obviously the guy hadn't seen Carrie well last night or he would have recognized her as the woman he'd arrested.

"So where did you meet this new lady friend?" Giordano asked.

"South Elgin," Jamansky said.

"Interesting. And she's already moved in with you? That's...fun."

"She hasn't moved in—not officially yet. I'm just helping her out. She's in somewhat of a bind. Although..." A sudden smile entered Jamansky's voice. "She's definitely showing her gratitude. I had to fight her off me this morning just to get to work on time."

Giordano laughed another booming laugh. "Nice. Don't worry, chief. I'll keep this between the two of us. I'd hate for Ashlee to find out when she gets back from vacation."

Jamansky's voice lowered again, so Greg didn't catch exactly what he said, but it sounded like something about how Ashlee could jump off a cliff.

A few more turns, and the car pulled to a stop.

"Bring this new girl of yours by tonight," Giordano said. "I want to meet her."

"No."

"Why not?"

Because you arrested her! Greg wanted to yell. Apparently, Jamansky lied to his own coworkers, too.

"Because she and I have better things to be doing than hanging out with you," Jamansky said.

The implications made Greg's stomach twist and turn like the car was. Another laugh. "I'll bet. Well, enjoy your night with her, chief."

A door opened, and the big patrolman got out. Then Jamansky backed out of the driveway.

Like Greg had wanted for a long time, he was suddenly alone with David Jamansky. But instead of planning how to maim the guy, all Greg could think about was where Jamansky would go next.

His house.

Carrie.

Greg had no idea what condition he would find her in. What had prison done to her? What had Jamansky done? Would she even speak to Greg after all she'd been through, all he could have prevented? Even if she didn't blame him, she should.

A minute later the car rolled to a stop. Greg heard the soft hum of a garage door opener. Jamansky pulled in and shut off the engine, and then the same sound of a garage door closed behind them, locking the two of them inside.

Greg's heart rate spiked. Carrie was yards, if not feet, from him. Freckled face, golden hair, and big blue eyes. He'd finally found her.

A sound broke through the garage, distinct and disturbing.

Barking.

Dogs were the last thing he needed right now—especially those dogs.

Or so he thought.

Jamansky spoke three words.

"Honey..." Jamansky sang out softly, "I'm home."

With a dark chuckle, the patrol chief got out. A door opened, a door closed, and Greg was left alone in the trunk.

forty-eight

Greg should have been happy. Carrie was free and alive. Whatever damage had been done in prison, slashes and bruises, physical or emotional, was hopefully on its way to healing. But he knew it wouldn't be that simple. The next ten minutes could make or break him—maybe even kill him if Jamansky had anything to do with it.

Feeling around, he found the safety latch and opened the trunk.

For a few seconds, he just looked around. Jamansky's garage was plenty big, but it was stuffed with junk, some piled as high as the ceiling. Blankets. Bikes. Tarps. Even a couch. Disgusted, Greg realized the clan's stuff was probably buried somewhere in there, like Carrie's porcelain keepsake and Zach's baseball. As if Greg needed another reason to loathe the man.

Shaking out of it, he forced himself to focus on what mattered. Jamansky had disappeared inside a door that probably led to a mudroom or kitchen. Greg needed a different door, preferably one that wouldn't get him shot or attacked by dogs. But there were too many piles to see around.

Carefully, he climbed out of the trunk and started searching.

His foot caught on something. He tripped. Not bad. Not enough to go down. But enough to alert the dogs.

Barking erupted on the other side of the door, loud and furious.

Greg dropped to the cement. Heart pounding, he hid behind the car, searching for a weapon. A shovel sat a few feet off. It would have to do.

He waited, holding his breath. More barking. Those dogs hated him. Could they tell it was him in the garage?

He braced himself for Jamansky to inspect, but instead, Jamansky yelled at them to shut up. It didn't work. The dogs kept barking at the door.

Greg heard footsteps storm through the house, as furious as the barking. Panicked, Greg slid to the side and grabbed the shovel. If he attacked first, he might have a fighting chance.

But instead of the door opening, the dogs quieted down. Then the garage fell silent.

Frozen, Greg waited several minutes to be sure. Then he started searching, deciding he definitely needed a different door to escape out.

Slowly and methodically, he started moving the piles of junk, box by box. With some digging, he found a side door that seemed to lead to the side of Jamansky's house—which would give him a chance to get his bearings. With the same maddening precision that helped him break into Kearney's group, Greg kept moving things, putting them back as he passed, until he was able to squeeze out that door.

It was early evening when he emerged on the side of Jamansky's house. The yard had minimal landscaping which meant no bushes to hide behind.

Crouched low again, he scanned the area. The next home was twenty feet away, also with little landscaping. Same with the one across the street. He'd landed himself in the middle of patrolmen heaven. Thankfully, the identical homes didn't have any windows on the sides, giving him a moment's privacy to figure out what to do next.

The dogs complicated everything.

Even if he could nab Carrie, they couldn't make a run for it without the beasts pursuing. And maybe that was the point, an easy way for Jamansky to lock her in.

Desperate, Greg crept along the dirt beds until he reached the corner of the house. Jamansky's backyard looked small, but backed into a thick row of trees. Two bushes sat next to the house, waist-high, on either side of a small cement patio. In between them, a full-length, sliding glass door led—hopefully—to the woman he loved.

Ducking low to escape a kitchen window, he ambled to the first bush. Not a perfect cover, but good enough.

His mind was a torrent of thoughts and emotions. Carrie. She was in there somewhere. And if she was in less-than-pristine condition, things were going to get ugly.

With a quick breath, he leaned sideways to peer through the sliding glass door.

Zach.

That was the first and only thing Greg saw. It was enough to startle him back. He clapped a hand over his mouth to stifle any sound that could alert the dogs.

Zach was there. His scrawny, bony body stood five feet from the glass door, complete with Carrie-colored rooster-tails sticking up in every direction. He stood next to a kitchen table with his back to the glass, blocking the view of anything else.

Greg strained to listen, picking up light conversation inside. The voices were soft, unrecognizable, and definitely not Carrie's. Nor Jamansky's. The voices erupted into brief but forced laughter. Zach laughed, too.

The kid was watching TV.

Moving out of the bush, Greg stole another peek inside. Zach looked to be in no worse condition than when Greg had last seen him. That was good. The kid was okay—at least physically. Then Zach shifted, and in an instant, he was forgotten.

Greg saw her.

Carrie sat on a black couch beyond the kitchen, watching the same show Zach was. Though the front curtains were drawn, Greg could still make out her delicate profile in the muted light, the soft waves of her wavy hair. His whole body stilled at the sight of her. She looked great. Amazing even. Not the deformed, broken image he had conjured up. The urge to hold her, to crush her to him, overwhelmed him.

He fell back against the siding. Carrie was happy. She was in Jamansky's house and she was happy.

Why?

"Hey, Carrie," he heard Jamansky call. "Want a drink?"

Unable to restrain himself, Greg leaned back around and glared inside. Zach left the kitchen and joined Carrie on the couch. Unfortunately, so had Jamansky. Luckily Zach nabbed the spot next to her. That left the tall patrolman to sit on the far end of the couch, loosening the beige tie around his neck.

As they all watched their show, Greg watched them. The longing kept him paralyzed. He wanted nothing more than to break down the door and take out Jamansky—and his dogs. But something stopped him. Several things didn't make sense. That Jamansky, of all people on earth, should be the one enjoying a nice evening with her, just the three of them, killed Greg.

Three, he suddenly realized. *Not four.*

Curious, he searched what he could of the small home, but he couldn't see Amber anywhere.

Jamansky suddenly leaned forward far enough to spot Greg. Greg ducked back against the white siding.

"Are you ready for that movie, Zach?" Jamansky said. "You're going to love *Batman.*"

"Sure!" Zach said excitedly.

Then it came.

Carrie's soft voice floated through the glass. "Isn't that kind of intense, David? Zach hasn't watched anything since he was little, and those were kid shows."

"Naw. Zach's a man now," Jamansky said. "Hey, Zach, be a man and grab us some popcorn. It's next to the fridge."

As Zach walked into the kitchen, Greg saw his chance. Unfortunately, so did Jamansky. The patrol chief slid across the leather couch and slung an arm up on the back of the couch—not exactly around Carrie's shoulders, but one step away from it. That left Greg two options: tap on the glass to get Zach's attention or break through the glass and rip off Jamansky's arms.

Zach stopped, suddenly spotting Greg. His blue eyes went huge.

Greg pressed a finger to his lips. "Shhh!" he begged.

The smile that lit Zach's freckled face was enough to give anybody hope. The kid turned and called, "Can I go out onto the patio for a minute, David?"

"No problem," Jamansky said, easing further into the couch. "Take your time."

Greg was momentarily tempted to change his mind—rip off Jamansky's arms first—but then Zach unlocked the door and yanked it open.

"Greg!" Zach called in an excited whisper.

Before the kid could blow his cover, Greg snagged his arm and dragged him behind the bush, out of sight. Once they were clear, Zach started jumping up and down.

"Greg, you're here! I can't believe you're—"

Greg threw a hand over the kid's mouth. "Shhh! You wanna get me killed?"

Zach peeled his hand away. "What are you doing here?" he whispered.

"First, where are the dogs?" Greg asked.

"They were being loud, so David put them in his laundry room."

Greg nodded. "Good. Make sure he keeps them there no matter what."

"Right, right," Zach said, still bouncing. "What are you doing here?"

"What am *I* doin' here?" Greg was unable to keep the bite from his tone. "Why are *you and Carrie* here? Of all the awful places to be, why *here?*"

"David got me out yesterday. He got Carrie out before that." Zach's freckled face wrinkled in confusion. "How did you get out?"

Greg took in the state of Zach's skin. Sunburned, peeling, with scratches and red spots on his arms. A small white bandage covered his palms. The kid wasn't as okay as Greg had originally thought.

"Are you alright?" Greg asked.

Zach shrugged. "They didn't saw my ankle in half, so that's good."

"What about Amber?"

"David is getting her out tomorrow, but how did you get free?"

Tomorrow?

Greg digested that. All three Ashworths would be free by tomorrow. Was it possible Jamansky would keep his word? Was he keeping them here until the exchange with Greg?

Frowning, Greg stared down at the grass. He could wait one more day for Amber, then he'd swipe the three of them. No negotiations. They'd just disappear from this house.

"Did you break out of prison?" Zach asked. "Oh, man, did you climb the fence to get out? Was it a barbed-wire one, or was it electric?" His eyes widened to the size of baseballs. "Did you shoot a guard? Did you kill someone to get out?"

Greg grabbed his shoulders. "What the heck are you talkin' about? Get out of where?"

"Prison. Did David get you out, too? But why didn't David tell us? Oh, wait, it's a surprise, right? You're going to surprise Carrie? That's it."

Zach's mouth was going faster than Greg could keep up. Greg threw a hand over his mouth.

"I wasn't in prison, Zach."

Zach shook free. "Yes you were. David told us you were arrested just like Carrie."

"Arrested?" The implications dawned on Greg. Jamansky told Carrie he'd been taken. Why? So she wouldn't go looking for him? So she might go to her house and not stay?

What other lies had Jamansky fed her?

The realization hit him full force. Jamansky wasn't planning on returning Carrie. There would be no exchange, not if she believed Greg was locked away forever.

Jamansky. Jamansky! JAMANSKY!

"Man," Zach whispered, still hyper. "Carrie's gonna flip out when she finds out you're free. Can I tell her? I'll go right now."

Greg couldn't answer. He wanted to see her, to stroke her honey-colored hair, to feel the warmth of her in his arms. He wanted all of it and a thousand more things. Instead, he straightened to his full height to peek through the kitchen window.

The love of his life sat watching a huge flat-screen TV from the comforts of a black leather couch, next to the man Greg despised more than anything. She wore a man's t-shirt and incredibly short shorts. Worse, she looked okay with the fact that the pathological lying vulture was claiming her as his own.

"Is she hurt?" Greg whispered. "Has Jamansky done anything to her?"

"I don't think so," Zach said.

At least she wasn't hurt. For now it looked like Jamansky was still playing the interested-guy card.

"Does she...talk about me?" Greg asked softly.

"No."

It was amazing how one flippant little word could completely shred a man. Greg glared down at him.

"She doesn't talk about anything right now," Zach clarified. "She's been really quiet. We're just waitin' for David to get Amber out so we can go home. Wait! Where's Tucker? Where's everyone, Greg? Carrie went home and nobody was there."

Greg didn't explain. Already the kid would struggle to keep his secrets. The Ferris Clan was providing the perfect hideout, but one slip of the tongue could ruin it all.

"I'll explain later, but nobody left. They're all just hiding."

Zach punched the air. "Yes! I knew it!"

Greg dropped back down beside him and threw another hand over the kid's mouth. "I'd rather not get my head blown off today. Would you try to keep it down?"

"Sorry."

"Is…Carrie really okay?" Greg asked.

Zach shrugged. "She misses everyone."

"But not me," Greg said more as a statement than a question.

"What do you mean?" Zach asked, giving him a strange look.

Greg leaned against the white siding and stared out over the small, trimmed lawn. "It's my fault that she was arrested and y'all were taken."

Zach's blue eyes hooded over, suddenly on guard. "No it wasn't. You weren't even there."

"I'm the one who told her to go that day, but it backfired. If I had come with you, I could have stopped it."

"So. How does that make it your fault?"

Greg blew out his breath. "It just does."

In a matter of seconds, the boy changed: shades, expressions, stances. Everything about him shifted into a kid void of emotion. "So Carrie hates you now?" Zach said in a voice that had aged five years.

Greg nodded slowly. "Do you?"

One of his shoulders lifted which was answer enough.

Greg studied the kid's wounds, wondering what he'd been through— what they'd all been through. Zach wouldn't even look at him anymore.

"Hey." Greg put a hand on his shoulder. "I'm glad you're okay now. And you said Jamansky's gettin' Amber out tomorrow?"

The kid nodded to the grass.

"Okay. That's good."

Zach looked back up. "But Jamansky said it was Oliver's fault that we got arrested. Oliver was mad at Carrie, so he arrested you, too, because Carrie loves you more. Jamansky said so."

Clearly Greg hadn't given the patrol chief enough credit. The guy could twist anything to his advantage. "Oliver's in prison, not me. Jamansky arrested him for helpin' your clan all these years. Zach, you gotta stay away from Jamansky. He's bad news. And by the way, all this stays between you and me. You can't tell Jamansky that I'm out here. And…" As painful as it was, Greg finished softly, "You can't tell Carrie either."

Zach shot him another strange look. "Don't you want to see Carrie? I thought you love her."

"I do." *Desperately.* "But I can't see her now. Not with Jamansky here."

"She doesn't like him, you know."

Greg rolled his eyes. Obviously. Or…mostly obvious because she didn't hate Jamansky like he did. If she did, she couldn't be sitting where she was, as calmly as she was.

"I'll ask her if you want," Zach said excitedly. "I can ask her if she still loves you."

Before Greg realized what he meant, the kid took off. Greg tried to snag his red shirt, but the kid was too fast. In seconds, he was to the patio and ran back inside.

"Hey, Carrie," Zach called out inside. "Can I talk to you for a sec?"

Very subtle, Greg growled to himself. Zach was going to get him killed.

Crouched behind the scratchy bush, Greg suddenly felt like he was back in middle school: the dorky kid watching the cute girl from across the way while his even-dorkier friend found out if she liked him—the whole time being eaten up by jealousy as she sat next to the other guy. Unable to stop himself, Greg rose tall enough that he could peek in through the window.

Carrie came, drifting into the kitchen. His heart stopped at the sight of her, just ten tiny feet away. He searched her for bruises, cuts, or scrapes. Mercifully he found none. Still, something was off. She looked thinner and paler than before, but that wasn't it. He took in the soft splattering of freckles across her nose and cheeks, the gentle wave to her shiny hair. Had it been anybody else, he wouldn't have thought anything was amiss.

Then he realized what it was. Her eyes. They looked dull and lifeless, like a light had been extinguished inside of her.

"What's wrong, Zach?" she asked, joining him in the small kitchen.

Facing away from Greg, Zach leaned close and whispered something in her good ear.

Greg cringed, imagining Zach's words. *Do you still love Greg? Maybe or probably not?*

She straightened in surprise and stared at her little brother for long enough to kill Greg twice over. Leaning forward, she whispered something back. A short answer. Then she went back to watch the movie.

That was it.

Carrie sat next to Jamansky, though she didn't sit as close as she had before.

Greg waited for some kind of signal from Zach. Yes? No? But the idiotic, immature, and incredibly short-attention-spanned kid was suddenly caught up in the movie. Greg's entire existence was put on hold so Zach could indulge in *Batman*.

Zach! Greg wanted to scream. *Turn around. Zach!*

After about the fifth time, Greg gave the window a soft tap. Zach glanced over his shoulder, surprised to realize there was someone in the world besides him.

But then Zach flashed a simple thumbs up.

Suddenly Greg didn't care how immature the whole situation was, he was flying. And he had completely decided on breaking Jamansky's left arm, quickly followed by—

"David?" Carrie said, interrupting his thoughts. The way the guy's name rolled off her tongue made Greg ill, but then she finished. "I've got a sudden headache. I could use some fresh air. Is it alright if I step out back for a minute?"

Greg's heart nearly burst from his chest. Carrie was coming to him.

Back.

To him.

He glanced down at his ratty clothes. It had been awhile since he'd seen clean water. Or a razor for that matter.

"Do you want me to come with you?" Jamansky asked.

"If you want," Carrie said indifferently.

"No!" Zach shouted at the same time as Greg thought it. There was a small awkward silence before Zach finished, "Who will explain the movie to me?"

Greg could have kissed that kid.

"Stay here and watch with Zach," Carrie said. "I'll just be a minute."

Holding his breath, Greg counted each and every one of her footsteps. At eighteen, the glass door slid open. When she stepped out onto the patio, and the sun hit her soft skin, Greg stopped breathing all together.

She stood perfectly still, hugging herself as the gentle breeze swirled her hair around her face. Her hair glowed gold, and yet her expression was one of immense sadness.

Greg felt paralyzed.

He waited for her to search for him, to see him crouched behind the bush, but she stayed staring off into space, seemingly unaware of him four feet away.

With a pulse to match a race horse, Greg whispered, "What's the weather today?"

She whipped around and searched for the familiar voice.

Overwhelmed by every emotion known to humankind, he allowed himself a quick breath before stepping from around the bush.

One hand flew to her mouth, the other clutched her stomach.

"Greg," she breathed.

He smiled. "Hey, beautiful."

forty-nine

Carrie stared at Greg for a long moment, pulse speeding up while she tried to convince herself that he was actually real. His brown hair, mussed and longer than he liked, his tanned face, his green eyes that seemed to carry the weight of the world and yet somehow penetrated her soul.

"Greg," she whispered again, tears pricking her eyes. Then she flew off the porch and into his arms where he spun her around and around.

Even after he set her back on her feet, she clung to him, arms around his neck, face buried in his shoulder. Even with the warmth of him, the strength of his arms squeezing her close, she struggled to believe it. Questions filled her mind. Zach told her to go outside in a few minutes if she still loved Greg. Such a strange request, but now...

She looked up into Greg's perfect face. "How are you here? I thought..." Her throat swelled. Her eyes overflowed. "Zach didn't tell me." She pressed her fingers to her trembling lips, but she was smiling as much as she was crying. "Are you real, or have I finally lost my mind?"

His thumb brushed the hot tears from her cheeks, then he leaned down and kissed her. The world swirled with warmth and assurance that he was very real.

When he pulled back, he lifted her chin. His thick brows pulled down as he studied her face, cheeks, and neck. "Are you okay? Are you hurt?"

"I'm fine," she said quickly. More than fine. "How are you here?"

His eyes flickered to the house. "Long story, and one we don't have time for. Jamansky's gonna come lookin' for you any minute. You should probably stand where he can see you so he doesn't get suspicious."

With great effort, she released herself from Greg's arms and went back to the patio. She looked inside. David sat next to Zach, but his gaze went to her, concerned. She turned away, keeping her back to the door where he could see her, but not her expression or talking mouth. She would have to stay perfectly still as she spoke, even though everything inside of her was bursting with excitement.

When she felt confident David would give her another moment of peace, she glanced sideways.

Greg's head was cocked to the side as he examined the clothes she wore. Heat filled her cheeks as she glanced down. Ashlee's ridiculously short shorts. The t-shirt she'd stolen from Greg's house.

"Is that my lucky shirt?" Greg whispered with a smile.

She tugged on the corner of the light blue UNC shirt. His favorite shirt had become her favorite shirt. It was too big for her and had faded with age, but she loved the feel of the worn material and the smell of the back woods. She'd worn it every moment since she'd taken it, even at night.

"They burned my mom's blouse," she said. It still made her sick with sadness. "And after you were arrested, I needed you with me somehow. So...I kind of stole it from your house. Sorry."

He laughed—louder than he should have all things considered. From his back pocket, he pulled out a little booklet and waved it around. Her weather journal.

"What?" she whispered with a surprised smile. "Of all the things you could have taken, you chose my stupid rain log?"

"It's not stupid, and it's mine now," he said, stuffing it back in his pocket.

Her smile grew. Needing to hide her excitement, she faced David's backyard and stared up at the blue sky. "Well, so is this shirt."

"Deal." He chuckled softly. "I guess that shirt still has a little luck left after all. It looks good on you, Carrie girl." At the sudden change in his voice, she glanced sideways again. Greg's eyes locked on hers, softening with a look that embraced her as much as his arms ever had. "Real good."

She lost herself in his eyes. There was so much to say, so much that happened, but she didn't know where to start.

"Zach said Jamansky is getting Amber out tomorrow," Greg whispered. "Is that true?"

"Maybe," she said quietly, turning back to face the woods again. "But he's been saying that for days. Something's wrong with freeing Amber, but he won't tell me. He just keeps saying, tomorrow, tomorrow. Everyday it's another tomorrow. I'm worried, but I don't know what else to do."

"It's okay. Maybe he'll come through tomorrow. If not, we'll figure somethin' out together."

"Together?" she whispered. A few tears fell down her cheeks. She couldn't help but steal another glance his direction. "You mean you'll stay?"

He smiled. "You think you could get me to leave you now?"

Her legs felt suddenly weak, yet at the same time she was flying. "I can't believe it. I'm getting my life back. And once we get Amber back..."

"We'll go home."

Home.

"Where is everyone, Greg?" she whispered urgently. "Please tell me they didn't—"

"Ferris," he interrupted. "They're all in Ferris, every last one."

"Ferris?" She closed her eyes in relief. "And Oliver?"

"Prison, since the night he dropped us off at home. Jamansky arrested him, sent him to Joliet's facility."

A pang of sadness twisted her stomach, quickly followed by anger. David had arrested Oliver. All this time, all the lies, but before she could reply, she heard something inside.

"I'm going to check on your sister, Zach," David was saying. "I'll be right back."

"No!" Zach said desperately. "I've never seen this part and I need you to explain it to me. It doesn't make sense."

Carrie's pulse jumped. Jamansky couldn't come outside. "Greg, I have to get back inside," she said.

"Go," Greg whispered. "We'll talk later."

Later. What a blessedly wonderful word.

As she turned to face the door, she noticed his expression had darkened.

"And for Jamansky's sake," Greg added, "he better stay away from you."

Heavy footsteps crossed the kitchen. Before David could reach her, she slid open the door and entered the house.

"Are you okay?" David said. He leaned down to examine her face. "Have you been crying?"

She wiped her cheeks. "Yes. Sorry. I was just missing Amber."

"Tomorrow," he said easily. "I'll get her for you tomorrow. Now come on. You're missing the movie."

As she followed him back to the couch, she bit back a smile and started counting the minutes until they could go home.

———— ◆ ————

Two hours after Carrie heard the TV shut off in the other room, she finally sneaked out of Jamansky's bedroom. She crept down the dark hallway and peered around the corner. David's black silhouette was barely visible, sprawled on the couch, but his snores filled the room.

All evening she'd tried to get back outside to Greg. Twice Zach managed to sneak food outside to him, but anytime Carrie tried to leave, Jamansky was at her side. Now he was dead asleep, Zach was conked out in Jamansky's bed, and she was wide awake even though it was after 1:00 a.m.

Bretton and Felix pawed the laundry room door, still shut away. They started to whine. They weren't happy that David had locked them up all night, but Carrie had insisted that they were irritating Zach. Now, as long as they didn't start barking, she could make it outside without them waking David.

No such luck.

The second she reached the dark kitchen, the dogs started to yelp. A few yelps turned into desperate barking. They wanted out.

Her adrenaline kicked in.

She rushed back to the laundry room door and put both hands on it. "Shhh," she whispered.

Sensing her presence, they went back to whining and pawing the door. She checked over her shoulder. If Jamansky woke up, she could claim she was just going to the bathroom.

Jamansky continued to snore.

Even if she managed to escape outside, the dogs would bark at the door until they woke David up anyway. She scanned the dark house, only able to come up with one solution. It wasn't even a great one, but she was desperate enough to see Greg that she grabbed the laundry room door handle and turned it.

She opened it a crack and knelt in front of them. Their damp noses poked through, excited for attention. She opened the door a little more and stroked their big heads.

"Shhh," she soothed.

Their tails wagged happily.

Standing in the dark hallway, she opened the door the rest of the way, releasing them. They followed her into the dark kitchen even as she told herself what a bad idea this was. But Jamansky kept sleeping, so she kept moving. If he woke up and questioned her, she could say that the dogs had woken her, wanting to go outside.

Maybe he would believe her.

They reached the sliding glass door. The dogs' tail-wagging sped up. So did their breathing. But no barking.

There was just enough moonlight outside for her to make out the basic shapes of Jamansky's backyard.

With careful movements, she grabbed their leashes and clipped them to their collars. Checking Jamansky one last time, she unlocked the sliding glass door and slid it open.

The dogs went first and she followed into the black night. She was about to celebrate—she had done it—but the second she closed the door, Bretton let out a low growl, quickly followed by Felix.

Greg.

"Don't move!" she whispered urgently. "Stay, Greg. I have the dogs."

She didn't even know if Greg was there, but the dogs were no longer happy and chipper. They had gone stiff, heads turned the same direction.

Mimicking Jamansky, she pointed a finger at them and firmly whispered, *"Sitz!"*

Both dogs obeyed, but they continued to search through the moonlight to the left, growls building inside their muzzles.

"Greg," she whispered more desperately. "If you can hear me, I'm going to walk out a ways. I need to get the dogs away from the house." Out of earshot of Jamansky.

She looked over her shoulder.

Jamansky's dark shape hadn't budged.

"Freund," she whispered to the agitated dogs. *"Freund."*

Again, she had no idea if she was talking to the wind. Greg could be asleep or ten miles away for all she knew. But she clutched the leashes and lead the dogs out across the dark grass. She hadn't dared to grab her shoes since they were past Jamansky. The grass felt cold and damp on her bare feet.

As she walked, she kept whispering, *"Freund. Freund. Freund."*

Bretton and Felix tugged on their leashes, wanting to go left and find whatever they had smelled or heard. Greg. But she held firm, keeping them moving straight ahead. The harder they tugged, the harder she pulled. She had to get far enough away that if they barked—*when* they barked—it wouldn't wake up Jamansky.

They reached the back fence that ran along all of the homes. It wasn't as far back as she hoped, but hopefully far enough.

"Sitz," she ordered again.

They obeyed.

"Good boys," she whispered, patting their backs. Begrudgingly, she decided they really were good dogs. Obedient, at least. It wasn't their fault their owner was a tyrant. "Now, let's see how you like my friend. *Freund,*" she started chanting again. *"Freund. Freund. Freund."*

After a minute of that, she called softly, "Greg?" Glancing over her shoulder, she said a little more loudly, "Greg? Come slowly."

In an instant, the dogs went on high alert. Their heads turned, their ears pricked up, and another growl built in their throats.

"Sitz," she said more calmly than she felt. *"Freund. Sitz. Freund."*

Squinting, she thought she saw movement. A moment later, a dark shape emerged in the moonlight, crossing Jamansky's yard with slow, easy steps. Greg's hands lifted as if that would ward off an attack.

"You sure this is a good idea?" he whispered to her, voice strained.

The dogs were definitely acting up. More soft growls.

"No," she whispered back. *"Sitz. Freund. Freund.* Please don't eat him."

When Greg neared them, she reached for him. "Here. Give me your hand."

Greg did as she asked, trusting her more than she trusted herself. Hoping she didn't end up ruining another of his hands, she placed his palm in front of the dogs. A peace offering.

"Freund," she begged quietly. *"Freund. Sitz."*

Both dogs sniffed Greg's hand. Then their breathing started to slow.

"Freund," she kept whispering. "That's it. Friends."

"Friends," Greg repeated softly. "Let's be buddies, okay, boys?"

Finally the dogs seemed to settle down. Bretton even leaned into Greg, begging for attention. Greg complied, scratching behind his ear, and Carrie straightened, breathing a little easier.

While he pampered the dogs, Greg shot her a look. "You..." he whispered, "are one crazy woman. How did you do that?"

"Sorry. I didn't know what else to do. They started barking when I tried to leave."

"Are they gonna freak out if I touch you?"

"I have no idea."

"Let's find out." Greg reached for Carrie's hand in the cool moonlight, interlocking fingers with her. When that didn't warrant any barking, he wound an arm around her waist. Then they both waited. The dogs watched them in the muted light, looking like they cared more about a nighttime adventure than anyone's current illegal status.

"Alrighty then," Greg said a little easier. "That woke me up."

"Sorry it took me so long to get out here," Carrie said. "I had to be sure David was totally asleep."

He pressed a kiss to her temple. "I'd wait forever if I knew you were comin'. Glad you warned me about those two, though. I nearly swept you off your feet back there by the patio. Doubt that woulda gone over well."

She stifled a laugh. "Probably not."

"Are you up for a walk?" he asked, squeezing her hand. "I scouted out a place that might give us some privacy. As I recall, you still owe me a moonlit walk, Miss Ashworth. And while this might not be our pond, it'll have to do. For now."

Happiness swelled inside her. "Sounds perfect."

He led her and the dogs along the fence through several yards. The patrolmen's homes were dark. A month ago, sneaking around like that would have terrified Carrie, but tonight she would have gone with Greg anywhere. Strangely, having the dogs made her feel safer, too. She just wished she knew the command for attack in case any of Jamansky's patrol friends surprised them.

For several minutes, they crept along the fence and low-lying bushes. Greg held the leashes, directing them toward a patch of trees behind one of the dark homes.

Greg let the dogs enter the woods first. They sniffed the ground, curious but still enjoying the adventure. Greg followed next, shoving low-lying brush and branches aside as he went.

"Are your feet gonna be okay?" he whispered back to her.

She nodded, even though the first of the twigs and dirt dug into the soles of her feet. They would be sore and scratched up tomorrow, but her eyes bothered her more. They struggled to adjust under the thick canopy of trees. The woods swallowed up the moonlight. But Greg and the dogs seemed to be able to see well enough to push forward until they entered a small clearing, safely out of earshot of the other homes.

Once they stopped, Greg turned and faced her. She waited for him to grab her hand or pull her in for another hug. But with the returning, intermittent moonlight, he looked worried, almost grim.

"Are you okay?" she asked.

"Are *you*?" he asked in return. "Are you really? And I don't want the standard Carrie answer. Zach told me some things today, and now..." He shook his head. "Tell me everything from the start. I've pieced together some, but I need to know what all happened."

A darkness filled her, darker than the woods. She shoved it aside before it could consume her.

"I'm fine now," she said.

That response seemed to upset him even more. When he had returned from military training, he'd told her everything, even the beatings. Everything with Kearney. With McCormick and Isabel. It had sickened her. Now he wanted the same, the whole story without filters or holding back. But she couldn't. Thinking about it hurt too much. If she had her way, she wouldn't have to remember what happened again. She needed to get Amber and Oliver safe, and then she needed to forget.

His brows pulled down, waiting.

She stared down at her hands that seemed to disappear in the darkness.

"The little Zach told me hasn't been good," she said. "He won't talk about it. The whole time–" Her voice caught, and she struggled to continue. "The whole time I thought Zach and Amber were together, but they were separated the moment I was arrested. For the first time in their life they were completely–" Her insides started to shake. "They were alone. And to think Amber's still stuck in the middle of it…"

He reached for her hands. Finally. Willingly she gave them, needing his reassurance that it was over. But he didn't interweave fingers like he normally did. Instead he held her hands, palms up, until they were visible in the moonlight. Once illuminated, he ran a finger over her wrists.

Her wounds.

When had he noticed them? How could he even see well enough to know they were there? Maybe Zach had told him, but she didn't know that Zach had noticed either. They were her own fault, though, fighting against the handcuffs when she didn't have a fighting chance. She'd barely noticed the cuts at the time. She barely noticed them now.

"And what about you?" he whispered. "How was it for you?"

Something about the way his fingers ran over her wounds pushed her over the edge. Her pulse sped up. Her throat constricted as she remembered the arresting officer, large and cruel. The guards searching her. Donnelle. Sicknesses. Jamansky's house. The memories slammed into her, every smell and sound, every moment of pain and loneliness. And yet worse was knowing that Amber and Oliver were still stuck in the middle of it—plus Crazy Marge, Lisbeth, and how many others?— enduring their own nightmares.

She withdrew her hands and let them drop back into the black, cold night where she could hide the wounds—and the memories.

"I'm fine," she said. Because she was now.

His chest moved in and out. His head started to shake. He took a step back, putting distance between them. Only then did she realize her mistake in withdrawing her hand.

She had pulled away from him.

"I'm sorry, Carrie. So totally and completely sorry I sent you that day. I never thought—"

"Don't," she cut in. "I'm the one who went without Richard. You told me not to go alone, but with the rain, I went anyway."

"Because I told you to go! I was so adamant about keepin' you away from Jamansky, and now…" He took another step away from her until his face was swallowed up in more darkness. "Carrie, I'm dyin' over everything you've been through—everything you're still goin' through. I don't know how to fix it or take away the pain."

"Please," she whispered, emotions rising against her will. He was pulling away like he had so many times before. Since the day his sister had died, he'd developed some warped sense that he was to blame for everything bad that happened around him. Jenna's death. His mom's. Things in the clan. Things at home. And right now, words were failing her when she needed them most.

What happened, happened, she wanted to say. It was over, done, finished. It was nobody's fault but the crooked world they lived in. She just needed him back. She needed him to hold her together before she fell apart completely.

"Please," she begged in a hoarse whisper. "Don't."

"Carrie..."

The coldness of the night pressed in around her, yet heat built behind her eyes.

"Don't let go of me," she whispered. "Please. Don't let go."

Slowly, he approached her again but he didn't reach for her. His hands stayed at his sides. He looked like a beaten man.

She reached out and grabbed his hands, winding them around her. "Don't let go of me."

His forehead fell against hers. "Carrie."

"Don't let go," she whispered. "Ever again."

They were the same words he'd once begged her. More than anything, she wished that life had allowed it to happen, letting them hold each other as long as they wanted, letting them just forget the world. She pressed her bad ear to his chest and kept squeezing, waiting, needing.

Slowly, almost imperceptibly, his arms responded, tightening around her until he was nearly crushing her. Suddenly it was as if he was trying to squeeze out every bit of hurt inside of her. And he did. With each breath she took, more of the pain subsided and her memories receded.

His chin rested on her head for a long time, the two of them listening to the woods and breeze whisper around him. He stroked her hair and she held him tight.

Then she felt something change.

His shoulders squared, and he stood a little taller. She felt him take in a deep, slow breath. When he spoke again, he sounded more like the Greg she knew, more like the confident Greg she had fallen in love with.

"Care to make it official?" he said.

Her head tipped back. "What do you mean?"

"I mean..." The filtered moonlight caught his face. He was smiling. "How would you feel about becoming a Pierce, Miss Ashworth?"

Her heart skipped.

His eyes, so steady on hers, so full of love and longing and everything in between, communicated his full question. A life together, working and surviving together. Neither of them had citizenship. Neither had much to offer besides themselves. But that was enough.

It was more than enough.

A smile spread through her. She wanted to shout and throw her arms around his neck, but in her current state, she was lucky to manage what she did.

A small nod and a big smile.

"Yeah?" he asked, eyes alight with hope.

Her eyes pricked with tears, but they were tears of joy. "Yes. Definitely yes."

fifty

"You gotta be tired," Greg said even as he stifled a yawn.

Awhile back, he had stomped down the vegetation and found a wide tree trunk for them to lean against. Then he pulled Carrie down next to him. The tree wasn't the most comfortable thing he'd ever rested against, but having warm Carrie snuggled into his arms more than compensated. The dogs sat beside them, dozing off and on as Greg casually stroked their backs.

Under the scattered moonlight, he caught Carrie up on his side of things. She was particularly interested in how things had developed with McCormick and Kearney, wondering if they could actually overthrow President Rigsby. He wished he knew. But anytime he pressed her about prison and her time away, she clammed up, answering his most basic questions. It killed him. The only time she opened up was talking about her friend Donnelle and the virus sweeping through the prison.

Though Greg hated to admit it, Jamansky had saved her life, getting her out when he had.

All things considered, heavy subject aside, he loved their time together. He liked hearing her gentle, quiet voice over the backdrop of night frogs and crickets. He loved feeling her in his arms, her softness and heat pressed up close to him. He loved the smell of her hair tucked near his face, and how she looked in his lucky shirt, moonlight dancing across her cheeks.

Mostly he loved that she'd said yes.

But the discussion eventually slowed, Greg's back ached from the stiff trunk, and he was fighting his eyelids to stay awake. As much as he hated to end this small piece of perfection, they needed to sleep if they were going to function tomorrow. With luck, in another twenty-four hours they'd have Amber and be on their way home.

"C'mon," he said, straightening. "I know you're tired and colder than you'll admit. Time to head back inside."

Standing, he grabbed her hands and pulled her up beside him. The dogs jumped up, awake and ready for more adventure.

"Do you think Richard and the others have any chance of getting Amber out?" Carrie whispered as they started back through the woods.

"Not likely. I found out the hard way that it's not as simple as we hoped. Unfortunately, Jamansky is Amber's best bet."

She looked less-than-thrilled by that.

Greg pushed aside a low-lying branch and let her pass.

"I just feel like he's stringing me along," she said, choosing her steps carefully to save her feet. "What if he never comes through? What if he's trying to keep me here permanently? What if he never lets me leave?"

That caught his attention. He tugged her arm to a stop. "What do you mean?"

She shook her head.

"Carrie, what do you mean?" he said, insides tightening.

Sighing, she stared out through the dark night. "One more day. That's all I think we should wait. If Jamansky doesn't come through tomorrow, then we should leave while we can."

"While we can?" He bent down to peer at her. "What are you not tellin' me? Has he threatened you?"

Even in the dark, he saw her roll her eyes. "You worry too much. I just think he's never going to get Amber, so why wait to go home? Maybe Richard, Ashlee, and Braden will have better luck. If not, we'll find another way."

Of course he worried too much, but normally Carrie didn't, which concerned him even more.

If she was worried about things here…

"Then we leave tomorrow night," he said. "No matter what. That means you definitely need to sleep."

Silently they worked their way back across the yards and lawns until they reached Jamansky's.

Carrie stopped and slipped her arms back around him. "I don't want to leave you."

He stroked her back, loving that she no longer hesitated to reach for him. If she wanted a hug or to hold his hand, she did, and he loved it.

He tipped her chin up and kissed her soundly. "Maybe I should come inside with you," he offered.

Her brows scrunched. "What? Why?"

He had plenty of reasons to want to be in there with her and Zach. More than anything, to be within hearing—and striking—distance if something happened. Not only was Jamansky scheming up something, he was predatory, unstable, *and* violent. If Carrie felt nervous, then it was worse than she was letting on. Greg needed to be close.

"How about I find a good spot inside to hide out," he said.

"No way. You can't. As much as I want you in there, it's not safe. Even if you hide, the dogs will track you down. Just stay out here until David leaves for work in the morning."

"It already is morning," Greg said. "Look."

He held up his watch. 3:48 a.m.

"Stay out here," she said firmly. "I'll be fine."

Trusting her judgment over his went against his instincts, but...she'd been at Jamansky's longer. She knew better.

She and the dogs started for the patio.

"Wait," Greg whispered. "Don't lock the door."

She turned. "It was locked before."

"I know." But it was a compromise he could live with. "If Jamansky asks why it's open, tell him you went out for early morning fresh air."

Nodding, she opened the door and disappeared inside.

———————◆———————

"What's this, Carrie?"

Jamansky pulled something dark brown from her hair. A piece of bark.

Carrie felt heat rush up her neck. "I...don't know."

His eyes narrowed on her. "Then maybe you can explain why there are dirty paw prints in my hallway?"

"I..."

Zach looked at her, panicked.

"I woke up early this morning," Carrie said. "The dogs seemed anxious to go outside, so I took them for a little bit. Is that okay?"

Jamansky fingered the tree bark. "How far?"

"Just by your patio, of course."

"Hey, David," Zach said suddenly, "can I take Bretton and Felix outside now?"

"For a few minutes," he said. "But stay close to the house."

"Thanks."

Zach snatched three pancakes from the plate—Greg's breakfast—and took off. Envious, Carrie watched her brother head outside with the dogs. When she turned back, Jamansky was still twisting the piece of bark around in his fingers.

She resisted the urge to finger comb her hair for more. Instead she grabbed his plate and headed for the sink.

"Did you sleep well?" she asked.

"Apparently too well," he muttered under his breath.

Her pulse sped up. He didn't believe her story. She turned on the water and slowly rinsed the syrup from the plates, needing a moment to compose herself.

"It's crazy how fast I've become accustomed to running water again," she said. "Even pancake mix seems like cheating."

"Yeah." She heard his chair push away from the table. He walked to the glass door and looked around. Carrie looked, too.

No Zach in sight.

Her stomach dropped.

Jamansky slid open the door. "Zach?" He whistled loudly. Bretton and Felix came racing back. Zach followed a few seconds later, out of breath.

"What the heck, Zach!" Jamansky snapped. "Where did you go? I said to stay by the patio, out of sight."

"Oh, sorry," Zach said, huffing. "We were just playing on the side of the house."

Jamansky slammed the door closed and locked it. "No more going outside today—for either of you. Bretton and Felix will be fine."

He grabbed a piece of buttered toast from the table. "I'm going to be late for a meeting. I'll be back later."

"Back with Amber?" Carrie said.

"What?" he said. "Yeah. That's the hope."

Hope? That didn't sound hopeful to her at all.

Her eyes flickered to the window, wondering how much Greg could hear. Maybe by the time Jamansky returned, they would be gone.

David stood in front of her. "Hey, I'm sorry I snapped at Zach. I just have a lot going on right now. But if things go well in my meetings, I'll have time to negotiate for Amber's release later. My meeting is near Joliet, and she's over that way. How about to celebrate, I cook a special dinner?"

That sounded a little better. Maybe he would get Amber after all.

"Okay," she said.

Jamansky glanced behind him. "Hey, Zach, what's Amber's favorite dinner?"

"Pizza," Zach said without hesitation.

Carrie scowled at that. Since when had Amber liked pizza?

Jamansky seemed to suspect the same thing. He turned back to Carrie. "What does your sister actually like? Make it something fancy. I can cook anything."

She looked up into his ice-blue eyes, trying to read him. His words sounded so confident that, without meaning to, she got excited. What if he actually did bring Amber home tonight? Carrie could have her family back in eight hours. Amber. Zach. Greg.

Smiling, she said, "Amber loves pasta."

"Perfect." He matched her smile. Lowering his voice, he leaned toward her, giving her another whiff of his aftershave. "Maybe after dinner we'll put on a movie for your siblings and go for a drive, just the two of us. What do you think?"

Her stomach flipped. While his offer implied several things, there was also a challenge in his eyes.

She couldn't risk angering him now. By dinner, they'd all be long gone, so she forced brightness into her tone. "Sounds great. Thank you, David."

"You're welcome," he said, obviously pleased by her response. Reaching up, he tucked a lock of hair behind her ear. "See you tonight, Carrie."

Then, so fast she wasn't sure it happened, he leaned in and kissed her. It was a fast kiss, barely a peck on her lips, but heat flooded her cheeks.

Zach's mouth dropped.

Snatching his keys, Jamansky headed out the door.

Minutes later, Greg tapped on the glass. Carrie had nearly finished cleaning up, but her skin still felt flushed. Keeping her back to Greg, she rubbed her lips back and forth a few times to erase the lingering, eerie feel of David on them.

"Good morning, beautiful," Greg said, wrapping his arms around her from behind. Turning her to face him, he kissed her soundly.

"I'm gonna puke," Zach said. "First Jamansky. Now you."

Carrie stiffened, waiting for Greg to pull back at the comment. It took him another moment, but when he pulled back, he was smiling. He hadn't noticed.

He brushed some hair away from her still-warm cheek. "You know, Zach, someday you might change your mind. Maybe when you know Delaney a little better."

"Greg!" Carrie said in dismay.

He laughed. "Sorry. Hey, what do y'all think about finding Zach's baseball today?"

"My baseball?" Zach asked. "Where?"

"I have a hunch it's in Jamansky's garage. Actually," Greg turned, taking in the luscious interior of Jamansky's house, "maybe we'll find a lot more. Man, just when I thought I couldn't hate the guy anymore. Here I've been worried that nobody was surviving in this economy. Apparently some are thriving. So let's do some hunting while Jamansky's gone. I've got a few items…that…"

Greg stopped, gaze slowly swiveling back to Zach. "Hold on. What did you mean, 'First Jamansky, now you'?"

Carrie picked up a napkin from the floor in order to shoot Zach a warning look.

"Uh…nothing," Zach said lamely.

"Hey, Greg," Carrie said quickly, "speaking of searching for things, I forgot to tell you something last night. I found some papers in Jamansky's office that I think you should see. Maybe they'll help us figure out how to get Oliver. Watch the road, Zach. Make sure he doesn't return while I show Greg."

Then she led Greg to the office doors. Finding her wire hanger, she let them inside. She showed Greg the letter from the Department of Investigations, including the one with the required repayment amount.

"I think Oliver and Ashlee are behind this," Carrie said.

He looked up. "Oliver?"

"Yes." She smiled. "Did I ever tell you Amber's theory about the two of them?"

Greg didn't seem to hear. He looked around, suddenly urgent. "Wait. What day is it?"

"Wednesday," she said, confused by his sudden change of mood.

"Wednesday. No. It can't be Wednesday yet. Are you sure?"

"Yes. What's wrong?"

In answer, Greg started shuffling through the papers on Jamansky's desk. "Does Jamansky have a map anywhere?"

"Wait! Stop, Greg." She grabbed his arm. "He'll know if you move things around."

"A map, Carrie. I need a map!"

Fear clawed at her. "There's one in his desk. Here." She crossed the room and handed it to Greg. "What's going on?"

He traced the lines on the map until he tapped on a spot south of them. "He said he had a meeting near Joliet?"

"Yes. Greg, what is it? What happened?"

He glanced down at his watch. "I'll never make it in time, but I've gotta try." He backed up, finally looking at her. "I'm real sorry, but I've gotta go. I'll be back soon."

"What? Where are you going?" she asked, panicking. He said he would stay. He promised to stay with her.

Greg raced into the kitchen. "Where does Jamansky keep his spare keys?" Like a madman, he threw open cupboards and drawers.

"You're leaving?" Zach asked, curious.

"Keys, Carrie!" Greg said. "I gotta go now if I'm gonna make it."

She pointed to a small box near the phone. "Go where?"

Greg snatched out some keys and ran to the door that led to the garage. She struggled to follow.

Once in the garage, he finally answered.

"I may or may not have agreed to meet with Jamansky this morning," Greg said. He grabbed a box and tossed it aside. Then he moved another.

Her eyes popped open. "You did what?"

He hefted a small couch up and out of the way. "He agreed to let me meet with Oliver today, but don't worry. I'll be back long before Jamansky returns."

He pulled a few more things out of the way until he revealed what he was looking for.

Her mouth dropped open. She started shaking her head. "No. No way! You can't take that, Greg. Are you crazy?"

With a slow smile, he ran a hand over the seat of a shiny blue—and very expensive-looking—motorcycle. "She's a beauty, isn't she? I found her yesterday when I was tryin' to break outta here. Barely a scratch on her."

"Whoa," Zach said, pushing out into the garage beside Carrie. "That's sweet! Do you know how to ride it?"

"Well..." Greg said. "My friend had one back in the day. This one can't be too different."

"Are you crazy?" Carrie exploded.

"Do you really have to ask?" He pulled out a shiny black helmet. He *and* Zach grinned like kids on Christmas morning. With the path cleared and motorcycle free, he tugged on the different parts to figure out what was what. "Front brake. Clutch. Throttle. I've totally got this."

He was serious. He was leaving.

On that motorcycle.

Carrie resorted to begging. "Please, this is ludicrous! Can we just talk first?"

His eyes finally met hers. "It's Oliver, Carrie. This might be our chance to get him out—or at least find a way. You really want me to miss that chance?"

"I..." She was at a loss for words.

Pulling on the helmet, he swung a leg up on the motorcycle. "Come on, baby. Work for papa." He turned the key, finagled a few things, and the motorcycle sputtered to life.

"That is *so* cool," Zach crowed.

Carrie couldn't even glare at her brother. Her heart pounded over the roar of the engine.

"Greg," she said in a whisper he could never hear. But he seemed to hear it anyway.

Smiling at her, he called, "Love you!" Then he pointed to Zach. "Push that button on the wall for me."

Zach did.

The garage door hummed open.

In a state of shock and horror, Carrie watched Greg peel down Jamansky's street.

fifty-one

Jamansky's toy was a little conspicuous, but one sweet ride.

The wind whipped Greg's clothes as he sped down the road. He stalled a few times, but eventually figured out what he was doing. From then on, he only stopped to check the map.

Finally he spotted Jamansky's patrol car in front of him.

From then on, Greg hung back, keeping Jamansky in sight only when necessary—which was a shame since the engine below him could easily double his current speed.

He noted every landmark, sign, and anything else that could get him back to Jamansky's house should they get separated. Mostly it was abandoned farmland, the same land he had passed through on his way to Logan Pond, though he passed it now at an exhilarating speed. The roads were empty.

As he neared Joliet, he ran through everything he needed to find out from Oliver. It had felt like a lifetime since he'd seen his patrolman friend at the hospital. He just had to figure out how to talk to Oliver without Jamansky eavesdropping.

He leaned right, taking a small bend in the road faster than necessary, and then he nearly ran off the road.

Jamansky was gone.

Greg hit the brakes. Somewhere, somehow, he'd missed a turnoff. Rather than trying to make sense of the map again, he spun around and sped back the way he'd come, checking every side road for the patrol car.

He only saw one road, virtually hidden past some overgrown trees. He chose it, hoping he was right. When he still couldn't see Jamansky, he went full throttle until he spotted the patrol car.

Greg slowed. Unless he wanted to walk back to Jamansky's, he couldn't lose his ride home by having Jamansky recognize the bike in his rearview mirror.

The second JSP came into view, Greg pulled over. He wheeled the motorcycle down into a low ditch and hid it in some tall weeds. Then he sprinted the rest of the way on foot.

JSP was huge, twice the size of the Rockford Women's Penal Institution, and enclosed by a concrete wall. According to Jamansky's instructions, Greg was to pass the outer wall, go to the next structure, and meet the patrol chief at the first entrance.

But the instructions were unnecessary.

Jamansky waited for Greg in the parking lot, leaned against his patrol car in full uniform, arms folded, typical sneer on his pretty-boy face.

"Pierce," Jamansky called. "It's been a while. I wasn't sure you'd make it."

Every moment, every memory from the last month—the last year—came slamming into Greg. His mom. Ashlee. Carrie. Oliver. Rockford vs. Rochelle. His entire body felt stiff with rage, but he forced himself to remain calm as he approached the patrol chief.

"How was the walk?" Jamansky said, noting how out of breath Greg was. "It's quite a ways, isn't it?"

"No worries," Greg said. "Somebody gave me a lift." That seemed to surprise Jamansky, but Greg went on quickly, wanting to get the whole mess over with. "Where are the papers to get me inside?"

"So," Jamansky said, "I guess you're still *dead*? When will you be done with your supposed secret mission?"

Greg said nothing. Just glared, waiting.

"I have the papers," Jamansky said, finally giving in. "First give me the money."

"Money?"

"I left you a note at that house. JSP is charging $500 for visits. If you want in, that's the price."

"Do you ever quit lyin'?" Greg snapped. "Or do the lies just roll outta your mouth when you sleep?"

Jamansky smiled. "Fine. That's *my* fee for getting you in to see Simmons."

It took every bit of restraint for Greg to keep from pounding the guy. Even if he had the money—or a tenth of it—he wouldn't use it to pay Jamansky's debt. If what Carrie had found was correct, Jamansky and Mayor Phillips would be rotting away in JSP soon enough.

Jamansky's expression darkened. Reaching into his pocket, he pulled out some permits. Greg flipped through them, noticing his authorization number at the bottom, along with his full name.

"These are sufficient to get me in without a card?" Greg asked.

"As long as I'm escorting you."

Greg looked up. "I get ten minutes alone with Oliver. That's what we agreed to."

"What exactly do you need to say to Oliver Simmons?"

"You've got a score to settle with him," Greg said. "Well, so do I."

Jamansky glared. "Not a chance. You talk, I stay."

"Fine. See you in hell."

Spinning on his heel, Greg marched back the way he'd come. Jamansky was desperate for his testimony against Oliver—at least, Greg hoped he was. But with each step, he started to wonder if he had underestimated David Jamansky.

"Five minutes!" Jamansky shouted. "You can have five minutes alone with him, but only if you sign the papers first."

Greg couldn't help but think how ironic it would be when Jamansky turned in the testimony of a dead special op. How well would that go over? Hopefully not well at all.

"I sign *after* I meet with Simmons—alone," Greg said. "That was our deal. Take it or leave it."

Jamansky's eyes narrowed to murderous slits. "I swear, Pierce, if you pull any stunts, anything whatsoever, you'll never see Carrie or her siblings again. Daylight either."

"Funny," Greg quipped. "I was about to say the same thing. Let's go."

As the two of them started across the parking lot for the building, Greg asked, "When do I get Carrie and her siblings back?"

"Next week at the courthouse, as planned," Jamansky said.

Unbelievable. But Greg kept up his side of the charade. "I expect everything with the deed to her home is in order?"

"Yes. I told you that I won't force Carrie to return against her will. If she and her siblings want refuge, I'm more than happy to offer it. I get the feeling she has moved on anyway. She got over Oliver pretty fast. She's over you, too. I'm thinking she's ready for a real man, someone who can fulfill all of her…needs."

"Carrie will never give you the time of day."

"You're wrong. She already did. Twice." Jamansky smiled. "Gotta love those conjugal visits."

That did it.

Greg grabbed his arm and, in one fluid motion, twisted it behind his back. Before Jamansky knew what hit him, Greg rammed him up against the nearest car.

"You really think I believe a single repulsive word you say?" Greg hissed in his ear. "You just keep dreamin', 'cause that's the only place you'll be with Carrie."

Greg shoved him hard into the car, and then turned and strode toward the building.

A group of prison guards came running out, drawing their guns. "Is there a problem, officer?" they called.

Straightening, Jamansky wiped his mouth. "No. We're here for an appointment. But do me a favor. Frisk him before we go in. I'd hate to have him pull any fast ones."

As one, the guards jumped Greg and threw him against the brick wall. They searched every part of Greg, finding nothing. Not even the tattered map since he'd left it with the bike. As if Greg was dumb enough to bring anything with him.

When it was clear that he was unarmed, two guards led them inside and down a long hallway, through several series of doors, and finally to an open area.

Another set of guards stood.

"Full treatment," Jamansky said to the next set of guards.

For a second time, guards frisked Greg. But the second search ended differently. They clamped cold metal restraints around his wrists. He had no time to question why they were handcuffing him. They were on before he realized what was happening.

All he could think was what an idiot he was, willingly walking into another of Jamansky's traps.

"What's this?" Greg asked, holding out his bound hands.

"Prison rules," Jamansky said. "They come off after the meeting."

Sure they would.

A last guard opened a door and ushered them into a long, small room with stools running up and down one side. A few people sat on the stools in there, talking on phones to inmates on the other side of a glass partition.

"Station number eight," the guard said.

For some reason, Jamansky followed Greg inside.

"I said alone," Greg growled, even though having his hands cuffed proved that he had less say than he wanted.

"I just want to say a quick hello to my old friend," Jamansky said. "I've missed him so badly."

Greg sat on the stool while he waited for Oliver to appear. None of the other visitors wore handcuffs.

Jamansky.

But Greg couldn't worry about that. He had several objectives in this meeting, and with only a few minutes, he ran through them quickly, organizing them in his mind to be the most efficient.

When Oliver came in wearing an orange jumpsuit, Greg tried not to react. His friend looked awful. Oliver's thin, dark hair was uncombed, he had thick scruff along his jawline, and he looked so thin that Greg wondered if they were starving him.

Jamansky waved excitedly through the glass like a school girl waving to her mother through the bus window. Oliver's eyes went from Jamansky to Greg and back. Then they hardened in anger.

Jamansky grabbed the phone receiver.

"Looking good, Simmons," he crowed. "I want you to meet the guy who's made tomorrow possible. I can't wait! It's going to be great!"

With that, Jamansky handed the phone to Greg.

"Five minutes," Jamansky said to the guard. Then he walked out.

When Greg turned back, Oliver was gaping. But the shock on his gaunt face quickly melted into a mask of indifference. Oliver stared straight at Greg, blank and dull, like Carrie had looked yesterday. It was the face of a survivor.

"You're working with Jamansky now?" Oliver said into the phone. "I suppose that's par."

Greg held up his hands, showing him the metal restraints. "Not exactly workin' with him. How else was I supposed to get in here to see you?"

Oliver's brows pulled down. "So…you're *not* helping him?"

Greg glanced over his shoulder. The prison guard stood watch, but the door behind him was solidly shut tight. While Greg hoped that meant Jamansky wasn't listening in, security cameras filled every upper corner.

With cuffs on, Greg clutched the phone and lowered his voice. "I'd love nothin' more than to see that guy rot in your place."

It was like watching a fire grow. Oliver's eyes lit with a spark until they were a blazing flame.

Suddenly, his words came out in a rush.

"What's going on, Greg? What happened since I left? Is Carrie okay? Has Jamansky hurt her? What about Ashlee? Have you seen her? Do you know anything about either of them, because—"

"Hold on," Greg said. "Slow down."

"No. You speed up!" Oliver snapped back. "I've been shoved in here with no word from anyone except Jamansky who comes in every few days to torture me with new tales of—"

"Carrie and Zach are at Jamansky's house," Greg cut in again. "He's keepin' them there."

Oliver's eyes popped open. "What? No! You have to get them out of there. Now!"

Greg shot him a pointed look. "Would you calm down a sec and let me talk?"

"Sorry. I just…" Oliver huffed. "Hurry."

Cupping his hand around the phone, Greg quietly explained how he was also at Jamansky's, only the patrol chief didn't know. They were just waiting for Amber, hopefully this afternoon. But when Greg mentioned the other plans for getting Amber, Oliver shot up.

"Ashlee? Ashlee's with Richard?" Oliver asked.

"Yeah," Greg said. "She came to Logan Pond right after Jamansky attacked her. She's actually been helpin' us a ton."

"And…is she okay?" Oliver asked. "Is she safe?"

"Very. Jamansky has no clue where she is."

"So she's been with you guys the whole time? She didn't get any letters?"

"What letters?"

"Never mind," Oliver said. "It doesn't matter now. She's safe. That's more important."

Oliver took this all in for a moment, small eyes darting around the small counter, seeing nothing, but thinking much. Then his gaze snapped up.

"Carrie's right. You need to leave Jamansky's tonight, no matter what."

"But Richard and the others have no way to get Amber out. They'll be lucky if they even get to visit her."

"Jamansky might have released Zach," Oliver said, "but that was just the bait to prove that he could. He'll never return Amber. Not when he can use her to keep Carrie from running."

"Why is he keeping Carrie in the first place?" Greg said.

"To blackmail me," Oliver said. "To force me to retract my testimony against him and Mayor Phillips."

Greg nodded, putting the final piece into place. "He told you he has her so you'll let him off the hook. Then he holds Amber over her head so she doesn't run. The guy is using Carrie to get exactly what he wants from both of us."

"Exactly. Can you get them out of there?"

"I can and will the second I get back. The question is, how the heck do I get you outta here?"

That seemed to catch the guy off guard. Oliver sat back, shoulders falling. "You don't. Just help me finish off Jamansky and the mayor. Can you break into my house? I have a file called 'Mileage' that I need you to send in for me."

"And when Jamansky retaliates?" Greg asked.

"He won't have anyone left to hit."

"Except you."

In his orange, over-sized tent, Oliver studied Greg with a look of immense sadness. "Not after tomorrow. But it doesn't matter. Jamansky can silence me or shoot me in front of the world, but I will take him and the mayor down with me."

Greg's brows lowered. Tomorrow. Tomorrow was Thursday.

Thursday.

His heart jolted.

"Shoot you?" Greg said. "What do you mean? What about the trial next week?"

Oliver gave him a strange look. "What trial? You think we get trials in here? No, I was convicted the moment they arrested me. I'm to be punished for treason against the state. You know, the whole firing-squad thing. I've heard they're going to televise it and everything. That should be fun. So take care of everyone, and take Jamansky down. That will be enough."

Thursday.

President Rigsby would be in Naperville Thursday. He was holding a public execution for traitors of the state.

Traitors.

Oliver.

"No," Greg said, dread spreading through him. "No, no, no."

They were going to kill Oliver.

The door behind them burst open. Jamansky came strolling in and met them at station number eight. He leaned down to see Oliver. "Did you ladies have a nice visit?"

Greg couldn't speak as he stared at the man who had spent six years of his life protecting Carrie and her clan—and was about to be executed for it.

"See you bright and early tomorrow, Simmons," Jamansky said happily. Then he turned to Greg. "Let's go."

Greg followed him back to the door, but at the last second, he ran back to station number eight.

"What are you doing?" Jamansky yelled. "Get him!"

Greg grabbed the receiver and hissed, "Be ready."

Oliver jerked back. "For what?"

He had no time to answer because the guard stormed over and grabbed his arm.

Holding strong, Greg shouted into the phone, "I hope you die for what you did to Carrie!"

Then he gave Oliver the look.

Be ready.

fifty-two

Amber heard a commotion in the hallway, people shouting. Suddenly the door to the communal quarters slammed open.

"Where is she?" someone asked. A man's voice.

Amber's heart leaped into her throat.

The man was back.

"Miss Ashworth is not available for release," Mrs. Karlsson said. "She knows sensitive information that—"

"Madam," the man growled, "if you do not move out of my way, I will have to take action against your establishment."

Amber threw the blanket over her head. The last time the man had nearly broken her. She'd given him five fake names, names of actors she'd seen in old *People* magazines, before he realized what she was doing. Furious, he had started twisting her casted leg. Harder and harder. When the pain became unbearable, she cried and pled with him.

"I don't know anything!"

That only angered him further.

She had screamed until she had gone hoarse. He promised that he would be back. Another form of torture. Anticipating pain often was worse than the pain itself.

And now he had returned.

"Fine," Mrs. Karlsson said. "The brat is right there. Take her."

The headmistress ripped off Amber's blanket, exposing her huddled in a ball underneath. Amber stayed facing the wall, already feeling her broken leg throb in anticipation of the next round of torture.

Tears pricked her eyes.

Mrs. Karlsson leaned over her and whispered, "Good riddance, mute."

Good riddance? The man was going to kill her? She'd been asking for death, begging for escape in any form, but now that it stood behind her, poised to stab her in the back, it left her shaking like crazy.

For five of the longest seconds of her life, Amber lay on her small blue cot, waiting for the man to strike.

Let it be quick, she begged him. *Kill me quickly.*

"Amber," the man said. His voice sounded different than last time, not like the whiny, librarian-looking brute who had twisted her broken leg. His hand went on her shoulder, tugging on her to roll her over. Her survival instincts kicked in, and she curled more rigidly into a ball.

"Amber, honey," the man said. "It's me…Dad."

Dad?

Her blinding fear melted into blazing anger. That voice was most definitely *not* her father's. After six painful years, she would recognize her father's voice anywhere. This voice was too rough, too old for the gentle, loving man her father had been.

How dare someone pretend to be him?

Her hands formed into rock-solid fists, ready to break another nose in this place. She didn't even care how he might torture her after. She would not go down without a fight.

"Amber," he said more urgently. "Just roll over and look at me, honey. Please. It's Dad. I'm here to take you home."

Mrs. Karlsson laughed. "After all she's done, she treats you as abominably as the rest of us. Her mother really must have ruined her in the years she had custody. I feel sorry for you, sir. Are you sure you want her back? We were finally making progress with her."

"Amber," the man said more urgently. "Please. I've come to take you home."

Something finally clicked. The voice. She found a face to match it. But it wasn't the face she first thought. It was a rugged face with a graying goatee.

Richard.

She rolled over, head twisting around before her awkwardly casted body could. She found Richard's wonderful, amazing, and perfectly familiar face just a few feet away. She threw her arms around his neck.

"Dad!" she said.

Richard O'Brien patted her back awkwardly. "Ah, there's my girl. Let's get you out of here, sweetie."

Sobs of relief erupted. Her shoulders started to shake.

"Dad," she cried, willing to call him any name in the world that he wanted. "I want to go home, Dad. Please take me home, Dad. Please, Dad. Please."

His own eyes filled. "Of course."

"How awful that her mother hid her from you for all these years," Mrs. Karlsson said. "I assure you that if we had known, sir…"

"I've found her now," Richard said.

With that, Richard scooped Amber up into his arms. Mrs. Karlsson set Amber's crutches across her lap. Then Richard Best-Man-of-All-Time O'Brien carried Amber out of the blue room and down the hallway. Mrs. Karlsson escorted him past the guards and toward the front doors, the same ones Amber had tried to escape out of the very first day. And suddenly the two of them were outside under the blue sky.

Amber took in a breath of fresh air. Then another. And another.

"Home," she said, warm tears streaming down her cheeks. "I'm going home."

"Yes," Richard's voice said, strained from the exertion of carrying her across the small parking lot. "But, unfortunately, I don't have any transportation, and it's a long walk. What did you do to your leg?"

Amber looked from her fractured leg to the tight muscles of his neck. How many miles away was home? Ten? Twenty? And she would be useless because of her stupid stunt.

"I'm sorry, Richard. I can use my crutches. I haven't tried them yet, but they can't be that hard."

"No worries. Here Ashlee and I were stressed about my scanty paperwork and story, but I think that poor headmistress would have paid me to take you. Sounds like you have been quite the troublemaker here, young lady."

Amber laughed, feeling close to delirium. "I tried, Richard. I really, really tried."

He smiled at her. "And what exactly did you do to your leg?"

Her gaze went back to the building that was quickly fading in the distance—and her future. "The window was higher than I thought."

Following her gaze, Richard stopped dead in his tracks. Then he shook his head. "We need to get you home."

Amber laid her head on his shoulder. She wanted to thank him but knew she would never do it justice. Besides, the farther they went, the harder the tears flowed, making it difficult to breathe normally.

One of the yard guards met them by the front gate.

"Papers," the man said.

"Can you stand for a minute?" Richard asked, setting Amber down.

She stood one-footed while he grabbed out her paperwork. She noticed the first paper had "Shelton Township" stamped across the top, making her curious about how he'd gotten her out. And what was that story about her mom stealing her from him?

Amber didn't know and she didn't care.

The guard scanned Richard's card, typed something into a computer, and pushed a button. And the gate slid open.

Richard went to pick her back up, but he was already sweating like crazy, and the guy was old enough to actually be her father. Maybe her grandfather. He didn't need to carry her anywhere.

"I can do it," she said. She straightened her crutches underneath her. She had gone from a mute, to starving herself, to refusing to move at all. Her body felt stiff. But she started pushing herself along the hot pavement. With each hop, she felt more confident. "I'll walk the whole way. We just might have to go slow."

"Well," he said, "I brought help."

"Help?"

"A few people are rather anxious to see you. One especially." Smiling, he motioned to a field ahead of them that was so overgrown with weeds it could have hid an entire mob of people. Or a clan.

Her heart jumped. "Who?"

"See that head of hair there?"

"Carrie?" Amber frantically searched for her sister's face hidden in that field. The last she had seen her, Carrie had begged her to take care of Zach. Amber had failed, but if Carrie was out, then maybe Zach was out, too.

It took her a second to spot the sandy blond hair that blended in with the golden weeds. But it wasn't a woman's head. It was a man's. And it was bouncing as he sprinted toward them out of the safety of the field, across the road into the wide open.

"Braden," she exhaled.

In five huge leaps, he was to them. "What happened to her?"

"Braden, get back!" Richard said, urgently glancing over his shoulder. "You promised to stay out of sight."

"Braden!" a woman said, coming through his same path out of the field, though at half the speed. Amber startled when she recognized her.

Ashlee Lyon.

Braden didn't seem to hear either of them. His eyes darted around Amber, from her cast, to her face. He looked so healthy and beautiful and just...there.

Suddenly he grabbed her crutches and handed them to Richard.

"Take these," Braden said. "Amber is mine."

No three words had ever sounded so wonderful in the ears of a sixteen-year-old girl. Braden whisked her up into his arms and started to run. Across the road, down a small embankment, and into the safety of the field.

As he ran, Amber laid a hand up on his face, somewhere in-between hyperventilating and hysterics. Between her stupid crying, and his frantic pace, his perfect face was a blurry, jumpy mess.

Finally they reached a clearing. The weeds had been stomped down to provide a spot to hide out. Several bags lay on the ground.

Braden stopped. The others caught up after a second, too. Ashlee Lyon started pestering Richard about what had happened, but Braden just stared the few small inches that separated him from Amber. He didn't speak and neither did she, as if both were beyond words. He bent his head to her. She reached her neck to him. Their lips met somewhere in the middle.

His kiss spread life through her, starting at her head and spreading through every cell of her body. When he pulled back, she wrapped her arms up around his neck and laid her head on his shoulder.

"Take me home, Braden," she said. "I want to go home."

He smiled. "Sounds good to me." He looked back at the others. "Are you guys okay to leave right away?"

"Wait!" Amber said suddenly. The field wasn't hiding her entire clan. Nobody was there except the four of them. "What about Zach? What about Carrie?"

"We were planning to go to Zach's next," Richard said. "And Greg's working on getting Carrie. But all things considered, I think we should drop you off at home first."

"No!" She squirmed out of Braden's arms. He set her back on her one foot. "No, I'm fine. Look. I want to go get Zach out. I need to be there when you get him."

"But…"

"Please." Amber's dark eyes filled. "I can't go home without my brother, alright? I made a promise to Carrie that I need to keep."

———◆———

"What happened to the trial bein' next week?" Greg asked Jamansky as a guard removed his handcuffs.

"Oh," Jamansky said. "They moved it to tomorrow. But don't worry. I'll still have Carrie and her siblings for you next week."

Greg forced himself to nod.

Sure he would.

"It's nice to see traitors like Simmons get what they deserve," Jamansky continued. "Don't you think?"

He still thought Greg worked on the same side of the law as him.

Greg rubbed his wrists. "You're gonna send Oliver to Rigsby's demonstration, aren't you?"

Jamansky chuckled. "You can thank me later. So does Simmons know that you stole Carrie from him? Did you tell him that's why you're stabbing him in the back, or can I tell him for you?"

He must have known he wasn't going to get a response because he smiled and handed Greg a set of papers. "Sign these."

Greg flipped through the documents. All sorts of accusations against Oliver. Some were true—assisting illegal clans—but plenty weren't. Jamansky had created a total smear campaign to get Oliver in front of the firing squad.

"The guy helped a few peaceful people survive the Collapse," Greg said. "He kept some women and children from starving. How does that make him a traitor to the country?"

Suspicion filled Jamansky's eyes. "Those people were illegals, living illegally on government property. They knew the consequences of their actions, and so did Simmons. Sign the papers."

Jamansky held a pen toward him.

Greg took the pen, fury building inside of him. His gaze traveled over the papers one last time before he decided enough was enough.

He snapped the pen in half.

Ink splattered everywhere: Greg's jeans, the floor, and even Jamansky's pristine, green uniform.

Swearing, Jamansky jumped back. He wiped his pants, smudging the ink further.

Greg threw the broken pieces on the ground. "I'm not signing a thing."

"We had a deal, Pierce!"

"I'm done makin' deals." Greg pointed at him. "And so are you."

With that, he started down the hallway.

"You'll never see Carrie and her siblings again!" Jamansky yelled after him.

Greg sped up. He had to get to Jamansky's house and get Carrie and Zach out of there before Jamansky could. His mind raced through the fastest way to disable Jamansky's car. Slash the tires, but he had no weapon. He'd have to do something to the engine. If only he'd thought to keep the keys with him, they probably had—

"Grab him!" Jamansky yelled.

Guards grabbed Greg from every corner.

Jamansky stormed down the hallway. "Search him. Make sure the prisoner didn't try to pawn off anything on him. And if it's not too much of a bother, keep him busy for a while for me, boys. I have somewhere I need to go and I don't want him following me."

Greg writhed, trying to break free of their tight grips. "Wait! I'm a special op, working in the Special Patrols Unit. You can't detain me."

"So he claims," Jamansky said at the door. "If I were you, double I'd double-check his story. Something doesn't add up." Then back to Greg, he added, "Carrie's mine. Have a nice life."

fifty-three

The seconds ticked by as Carrie waited for Greg to return. She was anxious for word on Oliver, and if there was any possible way to get her friend free.

Zach grew tired of watching movies and went searching for his baseball in the garage. That stressed her out, but he promised to be vigilant and leave everything exactly where he found it. That was more than Greg had done. Carrie fretted all morning about the havoc he'd left in Jamansky's den. Without a before-and-after picture, she had to guess on where to put things. Hopefully Jamansky wouldn't notice.

She was in the middle of making lunch for Zach when the phone rang. Bretton and Felix barked, anxious for her to pick it up.

"Not my house," she said to them, spreading the mayonnaise.

The answering machine picked up.

"Chief Jamansky," a voice said, "this is Cliff Watson from Central, the friend of Mayor Phillips. I wanted to let you know that, due to a scheduling conflict, President Rigsby moved up the demonstration to this evening at 7 p.m. I apologize for the late notice, sir. I tried to reach you on your mobile, and in your office—several times, actually—and couldn't get through, so I thought I'd try your home phone. I hope you're still able to make it. It would be such an honor to have you. We have you down for just the one prisoner, Oliver Simmons."

The butter knife froze in Carrie's hand.

"We will still provide transportation for your prisoner," the man continued. "I've already alerted JSP about the change in scheduling.

Also, Mr. President wants to keep things tidy, so if you still wish to participate in the execution, we will supply you with a standardized weapon and uniform. That means you need to be to the east gate by 6 p.m. Call me as soon as you get this with your size, and I will have both waiting for you."

Bretton and Felix started barking again. She ignored them, holding her breath.

"If you're unable to join us tonight, we understand. The execution of your prisoner will still go forward as planned. Again, I apologize for the last minute change, chief sir. If you have any questions, I can be reached at this number. There will be around twenty other traitors brought to justice as part of the president's presentation, so we should have a good turnout. Hope to see you tonight. United We Stand."

As the message clicked off, Carrie couldn't move.

Oliver.

Jamansky.

She didn't know what all of it meant, but she knew enough. Jamansky was going to kill Oliver tonight, at some demonstration—or not a demonstration. A mass execution by President Rigsby.

Her stomach rolled.

A public execution?

Oliver.

"Good to know," a voice said behind her.

Carrie whirled. The jar in her hand dropped, splaying mayonnaise all over the floor.

David Jamansky stood in his living room, front door wide open. Bretton and Felix were at his feet, barking, tails wagging.

"David," she said, pulse spiking. "I didn't hear—"

"Oh, I think you heard plenty," he said. Gaze never leaving her, he shut the front door and crossed into the kitchen.

Her thoughts raced. Why was he home in the middle of the day? Where was Greg? Had Greg followed him? Thankfully, Jamansky hadn't come in through the garage where Zach was searching for his baseball. But if Jamansky had parked in the driveway, Greg would have to dump the motorcycle somewhere else.

Jamansky.

David was going to kill Oliver.

Her entire body filled with horror.

363

As he reached the kitchen, she backed up against the counter, clutching the mayonnaise knife. But he wasn't coming for her. Eyes never leaving her, he pressed the button on the answering machine and played the whole, awful message over again. Every single word sickened her.

Oliver. They were going to kill him.

When it finished, he nodded. "I'll have to let Cliff know that I can make it."

"How could you?" she whispered.

"Simmons deserves it," he said, tossing his keys on the counter.

Carrie wasn't about to argue because she knew one thing:

She had to get out of there.

The sliding glass door was locked—one of the things she'd remembered to restore to its correct spot.

Jamansky followed her gaze. His jaw tightened. "Where's your brother? I told him to stay inside."

"He's not..." She swallowed. "Zach's not outside. He's actually in the garage. He thought he heard something out there. I'll go get him."

With swift, panicked steps, she practically ran for the garage door. She needed to snag Zach before Jamansky could see what he was up to.

When she opened the door, she gasped.

In spite of her warnings, Zach had torn apart a whole stack of boxes. Junk lay strewn about the cement. Even worse, one whole section was still empty from where Greg had extracted the motorcycle.

"Zach," she squeaked, voice too high, "I finished your sandwich. Come and eat."

"But I didn't find it yet," Zach said, tearing open the lid off the next box.

"Zach!" she said sharply. "Come now!"

"No," Jamansky said, joining her at the door. "Let him look."

Zach froze.

With the same ease, David sauntered outside, walking past shirts, dishes, and books heaped around. "So this is what you two do all day while I'm at work? What exactly are you looking for, Zach?"

Zach looked at Carrie. "Nothing. I'm sorry."

"Nothing?" Face reddening, Jamansky suddenly kicked one of the boxes, sending the rest of the contents sailing. "Nothing!"

Zach cowered. Frantic, Carrie motioned to him. Her brother ran back inside where she pushed him behind her.

Turning in a small circle, David surveyed the damage again, hands on his hips, chest heaving.

Don't notice the motorcycle, Carrie thought, heart hammering in her chest.

"I'm sorry, David," she said quickly. "I'll have Zach clean this up."

"Don't bother," he seethed.

Heading back inside, he passed them both up. When he finally faced them, his eyes zeroed in on Zach cowering behind her. "Zach, take Bretton and Felix out for a walk."

"A...a walk?" Zach said, still scared.

Jamansky crossed the kitchen and grabbed the leashes. "Yeah. Take them around the block. I think that they—and you—have been cooped up in here for too long. In fact, take them around the block several times."

"But," Zach said, "you said I shouldn't—"

"Things have changed!" Jamansky snapped. His dark glare went to Carrie. "Your sister and I are going to have a little talk."

The hair prickled on the back of Carrie's neck, but she nodded at Zach. If Jamansky was upset, if things turned ugly, she wanted her brother as far away from there as possible. Plus she had things of her own to say. Did Greg know what Jamansky had planned? Did Oliver? The execution was only a few hours away. There had to be time to stop it. Somehow she had to change Jamansky's mind.

Without argument, Zach quickly grabbed the leashes and left with the dogs out the sliding glass door.

The second they were gone, Jamansky locked it behind him, making Carrie's gut lurch. Locked in. But she told herself it was better that way.

"Where's Amber?" she said, forcing herself to stay on the offensive.

"Amber?" Jamansky gave a mirthless laugh. "Yeah, I saw her today. Pretty girl, that Amber. A lot prettier than you. I tried to get her out, but here's the thing. She doesn't want to go home. She told me that she wants to stay there forever. You see," he said, taking a step toward Carrie, "Amber enjoys her daily beatings. She doesn't...want...to leave."

Something cold ran down Carrie's spine. His entire being had gone dark with fury.

"More lies," she whispered.

"You think you'll get your sister back now? No. Things have changed, Carrie."

"Yes," she said, eyes pricking with tears as she thought of Oliver. "They have."

Namely that she was leaving.

She couldn't let Jamansky back her into the corner again, even though he seemed to be doing just that. She scooted to the right. He followed. She moved left and he mirrored her once again. He was pushing her into the corner of the kitchen, away from any doors and windows.

Clutching her butter knife, she searched the counters for something sharper.

"You've never liked the truth much, have you, Carrie?" he said. "But I have another secret for you. Guess who's sending Oliver to the firing squad tonight. Not me, but your new lover, Greg Pierce."

She searched his house. She couldn't make it to the back door. He would be expecting it. It had to be somewhere else.

"You don't believe me. You never do. But I'll prove it." He pulled out a paper and held it in front of her. "That's his name down there, Gregory Curtis Pierce. See his signature stating that Oliver Simmons is a traitor to the state? Pierce is the one sending Oliver to the firing squad. What do you think of that?"

Her eyes flickered to the counter, wondering to what lengths he would keep her there. If she ran, would he pursue her or just shoot? He was wearing his full patrol uniform with gun, Taser, nightstick, and who knew what else.

"Look at it!" he yelled, shoving it in front of her. "Look at his signature. He testified that Oliver spent the last six years protecting you. And now Oliver will pay the ultimate price. But I guess all's fair in love and war, right?"

Greg.

Suddenly she stared at Greg's name. The meeting. Where was Greg? What had happened to him?

The floor dropped out from under her.

What had Jamansky done to Greg?

Jamansky seemed to sense the change in her and smiled. "Tonight is going to be a new start for this country, Carrie. President Rigsby is in Illinois. He came to our area—*our* area—to turn the tide and squelch you illegals once and for all."

"Because killing us off one by one isn't good enough?" she whispered bitterly. "Now he'll kill us in groups? This is a public execution, David! A firing squad! This isn't the Middle Ages."

"Believe me," he said, ice-blue eyes as cold as steel. "Those people earned their sentences."

It had to be the counter. Her only way out, up and over.

She stole a few inches toward it. Once she cleared the counter, his living room would become an obstacle course with tables, lamps, and couches to dodge, but she was fast.

She would have to be.

Jamansky followed her gaze but misinterpreted it. "Oh, don't worry. Your brother won't last long outside. One of the other patrolmen will grab him. Zach will be back in DeKalb in no time."

Not if she got to Zach first.

Or Greg did.

Maybe that's where Greg was. He'd seen Zach wandering and both of them took off. She would catch up. They would take the dogs if they had to so Jamansky couldn't hunt them down. Wishful thinking, but it was the best she could do.

Plan in place, she straightened and looked him directly in the eye.

"I'm leaving now," she said.

Another dark laugh. "You're funny, Carrie. Very, very funny. You're not going anywhere."

Then he lunged.

He tried to grab her, but she was faster. She rammed the butter knife into his arm and spun out of his reach. He yelled in pain. She jumped onto the counter and scrambled across.

Front door.

She had to get to the front door.

Swearing, Jamansky followed.

Blood pumping, she dodged, swerved, and ran through his living room.

Tables. Couch. Front door, front door, front—

He grabbed her by the waist and threw her down. She crashed onto the floor, cheek slamming hard. Pain exploded in her head. He knelt over her, pressing his knee into her back.

"Maybe you didn't hear," he hissed over her, "but I said that you're not going anywhere. You're mine now, my little pet."

The air squeezed out of her.

She screamed with little sound.

He wrenched one hand behind her back. Familiar, cold, hard metal slid around her left wrist, clicking shut.

Blinding fear seized her. *Not again. Not handcuffs.* She couldn't let herself be taken again.

Frantic, she squirmed and buried her right hand under her. He shoved her onto her back, trying to grab her other arm. She flailed and kicked to get free, but he was twice her weight.

He caught hold of her right hand and pinned it to the floor, but in the process, lost track of the other hand, the one already cuffed.

Carrie swung.

With all her might, she swung her left hand around. The metal cuffs sliced across his cheek.

With a scream of rage, he fell back, clutching his face.

Carrie jumped up and ran.

Three steps and a gunshot exploded in the house. Dust particles rained down from the ceiling.

"Stop!" he shouted.

She froze.

Jamansky stood, rising to his full height, and pointed the gun at her head as more ceiling rained down on her. Blood ran down his cheek from an inch-long gash. His hand tightened on the gun.

"It's a shame," he said, huffing. "You and I were going to have so much fun, Carrie. But all you illegals are the same. Too stupid to know what's good for you. And you know what? I don't need you anymore. I'm done with you."

Carrie's chest seized. He was going to shoot her. She was going to die.

Zach, Amber, Greg.

He crossed the few feet between them and pressed the muzzle to her forehead. She squeezed her eyes shut as the gun pushed into her temple. He was just crazy enough to pull the trigger.

She braced for it.

Live free or die.

Live free.

Die.

But instead of shooting, he clicked the other handcuff around her right wrist. Both hands secured in front of her, he shoved her. She stumbled back, tripping onto the black leather couch.

"What are you going to do with me?" she said. "Put me in front of the firing squad like Oliver?"

He cocked his head, pensive. "You know, that's not a bad idea."

He pulled out his phone and pressed a button.

"Hey, Cliff," he said. "Yeah, I got your message. I'll be there tonight. Sure, sure. But I'm wondering if you have room for one more. I've got another rebel who will make a great contribution."

Listening, Jamansky paused to wipe his cheek. His hand came back red and bloody.

"Does she have the mark?" he asked. "Good question."

Stepping forward, he tugged Greg's lucky shirt away from her neck, exposing her shoulder. His hot fingers rubbed her skin, checking for a traitor's mark like Greg's. She squirmed free.

"No mark, but she's definitely a traitor." While he spoke, he kept the gun pointed at her. With a pause, he nodded again. "Great. I'll bring her in. Actually, are you taking kids?"

Lowering the phone, he said, "Hey, Carrie, how old is Zach? Twelve? Thirteen?"

She went cold. "No!"

"Oh, wait." His light eyes glinted. "Maybe we'll pick up Amber along the way. She's sixteen, right? We'll make it a family affair."

"David, no!" she cried. "Please."

Smile twisting into something awful, he spoke into the phone again. "I can bring in all three. Yes, great. I just have one stop to make along the way, and we'll be right there."

As he pocketed his phone, his smile grew. "They only have adults in the lineup so far, but the guy said they'd make an exception. Isn't that nice? I can't wait to see Simmons' reaction when he sees all of you march in. I hope President Rigsby lets you stand together."

"Leave Zach and Amber out of this!" she begged. "They've done nothing!"

"They lived," he said darkly. "That's fault enough."

Her heart pounded so loudly her vision was going in and out of focus. She stared at the gun. Maybe if he killed her, he might leave Amber and Zach alone.

Live free or die.

"It's a shame things had to be this way, Carrie," he said. "I think I could have really enjoyed you. Or maybe..." His eyes grazed over her. "I still will."

He slid his gun back in its holster.

Terror clawed through her.

She rolled, clearing the couch, but he was faster. He grabbed her arms and pushed her deep into the cushions. Then he brought his mouth down on hers. Hard. So hard she tasted blood.

She kneed him in the gut.

He fell back with a grunt.

"What are you doing?" she yelled, wiping her mouth with her bound hands. Her lip pulsed.

"Getting my payback," he said. "You owe me big time for all of your..."

He trailed off, suddenly listening. Carrie heard it, too. Barking at the back door. Zach and the dogs had returned. She couldn't see, but Zach started pounding on the glass.

"Good," Jamansky said. "Now I won't have to track him down. But he's going to have to wait a bit longer. I'm not finished with you yet."

He came at her again.

She rammed her feet against his chest, blocking him while her trapped hands reached up over her head. She scrambled around and found a weapon.

The picture frame.

"No you don't!" He grabbed her arms and pinned them up against the couch arms where they did her no good. He was over her. Dark. Heavy.

More pounding, and then shattering glass. The kitchen door. Zach had broken through.

On instinct, Jamansky looked up.

Carrie brought the frame crashing down on his head.

"Zach, run!" she shouted.

Only it wasn't Zach.

fifty-four

Greg dropped the rock and reached through the hole in the glass going too fast, being too careless. Zach held the dogs' leashes with all his might, feet digging into the grass. The dogs knew something was happening inside. They wanted back inside almost as much as Greg did.

Shards of glass cut Greg's arm, pain slicing, but he found the lock and twisted.

"I'm in!" he yelled at Zach. "Go hide."

Zach nodded quickly. "Got it."

Greg burst inside Jamansky's house. He slammed the door shut behind him, trapping the dogs outside where Jamansky couldn't use them as weapons. Then everything behind was forgotten.

"Greg!" Carrie cried.

Jamansky was doubled over next to the couch, holding his head. Blood streamed down his cheek and forehead.

"Pierce?" the guy said, looking dazed and confused, especially seeing Greg in his house. But his thoughts seemed to clear by the second. "You're a dead man, Pierce!"

"You first," Greg said.

Then he charged.

Glass crunching, Greg shoved aside a chair, leaped over a couch, and rammed into Jamansky. The two spiraled backward, landing on the lamp table. The table crashed to the floor.

Jamansky rolled and reached for his gun, but Greg was ready. Ready for payback. Ready for Jamansky.

With his shoulder, Greg barreled him back until he was up against the wall, face first, smearing blood into the paint.

"Carrie, go!" Greg yelled. "Get outta here!"

"No!" she cried.

Jamansky laughed, cheek to wall. "She's too attached to me. In fact, you interrupted our moment. So if you don't mind, I was just about to—"

Greg punched his kidney.

Jamansky grunted.

"What did you do to her?" Greg shoved him harder into the wall. "What?"

Jamansky didn't answer. Or couldn't.

Greg checked on her again. Deathly white, she looked rooted to the spot with shock. Then he saw her bound hands holding a broken picture frame. Revulsion swelled in him afresh.

He punched Jamansky again. The guy slumped against the wall.

"Carrie," Greg said, "get Zach and—"

Pain shot down Greg's leg. Jamansky's elbow rammed his thigh.

Greg's leg buckled. He dropped, but took Jamansky down with him. The two hit the floor hard. With a roar, Jamansky leaped up and swung. Greg caught his arm and twisted. He kneed him in the stomach and punched Jamansky's jaw. Jamansky's head snapped back. Another punch, and Jamansky was down again.

A blur of a leg came at him. Greg jumped out of the way, but a second kick caught him squarely in the chest. Greg fell back. He barely righted himself when Jamansky plowed into him, barreling him straight into the giant television.

Jamansky grabbed him by the neck and slammed Greg's head into the TV.

"How did you get free?" Jamansky yelled.

Greg grunted against the white, hot pain in his skull. "The guards are as gullible as you are. By the way, my buddies in the Special Patrols Unit are on their way. Carrie showed me every illegal thing you've been up to. They can't wait to—"

Jamansky rammed his head again.

Greg could hardly see through his dancing vision, but he finished. "—get their hands on you. Your blackmailing days are over."

It was a lie. Greg had barely escaped JSP, claiming his 'dead' status was part of Rigsby's demonstration and if they didn't release him at once, the president would visit them personally to find out why.

Nobody was coming.

"You'll be dead before anyone gets here," Jamansky said, squeezing the air from Greg's throat. "And the rest of us will be gone. By the time I'm done with Carrie, she'll only wish she was dead. And let me tell you, I'm going to love—"

A loud thud echoed.

Jamansky grunted and suddenly his weight was gone. He screamed in pain. Greg shook his head to clear it.

The only sound in the room was the dogs barking at the back door.

His blurred eyes lifted. Carrie stood four feet away, clutching a broken table leg in her bound hands. She had gone completely white.

Jamansky's gun perched inches from her nose.

But the guy wasn't looking at her. Blood oozed down the side of his face as he glared at Greg, nostrils flaring.

The ground dropped away from Greg. Jamansky was going to kill Carrie. Just like he'd killed Greg's mom. Greg was close enough to grab him, but not without the gun going off.

His hands flew up even though the gun wasn't aimed at him.

"Stop!" Greg yelled. "Don't shoot!"

"Oh, I'm not going to shoot her now," Jamansky said, heaving deep breaths. "Not until the demonstration. I'm going to put her right next to Oliver. But don't worry. I'll aim straight."

"Tonight?" Greg said.

"Didn't you hear? They moved up Rigsby's show. Turns out I didn't need your signature after all. They were more than happy to have three extra targets. Oh, and thanks for bringing Zach back. Now I don't have to go looking for him." Jamansky's expression turned murderous. "I guess that means I no longer need you."

The gun swung away from Carrie, but Greg had already ducked. A shot fired off, sinking in the wall over Greg's head.

Carrie screamed.

"I should have known you would follow me home," Jamansky said.

Greg straightened, hands high, feeling delirious with relief. Pointed-guns-at-his-head had become his specialty. And Jamansky stood just close enough.

"You mean, followed you *back* home?" Greg taunted. "Thanks for the lift. By the way, your Suzuki needs a little tune-up."

It took Jamansky a moment to understand. Then his eyes went wild. They flickered back to Carrie for a split second.

Just long enough.

In one fluid move, Greg dodged left, grabbed the back of the gun, and punched the wrist holding it. The gun twisted clean from Jamansky's hand. Jamansky screamed as the gun was yanked out of his fingers. His scream was cut off in a grunt as Greg kicked his chest, sending him backward into the couch.

By the time Jamansky scrambled around, the gun was up again, only in Greg's hands, pointed at Jamansky's blond head.

"Down on the ground," Greg ordered. "Down!"

Jamansky stared at his empty hands, confused. Little did he know that, at McCormick's order, Greg had practiced that move with Burke five thousand times. Disarming an attacker.

"I said down!" Greg roared.

Slowly, Jamansky knelt on the floor in front of the couch. His face was red. His cheek smeared with blood. His glare went back to Carrie.

"How long has he been here?" he asked. "How long?"

"Forever," Greg said. "By the way, we love your bed. Where did you get it, my neighbor's house?"

Then he kicked him again, slamming him the rest of the way down, flat on the floor.

"Grab his car keys," Greg said to Carrie. "And one of his uniforms. Turns out he's gonna help us get Amber back after all."

Carrie stood, eyes wide. "Greg, you're bleeding."

He didn't know where. He couldn't feel any spot that hurt more than any other. "Just get Zach and meet me outside." His glare went back to Jamansky. "I'll be out after I finish things."

"No need for her to leave," Jamansky said. "Zach just walked in the back door."

Carrie whirled around. So did Greg, seeing nothing.

Zach wasn't there. Nobody was.

The distraction had only been a second, an instinct more than anything, but that's all Jamansky needed.

Jamansky leaped up and caught Carrie by the waist. She had no time to react. Before Greg could think, Jamansky had yanked her violently in front of him, using her as a shield.

"Go ahead and shoot," Jamansky said.

Carrie kicked, writhed, and tried to break free. Jamansky just twisted her arm until she let out a yelp of pain.

Frantic, Greg dropped the nose of the gun, unable to point it anywhere near her. Jamansky dodged behind her, careful to keep himself protected as he started backing them up, back toward the front door.

Gun pointed down, Greg kept his finger on the trigger. Ready. "What do you want?"

"I have everything I want," Jamansky replied angrily. "Or I'm about to get it."

If he got her out that door, the game was over. Greg would never see her again.

His eyes swept every inch of both of them, looking for a spot. His aim was good, but it would have to be impeccable to get a shot off without hitting her. Knowing this, Jamansky's head stayed bent behind hers, his hands holding her arms back where Greg couldn't get them.

"If you want," Jamansky said, "flip on the television and watch the broadcast tonight. Carrie and the others will be executed in front of the entire world. Every person will see her head roll. In fact, for the rest of history, I bet the video of her death will be replayed over and over as the moment Rigsby turned the war in his favor. I can't wait."

Jamansky was right. The first public execution in America since cameras had been invented.

The footage would live forever.

They were nearly to the front door. Greg stayed five feet behind, gun still down, eyes still searching for a spot. He studied their feet, but they were moving too much. He watched Carrie's hands, but Jamansky's were hidden.

Then he noticed Carrie.

She locked eyes with Greg. Her brows lowered, but her eyes tightened in a clear, strong message. So strong that it stopped him in his tracks. Her jaw tightened, making sure he understood. Only he didn't understand what she meant, what she planned to do.

His heart raced, frantic.

Don't, Carrie! he wanted to shout.

But she was already moving.

Her arms lifted. Up over her head her hands went. Still chained together, they lifted until they were not only over her head, but behind Jamansky's as well.

Then she dropped them.

The metal chain fell behind Jamansky's neck. She yanked down hard at the same time she dropped, pulling her full weight down against it.

Caught off guard, Jamansky stumbled down with her. The two dropped with a sickening thud. Jamansky let out a scream of rage, but Greg watched, trying to dissect who was who. A web of flailing limbs. And then...

Bam!

The sound thundered through the house, but Greg had found the spot.

Bam, bam!

Two more shots. Jamansky dropped, body going still.

fifty-five

Greg said nothing as he sped down the highway toward Shelton, pushing Jamansky's patrol car to its limit. He just clutched Carrie's ice-cold hand.

Her lip was swollen and bloody, but the rest of her seemed unharmed. At least physically. She stared, unblinking, down at the towel she pressed against the wound on Greg's arm. She hadn't looked at much else, not the road, not even Zach in the back seat.

Greg understood.

Every part of him that wasn't throbbing with pain felt unsteady and shaky. He'd never killed anybody before. They had trained him to, but actually ending somebody's life?

He gripped the steering wheel, trying to block the picture of Carrie, trapped underneath the patrol chief's bloody body. The horror, the terror that seized Greg as he tried to see if he'd shot her, too. But she'd moved. Stumbling over, Greg helped to drag her out from beneath Jamansky.

For several minutes, he had just held her, burying her face against his chest as he surveyed the damage. Glass everywhere. Lamps and tables down.

And Jamansky.

Dead.

A shudder ripped through him. He glanced in the rearview mirror. Through the wire mesh, he saw Zach in the back seat, watching the world fly by out the window. Zach also had nothing to say.

It was too much, too overwhelming. And yet, they couldn't stop, or slow, or wait for their bodies to settle. They had to get to Naperville.

They had to save Oliver.

Somehow.

On top of being in shock, Zach didn't want to go home—or rather, he didn't want to go to Ferris, a new place with a new house without any of his siblings to comfort him. Zach wanted to go with Carrie and Greg to Naperville, but Carrie and Greg needed one less person to worry about.

With "Chief of Patrols" plastered on the side, Greg hoped they could get into the training facility—a place he never wanted to revisit. After everything, after Jamansky and Carrie and Isabel and McCormick, he couldn't believe he was going back to that place. He thought about pressing Carrie on the issue again, but she had been adamant.

"We have to help Oliver," she had said. *"Amber can wait."*

Oliver first.

Oliver.

Greg just had no clue how to do it.

McCormick might have trained Greg to kill. The Special Patrols Unit might have perfected his aim and taught him moves that had saved his life—and Carrie's—today, but Isabel was wrong about him. Greg wasn't a revolutionary. He was just a regular guy who wanted to live a nice, quiet life with a pretty girl. No guns. No running. No fear. He had tried to block those six weeks of Naperville training from his mind. But now, instead of heading home to start a picturesque life with Carrie, he was heading back into the thick of it—not just him, but Carrie, who insisted on going with him.

He had to talk her out of it. She had no idea what she was getting herself into—or maybe she did. Maybe she knew a thousand times more than he did because she had just come from Oliver's position.

She had almost lived Oliver's fate, too.

Greg took another shuddering breath.

Carrie squeezed his hand. "I know it hurts," she said, checking under the towel. "I'm sorry, but I have to keep the pressure on it. It won't stop bleeding. I think you need stitches."

"It's fine," he said. He could hardly feel it. He liked the pressure of her hand on his arm anyway. He needed to feel her close, warm, and alive. "I'll wrap it when we get home—I mean, to Ferris."

Zach sighed in the back seat. "Can't I just stay in the car in Naperville?"

Greg glanced at him in the rearview mirror. "No way. Sorry, buddy."

Zach leaned against the window. "We should have brought the dogs."

Another thing they'd turned down.

"I'm sure some patrolman will find Bretton and Felix and take care of them," Greg said. "They'll be fine."

Zach sighed again.

Carrie went back to staring at the towel on Greg's arm.

He reached up and stroked her cheek, needing to catch a glimpse of those baby blues, the window to her soul. She glanced up and flashed him the tiniest of smiles. Though it didn't last long, and though it was filled with heartache and weariness, the smile told him what he already knew: she was going to be fine, too.

Just get Zach home, he told himself. *Then convince Carrie to stay home, too.* If he could do that much, he might be able to think straight enough to figure out what to do next.

Greg had told Oliver to be ready. That gave him five hours to break the guy out. Somehow.

Think!

If he had until morning, like originally planned, he might have been able to pull it off. Isabel, McCormick, and Kearney's whole group would be gathering by morning. But President Rigsby's little "scheduling change" ruined everything. A twelve hour shift—one that Isabel and McCormick probably didn't even know about—and everything had fallen apart.

Jamansky's death had shaken Carrie enough. What would happen when it was someone she loved, like Oliver? On live television?

"What was that?" Zach said. He twisted around, trying to see out the back window.

"What?" Carrie said, turning.

Zach squinted. "I swear I just saw Braden."

"Braden?" Greg glanced in the mirror. Sure enough, a guy who looked a lot like Braden Ziegler had run into the middle of the road behind them, waving his arms over his head to get their attention.

Greg slammed on the brakes.

"Braden!" Zach yelled through the glass, waving uncontrollably. "It's Braden!"

———— ◆ ————

They were a tangle of arms.

Carrie couldn't stop hugging Amber, and Amber couldn't stop hugging her and Zach. They'd already cried and laughed and cried some more. Their group stood off the road in the bright sunshine, soaking in the joy of each other. Carrie squeezed her one-footed sister again and nearly toppled over. Amber didn't even complain. She just laughed along with the rest of them.

"I still don't understand," Greg said, staying close to the Ashworth knot. "Why'd they let Amber go?"

"Well," Richard O'Brien put a hand on Ashlee Lyon's shoulder, "this woman had the brilliant idea to draft a letter from Chief Jamansky on Shelton Township letterhead. In it, Jamansky demanded that they release Amber to her father—me. Didn't you put something in there about a long custody dispute?"

Ashlee Lyon smiled. "Yeah. It was a great story, if I do say so. I never thought they'd fall for it, but..."

"They couldn't wait to be rid of me!" Amber said happily.

Tears filled Carrie's eyes all over again. "Thank you, Ashlee. Thank you to all of you. I..." She looked from person to person who had come to her family's rescue. Unable to finish, she just laid her head on Amber and Zach's, hugging them tightly again.

"If we hadn't found that letterhead at Oliver's house," Braden said, "I don't think it would have—"

Greg turned. "Oliver's house?"

"Yeah," Braden said. "We stopped by Oliver and Ashlee's houses to grab stuff. Ashlee found the letterhead there."

Carrie and Greg exchanged a look. He still looked shaken from the fight, his tan skin was paler than before, but he seemed to read her thoughts. They had only been blocks away, two small streets over. Carrie had seen Oliver and Ashlee's homes on the maps. Two streets, and she hadn't known. Maybe if she had tried to go there...

She pushed the thought away, too overjoyed to let a detail like that bog her down.

"I'm just relieved it actually worked," Ashlee Lyon said. "If we would have known we were going to run into you, Carrie, we would have saved you some chocolate."

"No we wouldn't," Amber quipped. "It was *too* good. Sorry, sis."

Carrie laughed again. Good old Amber was back.

"By the way," Amber said, looking Carrie over, "nice shirt."

Carrie glanced down and smiled. Greg's light blue UNC shirt felt luckier than ever.

"Looks good on her, doesn't it?" Greg said. "I mean, I've always loved her in the blue blouse, but I think I've found a new favorite."

Carrie felt herself blush, but the comment pleased her more than she cared to admit. Ashlee hadn't noticed yet that Carrie wore a pair of her short shorts, but Ashlee was back in clothes that seemed better suited for her. And her nails were painted bright red again. Everyone looked wonderfully alive and healthy. She couldn't believe it.

"Hey, Zach," Richard said, "you should see the letter Ashlee wrote for you. It was another beauty."

Zach's smile faded. "You were coming for me?" His voice rose three pitches. "For me?"

The group sobered.

Amber rubbed her brother's mop of hair. "Of course. I didn't want to go home without you. Are you…" Her beautiful, dark eyes filled. "Are you okay, little bro?"

Zach looked at Carrie. Carrie looked at Greg, none of them anxious to share their side yet.

Finally, Zach nodded. "Yeah. I'm good."

That brought a return of smiles.

"I can't believe you walked that whole way," Carrie said, looking around at their flushed, sunburned faces. "Your poor leg, Amber. You have to be dying."

"She mastered the crutches pretty fast," Braden said proudly. "We've been following the road, careful to stay out of sight. But then Ashlee Lyon recognized Jamansky's car and started freaking out."

"You're lucky, Greg," Ashlee said. "I thought you were David. I was about to chuck a rock at you when I saw you driving. So…" She eyed the bloody towel Greg held against his arm. "How did you get Carrie and Zach, and why are you driving David's car? Considering dried blood is trailing down your arm, I'm guessing you had a rough day."

Jamansky.

Greg looked back at Carrie, and they held each other's gazes. The weight of the memory returned. His arm, cut and bleeding. He and Jamansky brawling, smashing into and over things until a few shots ended it all—ended David Jamansky.

Acid crawled up Carrie's throat. Her stomach churned, feeling the weight of Jamansky's body on her, no longer moving, but suffocating her all the same.

She swallowed. That could have been Greg, dead and lifeless.

Or her.

"How about we discuss that on the ride home?" Greg said.

"Yes," Carrie said, grateful for a postponement. "We actually need to get going." Because Oliver didn't have time for them to stand around.

"You mean we can ride the rest of the way?" Amber said.

Carrie hugged her sister again. "As long as you don't mind squishing in."

———— ♦ ————

Oliver kept his head down in the back of the armored truck. His only comfort came from knowing that in a few hours, maybe longer if Rigsby stretched out the drama, it would all be over.

Greg and Carrie—along with Zach—would be home soon.

They—along with Ashlee—would take down Jamansky.

That was enough for Oliver.

He closed his eyes.

I'm ready.

fifty-six

The clan huddled around the patrol car in Ferris. Everyone was there, including Jeff Kovach, who Carrie hadn't even been able to talk to yet. She was beyond relieved that Jeff had come back for his boys, but talking could come later. Celebrating could happen another time.

Now they had to move.

Fast.

Oliver needed help. Greg kept glancing at his watch, and Carrie couldn't help but do the same. Already it was after five o'clock, with time moving too swiftly.

Ashlee Lyon had taken Jamansky's death the hardest. Her eyes were still red and puffy from crying. The fact that he'd kept Carrie at his house made it worse. But as Ashlee heard about Oliver and where he was headed, her expression had turned to steel, feeling like Carrie felt. They had to find a way to help Oliver.

Carrie recounted the phone message as clearly as she remembered. It helped that she'd heard it twice. A man named Cliff Watson from Central. Scheduling conflict. 7 p.m. As she spoke, Greg's head started bobbing up and down, nodding with each thing she said. She could practically see his mind planning, giving her hope that he had something. His jaw, tight and confident, clenched when she finished.

"East gate?" Greg asked.

"Yes," she said. "Jamansky was supposed to be there an hour before everything started."

Greg glanced down at his watch. "Alrighty. I've got this. Wish me luck."

He started to move off.

"Whoa," Carrie said, snagging his good arm. "I'm coming, too. I told you that I'm coming, Greg."

"So am I," Ashlee Lyon said, stepping forward. "No offense, Greg, but there's no way you can do this on your own."

"I agree," Richard said. "I'd like to go as well."

"Me, too," Braden said.

Amber whirled around and stared at Braden. "No, Braden. Why do you want to go?"

Braden faced her, taking her hand. "This is our chance, Amber. If we can stop this, if we can help in any way, we can make things right for a lot of people, more than even Oliver."

Carrie watched the torture in her sister's eyes. At one point, Braden had wanted to become a patrolman—not to hurt people, but to try to make things right from the inside out. To become another Oliver.

Carrie nudged Amber. "I'll keep an eye out for him."

"As if you can," Amber growled. "Maybe I should just come."

"With your broken leg?" Braden said. "No way."

"Hold up, people," Greg said, lifting a hand. "We only took one of Jamansky's uniforms. I don't need anybody to go with me." He gave Carrie a look that said, *Especially you.* "If I can get to Isabel and McCormick in time, I might not even have to find Oliver. They might be able to take down Rigsby, and the whole demonstration will dissolve. I'll grab Oliver in the mayhem and be back before dark."

"And if not? What happens to Oliver?" Carrie said. Her insides tightened. "What happens to you?"

Sighing, Greg ran a hand over his thick, brown hair. "I know I gotta help Oliver—and I'll do all that I can to do it—but McCormick might not know about the schedule change. If he doesn't..." He blew out his breath. "We'll never get a chance like this again. I've gotta do what I can to help, Carrie. If I don't, there will be a million more Olivers out there. More Donnelles, Jennas, and my mom." He studied her, pleading for understanding. "I've gotta do the right thing. I've gotta warn them first."

Possibly at the expense of losing Oliver. She could read between the lines.

"I know," she said softly. "I understand, and Oliver will, too. You need to find McCormick and tell him. But you don't have to do it alone. Let me help."

"Us," Ashlee said firmly. "Let *us* help."

His jaw clenched again. "I don't need it. Once I warn them, I'll go after Oliver. You've got my word. Jamansky's uniform will get me into the facility, and that'll be enough. But if I don't go now, I might not make it in time. You gotta let me go."

Carrie saw the weariness in his eyes, his shoulders, and whole body, as if he carried the weight of the world.

"There's not enough time," she said. "You can't do it all, Greg, but the great thing is that you don't have to."

His dark brows pulled down in anger. "Look, you're either here, where I know you're safe, or by my side, where I can see you at all times. I'm not losin' you again."

"Ditto," she shot right back.

The two of them stared each other down in a faceoff of wills.

Ashlee Lyon stepped forward. "Then that settles it. You and Carrie stay together and warn McCormick of what's happening while the rest of us split up. Richard and I have our citizenship cards. We'll get Greg whatever he needs to get on the inside to Oliver. We'll meet back in the middle and go from there."

Greg hadn't even looked at Ashlee. He was still glaring at Carrie, breaths coming far too fast. "Not worth the risk."

Nodding, Carrie reached out and took his hand. "You're right. It's not worth the risk of losing Oliver *or* the chance to end this madness. Choosing one over the other is unacceptable. It's also not worth risking you going alone, so *no one* goes anywhere alone anymore."

His eyes widened, perfectly understanding her meaning—and reference. Going alone to Shelton to get Amber and Zach's citizenship had nearly cost her everything.

Before emotions could hijack her temporary bravado, she put on a brave face. "Five of us fit in the car. That's me, you, Braden, Richard, and Ashlee. So…am I driving or are you?"

"Excuse me?" Greg said.

Carrie held out her hand. "Give me the keys."

His eyebrow cocked. "You're gettin' a little sassy there, Miss Ashworth."

Even though she hadn't driven in six years, she held strong. "I guess I am. Keys?"

With a slow shake of his head, he fought off a smile. "Not a chance."

———•———

Richard and Ashlee dropped the other three off near the place McCormick planned to gather. If all went smoothly, Richard would drive Ashlee to the front gates where she would get the special uniform for Greg—the guy who, Carrie prayed, wouldn't join the firing squad because they already had Oliver by then.

Leading the way, Greg held Carrie's hand, pushing branches aside as they went. Braden followed. Carrie didn't allow herself to think of everything that could go wrong. She forced herself to stay optimistic. This could work.

It had to.

She lifted their entwined hands enough to see his watch. Six o'clock. One hour until the president's demonstration.

"I told McCormick and Kearney to hang west of the training grounds until it was time," Greg said to the two of them. "The woods here are thick enough to hide a large group. If they took my advice, they should be right about…" He paused and pointed. "Look. See the colors?"

Carrie nodded in relief. "You found them."

He looked less enthusiastic than she felt. Reaching up, he stroked her cheek, green eyes searching hers. "It's not too late to back out. You can still go back and wait this out with Amber and Zach."

That had been the hardest part, saying goodbye to her siblings after everything that had happened. Amber had cried, which made May Trenton cry. Even Zach had cried, clinging to her, which about tore her apart. But her siblings were safe. They would be taken care of, no matter what happened going forward.

Her thoughts raced over the plan: Ashlee and Richard were getting a uniform for Greg while he, Carrie, and Braden warned McCormick. Once those hurdles were cleared, Greg, posing as Jamansky, would take in his three prisoners—Carrie, Ashlee, and Braden—and lead them to where Oliver was being held. Hopefully. Richard O'Brien would pose as Greg's helper, wearing Jamansky's everyday patrol uniform. Between the five of them, they could do it. Strength in numbers. Once inside, once they found Oliver…well…they'd figure out what to do from there. Or that was what she kept telling herself.

So many things could go wrong, so many ways she could lose someone else.

Her gaze dropped to the bulge under Greg's waistband where he'd hidden Jamansky's gun. A shudder tore through her.

Leaning into Greg's warm, strong hand, she held his steady gaze and forced a smile. "This is the easy part." *The safer part,* she nearly added. "Let's go find McCormick."

The second they neared the camp, Carrie could tell that people didn't know about the change to Rigsby's demonstration. Several rebels were lazily setting up tents for the night, laughing and talking as if they had all the time in the world.

"I didn't know there would be so many of them," Braden said behind them.

Frowning, Greg surveyed the area. "This isn't even half, which isn't good. That means the rest are still comin'."

Two men approached them, holding rifles.

"What do you want?" one asked.

"We're here to see McCormick and Kearney," Greg said. "And we don't have time for the runaround, so let us through."

"Sure, sure," the first one said. "What's the password?"

"Password?" Greg snapped, growing angry. "How about this? Go tell Commander McCormick that Greg Pierce is back."

The rebel's eyes widened. So did Carrie's.

"Mr. Pierce?" he said. "I'm so sorry, sir. I didn't recognize you at first. But now…yes, come on. I'll show you where the leaders are."

Carrie looked up at Greg in surprise. He seemed equally taken aback.

He pulled her close and whispered, "That doesn't usually work."

"I guess you have a reputation," she said, smiling.

"Not a good one. These people have tried to kill me more than once."

That wiped the smile from Carrie's face. But as they started walking, she noticed a few people pointing at Greg. It seemed so strange. They knew who he was. Braden shot Carrie an impressed look.

Suddenly, a dark-haired woman broke through the group, running toward them full-speed.

"Greg!" the woman called, waving her hand. "Greg!"

"Isabel," he said, relaxing a little.

Greg's partner.

The dark-haired woman reached them. "I'm so relieved that you came, Greg," Isabel said. "I knew you couldn't stay away."

"Honestly," he said, "I hadn't planned to come, but there have been some changes. Here, let me introduce you first." Greg turned back. "This is Lieutenant Isabel Ryan—or former lieutenant, I should say. Isabel, this is Braden, a friend who volunteered to help. And this..." He wrapped a hand around Carrie's waist, bringing her slightly forward. Smiling for the first time since everything happened, he finished, "This is Carrie."

Dark eyes dancing, Isabel extended a hand to Carrie. "It's a pleasure to meet you, Carrie. I'm glad to see you safe and alive. This guy has been pretty worried about you."

"I'm glad to have him back," Carrie said. "And it's so nice to meet you, too, Isabel. I've heard a lot about you."

"Probably not all good," Isabel quipped. "How do you keep this guy in check? He's a loose cannon."

"I don't," Carrie admitted.

Greg huffed. "Alrighty. We've got things to discuss–that's why we came." Without preamble, he added, "Rigsby moved up the demonstration to tonight."

In an instant, Isabel sobered. "I know. We just heard. Kearney's talking with the other leaders right now about what to do, but it's not good, Greg. We're not ready—not at all."

"You've gotta be. You've gotta go in tonight. Where's McCormick? What does he say?" Greg asked.

Unexpectedly, her eyes filled. She looked from person to person, including the rebels who had gathered in around to hear. Finally she turned back. "McCormick was taken this morning."

"What?" Carrie and Greg said together.

"They took Uncle Charlie. They arrested him." Swallowing, her gaze lowered to the dirt. "He's scheduled to join the execution."

Carrie's stomach dropped. "No."

"How?" Braden asked.

In a rush, Isabel explained how Commander McCormick had been meeting with people on the inside, those on security detail that McCormick had known for years. Those people planned to get the rebels inside, but then one of them turned and exposed the whole group.

"As soon as President Rigsby found out," Isabel said, "he said he wanted McCormick front and center for the demonstration. The security guy barely escaped in time to tell us. And now..." She shook her head. "It's bad, Greg. I don't know how to get to McCormick, and we don't know how to get inside other than to just send everyone in for a major blow-them-out attack. That's what Kearney wants to do."

"No!" Greg said. "Too many innocent people will be killed."

"What else can we do?" Isabel said. "The guy who was supposed to open the underground gate was taken with McCormick. If I could even get in there, I could open the panel and get Kearney and the others inside, but I don't exactly have security clearance anymore. That place is hopping with guards, and we're out of time."

Carrie waited for Greg to say something, to tell Isabel of their plan to get inside. Maybe she could go with them. He just folded his arms, staring down at the dirt. So Carrie decided to go for it.

"Um..." Carrie said. "Maybe we can get you in."

"How?" Isabel said.

Again, Carrie looked at Greg. He wouldn't meet her gaze. Technically, the plan was hers and he hated it. He wanted to go in alone. No handcuffs. No using her and Braden as supposed prisoners. Just him, breaking in to free Oliver, alone. But now more than ever, Carrie saw the logic of her plan.

"It's hard to explain it all," Carrie said, "but Greg is going inside, pretending to be a patrol chief from our area who is scheduled to bring in three prisoners for the demonstration. Us. You can be one of the prisoners if you want. I think..." She shrugged, feeling stupid for being so bold. "I think we can get you inside."

It sounded so ludicrous, but Isabel's dark eyes lit up. She looked from Greg to Carrie to Braden.

"It'll work," Greg said with a reluctant nod. "I don't like it, but it'll work. We can get you in."

Suddenly Isabel whirled around and shouted, "Bring me Kearney! I think we've got something."

fifty-seven

Richard drove Ashlee right up to the east gate. Ashlee wore her own, nice clothes again, which helped. She didn't look so homeless anymore. And Richard wore Jamansky's uniform—a disturbing sight all things considered. But it fit him well enough, so Ashlee ignored that it used to belong to her ex-boyfriend. Especially since it got them through the first gate with a simple wave.

Ashlee had never actually been to Naperville. Now it was a flurry of activity. Officers, guards, federal patrolmen, and simple soldiers. They milled about the training grounds, getting everything in order.

"Just drop me off here," she said to Richard.

"But the people," he said, nervously scanning the groups lining the outside of the massive compound.

"It's fine. This is east, right? The message told David to go to the east gate. So meet me back here in five minutes."

Ashlee sounded braver than she felt, but she opened the door and got out. With a tall, confident stride, she approached the east entrance.

The guard at the gate took her green citizenship card and scanned it. She pretended to examine her dirty, rough nails, while she secretly held her breath.

The IDV machine beeped one beep and then a light turned green. She smiled. David Jamansky had done a lot of things, but he hadn't revoked her citizenship. Her picture lit up on the guy's computer screen along with her current job title—something else David should have changed but hadn't.

"How can I help you, Miss Lyon?" the guard said, handing her green card back. "You're not on my list of attendees." Though he didn't add anything else, his eyes grazed over her civilian clothing with another question. Why wasn't she dressed in uniform?

"I'm here to get the uniform for my boss, Chief Jamansky from the Kane County Unit. He's on the list for the demonstration today, but he's running late."

"Sorry, but your boss will have to pick up the uniform himself."

"I understand. Only he's super late." She shrugged helplessly. "He asked me to get his uniform for him so he can go directly to the facility and change there."

"We have changing rooms here."

She looked to where the guard pointed. Other patrolmen were coming out of the bathroom, dressed in matching all-black uniforms. The uniforms weren't like typical federal patrol uniforms, though. They were much fancier, with a red stripe on one leg, and a blue stripe running down the other. Over the right breast was a single, white star—the new symbol of Rigsby's message. Below the star read, "United We Stand." An ironic statement considering the massacre that was about to happen.

How could those people walk so tall, and laugh, and ignore the Medieval-type slaughter about to happen? How could they be okay with this in any form? What happened to America being the land of the free and the home of the brave? All she saw were a bunch of cowards, cowards in fancy black uniforms.

Working to keep her face even, she acknowledged the changing rooms with a nod. "I see. It's just that he's checking in some last minute prisoners, and he's worried that he won't make it back in time. Does your file there say anything about him bringing in extra traitors?"

She had no clue if there was such a file, but it seemed like something the government would require.

Sure enough, the guard pulled up another screen. "Yes. He's slotted to bring in three others besides the original one."

A name flashed up on the screen beside David's.

Oliver Gerard Simmons.

She stared at his name a moment too long before she caught herself.

"Right," she said, voice tighter than before. "And he's delivering the three of them to Cliff Watson. Do you know where Cliff is? My boss is looking for him on the north side but didn't see anything there."

"Cliff's at the next entrance down."

"Great. Then is it alright if I meet him there with the uniform? I'd hate for him to be late for everything. My boss doesn't want to miss the celebration." She finished up with a flutter of her eyelashes, something that sometimes worked.

When Ashlee walked back out to the car two minutes later, carrying the black, fancy uniform, she wanted to feel victorious. She had done it. But time was moving too swiftly. Oliver was in there somewhere, and the firing squad was gathering, nearly ready.

Richard gaped at her as she opened the back door of the patrol car and set the clothing bag safely inside.

"You did it," Richard said. "How?"

"Just go," she said urgently. "I'll explain as you drive. Go!"

As he pulled out of the parking area, she stared back at the massive training compound. What if they weren't fast enough? What if Greg couldn't pass himself off as Jamansky? Even if he could, what if it was already too late?

"Any other instructions?" Richard said. "Did they tell you where Greg should go?"

"They'll give Greg his weapon on the platform. It's standard issue, so I hope he knows how to use it. Can you drive any faster?"

The rebels were waiting for them when they returned. Braden met Richard and Ashlee at the car.

"You did it!" Braden said happily. "I can't believe you got it."

"Don't sound so surprised," Ashlee said sharply. She scanned the growing crowd of rebels milling about the woods. There seemed to be hundreds of them, but she couldn't see the most important ones.

"Where are the others?" she asked. "Where's Greg?"

"Right here," Greg said, striding toward them. A small entourage of rebels followed him, including Carrie. He made quick introductions, introducing the key people, but Ashlee barely paid attention. She shoved the uniform into his arms.

"You're out of time, Greg," she said in a rush. "You need to go. People are already changed and ready, so go fast. Shoes are in the bag."

Taking the clothing bag, Greg ducked down inside of the first tent.

Ashlee stood against the car. Her stomach kept doing flips. If she didn't calm down, it was going to empty itself. She needed to be doing something, not thinking.

"Hey, Richard," she said. "Let me adjust your uniform before we head out." Grabbing his arm, she ripped off two gold bands from Jamansky's green uniform sleeve. A few loose threads hung remained, which she quickly tore away. "There. You just went from patrol chief to lowly patrolman's helper. They shouldn't question either you or Greg."

Richard nodded. "Thank you, Ashlee. We are all indebted to you. So is Oliver."

Oliver.

Her gaze dropped to her hands which felt suddenly jittery. She balled them against her stomach. "What if we don't get there in time?"

"We will," Carrie said. "Don't worry. We'll make it happen. But...actually..." She glanced back at the group before looking at Ashlee again. "There's been a change of plans. We actually don't need you to go with us anymore, Ashlee. You can stay here until we're back."

Ashlee's head whipped up. "What? Why not?"

"Because I'm going in your place," a woman said, joining them. She held out a hand to Ashlee, but Ashlee was too appalled to shake it. "I'm Lieutenant Isabel Ryan. Thanks for letting me take your spot. It's just the thing we need to break the rest of this sorry lot inside, so thank you." To Carrie, Isabel added, "Is Greg ready yet?"

"He's changing now," Carrie said.

"Wait!" Ashlee said, panicked. "I need to be there. I need to help Oliver."

"We can't risk you being seen again," the lieutenant said. "Besides, we've been talking strategy, and it's all worked out. Braden and Richard will help me clear the corridors while Greg and Carrie work on freeing your boyfriend and the commander."

Ashlee's eyes widened. She felt heat creep up her neck. "Oh, Oliver's not my boyfriend. He's just someone I know—a coworker."

"My apologies," Isabel said. "When they told me you volunteered to help, I just assumed."

Before Ashlee could explain, a rough-looking guy strode up to them. "Isabel," he said. "One last thing."

Isabel gave Ashlee an apologetic look. "Sorry. I need to speak with Kearney. Thanks again for letting me take your spot."

As Isabel and the rebel leader started going over the last minute plans, Carrie, Richard, and Braden huddled close, also reviewing what needed to be done.

Ashlee stood alone.

They really were going to leave her behind.

Frantic, she broke into Carrie's small huddle. "Please don't forget Oliver with everything else. I mean, of course you guys won't, but if you see him, will you tell him that I'm here? Even if it's too late, just let him know that I came."

Even if it's too late?

What was she saying? Why would Oliver care that she'd come to Naperville? But after the two letters he'd written via Reef, she wanted him to know that she had changed. For the first time in her life, she was proud of who she was. And for whatever reason, she wanted Oliver to be proud of her, too—which was so stupid. The guy was marching to his execution.

"It's going to be okay," Carrie said. "We'll find Oliver, and then we'll all go home. Just wait here for us to..." She trailed off, gaze lifting over Ashlee's head.

Ashlee turned to see what she had.

Greg had climbed out of the tent, wearing the all-black uniform meant for David Jamansky. It fit him well. A little long on the pants, but otherwise a good fit. He'd combed his hair and somehow managed a shave, too.

"Wow," Isabel Ryan said, breaking away from her conversation with Kearney. "You clean up pretty well, Pierce. Very official. This might actually work."

Ashlee nodded, regarding him again. "You look like the other officers I saw, Greg. It's perfect."

Seemingly nervous, Greg walked straight up to Carrie, brushing down the front of his uniform. "Is it okay? You look a little spooked. Sorry. It's not like I want to be wearin' a fed's uniform."

Carrie did look a little spooked, but she shook her head. "It's not that. You look great. Really great. It's just...uh..." Carrie's cheeks colored, making Ashlee smile a little. It was cute seeing her flustered around Greg in his fancy uniform. In a boring t-shirt and ratty jeans, the guy had been nice eye candy. Now, with his slicked-back hair and broad shoulders, he looked regal. Yet he only had eyes for the sweet, warm-loving Carrie Ashworth.

A twinge of jealousy shot through Ashlee. Not that Greg was looking at someone else. She didn't care about that. But that Carrie had someone who could look at her so thoroughly, so completely, as if her opinion—and her opinion alone—was the only thing in the world that mattered.

"Sorry. You look great," Carrie said, finally composing herself. "Very convincing. Is your arm okay?"

He lifted it, but his wound was covered in the black, long sleeve. "I wrapped it real tight. As long as it doesn't start bleeding down my hand, it should be just fine."

"Ah, Pierce," Isabel Ryan said, "you would have made a good soldier. It's a shame."

"No," Kearney countered. "He's got rebel blood in him, through and through."

Greg rolled his eyes, but turned his attention to Ashlee. "Has Jamansky ever met this Cliff guy before? Will Cliff know what he looks like—what I'm supposed to look like?"

"I've never heard David talk about him before," Ashlee said. "I think he's a friend of the mayor's, so let's hope not. He'll be at the second entrance. He's expecting you and the three prisoners, so you really need to hurry."

"Alrighty. Now for the worst part." Greg pulled out three sets of handcuffs. He clicked the first around Braden's wrists easily enough. Isabel's, too. But when he faced Carrie, he stared down at her outstretched wrists, wrists that hadn't even fully healed yet. His Adam's apple bobbed once. Slowly, he shook his head and whispered, "I can't do it."

"I'll be fine," Carrie said. "Once we're inside, you can release us. It's a good plan."

"It's a horrible plan," he countered angrily.

Carrie looked up at him, and for the second time it seemed like the two of them stood alone in the world. "My siblings are safe, Greg. That means more to me than anything. This is our only way inside. Even if the worst happens and you and I don't make it out…" She tried to smile, but it looked weak and tentative. "It will still be worth it."

"Live free or die," a rebel said behind her.

The second he said it, the motto caught on like wildfire. The whole group of rebels started chanting it. "Live free or die. Live free or die."

Greg scowled at them. "You're not makin' me feel any better." Turning back to Carrie, he sighed a deep, weary sigh. "Think the early American patriots felt prepared for what they had to do?"

"Probably not anymore than we do," Carrie said. "They were just regular people who hoped for a better future. They were willing to try, and we have to as well. It's time to live free."

"Or die trying," he finished softly.

He clicked the handcuffs around her wrists, and then lifted her bound hands and kissed the back of them. Then he straightened, standing tall in his black uniform, and surveyed the group of mismatched people, from trained army commanders, to simple everyday-citizens-turned-rebels. All of them waited for him to make the first move. Get Isabel on the inside. Help the others follow. And then take down the president.

Hopefully not forgetting a semi-awkward, semi-balding patrolman named Oliver Simmons.

"Alrighty," Greg said. "Time to move out."

Ashlee's heart felt heavy as they headed for Jamansky's patrol car, knowing they were leaving without her. She hated letting them go in her place—especially since she was the only one there with nobody left to live for.

As Richard opened the back door of the patrol car for his three "prisoners," Ashlee ran up to him.

"What can I do?" she asked. "Give me something to do while you're inside, or I'll go crazy."

Richard O'Brien pulled the car keys from the green, stolen patrol uniform. "Would you like to be the chauffeur? We'll probably be coming out on a dead run."

Ashlee nodded. "I'll wait outside of the gate. I'll wait all night if I have to." And hopefully her wait wouldn't be for nothing. Because she didn't know what she would do if these people she barely knew—but already considered her as a friend—never came back.

fifty-eight

"You're late," a guard said.

"Tell me about it," Greg growled. He was wrestling with Isabel who was putting on a better "traitor" show than Greg had bargained for. She writhed all over the place. With all of her training, she was strong and fast. His stiff, black uniform made it hard to keep hold of her. He wanted to poke her and tell her to cool it. Richard, looking surprisingly formal in Jamansky's green uniform, held Carrie and Braden's arms tightly. Both of them remained perfectly compliant.

The guard typed something into his computer. "Your name?"

"Chief David Jamansky," Greg said, still struggling. At the same time, he worked to control his southern accent so he didn't sound like an outsider. "Any idea where Cliff Watson is? I'm supposed to deliver these three to him."

"Yeah," the guard said. "Cliff just went back that way."

Once the information came up on the screen, the guard studied Carrie, Isabel, and Braden, looking suddenly suspicious. "This says two of the prisoners are teenagers."

Braden and Carrie, the younger ones, were nineteen and twenty-three. Obviously not close enough to teenagers.

"The rebels exaggerated their ages," Greg said, thinking quickly. "To get out of full prison sentences. Believe me, they're not kids."

"Alright. They're about ready to start, Chief Jamansky. Give me your papers, and we'll get you through quickly."

Isabel suddenly jerked to the side, nearly yanking Greg over. "I won't go down without a fight, you Nazi scum!" she yelled. "You're going to regret—"

Greg whirled and whacked her across the cheek. He hated doing it, but she'd told him to. With a cry of pain, she doubled over.

Hand stinging, Greg said to the guard, "I'm going to miss the whole thing if I don't hurry. Come on. Let me through."

"Fine." The guard waved them back. "If you need help with that dark-haired one, ask the guards at the checking station. They'll help you escort her back to the holding cell."

"Thanks," Greg said. "I won't be sorry when her head rolls."

The guard laughed and pointed down the hallway. "First corner on your left. Once they've checked the prisoners, follow the hallway from there. Cliff Watson should be near the elevator."

Greg yanked on Isabel and started forward. Richard and the others followed.

As they cleared the first corner, Greg's heart rate kicked up a notch. He'd been in this spot before. The cubbies. The poorly-lit hallway. Down the first cubby, sumo-sized guards had strip-searched him and found the marks on his back and shoulder. Then they'd beaten the snot out of him.

If any guards recognized him today...

His mind screamed at him for dragging Carrie into this. Carrie. Braden. All of them.

He leaned close to Isabel and whispered, "Check the prisoners for what?"

"They're just going to frisk us," Isabel said. "Make sure we didn't sneak in any weapons."

Frisking was okay. Anything more and Greg would have to snap a few necks. His gaze flickered back to Carrie. She flashed a quick smile. *So far, so good,* she seemed to say. He wished he felt the same.

Facing front again, he caught sight of the bright red spot across Isabel's cheek.

"Sorry about that back there," he said.

"Don't be. You hit like a girl." Then Isabel also smiled.

Greg told himself to calm down. This could work. Carrie and Isabel obviously thought it would.

A new group of guards met them, thankfully none that Greg recognized.

"What's this?" one of them asked.

"Latecomers," Greg said, trying to sound official again. "I'm Chief Jamansky from the Kane County Unit. Let us through. The guard back there said they're ready to start."

"We'll be fast."

The guards circled Isabel, Carrie, and Braden. "Hands on your heads," they ordered. "Feet apart."

Greg cringed as they started frisking Carrie and the others. Pockets. Pants. Even patting down Greg's lucky shirt that Carrie wore. Intrusively, they checked every possible spot for weapons. Handcuffed and helpless, the three of them complied, though Carrie's neck turned a splotchy red.

Once the guards finished with the prisoners, they turned to Greg and Richard and did the same, patting them down. Greg panicked. He hadn't been expecting that. Sure enough, a guard extracted Jamansky's gun that Greg had stashed inside of his belt.

Scowling, the guard held it in front of Greg. "No outside weapons, chief. They're providing a weapon for you."

"I knew that," Greg said. "Sorry. I dumped all my other guns. I forgot that I keep that baby tucked in there. Can I have it back after the ceremony? It's my good luck charm."

The guard tossed it in a bucket. "Sure. Check back here after, and we'll have it for you."

"Thanks."

As they moved down the long, empty hallway, Greg glanced back at Carrie. Hands still bound in front of her, she seemed to be holding up just fine. He didn't know how. He felt like he could sleep for a week.

He scanned every door and corner coming up for a dark spot to hide. Isabel did the same. She pointed at a door to the side, a women's bathroom, and motioned to Richard. Taking the cue, Richard darted inside and was back out in seconds.

"It's clear," Richard said.

The five of them ducked inside of the women's bathroom. Isabel searched every spot, checking the vents and air ducts.

Stopping near the sinks, Isabel pointed upward. "There's a room right above us that connects to McCormick's old office. I can make it from there. Braden, Richard, this is where we break off. Let's go."

Greg fished out the handcuffs and released Braden and Isabel, but not Carrie. Carrie would remain his decoy prisoner until they found out where Oliver and McCormick were being held.

"Good luck," Braden said to Carrie.

"Be safe," Richard added with a look meant for Greg as much as anyone. Richard O'Brien seemed to be the only other person who saw the endless potentials for failure in this plan. The man seemed to have aged a decade over the last week.

There were a thousand things Greg wanted to say to his stepdad—and to Braden who was too naïve to realize what he'd volunteered for—but already Isabel was up on the counter, pushing ceiling tiles aside. Greg had no clue how they would get up and through, but he trusted Isabel to make it work.

"We'll see all of you soon," Carrie said, remaining the optimist Greg needed her to be. Yet under the bright bathroom lights, her skin looked pale, her pupils, wide as she watched them climb onto the counter. She was more frightened than she was letting on.

Greg faced her suddenly. "Go with them." He motioned to the others. "Go. I'll be fine. I know what I'm doin' now."

She shook her head.

"Or stay here as a lookout," Greg tried desperately. "Please."

"If you don't have me," she said, "they'll just send you straight outside to the platform. You need me to get to the holding cell. We stay together, so let's go."

Without further argument, she started for the hallway.

Greg followed. He took her arm, keeping her close to his body, closer than an officer should keep a prisoner, but he couldn't help himself. He needed to feel her warmth, to inhale the scent of her hair one last time in case something went wrong—on either side of this insane plan.

He leaned down and whispered in her good ear, "As soon as we figure out where the holding cell is, I'm gonna release your cuffs, and then you and I are gonna hide until we figure out what to do next."

Her head fell against his shoulder for the briefest second. "Sounds good."

Sudden footsteps broke out in front of them, around a corner out of sight. Greg stepped away from Carrie just as an older man with large glasses came into view. The man strode right toward them, wearing a federal patrol uniform.

"Chief Jamansky, I presume," the man said, extending a hand. "It's so good to see you, sir. I'm Cliff Watson, Mayor Phillips' friend. We spoke on the phone. Thank you for joining us today. Glad you finally made it."

"Barely in time," Greg said.

"Well, it's an honor to have you." Cliff glanced sideways. "You only brought the one prisoner after all?"

"Yeah. I ended up shooting the younger ones," Greg said. "They were causing too much trouble. This one is pretty docile, though. Plus I thought she'd look good on the big screen."

The second he said the words, his insides crawled—especially as Cliff looked Carrie up and down long enough that Greg wanted to punch the guy.

"I agree," the man said. "She'll make a nice addition to our sorry group. They're an ugly bunch. Here, chief. I'll walk with you and show you where to take her. Then I've got your weapon ready."

"Oh," Greg said, pulse jumping, "just point me in the right direction. I can find the holding cell myself. I'm sure you have a lot of last minute preparations."

"It's no bother. Everything is all set. I need to explain the procedures to you anyway."

Cliff started off.

Frantic, Greg tried to hang back with Carrie, but the man just turned to face them as he spoke, like a tour guide, giving details while walking backwards.

"We only have about ten minutes in which I'll get you your weapon," Cliff said. "Then when we give you the signal, all of you on the firing squad will march, single file, out onto the platform. Try to make it look like you practiced with the rest of them. Left, right, left. I'm sure you remember from your training days. You'll stand at attention during the rest of President Rigsby's speech. I apologize that I don't know how long that will be. They don't tell us that kind of thing."

Greg was hardly listening. He was in full freak-out mode. He had nowhere to stash Carrie. The hall was bare, and the man's eyes stayed on them, which meant Greg would have to take Cliff down. Considering that the man was armed and Greg wasn't, that wasn't a happy prospect.

Greg's grip loosened on Carrie's arm. With his eyes, he tried to tell her to run.

Go!

She saw and ignored his warning.

The hallway was long, blank, and void of hiding spots. There was nowhere. He pushed her away anyway. She came right back.

Cliff slowed. "Ah. Here we are, chief sir."

A giant holding cell sat in front of them. Inside stood a few dozen people, hanging around the bars. They didn't look like a bunch of rebel traitors. They looked like hungry, homeless people somebody had pulled off the street. A few wore orange prison uniforms, others wore blue municipality work outfits, but most wore regular civilian clothes like Carrie. They watched the movement around them with expressions that looked like they'd already given up.

Even more frightening, the firing squad stood outside of the bars in black uniforms identical to Greg's. Most were looking out the open doors to the outside compound, talking about how things would play out and who should march in first. Early evening sunlight streamed in from the outside. So did the sound. The noise of a crowd in the commons area floated through, everybody waiting for the show.

Though he couldn't see, Greg guessed that some soldiers in that crowd outside—maybe even most—didn't want to be there. They'd been recruited to fight Rigsby's battle. They would pretend to cheer, but Greg knew better. Greg hoped Kearney remembered Greg's warning. Leave the innocent out of the fight.

Carrie gasped softly behind him.

A man in the back of the cell with dark, receding hair and a long, thin face moved forward to the bars. Oliver. His shadowed eyes were huge as he watched Greg and Carrie approach.

Greg gave Oliver a sharp shake of the head. *Don't react.*

Greg knew it looked bad: him wearing a firing-squad uniform, Carrie in chains. *Just trust me,* he begged Oliver silently. *Don't react!*

Carrie seemed to compose herself first. Then, thankfully, so did Oliver.

Oliver stood next to a man curled up in a heap, groaning on the floor. The broad-shouldered man wore the same everyday clothing he had been wearing when Greg had seen him last.

Commander McCormick.

From the little Greg could see, it appeared they'd beaten his former commander, but Greg couldn't tell how badly.

Greg's pulse thundered in his ears. This was not going to end well. Carrie. Oliver. McCormick.

All of them.

A large screen over the heads of the firing squad showed the countdown to the broadcast. Five minutes and twelve seconds. A flag waved behind the numbers—the new flag of the United States with thirteen stripes but only one star in the blue corner. The clock on the screen ticked down. Five minutes. Four minutes and fifty-five seconds.

Greg tried to push Carrie away again, but somebody suddenly called his name.

"Pierce?" One of the black-clad soldiers moved through the group. "Hey, is that you?"

Greg froze.

Burke, a guy who had been in Greg's special op group in this very place, came forward, smiling. "Dude, what happened to you? I heard you were kicked out of our group when you disappeared. I thought McCormick shot you for mouthing off or something."

"No. Reassigned," Greg said evenly, eyeing Cliff who listened, but hadn't noticed the slip of the tongue.

Pierce.

Not Jamansky.

Greg's eyes darted around the small area for an exit. Backwards wouldn't work—nowhere to hide. It would have to be forward, beyond the holding cell, into another hallway which could lead to anywhere.

"You'll never believe who we nabbed this morning," his former comrade continued excitedly. Burke pointed to the holding cell. "Look who turned traitor on us. Commander McCormick. Can you believe it? McCormick quit his job earlier this week, but Oshan found him this morning, trying to weasel his way back inside. President Rigsby totally went ballistic when he found out. Now he wants McCormick front and center on the line, which makes him my target." Burke's smile faltered a little. "Crazy, huh?"

McCormick didn't turn at the mention of his name—or Greg's voice. Greg wondered if the guy was even conscious.

"Yeah," Greg managed. "Crazy."

Growing anxious, Cliff Watson stepped forward and reached for Carrie. "Here. Let me take her for you, chief. I'll put her in the cell with the others."

Greg's grip clamped iron-strong on Carrie's arm. "No. I got it. Just a minute."

Burke, still celebrating the reunion, called over his shoulder, "Hey, Oshan, guess who walked in. Remember this guy from our group?"

Straight from Greg's worst nightmare, from the middle of the firing squad, another of his fellow trainees strode forward, excited to see him.

"Gregory Pierce!" Oshan called. "What's up, man?"

Cliff Watson whipped around. "What did you say his name was?"

Greg froze.

Carrie suddenly yanked on his arm, pulling him back away—only back was the wrong way. They'd never make it.

Oshan didn't seem to hear Cliff's question, and neither did Burke who, instead, gave Greg a strange look.

"Hey, Pierce," Burke said, pulling out his clipboard. "I don't remember seeing your name on my list. I'm in charge of the firing squad, but I would have recognized your name. Yeah. There's no Greg Pierce on—"

Greg saw the movement.

Time slowing, he watched Cliff Watson reach for his gun.

With one step, Greg swung wide and punched Cliff Watson clean in the jaw. Cliff stumbled back into the bars of the holding cell. Grabbing Carrie's arm, Greg leapt forward, plowing over Burke and Oshan. He sprinted forward, breaking through the stunned group of soldiers.

"Stop him!" Cliff roared.

Shouts echoed through the room.

Bullets fired off.

Within seconds, Greg and Carrie were tackled to the ground.

fifty-nine

Burke and the others threw Greg and Carrie into the holding cell with everybody else. The metal bars clanked behind them.

"No!" Greg pounded the metal bars. His wounded arm throbbed with pain, but he kept pounding. "No!"

Oliver rushed over to them. "What happened? Why are you here?"

"Oh, Oliver," Carrie said. She tried to hug him, but her bound hands prevented even that. "I'm so sorry."

"It's okay," Oliver said. "I'm okay. Well, not really. Why are you here?"

Oliver glared at Greg with a lecture Greg didn't need to hear. Greg hated himself so deeply, so thoroughly, for leading Carrie into something that had put her at death's doors—again—he couldn't even bear to look at her. But he could release her.

He reached into his pocket for the key, and unlocked her handcuffs.

"Can you help McCormick?" he asked.

With a nod, Carrie rushed to the back wall. "Commander McCormick, sir?" Kneeling, she pushed her hair back away from her face and tried again. "McCormick?"

The older commander groaned, but didn't move much. From the little Greg could see, his face was bruised and bloody. He wasn't dead, but what did that matter? He would be dead soon. They all would be.

He pictured Carrie standing in front of the firing squad, eyes wide with terror.

His stomach rolled.

Two minutes and thirty seconds until show time. How long after the broadcast started before they hauled them out onto the platform? Counted to ten? Started shooting?

Greg paced. All the other "traitors" in the cell watched him. In and around bodies he paced, by Carrie and McCormick, past Oliver and back again. The cell felt impossibly hot and grew hotter by the second. Sweat beaded down his face.

Isabel needed to hurry. That was it. They'd gotten her inside. She would kill Rigsby, the broadcast would never happen, and…they'd all be shipped to Joliet's State Penitentiary, but at least they would be alive. But if Isabel didn't move fast, everything would be—

A roar went up outside.

"There he is," Burke announced to his squad. "The president has arrived. We'll be up soon, gentlemen. Be ready to march."

"No!" Greg shouted with another pound on the bars.

Isabel was supposed to stop President Rigsby before he ever made it to that southern tower.

Where was she?

The television screen over Burke's head flickered to life. In an instant, President Rigsby's face filled the screen, smiling and victorious. His dark, dyed hair was slicked back, his suit and tie looked pristine. That same face had been plastered everywhere lately: every *New Day Times* issue, every single bill of the new, red currency. In person, the president looked at least a decade older than his photos with wrinkles and tired skin. Yet he still had the slimy, fake smile—and hair—of a politician. He held his hand up in one long, waveless wave.

Cheers echoed through the training facility. From the tops of the guard towers all the way to the holding cell, loud cheers sounded. And then it started. The chanting.

"United we stand! United we stand!"

Carrie, who knelt next to McCormick, turned toward the screen. She and Oliver had propped the commander up in a semi-sitting position, leaned against the back wall. McCormick's eyes were opened but didn't seem to see anything.

But Carrie did. Her gaze went to Greg.

"United we stand! United we stand!"

Those huge, blue eyes just stared at Greg. They started to fill. With a blink, a few tears slid down her cheeks. She knew they'd lost. She knew they were dead. He felt like his heart was being ripped from his chest.

"United we stand! United we stand! United we stand!"

Each time grew louder, and with each notch in the rising volume, Rigsby's smile grew. His hand stayed up, victorious. He had them, and he knew it.

Rigsby was going to win. He would snuff out the rebellion, killing all who opposed him, and ensuring his grip on America.

Sudden rage filled Greg. He whirled around and shook the bars.

"Burke, listen to me," Greg said. "You can't do this. This isn't right!"

"You dug your own grave, Pierce," Burke said without turning away from the overhead screen.

Cliff Watson approached the bars. A bright red spot covered his cheek from where Greg had punched him. He glared at Greg through the bars.

"You will change out of that uniform this instant," Cliff said. "I will not have you marching out there, dressed as—"

Fast as a viper, Greg reached through the bars to grab him by the neck.

The man barely jumped back in time. "Sergeant Burke, sir!" Cliff called. "We can't have that man out there wearing the same thing the rest of you are wearing."

"What would you have him wear?" Burke said, still distracted by the broadcast. "It's not like we have a change of clothes. It's fine. Just throw a bag over his head. No one will care."

From the large, overhead screen, Greg saw the president wave his hands in a downward motion, trying to get the soldiers-in-training to quiet down enough that he could begin.

"Good evening," President Rigsby finally started. "I thank you for so graciously hosting me at this magnificent training facility." There was a slight delay between real time and the broadcast on the television, making everything sound in stereo. "It is an honor to look into your bright faces tonight. You, my friends and soldiers, are the future of America!"

That brought another round of cheers.

Greg needed to kick something. Where was Isabel? From the camera angle, it looked like Rigsby stood where McCormick assumed he would, in the upper southern guard tower. So what had happened? Isabel should have let Kearney and the others inside by now. Where was everybody?

Or were they about to join Greg and Carrie—and too many others—in the massacre?

"As you know," President Rigsby said into his microphone, "the last six years have taken its toll on our precious country. At the heart of our economic struggles…"

Greg couldn't stand to hear another word. Not a single one. As Burke's guys nodded in agreement, he grabbed the bars and rattled them again.

"Burke, listen!" Greg yelled. "Oshan, don't be a part of this. This is gonna be a massacre, the first execution like this in the history of our country. This is wrong!"

The only response was President Rigsby's voice.

"Some have taken advantage of our economic struggles. They have trampled the very laws under their feet that you are fighting to protect," the president said. "They've stolen your dignity and sense of safety. If we are to regain our former greatness, these illegals must be eradicated. A nation cannot be strong if its people are not strong, and we must be strong!"

The crowd cheered again.

Strangely, Greg realized that most of the cheering was coming through the television speakers and not the open door, as if they were supplementing the broadcast with extra applause and cheering.

"Burke!" Greg snapped. "These people have done nothin' wrong. *Burke!*"

Burke gave him a *buzz off* wave.

"Now we must do what must be done," President Rigsby continued. "That means rooting out the traitors among us, even at the lowest levels."

Traitors.

Greg spun to the person next to him. "Why were you arrested?" he asked loudly.

The man looked startled. "Uh…I was living illegally on government property."

"How does that make you a traitor worthy of death?" Greg said.

The man shrugged.

Turning, Greg took in the next person, an older woman slumped at the shoulders and so thin that the bones on her hands looked skeleton-esque.

"Why were you arrested?" he asked loud enough to drown out the president.

"I've been illegal since the beginning," she said. "They caught my clan a month ago. They took my granddaughters...and..."

As she broke down crying, a man grabbed Greg's arm.

"They arrested me and my family because we wanted to leave Aurora's municipality," the man said. "Have you seen those places? We couldn't stay there."

All at once, people around Greg started telling their stories. Unable to pay dues. Stole medicine for a child. Simple people who had been in the wrong place at the wrong time.

"Burke, are you listening?" Greg yelled through the bars. "These aren't traitors to the country. These people don't deserve to die."

Burke's shoulders stiffened. He could hear Greg well enough, but he pretended otherwise.

"How many of you had a fair trial?" Greg called to the holding cell.

"Silence!" Cliff Watson shouted back. "Not another word!"

"How many?" Greg said anyway. "How many went through the legal system? After y'all were charged and arrested, how many had proper sentencing? How many had a lawyer? Had their rights read to them?"

Burke's curiosity betrayed him. He glanced back. So did several others in the squad.

Not a single hand rose.

"Pierce," Burke growled, "if you don't shut up, I'm going to have to shoot you before I shoot you."

Greg glared right back at him but spoke to those locked up. "How many of you know somebody who died because of Rigsby?"

Every hand shot up, including Oliver, Carrie, and McCormick's.

For a second time, Greg's eyes locked with Carrie. He counted every person she had lost—they had lost. Her parents. Jenna. Greg's mom. Richard's first wife. Women Carrie had met in prison. People in Kearney's camp.

"How many," a weak voice said from the back of the cell, "know people who have died from this virus Rigsby created?" McCormick tried to sit taller and ended up coughing. But he continued. "How many watched them die in your arms?"

Hands stayed up.

That did it.

Burke whirled around and stormed over to the holding cell. "So help me, all of you just shut up!"

"Or what?" Greg challenged, separated from his former comrade only by metal bars. "You can't kill us. Not yet. Not here. Not so privately. So what are you gonna do?"

Burke reached down to grab the nightstick he no longer wore. His hand came back empty. If he stood even a foot closer, Greg could have grabbed him and shaken some sense into him.

"You will not silence us," Greg said, chest heaving. "Not until our last breath. Look around, Burke. Open your eyes. This is wrong, and you know it."

Burke turned to Cliff. "I'm done with this. Give me a gun!"

"Yes, sir."

Cliff Watson shuffled out of the room.

"If you go through with this," Greg continued, glaring through the bars, "if this brutal, barbaric execution is televised for the whole country to see, it'll start a full-scale retaliation like this country has never seen before. Human life will no longer be sacred. Blood will be spilt on both sides." He looked Burke directly in the eye. "Don't let that happen. Stop this."

Oshan watched them, waiting, looking unsure. The others did, too.

The president's voice rose theatrically. "We will stamp out this resistance! Your children and your children's children will hail your names as the ones who returned America to its purest form. Today we start that purification. Today we will remove the undesirable elements from among us."

"That's our cue," Oshan said. "Burke, we're supposed to march them out now."

Cliff returned, wheeling in the cart of laid-out rifles. He started handing them out. That seemed to break the tension. The firing squad refocused, lining up, now armed and ready.

Somebody took Greg's hand. Carrie. She'd given up helping McCormick and joined Greg by the front of the cell, preparing to march out with him. Her hand felt as cold as he suddenly felt. Clinging to him, she looked up at him, blue eyes filled with tears. They would stand together out there. They would fall together.

Carrie.

410

"Guess how she and I got inside today," Greg said. "Not a single card. Not a single paper. All I had to say was that I'd brought in more prisoners for the execution, and they waved us right through. Do you know a single name of the people behind me, Burke? Do you know their crimes? For all anybody knows, I picked up three random citizens on the street. But who cares, right? Rigsby has to have his demonstration."

"Three?" Cliff said, turning.

Greg didn't even bother rubbing it in the whiny guy's face that three of their original group now wandered freely through the training facility.

"As if that isn't bad enough," Greg said, voice rising, "the guy I was impersonating wanted to bring in teenagers. Children, Burke! To be shot on live television. And you wanna know what your buddy, Cliff, there said? Sure. Bring them on in. The more the merrier. Are you listening to me, Burke? Do you realize what this is?"

"She's pregnant," Carrie said, gesturing to a woman huddled on the floor. "This woman beside me is pregnant."

For a second time, Burke's eyes betrayed him. He glanced back to see the woman, and flinched when he spotted her bulging stomach.

"This is wrong," Greg said. "I know it, McCormick quit his job because he knew it, and you know it, too. So listen to your gut and do something while you can. Don't let these people die."

"Burke," Oshan said nervously, "Rigsby is stalling out there. He's just saying the same thing over and over, waiting for us to bring the prisoners out. We need to move."

"We will bring these traitors to justice!" the president roared, throwing a fist in the air. "United we stand!"

The crowd chanted again, but the longer they chanted, the more obvious it became that it wasn't the crowd outside at all. It was all broadcast garnishing.

Burke locked eyes with Greg, hard as steel.

Greg shook his head. "For all you know, the guns will be aimed at you next. America is better than this," he said, borrowing a phrase Carrie said months ago that stuck with him. "This is *not* who we are."

Cliff Watson huffed. "I've heard enough! Release the prisoners now. We're taking them out."

Burke shoved a finger in his face. "I'm in charge here. We don't move until I say move."

"Greg," Carrie said, nudging his arm.

He turned to see Oliver working toward the front of the cell, holding Commander McCormick up by the waist.

"Burke," McCormick said weakly. "Oshan. All of you. We've worked together for a long time. You know that I am a man of principles, and so are you. Do the right thing, gentlemen. You're the only ones who can now."

Burke closed his eyes for five full seconds. Then, with a huff, he shook his head and reached into his pocket. "I can't believe I'm doing this."

Greg held his breath.

Extracting his keys, Burke unlocked the holding cell and motioned to the people inside. "Get out of here before I change my mind."

Greg jumped into action. He ushered Carrie out first.

"Go," he told her. "Down the hallway back the way we came. Show the others where to go. I'll make sure we get all of them out."

"No!" Cliff yelled, running forward. "You can't let them—"

Burke rammed the butt of his rifle against the back of Cliff's skull. Cliff Watson dropped onto the floor with a thud, unconscious.

The squad guys stared in shock. Greg pushed the prisoners out of the cell faster.

"What are you doing, Burke?" Oshan yelled. "You can't ignore the president! You can't just let them go!"

"Yes I can," Burke said. "And so will you. We're going to do what our commander trained us to do, Oshan. We're going to do the right thing." Burke turned back to Commander McCormick and came to a full salute. "Sir, what are our orders?"

Startled, McCormick stopped in the cell door, leaning heavily against Oliver. Carrie had the group halfway out of sight, but she stopped as well, watching things unfold like Greg was.

Slowly, one by one, the men in black, crisp, identical uniforms mirrored Burke and came to a full salute. In seconds, two dozen men were saluting a man that some of them barely knew, all for the hope of something different—something better and less barbaric.

Face pinched with pain, McCormick nodded. "That's more like it, gentlemen. Now, shut those outside doors. Lock them down, and let's move. We're heading the other way, into the heart of things. We've got to stop Rigsby, and we don't have much time. Burke, give Pierce a weapon."

One of the men rammed the doors to the outside shut with a loud *bang.* Sergeant Burke raced over to Cliff's rifle and tossed it to Greg.

Greg caught the gun, freezing with indecision.

Waving the last of the people past her, Carrie watched Greg, waiting for him to follow.

He gripped the gun. "Hide them in the women's bathroom," he called. "I'll come back and help when I...when we..." His voice failed him. He couldn't finish. Their chances weren't good. They were outnumbered a thousand to one. Carrie seemed to know it, too.

Swallowing, she nodded. "Go."

Then she took off, running behind the others.

When Greg turned back, Oliver Simmons blocked him. The guy still wore his orange prison tent, looking pale, tired, and weak. Hopefully he still had enough strength in him to do what had to be done.

"Help Carrie get those people to safety," Greg said. "In fact, take this gun. You'll need it. There are guards everywhere."

Oliver pushed the rifle back at Greg. "You go with Carrie. I'm going with your commander. I need to see this through."

Burke, Oshan, and the others huddled around McCormick as he gave quick instructions about where they were headed and how to reach Rigsby.

Somebody pounded on the outside doors. "Hey, what's going on?" a guy's muffled voice called. "Open up!"

"No," Greg said back to Oliver. "I already know the plan. Plus I've gotta help Isabel and Kearney—somethin' must have gone wrong gettin' the rebels inside. But Ashlee's waiting outside. She has Jamansky's car, so just—"

Oliver's eyes popped open. "Ashlee's here?"

"Open up!" The pounding grew louder outside.

Greg turned Oliver around. "Yes! It's gonna be a bloodbath, but I've been trained to do this. Get out while you can. Get Carrie and the others safe."

"You've had a few weeks of training, Greg!" Oliver shot back, digging in his heels. "I've been Rigsby's slave for years. *Years!* I know how to hunt people, and right now, nothing would make me happier than using the gun meant for Jamansky to right some wrongs. So go with—"

An explosion blasted the hallway.

The blast of air knocked Greg off his feet. He fell back and threw his arms over his face to block the dust and flying cement chunks. He coughed and still couldn't find clean air.

They'd blasted a hole in the wall.

The president continued to drone on over the chaos, but the outside guards had blasted a hole in the wall. It wasn't large enough for a person. Not yet. Greg heard people shouting on the outside, ready to set off the next bomb.

McCormick lay on the ground, moaning.

As one, Greg and Oliver jumped up, grabbed each of McCormick's arms, and ran.

They sprinted the opposite direction of Carrie, dragging McCormick along with them.

sixty

Carrie braced against the bathroom wall for another explosion. The first one had sounded like a bomb.

Greg.

Tears stung her eyes, but she fought them back. There wasn't time.

Half the fugitives stood in front of the bathroom door, blocking it. The other half listened in fear like Carrie was. Their faces were damp with perspiration, their eyes etched with fear, but they all stayed silent, waiting.

Footsteps raced down the hallway on the other side of the door. Guards shouted, running toward the explosion. Thankfully, the footsteps passed the bathroom up and kept racing down the hallway.

Gone.

Carrie had to get those people out of there.

They could go out the front entrance she and Greg had come in, but she doubted that the soldiers—even with the explosion—had left the entrance to the compound unguarded. If any guards came back, searching for them, they would check the bathroom. They could easily shoot through the blocked door. These people could still die.

She spun around.

For the second time in a day, she scrambled over to a counter and climbed on top of it. Her head whirled with the adrenaline and rise in elevation, but on top of the counter, she went on tiptoe. Reaching as high as she could, she pushed the same ceiling tile out of the way that Isabel had.

The space above looked dark and small. Strangely, she could hear the broadcast even better with the ceiling tile gone, as if President Rigsby was speaking to the walls themselves. The man was insane, continuing while the training ground was under siege.

She had no idea where Isabel, Braden, and Richard had gone, or what might be up there, but she reached up and grabbed the sides of the opening. One side felt stronger than the other, strong enough to support her weight, but on tiptoes, she could barely catch hold. Even then, she'd never done a pull-up in her life.

"What are you doing?" a man from the group said, running over to her.

"My friends went up this way," Carrie said. "Can you give me a push? I think this is a way out."

"Hold on," he said. "I'm from Kearney's group. Let me go first."

"Kearney's group?" she said in surprise. He looked as rough as the others who had been in the holding cell, but maybe not so beaten down—or skinny. His body looked rock-hard and solid.

"I came with McCormick this morning," he said. "I was taken with the commander. I've been a rebel for years—one of the few in that holding cell who probably deserved to die—so let me do this. Just give me a second to get up there."

He climbed up beside her on the counter and used his incredible arm strength to pull himself up into the hole. He started to flounder, but she grabbed his foot and hoisted him the rest of the way in. He disappeared into the darkness, scuttling through the ceiling.

"I think it leads to an office," Carrie called. Whether that office would be empty or a safe place to hide two dozen people, she didn't know, but it had to be better than an unlockable bathroom on the same level as the action.

A minute later, the rebel poked his face back out of the hole. "Found it. Send people up. I'll pull them through."

More footsteps and shouting in the hallway.

Carrie hopped off the counter and ran back to the group. "Go," she said quietly. "One by one. Help each other up. That man will tell you where to go from there. Please hurry."

The people moved, and climbed onto the bathroom counter. Like a giant vacuum, the ceiling started swallowing them up until it was just her and a huge guy left blocking the door.

"Go," Carrie said to the big guy. "I'll come up last."

"Sweetheart," he said, "I'll break the ceiling if I go up—or someone's arm. I'll just hide in one of the stalls and hope I don't scare the daylights out of any nice ladies coming in."

Another explosion shook the compound. The bathroom walls reverberated. The sound echoed right through to her heart.

Greg.

He was out there in this.

"Come on!" the rebel urged from the ceiling. "We're out of time."

The big guy nudged Carrie away. "Just go. I'll be fine."

She raced over to the counter and caught hold of the rebel guy's arm. With incredible strength, he swung her up and inside the dark ceiling cove. Another wave of dizziness assaulted her. Heights weren't her friend. Neither were dark, tiny, enclosed spaces.

"Lean your weight to the right on the scaffolding," he said through the semi-darkness. "Then follow the others toward that light. It goes straight up into an office."

She nodded. "Thank you."

"Jershon," he supplied. "I'm Jershon."

"And I'm Carrie. Thank you, Jershon." She motioned down through the hole. "Is there any way to get that man up? He says he just wants to hide, but those guards could come back any minute."

"Hey, big guy," Jershon called down. "Come on. Give me your hand. We'll get you up."

The man shook his head. "I'll just hide."

"Yes," Carrie said. "You're going to hide with us. Come on. We can do it."

Lying flat on the dark, dusty framework, she reached her hand down. Jershon did the same.

The shouting grew in the hallway. The guards were returning. The big man shoved his weight against the door. He waved wildly at Carrie and Jershon to leave.

"Open up! Open up now or we'll shoot!" someone shouted.

Something rammed against the bathroom door. Carrie's heart jolted. The big guy planted his feet, pushing back against—

Carrie was suddenly yanked up into the darkness. Before she could stop him, Jershon had slid the ceiling tile back into place.

"Go!" he hissed at her.

Frantic, Carrie started crawling.

She only made it a few steps when sudden gunfire rang through the bathroom below them.

Carrie froze as if a bullet had struck her. She clamped a hand over her mouth to keep from screaming. The man blocking the door. They'd shot him. Squeezing her burning eyes shut, she listened for his scream, his grunt, or anything to let her know that he was still alive. Nothing from the man, but heavy footsteps sounded through the bathroom.

Stall after bathroom stall door banged open.

"Clear!" one guard yelled. Then they took off, racing back out.

Carrie's breathing sped up. That man was dead. She didn't have to see to know.

In the semi-darkness, Jershon waved her onward, but she couldn't move. Paralyzed, she pictured that man's face, lying on the bathroom floor, never to move again. Like Jamansky. Like Mariah, and Jenna, and everyone she'd ever watched die. Too many deaths. And what about Greg?

But...

Two dozen people still needed her. She had to get them to safety before they followed the same fate. So she forced her frozen limbs to move again. One hand in front of the other through the dusty, dark space.

As she neared the opening, someone reached down and pulled her up into the office.

"Well," a man said, gripping her tightly, "there's a face I'm happy to see."

Surprised, Carrie looked up and saw an older man with a graying goatee and long ponytail.

"Richard!" She threw her dusty arms around him. "You're still here?"

"Isabel and Braden left me to be the lookout," Richard said, "which is apparently the only thing someone my age is good for." He paused to lend a hand to Jershon, pulling him into the office as well. "I've been waiting for them to come back this way, but then this group of ruffians suddenly emerged from the bathroom." His smile faded, noticing Carrie's expression. "What happened? What is it?" Stiffening, he looked back down into the dark hole. "Where's Greg?"

Carrie explained quickly. Greg and Oliver. McCormick. The firing squad. At the same time, her gaze swept over the office. No windows, and only one door out. She could hear the president's speech still going on outside, but otherwise, things seemed quiet around them, at least to her less-than-perfect ears.

"Do you know a way out?" she asked.

"I've done a little searching," Richard said, "but as far as I can tell, the only way out that doesn't take us past the grand proceedings is back the way we came, through the bathroom."

Carrie shook her head. "Too many guards. There has to be something else."

"I can get us out," Jershon said, breaking into the conversation. "McCormick told us every possible exit in case we were split up. There's one not far from here, through a back access. If you'll allow me, Miss Carrie, I can lead us out undetected."

Startled, she looked at Richard, but Richard was looking at her as well, as if expecting her to decide.

"Um," Carrie said, "that would be great. We'll follow you as soon as you're ready. Thank you, Jershon."

"No, thank *you*. And when you see him," Jershon added, "thank your guy Greg for me, too. I'm indebted to him now—twice."

Her eyes widened. "You know Greg?"

"I met him briefly the first time he came to Kearney's camp. I'm sure he doesn't remember me, but when he and Isabel were found out as spies, Kearney wanted to kill them. Isabel chucked a grenade. In the chaos, I lost track of my son. He tripped over someone—Greg—who had recovered his gun by then." Jershon paused, face tightening. "Greg was about to shoot my son. It would have been self-defense. But when he saw that he was just a kid…he chucked the gun and ran. So I'm indebted to Greg double-fold. For the rest of my life, I will always remember Greg Pierce—and you, Miss Carrie. Will you please thank him for me?"

Her throat thickened. "I will." And then she forced herself to add two words. "I promise." Because that promise meant that she would see Greg again.

With both of them alive.

"Alright," Jershon said to the group. "From here on out, there's no sound. We're heading out into the open, so stay close."

———◆———

"That way!" McCormick pointed. "Down to the tunnels."

Greg and Oliver raced, unable to be gentle with the commander like they should have been. They each slung one of his arms over their shoulders, carrying some of his weight. While the commander could walk, he was slower than they needed to be. They practically pushed him along as he ordered the group where to go. Anytime they jarred him, he yelled out in pain.

"Is it your ribs, sir?" Oliver asked him. "If so, take slow, easy breaths. It will help."

Commotion reigned out behind them. Heavy footfalls. They were being pursued—which wasn't all bad. Greg figured if they came after them, Carrie might have a chance to get the others free.

Half of Burke's men stayed in front, scouting out the way. The other half brought up the rear, rifles up, keeping watch. Every few minutes, somebody shouted out a warning and shots were fired. Greg never checked to see who or what. He kept racing through the compound, holding McCormick up as he showed the way.

Burke and the others stopped at a steel door.

"Locked!" Burke called back. "Security access only. Now what, sir?"

"The card," McCormick said, voice strained. "In my breast pocket. Grab the card."

Greg pulled out McCormick's security card with his photo in the corner, and handed it forward. Burke swiped it through the security panel. A light flashed green, and they were in.

Down they climbed into the deep recesses of the training grounds. The lower they descended, the quieter it grew. Greg hadn't even known the compound had tunnels beneath it. Motion-detecting lights flickered on ahead of them.

Finally, the stairs ended. A long, straight tunnel lit up in front of them. The air was cool and stale in the tunnel, and the only sounds came from the beat of their footsteps and the president's speech, piped into overhead speakers.

Greg would have gladly shot out the speakers if he knew where they were—or if he still had a gun. Oliver held the one he'd been given. Even with all the chaos, Rigsby kept up the charade of a normal, everyday speech for the sake of his beloved live broadcast. The guy was certifiably insane.

"We've overcome many hurdles," the president was saying, his voice echoing down the long, straight tunnel. "Fighting for things we believe to be right and good…"

Annoyed, Greg used the opportunity to catch McCormick up on the little he knew about Isabel's plan. The commander's face was purple in some places and bloody in others, but he nodded, listening.

"She was gonna get Kearney and his guys inside," Greg said, "but I haven't seen them. And since Rigsby's still droning on, that can't be a good sign."

"Then it's up to us to finish it," McCormick said. "Wait. Stop, please." He twisted free of their grasp. "I can make it on my own now."

"Are you sure, sir?" Oliver said. The commander's face was flushed and red from exertion.

"Yes," McCormick said. "I need to get my feet under me before the fun starts."

Fun.

McCormick threw a hand around his middle, as if holding himself together, but then he started off, somewhat hunched over. Greg and Oliver followed, each ready to jump in and help if needed. But McCormick's strides grew steady and solid. Whatever injuries he had were on the upper half of him.

"Is Ashlee really here?" Oliver asked under his breath.

Greg shot him a dark look. "Of all the things to worry about right now?"

"Sorry," Oliver said, instantly contrite.

It took a moment for Greg to realize why Oliver's thoughts were on Ashlee. Carrie wasn't far from Greg's own worries.

"Ashlee's outside waitin' for us," Greg offered. "You know, she's not half bad. She's helped us a ton. She's kinda part of our clan now."

Oliver stopped. "Really?"

"Keep movin'!" Greg growled. "Come on. Focus."

"Sorry."

Oliver started jogging again. The tunnel seemed to last forever. Lights only flickered on in small sections, barely illuminating the area before them.

"Jamansky might be dead," Greg continued after a moment, "but I'm guessin' all your sleuthing with Ashlee will be enough to finish off Mayor Phillips so he can't train up a new round."

Oliver nodded several times. "Good. I hate that guy almost as much. And Ashlee is...she's..."

"Probably freakin' out about now, but she's safe. She's the one who got me this uniform." Greg paused to catch his breath. "She wanted to come with us to get you, but since we came in the same way she already had, I didn't think it was safe."

"Right. Good. Safe," Oliver huffed.

"You know...Carrie thinks Ashlee kinda has a thing for you."

Oliver glared sideways at him. "Not funny, Greg."

"I wasn't tryin' to be."

Somehow Oliver sped up, pulling ahead, but Greg could have sworn a tiny smile was tugging upward on the guy's mouth.

Burke and the others finally stopped, letting the rest of them catch up. They'd come to an intersection.

"This is where we split up," McCormick said, a little breathless. "There are counter snipers on every corner. Oshan, you're my best shooter. Take three guys...that way to the west tower. Plan on heavy guards once you exit the R corridor." His grip tightened around his middle section. "Take out who you must. Once on the tower, nothing fancy. If you can get in a shot of Rigsby, do it."

"Sir, yes, sir," Oshan said, snapping to attention. He pointed to a few men and took off in that direction.

"The rest of us," McCormick said, wincing with a sudden stab of pain, "will take a direct approach. We go directly after Rigsby."

Burke took the lead again. Guns raised and ready for anything, they started forward, though at a slower, more-ready pace.

Greg glanced down at his watch. Seven minutes since he'd left Carrie. With luck, she and the others were outside, free. He tried to picture her breaking out into the sunshine. She would meet up with Ashlee, and if the two of them knew what was best, they would race away, get as far from here as they could. He held onto that vision to make moving deeper into the compound more bearable.

Burke and the others reached another thick door and stopped.

"Is this the one, sir?" Burke called back.

"Yes." McCormick leaned against the tunnel wall to catch his breath. "The president will have...well-armed agents surrounding him." He pounded his chest in frustration. "Ah, I don't have time for this."

Greg started to move toward him to offer help, but the commander waved him back.

"I'm fine. We need to move," McCormick said. "Somebody find me an elevator!"

"On it, sir," Burke said, reaching for the door.

"And Burke!" McCormick called. "If you see any rough-looking, homeless, bearded guys, don't shoot. They're with us."

Nodding, Burke exited the tunnel with another guy. The rest waited, catching their breath.

Sudden screaming broke out over the speakers. Shouts of alarm. Greg and the others turned, as if they could see what was happening on the outside. Chaos had erupted in the compound, and amazingly, the president wasn't speaking anymore.

The president wasn't speaking.

"Rigsby?" Greg said. "Do you think they got him?"

McCormick nodded. "Let's hope so."

Greg wanted to cheer, but he didn't dare. Not yet. They listened another moment. Any excitement turned to dread in Greg's gut as sudden pops of gunfire sounded through the speakers. People shooting.

"Isn't it too soon for Oshan to have gotten the president, sir?" Greg said.

"Yes." McCormick smiled a slow smile. "But not too soon for Isabel. Way to go, girl. That means it's time to move, gentlemen."

"This way," Burke said, waving them through.

sixty-one

Burke and the others plowed through a group of armed guards with a precision that was both sickening and incredible. Bodies lay strewn about—only these bodies were dressed differently than the other guards in the compound. They wore dark suits and ties.

The president's entourage.

Greg followed Burke's group to an elevator that barely fit them all. When they emerged on the fourth floor, a different set of armed people met them. No suits. No ties. No uniforms. These soldiers looked like they lived in the backwoods.

Kearney's group.

Guns pointed both directions in a momentary, startled stand-off.

"Hold your fire!" McCormick yelled, pushing to the front of the elevator. "Hold your fire! It's me. Where's Kearney?"

"Over here," Kearney called back. "Is that McCormick?"

Strangely, when the rebel leader broke through his group, he was smiling. Greg had never seen the bearded guy smile before.

"You're out, sir," Kearney said. "We were worried that Rigsby added you to the lineup."

"He did," McCormick growled. "But Pierce's slick tongue got carried away with him—as usual—and somehow he finagled us out. Report."

Kearney's smile grew. "We made it through. We got him, sir. President Rigsby is down."

A shout of victory rang through both groups. Even Greg felt the thrill of it. They'd gotten the tyrant. President Rigsby's reign of terror was over.

But McCormick seemed less-than-thrilled. He nodded soberly. "Dead or just down?"

Kearney's smile faltered. "Not sure yet. We lost contact with Lieutenant Ryan. She's still up there."

Isabel.

Face grim, McCormick glanced back at Greg. Losing contact was never good. "Then we'll not be celebrating just yet," the commander said. "Where are your people stationed?"

As Kearney caught him up, Greg spotted a man off to the side who looked younger than the others and twice as pale. Braden Ziegler. He gripped a rifle, pointed down, and watched the chaos, frightened. Beyond the mayhem, gunfire sounded through the walls of the compound. Fighting had broken out everywhere. It sounded bad. Standing off to the side, Braden looked like a lost kid.

Greg strode over to him. "Braden, looks like you've been busy."

Relief washed over his young face. "Greg! You made it. Oh, I'm so glad. Wait, is that Oliver?"

Oliver rushed forward and shook his hand, looking out of place in his bright, orange prison uniform. "Good to see you, Braden. So good."

"What happened?" Greg asked. "When did you last see Isabel?"

"A while ago," Braden said. "As soon as we let Kearney and the others in, she told me to stay here. I've been here ever since, waiting."

Greg would thank Isabel later. Braden might have the heart of a warrior, but he spent his days milking goats, not shooting guns.

More gunfire sounded outside, but who was shooting whom? Military or rebels? Probably people dying on both sides—which was unacceptable.

Feeling sick, Greg looked at Oliver. "How do we stop this?"

"I...I don't know," Oliver said, scanning their surroundings. That particular hallway had no windows. It seemed to lead to small, inconsequential offices. Oliver shook his head. "We need to see what's happening. Maybe we should head up top to see if we can figure out how to stop it."

"Somebody needs to go up there," Greg agreed, growing more concerned with every pop of a gun. "But not us."

He stormed over to the two leaders discussing strategy. "Call off your guys," Greg said to Kearney. "Now. They're killing innocent people."

Kearney glared right back. "My people are taking control of this compound. Rigsby has people stationed everywhere."

"And how are your guys distinguishing between Rigsby's cronies and kids who were pulled off a farm?" Greg challenged.

"What's the difference?" Kearney said with a shrug. "They've all sworn loyalty to the tyrant."

Greg's temper snapped. He threw his hands into the air. "If you'd just listened to me, you'd know that most people out there are here by force, and your guys are killing them. How's that any better than the scheduled execution?" Exasperated, he turned to McCormick. "Sir, you gotta get up there."

"Up the tower?" McCormick said in surprise. "Why?"

"With all due respect, sir, those are your troops they're killing, not Rigsby's. Somebody's gotta put a stop to this, and that somebody has to be you."

McCormick thought about that for a second before he nodded. "Fine. Pierce, you're with me. You, too, Kearney. Will somebody please get Pierce a blasted gun?"

When they burst out onto the tower platform, Greg saw more bodies down, but one caught his full attention. A tall man with slicked back hair and a dark, pristine suit lay in a smear of his own blood.

President Rigsby.

Nobody hovered over the president's dead body. It had been abandoned for self-defense. The rebels crouched behind the waist-high wall, shooting blindly into the crowd.

"Nice of you boys to finally show up," Isabel growled. Greg whirled around and spotted her behind them. "Get down before you're shot, idiots!"

Greg didn't.

His gaze swept over the fleeing crowd below. It was chaos, with very few soldiers-in-training firing back. Greg checked the other towers. Oshan stood on one, and Greg couldn't see any more of the president's henchmen even though Isabel's group was still firing freely.

"Lower your guns!" Greg shouted. "Cease fire, cease fire!"

"But, sir," one of them said.

"Do it!" McCormick ordered.

As Isabel and the rebels lowered their guns, Greg followed McCormick and Kearney through and around the bodies, heading for one destination.

The microphone.

"Are the cameras still rolling?" McCormick asked.

"Let's hope, sir," Greg said. "Because everybody watchin' the broadcast right now is just as scared as us—maybe even more so."

With a quick nod, McCormick stepped up to the microphone.

———◆———

Carrie, Richard, and the others followed Jershon through the back hallways. At each corner, he stopped and checked around before waving them onward.

Their group was nearly to an emergency exit when the speakers suddenly crackled back to life.

"My fellow friends and comrades," a voice said loudly, voice echoing through the compound.

Carrie stopped.

People bumped into her, but she held up a hand, recognizing that voice.

"My name is Commander Charlie McCormick from the Federal Special Patrols Unit. Beside me stands Kearney, who leads the resistance in this area. We stand together to inform you that President Rigsby has been killed."

Carrie's hand flew to her mouth. Gasps of shock sounded around her.

"Oh my," Richard breathed. "They got him."

Rigsby was dead.

Yet gunfire still echoed in the background.

"We're in the process of detaining those closest to the president," McCormick continued loudly. "Now I beg you to stop the violence—not just here, but all within the sound of my voice." An edge crept into his tone. "President Rigsby will not kill another American so long as I can help it. I order you to cease fire!"

"A screen," Carrie said urgently. "I need to see a screen!"

They had passed one a few minutes ago. She spun around and ran back to it.

"Where are you going?" Jershon called.

For whatever reason, the others followed Carrie.

Carrie stopped at the large television mounted on the wall. On screen, McCormick stood tall with Kearney behind him. And on the other side of them…

One hand went to her mouth. The other clutched his lucky shirt.

"Greg," she whispered.

Greg was there, alive. Oliver, too, stood farther back. Both looked determined, almost triumphant.

"We must stop ending lives and start saving them," McCormick continued loudly. "That begins here and now, but it doesn't end here *or* now. Every state, every county, every precinct within the sound of my voice, I urge you to stop the violence. With Rigsby's death, those days are behind us. It is time for peace to become our new motto, our new way of—"

"Halt!" someone barked, running up to Carrie's group. A guard held a rifle, pointed directly at Carrie. "Halt right there! Hands on your heads. Down on the ground. Maynes, I found them! Get the others." His grip tightened on the trigger. "Down on the ground, all of you! Down!"

Carrie's heart pounded in her bad ear.

Reluctantly, she obeyed.

She dropped first to her knees, caught one final look at Greg on the screen, and then lowered the rest of the way down, pressing her stomach flat onto the cold tile with everyone else.

Other guards ran in and surrounded their haggard group.

"Don't move a single muscle, or we'll shoot!" they yelled.

Above them, McCormick continued. "All hospitals and medical units, I urge you—no, I beg you—to open your doors to those who are sick and dying. Stop checking cards. Stop saying who is a citizen or not. We're all Americans—but more than that, we're all human. We all deserve to live. If you have access to the cure, give it out, duplicate the formula, I don't care. Do anything you can to save our people."

"Quiet!" one of the guards yelled. But he wasn't yelling at Carrie's group. They were all devastatingly silent. He yelled it at his partners. "Shut up. I want to hear this. He's talking about the cure."

"We can rebuild later," McCormick boomed. "We can fight about laws and cards and citizenship another time—and we'll have to. We'll need to spend time untangling ourselves from the laws Rigsby created that have enslaved us for too long. But today, I beg every one of you with everything that I have to *save our people*." He accentuated the last three words, so nobody would misunderstand. Our people. Our country. Truly united.

Carrie's eyes burned. Tears leaked across the bridge of her nose, dripping onto the hard, cold floor. But they weren't tears of fear or sorrow. They were tears of relief.

Rigsby's reign was over.

They had done it.

Next to her, Richard lay with his cheek pressed to the tile. His hand slid across the cold floor and snagged hers. He smiled weakly, as if he could feel it, too. No matter what happened now, no matter what happened in the next few minutes or whether they lived or died, they had won. She had seen it in Greg's face. She could hear it in McCormick's voice now. It was over. The worst of it was behind them. A brighter future for Amber and Zach. A brighter future for America.

A few more hot tears slid down her nose.

"We have fought too many battles," McCormick shouted, "overcome too many obstacles since the creation of this great country to let *one* man destroy it! So I say it's time to end the conflict. It's time to live free. Choose life. Choose liberty. Choose to put down your weapons and help us save America—and choose to do it *now*!"

Out of the corner of her eye, Carrie saw a movement, slow but unmistakable.

The guards around her started to lower their guns.

Her breath caught in her throat.

Gaze flying from person to person, she watched it happen. The muzzles of each rifle lowered until they hung loosely at the guards' sides, no longer a threat.

sixty-two

Carrie and the others gathered around Jamansky's patrol car in the bright sunshine. She blinked against the brilliant light, and her head spun with all the events of the day, but her soul filled with joy.

Ashlee's face was vibrant as Carrie and Richard told her about how they had been released. Once the guards had disarmed, they had stared at each other, unsure what to do next. Then slowly, they started helping Carrie's group to their feet.

Carrie still couldn't believe it.

With a squeal of joy, Ashlee kept hugging random people, people from Carrie's group, or complete strangers running out of the compound. Carrie smiled at it all. She was thrilled, too.

But still no Greg or Oliver.

Braden emerged a short time later with many of Kearney's group. Braden found them by the car and told them all about how Greg and Oliver had shown up and then convinced McCormick to barge up into the tower and onto the broadcast. Because of the ridiculously loud speakers, Ashlee heard Commander McCormick's speech. They all had. It was amazing and perfect. It had saved their lives.

But...

The longer it went, the more conflicting Carrie's feelings became. Relief. Joy. But also worry. Overwhelming worry, strong enough to make her insides tremble. She wrapped her arms around herself. Most of the fighting had stopped, but occasionally she heard a random gun fire off. Each time, her stomach clenched.

Where were they?

Turning, she checked the main entrance to the Naperville facility again. The stream of people filing out had slowed to a trickle, as if everyone who wanted to leave already had—or everyone who was able to leave.

What if they'd been caught in the crossfire?

Once her own small group of prisoners had reached the outside, they'd hugged and cheered and hugged some more. But eventually they'd broken apart. Only a few remained in the parking lot with her, as if they didn't know what to do or where to go next. Some had been imprisoned for years. That seemed to be the general feeling all around: what should they do next?

Rebels, soldiers from the compound. People on both sides looked a little lost. She watched their excitement as they exited, but once in the parking lot, disorientation seemed to rule. Carrie knew what she needed to do next, though. She needed to find Greg. The longer it went, the more her insides tied in knots.

She looked up at Richard. "Are they okay?"

"They'll be fine." Richard glanced back at the large facility. "They have a lot to sort through right now. I don't envy Commander McCormick."

Nodding, Carrie told herself to stay optimistic, but as more people drifted away, the rest of them grew silent. There was nothing more to say. She, Ashlee, Braden, and Richard stood there, watching the doors.

A woman from her group walked up to Carrie and hugged her for the fourth time. "Thank you, Carrie," she said. "Thank you for saving us."

Carrie smiled. "It was all of us. We did it, didn't we?"

"Yes, we did," the woman said with a laugh. "Now, if you don't mind, I'm going home. I haven't seen my husband in four years. Do you think he'll still take me back?"

"Of course he will," Carrie said warmly. "Go home and spread the good news that—"

Ashlee's fingers suddenly dug into Carrie's arm.

Carrie twisted around. The sun was too bright, too blinding.

Desperate, she shielded her eyes.

Striding out of the compound was a man in a black, crisp uniform. A red stripe ran down one of his pant legs, a blue one down the other. His brown hair was longer than he liked, and totally messed up. A line of dried blood ran down his hand, but he was smiling as he talked to the guy next to him: a tall, thin, tired-looking man who wore an orange prison jumpsuit.

Suddenly the two men caught sight of Carrie and the others from Logan Pond.

Greg's smile faltered. He stopped in the bright sunshine. Then suddenly he broke into a dead run, sprinting across the sidewalk and over the parking lot.

Carrie met him halfway, laughing and crying together.

He scooped her up and spun her around several times. Then he kissed her soundly and entirely. Once he set her back on her feet, Carrie stroked his cheeks, checking his arm, and feeling his skin.

"You're okay," she said. "You're okay, you're okay!"

"I'm better than okay," he said, kissing her again. Then his arms enveloped her, pulling her close against him in a tight cocoon. She pressed her good ear to his uniform until she heard his steady heart beat, swift and strong.

Out of the corner of her eye, Carrie saw Oliver slowly approach the woman standing near the patrol car.

After hugging practically every single person coming out of the compound, Ashlee Lyon seemed hesitant, almost shy in front of Oliver. She brushed wisps of blonde hair away from her face and then clasped her hands in front of her, bright red nails and all.

"Oliver," she said with a controlled smile. "I'm so glad you're safe. I've been so worried about you."

"Look," Carrie whispered, nudging Greg.

His grip loosened around her enough that he could watch the interchange.

"It's good to see you, Ashlee," Oliver said. "Uh…thank you for your help."

That seemed to melt her.

With a cry of joy, Ashlee threw her arms up around Oliver's neck, startling him. Then she started to cry. His eyes flickered nervously over to Carrie and Greg, both of whom just smiled in return. Though it took him a second, Oliver's arms eventually folded back in around Ashlee.

Greg leaned down to Carrie and whispered, "Think he can handle her? She's a bit of a fireball."

Oliver started to pull back as if he might release Ashlee. He'd always been awkward with physical affection, but Ashlee kept squeezing the life out of him. Though Carrie couldn't hear, the woman was talking a mile a minute, telling him everything that had happened since his arrest, while her tears bathed his orange uniform—and smeared her heavy mascara. Finally, he couldn't seem to resist. He hugged her again.

"It's okay," Oliver's gentle voice said. "It's all okay now."

Carrie's smile grew. "I think she's wonderful for him."

Nodding, Greg lifted Carrie's chin, pulling her thoughts back. His eyes took in her face, her hair, her everything.

"I think *you're* wonderful and amazing and beautiful," he whispered with a smile. His forehead fell against hers and his eyes closed. He cradled her face in his hands, stroking her cheeks with his thumbs. "We did it, Carrie girl. Can you feel it? I know there's a world of work to be done, but things are gonna change. Can you feel the change in the air?"

She thought back to all of Greg's plans through the years—not just for the clan to buy homes or find a way to earn a small bit of money to get them legal, one by one, but his dreams he'd had since he was a kid, his dreams for the future. For the first time since she'd met Greg Pierce, those dreams were a possibility again. For the first time in six years, she felt like she could breathe, finally breathe free. Hot tears of gratitude filled her eyes.

Words failed her, but she nodded with a smile. Then she buried her face against his chest and held him tight.

When she felt in control of herself again, she took his hand and led him over to the others.

"What do you say we all go home?" Carrie said happily. "You too, Oliver. I think it's high time you move into our neighborhood."

"Me?" Oliver looked taken aback. "But..." He looked around the group. Richard, Braden, Ashlee, and Greg all nodded. "Are you sure the others will...will they let me join?"

"Yes," Ashlee said, smiling up at him. She took his arm and didn't look like she was going to ever let go. "I'm very sure."

"No, not me." Oliver shook his head. "Not after everything."

"Now, more than ever," Greg said, "you're part of our clan, buddy."

"Definitely," Braden added. "There's plenty of room in Ferris. Oh, by the way, we had to move. We're in Ferris now. Did anyone tell you that?"

"How about we stop by your house on the way?" Ashlee said excitedly. "I'm sure you don't want to wear that prison uniform forever. No offense, but orange isn't your color. Oh, and I got your letters and broke into your house. Your paperwork was perfect! I submitted everything. I hope Mayor Phillips rots forever."

Oliver's small, gray eyes widened in a look of horror. "You got the letters?"

Ashlee smiled shyly again. "Both of them. Or did you send others?"

"Oh, um…no, just the two." He scratched his receding hairline. "But you see, Reef, this guy I knew, he just…he wrote all sorts of crazy stuff that…well…" He winced. "I'm really sorry."

"Don't be," Ashlee said with a laugh. "I thought they were perfect—unless you didn't mean it."

"No, I did. I just…"

She smiled again. "Then they were wonderful and super sweet. So…let's get your stuff and head back to this Ferris place. It's not half bad. By the way, do you have any chocolate in your house? We're going to need chocolate. A lot of it."

That brought a quick round of laughs from everyone. Everyone except Carrie. She surveyed the faces of the people who meant the world to her, and yet her heart felt heavy.

"What's wrong?" Greg asked, squeezing her hand.

"No offense," Carrie said to the group, "but that's not what I meant. I don't want Oliver to go to Ferris."

Oliver paled, registering his shock. "What? Oh. I mean, okay. I understand."

"Carrie!" Ashlee said sharply. "What the heck? You just said…"

With a slow smile, Carrie continued. "I don't want Oliver to go to Ferris because I don't want any of us there." Her mind raced over the events of the day and the full implications. Jamansky. Rigsby. "What do you say that we go *home* home?" She looked up at Greg. "To Logan Pond?"

Like she had done, Greg seemed to weigh everything that had happened and what that might mean for their future. He scanned their small group of friends and suddenly grinned ear to ear.

"I say that sounds just about perfect. Let's go home." He held out a hand to Ashlee. "Give me the keys."

OF HAPPINESS

epilogue

A woman entered the store with sun-baked skin. She looked around nervously. "Are you guys open? I saw the sign outside, but I wasn't sure."

Carrie strode forward. "Yes. Come on in. We just opened this morning." *But haven't had a single customer yet,* she added silently. "What can I help you with?"

"Well…" The woman looked around, eyes sweeping over the roughly built shelves and the old table that stood in the front of the store. The table held all of the fresh items: baskets of ripe tomatoes, plump squash, freshly baked bread, and the noodles Amber had rolled out the night before. The shelves held more homemade things, like blankets and wrapped-up fuller's soap. The woman finally seemed to relax. "It all looks so wonderful. Wait. You have cheese?"

"Goat cheese," Carrie said, thinking how excited Braden and Amber would be that she'd noticed his cheese first. "And there are eggs in the container down there."

"This is so great," the woman said.

"Thanks!"

While Carrie would have loved to watch the woman shop—analyze every tiny thing she picked up and why—she decided she better get a handle on herself before she creeped out their poor first customer.

Taking a step back, she said, "Let me know if you need help with anything. I have to grab something from the supply room. I'll be right back."

Carrie fought off a smile as she walked out, but by the time she entered the back room, she was grinning like a little kid. She couldn't help it.

With a shake of his head, Greg laughed. "Are you gonna react like this to every customer?"

"Probably," she admitted.

"Good." He stood and kissed her forehead. "I'm about done labeling these tomatoes, but you didn't tell me what kind they are."

She looked at him in dismay. "Those are pear tomatoes, Greg. They're my favorite. I've only talked about them every day since…"

Her words trailed off as she realized he was smirking at her.

She swatted at him for making fun of her obsession—especially since he had plenty of his own. Chuckling again, he caught her hand and pulled her close where he could snuggle his face into her neck.

The back door to the store swung open.

"Hey, guys," Delaney said, striding inside with her black braids swinging. She barely spared them a glance as she carried in a large, heavy box. "Hope I'm not too late."

Extracting herself from Greg, Carrie walked over and took the box from Delaney. She knelt over the Sprucewood contributions, admiring the beautiful handiwork—rows of hand-woven rugs, and knitted socks folded up.

"These are perfect," Carrie said. "Tell your mom she's an angel."

"Okay," Delaney said brightly. Then she looked around. "Is Zach here yet?"

"He should be here in a minute," Greg said. "He's helping Amber and Braden sort the baby chicks."

"Oooh, can I buy one? I love baby chickens!" Delaney said.

"I think your mom already ordered twelve," Carrie said.

"Yes!" Delaney said with a whoop of delight. The girl was the epitome of sunshine. It was hard not to smile around her. "Can I wait for Zach here?"

"Sure," Greg said. "You can give me a hand labeling the rest of these…um…" He glanced up at Carrie. "What kind of tomatoes are these?"

Rolling her eyes, Carrie took the first batch from him and went back into the front room.

As the woman browsed, Carrie busied herself behind the counter. She adjusted the stack of herbal seeds, lining them up alphabetically for the twentieth time until there was nothing left to do but wait.

Her eyes flickered across the street to the police station, wondering how Oliver was doing, adjusting to his new role as Sheriff. Ashlee claimed he was doing an amazing job—of course, Ashlee thought everything Oliver did these days was amazing. But Oliver was still Oliver, always stressed about doing the right thing. While the situation around the country had definitely improved over the last two months— all of Rigsby's "emergency laws" had been repealed—there were still pockets of supporters causing havoc and staging violent protests. Until the presidential election in a few weeks, things would remain in limbo. Oliver spent most of his days buried in paperwork, working with the new mayor, and training his newly-hired policemen on the new laws—or rather, a return to the old laws.

Carrie would take him some bread and jam for lunch when she got a free minute. If she got a free minute. Maybe they would be swamped with customers all day.

Hopeful, she watched the few people walking Shelton's small Main Street, but none were heading toward their shop on the corner.

Yet.

The woman grabbed a small basket of pear tomatoes and added them to her pile. Carrie smiled smugly. See if Greg teased her about them now.

With that, their first customer approached the counter and spread out her things. She picked up one of the small bags of herbs.

"What's this one?" the woman asked.

"Rosemary," Carrie said proudly. "It was my mom's favorite."

"Oh, I love rosemary. It makes the best chicken." The woman opened the small bag and inhaled. "What great memories this brings back."

Five minutes later when Greg walked into the front of the store, Carrie was chatting happily with the older woman—Serena—all about the best way to dry herbs. Carrie made sure to give Greg a pointed look so he wouldn't miss the pear tomatoes on the counter. Greg pursed his lips and nodded, impressed.

Spotting him, Serena stepped back. "Goodness, I should get going. I'm talking your fiancée's poor ear off."

"Oh, no worries," Greg said. "She loves it."

Carrie kicked him softly behind the counter. He was on a roll today.

"It's great to meet you, Serena," Carrie said. "We're just getting up and running, but we hope to continue adding to the inventory. Depending on the season, we'll have different plants and seeds available, chickens and goats for sale out back, plus handmade items from people in the area."

"Oh, I'll definitely be back," Serena said. "It's so lovely to have a place like this here in Shelton again. It reminds me of my early days walking Main Street with my mom."

"Me, too," Carrie said fondly. In fact, memories of her mom—and Greg's—had filled her thoughts the last few days as they'd prepared to open shop. Both mothers would have been thrilled for them.

Greg put an arm around Carrie's waist and gave her an affectionate wink. While he could never resist the chance to tease her, he also knew that she was in little farmers' market heaven.

Serena cocked her head and studied him. "You know, you look familiar to me. Have we met before?"

Carrie felt Greg stiffen next to her.

"Don't think so," he said quickly.

"Are you sure? I could have sworn I've seen you somewhere."

"I just have one of those faces," he said.

It was Carrie's turn to fight off a smile. Greg hated this, but she didn't mind so much.

Serena continued to study him until her eyes suddenly widened. "The broadcast! You were there. I knew I recognized you."

Even with her bad ear, Carrie heard him groan under his breath. Every time they replayed the footage, he was there beside McCormick, standing tall and regal in his uniform. About the only thing Greg ever said about the footage was that his shaggy hair looked ridiculous, *"flapping around in the wind like that. They didn't even get my good side."* But with the upcoming elections, the networks kept replaying the footage. The attention was bound to get worse.

"So I guess I know who you two are voting for," Serena said with a knowing smile.

"Yes," Carrie said. "Charlie McCormick is a good man. He would make a great president. Have you decided who you are voting for yet?"

"I'm not sure, but I've liked all that McCormick has to say." With that, she lifted her purse and pulled out her wallet. "Now…I really better be going. How much do I owe you? I ended up getting more than I anticipated. I hope I have enough."

"It's thirteen dollars," Carrie said, having counted it up practically as the woman grabbed each item.

Serena pulled out some wrinkled, old green bills and counted them one by one, as if each was precious to her. They were about to be precious to Carrie, too. With things in the country pulling back together, the first of the banks planned to reopen. Supposedly she would be getting a portion of the money back that her parents had left in the banks before they had collapsed, but Greg said not to count on that. She needed money of her own, in hand, so when her first rental payment on her home in Logan Pond came due, she would be ready.

"Oh dear. I'm a little short," Serena said. "Can you save these tomatoes for me? I'll come back later today. I just need to run home first."

Carrie would have been fine with that if Serena hadn't pushed away the basket of pear tomatoes. Then it felt like an insult. But she forced herself to smile. "Sure. I'll save them."

"Thanks." Serena gathered up her items. "I'll be back soon."

"Bring friends," Greg added.

The woman laughed. "Of course. By the way, when are you two getting married?"

"She's makin' me wait until spring," Greg said with a roll of his eyes.

"Spring flowers are my favorite," Carrie said. Even as she said it, she could hear how lame that sounded. Who chose a wedding date based on which flowers were in season? "But who knows," she added quickly. "He might be able to talk me into something sooner."

Greg's head whipped around, green eyes going wide. "You serious? You'd move it up?"

She shrugged nonchalantly, but her stomach filled with butterflies at the idea. "Sure. Why not? I love fall flowers, too."

Greg gaped at her, making Serena laugh.

"Well, congratulations, you two. You're a cute couple."

"Thank you," Carrie said.

Heat crept up her neck as she felt Greg's eyes still on her. He loved to surprise and shock her all the time. Every once in a while, it was nice to turn the tables on him.

She picked up the yellow pear tomatoes and set them behind the counter, where they would probably sit until she gave up hope of Serena returning. Because who would come back for a few odd, pear-shaped tomatoes that only Carrie was obsessed with?

Suddenly she turned back.

"Wait," Carrie called. Serena was nearly to the door, but Carrie held the small basket of tomatoes toward her. "Here. Take these. They're a gift from us."

Serena looked startled. "Are you sure? I don't mind returning."

Carrie's gaze swept over their small store on the corner of Main Street in Shelton, Illinois. The streets were no longer empty. Even beyond their little downtown, the world was coming back to life. Like a flower slowly blooming in the spring, each day new people appeared, emerging from their dark hiding places. Serena might be their first customer, but she wouldn't be their last.

"Take them," Carrie said with a smile. "Please."

"Trust me," Greg added, "nothin' would make her happier."

the end

more

Meet the citizens, explore Logan Pond, find out which citizen you are, and discover more content at www.rebeccabelliston.com.

(scan QR codes)

Website

*Meet the Citizens
Explore Logan Pond*

*Take the Quiz
Which citizen are you?*

CITIZENS OF LOGAN POND TRILOGY

Life

Liberty

The Pursuit

Thank you for reading *The Pursuit*! This project has been near to my heart for many years, and it's been fun bringing it to life. Word of mouth is an author's best friend. If you have a moment, please leave a review for *The Pursuit* and tell your friends. Thank you!

acknowledgements

While I can write 140,000 words, I'm not always great at expressing my appreciation in person. But so many people inspire me to write and even just to smile.

My readers. Thank you for all your kind notes and enthusiasm about this little band of citizens. I love you guys!

A huge thanks to my husband, my dad, Laura, Katelynn, Sarah, Sharon, Annette, Lucy, Cindy, and Stephanie who read, proofread, and gave me suggestions that helped to shape this book. Your support means the world to me!

And lastly, thank you to my Father in Heaven for the many blessings and liberties he has given me. Writing this series has given me a deeper love for this land and the freedoms I enjoy.

Rebecca Lund Belliston is the author of the bestselling dystopian romance trilogy, *Citizens of Logan Pond,* and the contemporary romantic suspense novels, *Sadie* and *Augustina.* Rebecca also composes piano and choral music in the religious and classical genres. When she's not writing books or music, she loves to play tennis, make sarcastic comments, and cuddle up with a good book—usually not at the same time. She lives in Michigan with her husband and five kids. Visit her website for characters, maps, music, and other fun freebies: www.rebeccabelliston.com.

CONNECT :

Website: www.rebeccabelliston.com
Facebook: @rebeccalundbelliston
Twitter: @rlbelliston
Pinterest: @rlbelliston
Instagram: @rebeccabelliston

SUBSCRIBE:

CPSIA information can be obtained
at www.ICGtesting.com
Printed in the USA
LVOW04s1504131016
508637LV00016B/1302/P